I0738406

Unless the living entity forgets his real identity, it is impossible for him to live in the material conditions of life. Therefore the first condition of material existence is forgetfulness of one's real identity. And by forgetting one's real identity, one is sure to be afraid of death, although a pure living soul is deathless and birthless.

Srimad Bhagavatam

# Ocean of Milk

# Ocean of Milk

Belinda Aycrigg

99% Press

Published by 99% Press,
an imprint of Lasavia Publishing Ltd.
Auckland, New Zealand
www.lasaviapublishing.com



ISBN: 978-0-473-40419

# Acknowledgements

Heartfelt gratitude goes to my primary supervisor at AUT, Siobhan Harvey, who with all the expertise and tough love of a tiger mother pushed me to develop a very shitty first draft into something else. I will remain eternally grateful to Mike Johnson for recognising the potential in that something else, his offer to publish it and his unstinting encouragement (and patience) throughout the whole process.

I also appreciate the other Masters of Creative Writing lecturers, James George and Bianca Zander, whose very able guidance helped to shape this book.

For inspiration, support, spot on feedback and writerly fellowship I would like to sincerely thank my alumni group, Kirsty, Jacquie, Thalia, Michael and Helen, and my AUT cohort buddies Lorraine and Maris. I am particularly grateful to Lorraine and Kirsty for taking their precious time to give me detailed, illuminating and pertinent critiques of the whole manuscript.

Many people have freely given of their knowledge in specialist areas. My appreciation and gratitude go to Amee Nicholson for her expertise on the subject of CYFS, Kaye Marson for kindly giving me the benefit of her years of experience in the psychiatric field and

Constable Kelsey Lynam for her generous spirit and enthusiasm in explaining police procedures and showing me relevant areas of Auckland Police Station. I also thank Morgan Tims for going out of her way to provide further details on mental health facilities and Massey Early Childhood Centre for welcoming me in. I must add that all wild extrapolation over and above the basic facts provided by these experts is purely my imagination.

I would like to express my deep appreciation for the enthusiasm and encouragement I received from Dr Laura Markham for me to include references from her ground-breaking book 'Peaceful Parent, Happy Kids', a book that had a significant impact on my work. Also my thanks go to Marian Lizzi, Editorial Director at Penguin Random House for kindly giving permission in this regard.

My sincere thanks to Ramiel Nagel for granting permission to use excerpts from his book 'Cure Tooth Decay' and to Dr Louise Porter for generously allowing me to quote from her book 'Children Are People Too', (now called 'Parental Guidance Recommended').

It has been a real pleasure to get to know and work with the team at Lasavia. I am deeply grateful to you all. Mike of course who is the inspiration behind publishing literature that otherwise would not see the light of day. Thank you for having the vision of an alternative press that supports and encourages writers. You have gathered round you a wonderful team. Thanks to Irena for reading and rereading my work despite the demands of small children, for the encouraging and warm skype calls and having an almost sixth sense about what works and what doesn't. Thanks to Odette for your eagle eye, for being a pleasure to work with and for going above and beyond the call of duty in suggesting changes (eg the ending!). Thanks to Jenn for your great talent, friendliness and patience in working with me on the cover. Thanks goes to Daniela and Rowan for layout, design and marketing and for your generosity.

A huge thank you and kudos to Chandra Palmer for being able to decipher my totally illegible scribble and convert it into a workable manuscript. Thanks also to all the folk at Massey Library for providing a conducive workspace, friendliness and encouragement.

And beyond thank yous, my love and deep appreciation goes to my family whose support and patience made this journey possible and enjoyable. Among things too numerous to mention, thanks to David, for always having complete faith in my abilities, even when I have none; Rama for pushing me to do a Masters in Creative Writing, for constant encouragement, and the brilliant original idea for the cover; Rahul for his honesty and loyalty to family; Kim for always being interested in my book talk. And of course not forgetting... an ocean of thanks and love to my wonderful grandsons Manu and Samba - both the reason and the inspiration for this book.

Finally, I owe the greatest debt of gratitude to my teacher A.C. Bhaktivedanta Swami who not only introduced me to the ancient Vedic culture which underlies this story, but empowered me to write about it.

For Manu and Samba

# Prologue

By the laws of Manu, a woman should never be blamed. On the contrary, women, children, indeed all innocent creatures, are to be protected, cherished.

However, I am no ordinary woman.

The eyes glistening in the last merciless rays of the sun acknowledge this. Some turn away, some are liquid with compassion, begging my understanding. Yet the eyes of those arbiters who determine destiny, burn with purpose. It suits their purpose no doubt.

Against this silent collusion, the whispering of the ivory waves as they rise and fall, skittering up the shore, teasing me, tossing gems capriciously at my feet, "Come play!"

But no. No more play.

Behind me, the Parijata tree etches a filigree of stars against the firmament. Its nostalgic perfume chokes me. Birds swoop in exultation, weaving kaleidoscopic colours. I used to delight in them, their orchestra. Now their song is a cruel taunt, "Look at us! We're free!"

It seems so unfair!

Yet I have enjoyed intense pleasure. Maybe beyond the imaginings of some. Ha, I hear the others enjoying now, their laughter echoing from the caves of Trikuta Mountain, its glorious peaks shining gold, silver and emerald. Soon the revellers will skip to their palaces. Skip? Fly! To adorn themselves for their nightly pleasures: the beautiful dancing girls, the musicians taking up their instruments of pearl and amber. Ah! All is alive; all is delightful.

And I deserved it. After countless years of austerity. Did I not? But now...

I couldn't suppress my laughter. Although I turned my head to one side and covered my face with my shawl. He was so ridiculous a spectacle! The great master, bent in eight places, like a gnarled old tree, dragging himself along. Such an anomaly. Why would *I* take orders from such? And of course there was the occasion when the greatest of all the masters, Narada Muni, was by his own sweet will, honouring us with his presence. Absorbed as I was in merriment, sporting in the fragrant river of mango juice with the sons of Kuvera, I barely noticed his presence.

Yes, I forgot. I'm willing to admit. I thought I was invincible. From the highest celestial realm to the lowest hellish planet, all places of misery, of birth, of death. We all know it. But still.

I step into the flowery canopy of the swan aeroplane. The stamens of its blooms point accusing fingers, enveloping me in a fragrant prison.

I didn't think I would require a conveyance; I could have made my own way. Am I to be shorn of all my powers? However, I won't stoop to argue. I shiver, maybe for the first time ever and clutch my gossamer shawl about me. As the swan rises gracefully from the shore, I look down on the white ocean, then quickly avert my gaze. They shall not have the gratification of seeing my tears.

# Chapter One

# Fugue I

Hey! Where are you going? Stop!"

Good question. Where am I going? I have no idea.

My feet are heavy as stone, colliding with hard ground that stabs my soles at every step, as I wend my way between metallic box-like creatures with gaping mouths and bulbous eyes, standing row upon row.

Suddenly one is upon me, squealing and screeching and I tumble before it to the unforgiving ground. The woman with the dull parchment skin and the man with intense eyes are leaning down and pulling me up.

"Are you alright, Amalia?"

"Ama, what's going on?"

Two small people, one dark and one fair, stand watching. One of them has a finger in its nose. The other carries a small branch.

A face emerges from within the squealing creature, an ugly, flabby face, etched with lines, howling, "she just ran straight out in front of me."

Intense Eyes leads me away from the creature, while Parchment Skin addresses the ugly face. "We'll take her in and check her over, but I don't think you hit her, did you?"

Another person joins us as Parchment Skin takes tight hold of my arm. Sharp pain courses through my body. Wrenching my arm away, I struggle to break free.

"Am!" shouts Intense Eyes.

One of the small people is crying. I feel like crying too. And all of a sudden, so drowsy.

Well, I didn't know what else to do. I'd woken up to find myself on a bed of some sort, in a hard, harsh place I didn't recognise. There were no beautiful people or fragrant breezes, only acrid smells catching in my nostrils and people with dried up parchment skin.

On first opening my eyes, I beheld a huge claw poised above me, ready to strike and in shock I sat up, whereupon a maroon-clad person at the end of the bed disappeared out of a doorway, yelling, "she's awake!"

Throwing back the bed covers, the sight of my own brown parchment legs gave me such a fright, I leaped to the floor. I think I must have screamed.

Then a man with intense eyes clasped my hand. "Am, it's okay, we're here."

His touch was gentle, but sensing he might be about to embrace me, I lunged for the doorway.

My flight was impeded, however, by the arrival of a woman with parchment skin, who led me firmly back to the bed, saying in an iron voice, "I don't know if you should be out of bed yet."

Upon her breast was a brooch marked 'Hilary', which, I couldn't help noticing, added nothing to her beauty. She instructed me to sit down and I wondered who this dull woman was, to be giving *me* orders? But then she turned away to attend to a one legged creature beset with lights and orange tentacles.

At which I took the opportunity to flee.

Fleeing seems to be what I do, a small lady explains, her black eyes boring into me through a glittering eye mask, while Hilary Brooch of the parchment skin nods and squashes her pallid lips together. Finding their lives to be untenable, some individuals attempt to flee and start afresh, create a life anew, she says. That's what they assume has happened to me. Why I ended up on the shore unconscious with no indication to suggest who I was or where I had come from. And now, with no memory of anything.

Anything before the shore, that is. I well remember the shore. The sea swirling at my feet, iron grey and hissing. The sky devoid of sun. No sun! I was shivering. There was rain falling too. Not gentle refreshing rain, but rain hurled like so many daggers from the sky. I could not understand what sort of land this was. Beyond the shore, a dark shadow loomed out of the ground. I thought perhaps it was a mountain. It seemed to disappear into darkness. Yes, and the wind was no tender teasing breeze, rather a howling fiend. In the distance, I noticed a shadowy figure struggling, hunched no doubt against the wind. Around him or her, another shadowy figure on four legs leaping, running. And further off, a few spots of light. I wondered if they might indicate shelter? However, the force of the wind pressed me back, hindering my progress. Truth to tell, I felt shorn of all power. In the end, I managed to drag myself to the foot of the mountain, if such it was, and curled up on the sand.

Which was where I was found. Unconscious. Despite this, Glittering Mask reassures me, she's had a good look at the sea tea scan and she's quite happy with that. There's no head trauma. On the glasgow coma scale I have scored satisfactorily, and here she smiles encouragingly, as though I should be delighted. I am to be watched closely, however. If there are any signs of concussion, any at all, we must contact our gee pee. A letter will be sent to us to arrange a follow up appointment. Other than that, here she addresses Intense Eyes quietly, I should see a psychiatrist about the fugue, cause unknown, most likely trauma. Hilary Brooch smiles and nods at this unfathomable speech, while Intense Eyes' gaze shifts restlessly from Glittering Mask to me. The small dark person is crying again.

The fair one tugs my hand. "Mama's milk!"

"You can't have Mama's milk now Sammie, Mama's not very well."

Next thing I know, Hilary Brooch is taking my garments off behind a drawn curtain of indescribable cloth, and strapping me into something cold and tight and leaden (almost as bad as the terrible cylindrical creature which earlier swallowed me in its maw), which she calls my 'own clothes'. I'll feel more comfortable in them she assures me. Voices rise and fall around us. Harsh light pours down; it is not sunlight. Orders issue forth from all sides: STOP! Clean your hands! Emergency! Danger! Warning! Do not fill above the line. Microshield (which doesn't look like a shield) kills bacteria! Keep out of reach of children. Wait! Have you removed all wrist and hand jewellery?

Then I'm 'ready to go home'.

Intense Eyes puts his arm underneath my arm, holding me up. Small Dark holds my other hand.

Small Fair stands before me, arms raised. "Cawwee!"

"No Sammie, remember I told you, Mama's not well... she can't carry you."

"Sam*mie*, you have to walk!" Small Dark orders Small Fair.

I know how you feel Small Fair. As my feet contact the hard ground, every step is a struggle. I would like someone to cawwee me too.

Obediently following orders on walls (EXIT →), past a one legged COW, (Unplug COW before taking away!), into a silver-doored box, which demands that Kids need hugs not bugs. Immunise! and sinking, sinking, while Small Dark and Small Fair engage in some sort of contest regarding silver discs on the box's wall. Then out amongst the vast field of metallic creatures, where thin trees sprout from the ground like one-legged giants, waving dull swords. A continual roaring sound and fiery odours assail me. There is no sun. Only varying hues of grey moving slowly and ominously above.

"I'll open the door," says Small Dark, holding aloft a

handful of silver amulets, presumably as protection from the creatures.

There is a squealing cry and a glum looking creature's eyes flash. Small Dark opens up a great hole in the creature's flank and tosses the amulets inside.

I touch the creature's metal surface, wondering at its round black feet and soft belly. As Small Fair clambers into the creature's maw, I can't help a gasp.

"Silly Mama!" says Small Fair, and then, "I want Mama to do my buckoos."

"Mama's not well I told you, I'll do them…"

An ear-piercing wail emanates from within the creature. Intense Eyes sighs, leaning his arm along the edge of the black hole. "He always wants you to do them."

Always?

Small Fair peeps out expectantly.

With great trepidation, I lean into the hole. "Can you show me how I do your buckoos?"

"No, *you* do my buckoos!" Small Fair pushes his lips into a pout.

"I don't know how to do your buckoos." I search vainly within the creature's belly. "I don't know what your buckoos *are*." I don't know *anything!* I don't even know my own voice.

"Oh," Small Fair appears to consider this. "Woll… this is how you do it. You take this bit and you put *this* in here… and this bit goes…" He pulls two strangely formed black shapes together.

"No," says Small Dark, leaning over, "you put that bit in there and that bit…"

"No you don't... That bit doesn't go in there," protests Small Fair.

"Sam*mie*! You don't know how to do it. I do. I'm the oldest. I'm six and a quarter."

Intense Eyes inserts his head into the belly. "Stop arguing boys. I'll do it."

"No! I want Mama to do it!" Small Fair utters another loud squeal, obliging me to clutch my ear in pain.

Then Small Dark leans into the hole. "Usually, I sit in the front. In fact, I *always* sit in the front... except today, because you're not well. Soon I won't even need my seat." As he helps me attach my buckoos, he assumes a very serious expression. "You *must* put your seat belt on, otherwise the policeman might come."

Then it's driving home. Wherever that might be.

If I knew how to undo my buckoos. If I wasn't feeling so soporific. If we weren't going so fast. I'd leap right out of this creature's stomach, I would!

The roadway appears to be a petrified sea on which sail endless creatures with varying expressions from sneering grins to taunting grimaces. Low, sleek and serpentine or sturdy and elephantine, the creatures can be any one of a limited spectrum of dull colours, while inside, people sit erect like statues as they glide along. Sometimes, four people are swallowed by a creature, sometimes two, often one all alone. Where are the creatures rushing to?

All about us, trees continue to hurl great arms laden with dull green weapons, so many warriors lining the route. Black holes like empty eye sockets stare out of towering monoliths as they soar from the ground on glittering word encrusted feet. Words! Words are incessant as the waves of the ocean. On huge pictures, on small poles. Vote for Us! The Back Seat's No Safer, Belt Up! Wrong Way! One Way! Stop! No Entry! No Exit!

By my side, a man who calls himself my husband, manoeuvres a black wheel with his hand, while behind us sit two small people who seem to think I'm their mother. Can it be? I swivel round as far as my buckoos will permit and scan their faces for clues. How can a mother forget her own children?

Unlike Hilary Brooch, Small Dark is soft and dusky, a dark rain cloud mixed with thunder and lightning. His hair curling in little tendrils round his face. He squeezes his mouth into funny shapes, pulling his lips from side to side and moving his eyebrows up and down, one up, one down, above his cat eyes.

"You can't do that, can you?" he says.

Is this what we're supposed to do? I try to oblige by moving my eyebrows, though truth to tell, they don't feel like my eyebrows. "Am I doing it?" I whisper in the voice that doesn't sound like my voice.

He glares at me. "You're not supposed to be able to do it. You didn't *used* to be able to do it. Dada can't do it, nor can you Sammie can you? Because you're only three and three quarters."

However, Small Fair doesn't answer; he's fallen asleep, his little head flopping against the edge of his miniature seat. Golden hair pokes out of his head in all directions like kusa grass. A few tiny brown dots sprinkle his milky skin with stars. Long dark lashes flutter against his cheeks. He must be dreaming. His mouth is as pink as the first blush on fruit. He is the sun to Small Dark's night.

Sunny and Moony.

When I finish scrutinising the Sunny one, I look back at the Moony one, fearing a fresh onslaught of facial contortions, but his features are still. He too is asleep.

"They were up early this morning." This man who believes himself to be my husband turns intense eyes upon me. "You know how Mattie never usually goes to sleep…"

"Oh."

"Well of course he does. I mean…"

The husband's face starts contorting like Moony's. I wonder if this is how we are to communicate? But then his eyes fill with tears.

"Do you really not remember anything? Don't you remember… the boys? Don't you remember… me?"

I touch a single tear coursing its way down the husband's cheek. He possesses the darkness of Moony and the light of Sunny. But it's not sunlight. No. His light is from Saturn or Mercury if such a thing could be. Emotions sweep his face like the shifting grey of the sky above.

"It wasn't that bad was it? Before? She said you must have had a trauma but… did you? You might have been a bit low…"

My inward eye unfurls back through its brief contents: the creature, my 'own clothes', Glittering Mask, the cylindrical creature, the tentacled creature, the mirror, drowsiness, sharp pain, the silver doored box, Hilary Brooch, a threatened embrace, intense eyes, brown parchment skin, fair and dark sons, a strange bed, curling up beneath a mountain, battling wind, figures on the sand, rain falling like needles from a darkening sky, black clouds, a hissing ocean.

Nothing.

Even if I could undo my buckoos, even if we weren't rushing at such speed, where would I flee?

Chapter Two

# No Exit

We will soon arrive at the place called home. Where, the husband tells me, we've lived for three years. The road, climbing through trees and meadows, becomes rougher, full of small stones, like journeying over choppy waters. To our left, in the distance, an ocean spreads white and grey around a small island on the horizon. Something stirs within me. It's a sight I must have seen countless times. Flanking the road, long grasses topped with plumes wave in the wind. They seem welcoming enough. Yet it feels colder if that is possible; the sky seems to grow darker. Words become scarcer and less bossy.

How long we have travelled, I can't say. The sun's sporadic appearance makes it hard to ascertain and I'm drowsy. Between learning about plastic and other useful facts, I drift in and out of sleep, along with the sons. Intermittently, the husband talks to himself, a square metallic locket dangling from his ears on a white thread. It seems an unusual way to wear it, but how can I judge? I hear him recounting the story of how they found me. I say, yes I know. But he just carries on talking, as though I'm not here.

"There's only one problem though," he says at the end of the tale, "she can't remember much." And here he pauses for a while. "They say it should right itself soon... with a bit of help."

Yanking the necklace out of his ears, he turns to me. "That was your mother."

After a while, the road peters out into a meadow and the creature stops beside a squat brown building. Before I can really take it in, however, the creature is assailed by a monster, beating its urgent wings against the windows and screeching like a demon. Is it a vulture? It appears to be a four-armed bird with two heads. I cry out, shrinking into my seat.

"Hey, hey... what's wrong?" The husband seems surprised.

The sons! I turn round in alarm, fearing for their safety. I hope they still have their buckoos on!

Sunny is saying, "I want Mama to undo my buckoos!" as clawed hands reach in for him. Moony, his finger in his nose, gazes off into the distance.

Then the clawed hands reach in for me.

As I emerge, trembling, from the car creature, the four-armed monster grabs me in its many arms. I try to flee, but soon find myself clutched by *six* arms. Plus Moony's feet. All accompanied by Sunny's wailing, which again fills my ears with pain. Pain! I'm reminded of another pain, a searing pain in my arm, while similarly being held by many arms. Fearing a repetition of that agony, I abandon my struggles, allowing for a more sober inspection of the monster. And lo! It is not a monster after all. No.

It is my mother and father.

We make our way along an earthen path, Moony walking on his hands, his feet in my face, then tumbling into long wet grass with a "whoooaaaa!", Sunny in the husband's arms wailing, "I wanted Mama to do my buckoos!" and me held firmly by the four armed monster, who is not a monster after all. The all-pervasive roar has been replaced by a discordant clucking and screeching. The fiery aromas by the scent of rain and wind. Ascending steps, passing through a wide transparent doorway, we are home.

Sunny disappears through another doorway, "I want to watch something."

The others follow him, shouting variously, "I'll make coffee!" "I'll make us some tea!" "I better get the boys something to eat they'll be hungry!" "But aren't you both hungry?"

Moony remains in the room, poring over boxes full of multifarious coloured cubes which he proceeds to affix, one to another.

And what am I to do? Hover on the threshold? Reacquaint myself with the home?

This room is not so beautiful. I'm disappointed. It does not inspire me to take possession. What must I have been thinking? The proportions I find to be cramped, the surfaces of the walls crumbling, the couch of wretched materials, not gold, ivory or coral. I wander round the poky room with its suffocating ceiling, stroking the brown substance of which all is wrought - the window edges, the chair arms, the floor. It feels marginally less repulsive than plastic. What can it be?

A blue carpet, neither plush nor soft, is strewn with Moony's cubes and white particles. Withered curtains droop from brown poles. No wonder I ran away. But wait... Are those *elephant* heads at each end of the poles? I feel a slight lifting of my spirit. If only they weren't brown.

I'm surrounded on all sides by gloomy furniture, one crammed full of, I think, parchment, another sagging miserably in a corner. To my astonishment however, as I draw nearer I discover four startling personages flashing out of its miserable depths. Better than elephants! Not brown! A sultry youth, brilliant as an Indranila gem, holds a flute to gently smiling lips; at his side, a glowing damsel offers benediction. Beneath them, a man of ashen hue sits astride a great bull, a crescent moon and raging river adorning his crown, a writhing snake around his neck. I feel a tremor through my body, tears well up. And behold! Here sits a fearsome woman upon a tiger clutching weapons in her many hands. My limbs burn. I wheel round, anticipating the arrival of parchment skinned people, brandishing lances to pierce my arm. But no, there's just Moony, intent upon his cubes. I bend down to see what he's doing.

He tells me he's making a Panzerkampfwagen. "It's a type of tank," he says.

I reply that I don't know what a tank is. Meanwhile, Sunny

appears in the doorway bearing a square object. He plops it amongst the cubes and particles, and as he prods and pokes it, pastel coloured creatures come to life within. Moony abandons the cubes to gaze unblinking as a strange, tiny world unfolds. A strange, tiny world within a strange, larger one.

Suddenly I'm exhausted. My feet are as heavy as stones on the dull brown floor. Outside, the grass sways like an ocean rippling in the breeze, while long fingered bushes beckon. At the foot of a hill beside the home, a vast forest stretches away to the horizon. I could just walk away. I could just…"Ouff!" My nose crashes into something. Oh, it's the transparent doorway.

A bitter, nutty smell pervades the room. It's not unpleasant.

"Tea!" "Coffee!"

The mother and father place steaming vessels (not gold or even silver, but some earthen material) on a low table, (brown), followed by the husband, bearing a large platter of spongy objects. The mother gently leads me to the wretched couch, coaxing me to sit, which, despite the aesthetics, is something of a relief. Indicating the platter, she tells me to 'tuck in' and gazes upon me, whilst I simultaneously behold her. Her parchment skin is etched by fine latticework. She's no vulture, rather, a small bird, with shining eyes darting here and there. Kind eyes, gentle eyes, which fill with tears.

"Tea?"

On another chair, the father. With different eyes. Eyes hidden under the shadow of an overhanging brow and thick, slanting eye masks. His lattice pattern is different from the mother's. More sparse, more carved. Raising a vessel to fleshy lips, he quaffs deeply, observing me through his shrouded eyes. With a slight lift of his brow, he juts his chin at a vessel of black liquid.

"Coffee?"

"Well, maybe she wants tea?" says the mother.

"Coffee is better. Especially mine, eh, Beti? Always you like my coffee."

The mother and father watch me intently.

"I don't know... I'll have both... "

"Oh, you're just the same as ever!" says the mother delightedly, hope in her eyes. "Eat up and then we can talk."

The husband says, "Turn that off now boys, and come and eat your lunch."

The terrible wail from Sunny is now echoed by Moony. After an excruciating interlude, it dies away. Then Sunny is climbing onto my lap and snuggling in close. He smells sweet like fruit.

"Mama's milk!"

The father appears furious, the mother anxious.

The husband says, "Sammie..."

However, Sunny, undeterred, wriggles his tiny hand under my suffocating tunic. To my great surprise, it doesn't feel alien and I seem to know what to do. Soon he's sucking contentedly at my breast. A mantle of peace softly envelops me for the first time in memory, as the milk flows.

He pops his head up. "It's diffwent."

The mother and father exchange glances.

"It's yum," says Sunny, resuming his drinking.

So, tea or coffee? It seems like an important decision. I thought I'd tried coffee in the hospital mansion but the father says that wasn't actually coffee. The spongy objects, 'sandwiches', are served on small platters and chewed delicately by the mother, in between dabbing her mouth with parchment. While the husband, (seated on a vast clay coloured cushion on the floor) tears off great mouthfuls in between gulps of either tea or coffee. The father reclines on a low red chair, legs outstretched. Producing a white cloth from an aperture in his leg covering, he squashes an errant drop of coffee spilt on his brown tunic. On the wall behind him is a large picture of what look like spheres floating in the heavens. A red arrow pointing to one sphere, is inscribed, YOU ARE HERE.

"How's the coffee?" asks the father.

I take a small sip and almost spit it out. "Bleah! It's so bitter!"

"Maybe you need some sugar?" offers the mother jumping up and disappearing through the doorway to the unknown.

"And milk..." says the husband, following her.

"Normally you are not taking milk or sugar," grumbles the father.

I attempt the sandwich. It tastes and feels like sand on my tongue. And my mind fills up with pain. But there is a roaring in my belly which is yet unassuaged. I rise up a little shakily. Maybe this time I can make it through the door.

Just as I place my hand on the door, however, I am again enwrapped by several arms and returned firmly to the couch. The mother rushes into the dark doorway and returns bearing a receptacle of different coloured shapes. Fruits?

There is whispering around me. "Should we call the hospital?"

Then, "Have some fruit, maybe after a trauma something light?"

Crawling over, Moony plucks an orange globe from the receptacle, so I follow his lead, picking a long yellow shape, marked 'FairTradeOrganic'. I wonder briefly why the fruit is labelled. Do other people also have trouble remembering? The growling in my belly is insistent however, and I desire only to eat. For a moment, it is a puzzle *how* to eat. Then I see Moony pulling off the outside of his orange fruit. Everyone becomes still, as I peel back the fairtradeorganic's outside and sink my teeth into its flesh.

"Silly Mama," says Sunny, "you don't even like bananas."

"So," the mother places her small platter neatly on the table, "what did the doctor say, Jay?"

"Ah, Doctor Chaturvedi…"

The father looks interested. "Oh yes. Doctor Chaturvedi is it? What was his diagnosis and recommendations?"

"Yes, Prof. One of your lot. What a surprise." The husband takes a quick slurp from his vessel. "And *her* diagnosis, as I told you on the phone, was possibly a fugue episode."

"I looked it up on the internet," says the mother twisting her hands together. "It happened to Agatha Christie. After her husband had an affair."

Everyone is silent for a moment. The mother's eyes dart anxiously round. I follow her eyes hoping for some elucidation. None is forthcoming.

The husband says quickly, "Yes, well... It could take six months, but generally it's less, for all the memory to come back. She suggested Ama should get psychiatric help, but I'm not that into..."

"You must do the right thing, Jay. If the doctor says..." begins the father, placing his empty vessel on the table and shaking out his large white cloth.

The husband turns his saturnine eyes upon him. "And you'd know what the *right* thing is wouldn't you my dear *Prof*."

Rising off the couch slightly, the mother attempts, "Let's try and work together on this for once. We could..."

But before we can find out what we could, the husband is sitting up straight on his cushion. "I suggest we go to Doctor Ganesh first, and then..."

And the father sits erect in his chair. "No! You must go to proper doctor..."

"He *is* a proper doctor!"

"I have one colleague..."

"...who'll just fill her full of chemicals."

Discordant notes shoot back and forth, out of time and off key. My ears burn. The sons, curled up on the blue carpet, only have eyes for their little world in a box. Meanwhile, outside the transparent door, the plant's long green fingers beckon...

Placing a gentle arm around me, the mother says, "Now, from what I read on the internet, if you try and jog the memory it can help." She appears to gather her courage. "I have an idea... why don't we find out what you can remember ... and what you can't?" She looks round hopefully. "What do you think?"

Carefully folding his white cloth, the father inserts it into his leg coverings and with a loud snort, rises solemnly to his feet. Piling small platters and vessels one atop the other, he marches out. There's a loud clatter followed by the sound of gushing water.

The husband raises intense eyes to the ceiling and shakes his head. "I guess we could." He refocuses his eyes on the mother. "You mean like… what's your name? Who's the prime minister?"

Wild crunching and crashing emanate from the doorway to the unknown.

The mother squeezes my hand and smiles. Her whole demeanour brightens. "That's right. Those are the questions they ask to see if you have dementia. They did it with your Granddad, do you remember?"

I look down at the brown parchment hands, clasped in the mother's paler ones. Striding in, the father scoops up the remainder of the vessels and sweeps out again.

Releasing my hand, the mother says, "No, you might not remember that. You hardly saw him." And at this, for some reason, she stares angrily after the father's disappearing back.

Then suddenly, all eyes are upon me. "What's *my* name?" asks the husband.

"Oh… er…" I feel a bit like I did in the hospital building when they were asking me so many questions and shining blinding lights into my eyes, "Husband?"

"No… you don't call me that… You call me my name, which is…"

The father appears in the doorway. "What's *my* name?"

"Father?"

"No my *name*..." He stands, arms folded upon his chest, before the planet picture, the YOU ARE HERE arrow aimed at his left hip.

"Oh... Prof?"

"No, that is what your husband is calling me. My *actual* name is... "

Sunny suddenly emerges from his little world. "What's my name?"

"Sun... I mean Sammie?"

"And mine?" A disembodied head appears from under the table.

"Moon...?"

A dark cloud crosses the face of the moon. The dark son's brow glowers and he leaps up, clenching his fists, his lips a downturned crescent. "That is *not* my name!"

"No, no I know it's Mattie. It's just that you remind me of..."

As his son stamps towards me with hunched shoulders, the husband puts out a warning hand "Mattie..." Then he's up and chasing around the room after Moony... er... Mattie, who dodges this way and that, before collapsing onto the floor in laughter.

"That's what you're supposed to do when Mattie has a meltdown. Unless of course, he has too many emotions in his backpack," says the mother sagely. "But," she brightens, "the main thing is... you remembered the boys' names! Of course you did. You couldn't forget them!"

Everyone looks at me for a moment. Hope in their eyes.

Then Mattie happily grabs the small picture box from

amidst the sea of blocks. "What's this called?"

"I don't know."

"No, you say 'Pass'. That's how you play it. We did it at school." He runs over to the window. "What's this?"

"A window?"

"No, but this?" He points to the ubiquitous brown substance encircling the window. "What's it made of?"

"Er... pass."

"It's made of wood."

"It's made of twees!" Sammie jumps up and grabs an article from the shelf of parchment. "What's this?"

"Pass."

"A book! It's made out of twees too! Look!" Sammie brings me the book and opens it on my lap. I hear a faint murmuring.

"Oh, I know what a book is... It just didn't look like a book..."

"Woll... look at this." He lifts a morsel of parchment within the book. "See... *Where does the cow live?* Then you open the flap and it says... What does it say again?"

"*In the field.*" Mattie comes over and joins us.

"And this one, *Where does the pig live?*"

I now know where the pig, the cow, the chicken and the sheep live. I know what rhymes with hen and rock. I know my colours and my numbers up to ten. So much knowledge under little flaps in Sammie's books. And soon after that, it's time to find out where *I* live.

I'm informed our present poky situation is the living room and when we go through the doorway to unknown regions, that is not the dying room, but the kitchen. It has a silvery metal 'sink' with 'taps' from which water flows, where Prof wields sway over submissive utensils. Then there are mystifying metal boxes...

The fridge: a hulking contraption of ice or frozen water, which makes me shiver. I try to put my cheek to it but the mother, (now known as 'Nani'- "Silly Mama, *evewyone* knows that!" Sammie informed me when I'd said "Pass." And 'Nani' had sort of wilted when I knew where the cow lived but not her name.), gives an alarmed yelp and tells me not to as it will stick.

The woodstove: black with legs and two small doors opening onto a cavity for burning trees. Poor trees. So many of them dead! I plunge my fingers into the grey wood dust and put them into my mouth. Nani's eyes open wide. The dust tastes of sand. I wonder if this is what sandwiches are made of? But I don't ask. Apparently, you can use the woodstove for cooking and for keeping warm. The husband says it's a brilliant environmentally friendly stove. The father... Prof, says it's very primitive and just makes more work for me.

The oven: a grey box topped with iron racks, as heavy as an elephant. This is the real oven, where Prof tells me, I can cook when I am back to normal.

All along one side of the kitchen, there are small brown doors – more deadened trees – with handles on them. I feel like weeping. On either side of the sink is a long shelf of metal, on which sit utensils and vessels, now pristine and wet.

The sons take me excitedly round the house, showing me every room. "What room is this?"

The toilet I already know from the hospital mansion. The bedroom contains a large bed and the bathroom contains a basin and a bath, which is a huge white metal basin you can lie in. Mattie and Sammie both jump in to show me and twist the metal taps. Nani tells them to get out because they still have their clothes on. I think I'll be able to remember bedroom and bathroom.

Then we all squeeze into the sons' bedroom, while Mattie and Sammie jump up and down on the top bed of two beds joined one on top of the other with wooden posts. Mattie tells me he has the top 'bunk', which has a cover on it with a strange object with wings called an aeroplane. I feel as though I know what an aeroplane is. Nani looks hopeful. But the aeroplane I know looks nothing like that.

"It's fun for the boys having someone who knows less than them, especially Sammie. No one ever knows less than Sammie," says the husband.

Nani, squashes her lips together, the lattice work furrowing deep in her forehead. She takes my hand and sighs. "Don't worry you'll soon be back to normal, sweetheart. It seems that you're remembering so many things already aren't you?"

"You're a quick learner." The husband smiles at me encouragingly. "Who knows? You may even catch up with Sammie before too long." He ruffles Sammie's golden hair. "You can have a race!"

Sammie puffs out his chest and pouts his little ruby mouth. "Silly Mama. I know heaps more than you."

"What I don't understand," I say, "is how I know some

things and I don't know others... I remember how to read. I know how to speak. Why can't I remember everything? And why did I go?"

My father observes me with his hidden eyes. "Ah Beti, it is a question of certain areas of the memory banks only. Different chemical synapses firing. Psychiatrist would be able to know the reason..."

"You must've blocked out certain parts of your memory, sweetheart." says Nani quickly, dabbing her eye and giving me a warm embrace. "I think you were probably... quite depressed."

Prof, stands in the hallway outside the sons' bedroom. The name is not self-explanatory and no one has told me what you do in a hallway. "I think we must not raise our hopes up. We must not live in pretence." He shakes his head back and forth. "Arey. My own daughter, not knowing her father's name..."

The light in the room is fading.

"On the light, Mattie," says Prof.

"*I* will!" yells Sammie.

"Sam*mie!*" shouts Mattie.

They both launch themselves on a small ivory plaque on the wall, which is possibly not ivory but plastic. The living room comes alive! Two round orbs, protruding from a wall, emanate a glow as bright as day. They're like full moons.

"Are they pearls or diamonds?" I ask.

Mattie jumps onto the couch and shouts in my face, "It's electricity!"

Sammie assumes a very superior expression. "Silly Mama."

I reach out to touch one, but before I can, Nani grabs my hand. "Ooh, don't touch angel!"

Husband stands watching, his hands tucked into his leg coverings. "We never used to have electricity. We were going to be self sufficient..."

At which, the discordant orchestra starts up once more.

"Laundry by hands! So much squeezing... "

"...off the grid..."

"...like Indian woman in the village... I did not raise my daughter..."

"...not using up the earth's resources, the oil... depending on corporations..."

"...to be dobi wallah. I came to this country..."

I put my hands over my ears and stamp my foot. A contrary little synapse within me screams, "It's not fair! If I wanted to do fugue why shouldn't I?" Then, before you can say ´electricity`, I wrench open the door and plunge into the dark night.

Then I stop. I look up to see the vast heavens, the planets appearing one by one like so many electricity orbs. And is it my imagination, or are they in the shape of an arrow? As if I am an insignificant particle, lost amongst the debris on some massive carpet and a giant arrow is aimed at me! YOU ARE HERE...

Another synapse, somewhat bossy, then says, "You can't go running away when you've got kids!" I wonder at its audacity in giving *me* orders.


Re-membering. Day One:

fugue, hospital, vitals, machine, nurse, toilet, toilet paper, empty your bladder, bowel motion, Glasgow coma scale, gee pee, sea tea scan, COW, lift, car (not creature, not alive), injection, blood, sedative, road, motorway, road sign, policeman, plastic (solidified oil), basin, taps, windscreen, phone, tablet, coffee, Beti (a term of endearment meaning daughter or darling in Hindi – a different language, spoken by the father or Prof. Imagine! Not everyone talks the same language; perhaps because they are from a different realm, or perhaps because they have forgotten some of it like I have. Either way, this can cause serious misunderstandings of many things, including, for example, agatha christie. I must conclude this to be the reason things are labelled as in fairtradeorganics), tea, sugar, machine, glasses or spectacles (eye masks: small windows you can see through), windows I already knew. I thought they were made of jewels or crystal for some reason, but no, it transpires they are composed of the same substance as the eye masks: glass (a shiny, transparent substance made of none other than fused sand! ), which reminds me... sandwiches, (not from the shore nor from wood dust), wood dust, woodstove, fridge, oven, bathroom, bedroom, bunk, aeroplane. (again, I thought I knew it but I didn't) books (likewise), knives, where the cow lives, where the pig lives etc, numbers to ten, Panzerkampfwagen, tank, steering wheel, handkerchief, electricity, electric light, chemical synapses, deadened trees, wood, Lego, bananas.

# Chapter Three

# Archeology and Anthropology

Y ou slept well." Two startling eyes, surrounded by dark tangled locks look down on me. "You just slept twelve hours." The eyes, (where have I seen them before?) are accompanied by full lips which lift slightly at the corners. "You went out like a light last night. You probably needed it."

I gaze around me at white walls, a dark red cloth decorated with yellow shapes suspended from some sort of pole, a small furniture piled high with parchment by the side of a bed. A wrinkly sort of bed in which I find myself prone and gripping tightly onto a rough textured covering.

The eyes get closer, together with an earthy smell, mixed with something like herbs. The hair brushes my cheek as the lips softly touch my forehead.

"Hello Am. How are you feeling?"

I sit up with a jolt to find a woman with brown tousled

hair staring at me in shock. Where am I? Who is that woman? Who is this man?

Seeing me staring at the woman, the man says anxiously, "Am, it's you. It's the mirror. Did you forget?"

The mirror!

Oh, yes. Yes, it's returning now... Yesterday... was it yesterday? The intense-eyed man telling me so many things. Riding in the dead creature. Not a creature! (Silly Mama). No! Wrought of metal, but with the *power* of so many horse creatures. Which runs on oil derived with great hardship from the centre of the earth planet and it would be so much better if it could run on electricity. Electricity! Oh yes and *plastic*, (also made from the oil from the centre of the earth planet). A tiny *plastic* screen folding down to block out the sun, and upon that tiny screen, a tiny mirror.

Looking up from time to time as we journeyed yesterday, I would catch sight of a lifeless woman staring out of that tiny mirror. And so terrifying a sight was this, that *if* I had known how to release my buckoos... However, that wasn't the worst.

Worse, much worse. In the hospital mansion, above a marble bowl with silver levers (Wet hands! Rub hands!), there appeared to be a window. On the far side of which lurked a creature, watching me with suspicious deadened eyes, her muddy skin taut around her cheeks, her insipid lips pinched in misery. As I held my hands under the gushing water, so did she. Then, Hilary Brooch told me... indeed, she *insisted*, that the woman was me. Me!

No, I told her. That is not me. That, and here the woman

through the window pointed at me, is an imposter.

The woman in the mirror today doesn't look much happier, but at least she's not aiming her accusing finger. On the other side of the mirror, there is no woman with brown clumped hair, brown eyes, brown lips, brown parchment cheeks, brown ears, brown clothes. No, that woman is in *front* of the mirror. On the *other* side of this mirror is a big cupboard, which as far as I know, contains no women or even cups, just clothes. My clothes. Yesterday I didn't know which was better, the bossy hospital tunic, telling me all over it was property of the hospital, (I reassured it that I certainly would not remove it from the place where it belonged and Hilary Brooch looked at me strangely), or *my* clothes, which said nothing. So dull. And worse, when Hilary Brooch dressed me, (I didn't know where to put what), sad pictures invaded my mind. Could they have been memories? If so, everyone will be happy. Except maybe me.

If I walked through the back of the cupboard of quiet but sad apparel, I would find myself in the bathroom, where Sammie is to reacquaint me with teethbwushing (while I try to avoid looking in the mirror). I don't walk through the cupboard though, I just follow Sammie obediently down the hallway.

"Woll, you get your toothbwush," he explains. "Mine's a giwaffe." He shows me a creature, (dead, solidified oil). "See? It's purple and owange... my favowite colours."

"Do I use this one?" I ask picking up a similar creature from a sand glass vessel at the side of the basin.

"No, silly Mama. That's Mattie's. This one's yours." He pulls out a rigid green snake topped with tufts of fur and places it in my hand. Then, clenching his tongue between his lips, he squeezes a brown worm from an object called 'Naturepaste', and lays it onto his giwaffe's fur.

I think the Naturepaste is a book as it's covered in writing. But when I start to read it, Sammie grabs my hand. "Come *on*, Mama!"

So, clenching my tongue between my lips, I give the Naturepaste book a vigorous squeeze and out shoots a long serpent!

"Silly Mama," sighs Sammie. "That's far too much."

We have to turn on the tap and push the serpent down the hole in the bottom of the basin. It smells herby like the husband.

I pick up my toothbwush ready to try again, but suddenly experience a sharp pang of loneliness.

"Can we go to the museum, ple-e-ase," begs Mattie, hopping from one foot to another by Prof and Nani's car.

"The sun's shining. We should do something outside," says Nani.

And indeed it is! Among the (many) things I seem to have forgotten is how capricious the sun can be, a bit like me, suddenly disappearing without warning. Yes Nani, I also wish to luxuriate in the sun. And breathe in the smell of fresh grasses which hover on the breeze today. Even the birds sound less strident. Maybe they were arguing yesterday. Maybe they're happier with the sun pouring on their feathers. Their clicks and chattering and whistling, well you couldn't call it musical, but it has its own rhythm, it's not totally devoid of harmony. Not like some voices.

Prof's tunic shouts, "Do It Yesterday!"

"A-ah!" moans Mattie.

Nani, does not respond but takes my hands (with which I was about to cover my ears) in hers, settling her gentle bird eyes on me. "You two need to spend quality time together; it might be just what you need."

Prof, is studying a dial on an unbeautiful bracelet on his wrist, like the dials in the husband's car. "If we are going to go, then let us go," he says in definite but not such strident tones as his tunic.

Where they will go, finally, I'm not sure. I wonder what a museum might be? Where the sun does not shine? It must be glorious indeed for Mattie to prefer it to sunshine. The parents and sons depart in Prof's blue car, Mattie in the front, leaving the husband and me alone to spend quality time, a concept with which I am yet unfamiliar.

So, here we are, sitting side by side on the orange couch, me on the very edge, shuddering at the sensation of the cloth, gazing at the elephants and the ugly furniture with its not ugly contents from time to time, for some encouragement, and the sun streaming in through the transparent sand window. I look outside longingly. But, it seems that quality time is to occur inside, out of the sun. Like the museum. We are set to do some serious re-membering and a 'hole in the ozone layer' might impede our progress. And after all, what do I know?

However, as the husband says, I'm a quick learner! I now know so much more than I did. Important things. For example, that the whole house is made of trees, not just the floor, which I personally 'sanded' and 'polished' with organic oil. Imagine! I bend down to feel it and smell it. It smells faintly of fruit.

The husband watches me, his fervent eyes softening. "You're like a toddler. Like Mattie used to be. Touching everything. Putting everything in his mouth!" He stops to consider this for a moment. "You're living in the present aren't you? Amazing. The Power of Now…" He laughs. "All that good stuff… I almost feel a bit jealous." He lifts one foot onto his thigh. "Okay, where shall we start…? I suppose that's a rhetorical question, since you don't know anything…"

"I don't not know *anything*," I say, sounding a bit like Mattie.

"No. You knew what a book was, sort of. But that's not surprising. You love books. We both do. Just look around you." He indicates the dull furniture, overflowing with books.

A quiet hum begins to sizzle, accompanying the birds' squawking. It's slightly off key.

"And as I say," continues the husband, "you seem to be a quick learner." He lifts one eyebrow. "A real sruti dhara."

I nod. "One who learns by hearing once."

The husband seems surprised. "How did you know that? You must be remembering something."

"Yes, some things… "

"Ah well, how do swallows know to fly north? From the Great Soul comes all knowledge and remembrance." He puts his hand on my heart. "In here."

He looks into my eyes. I gaze into his flashing ones. Birds chatter. Intense eyes blaze. The husband swallows. My heart flutters. I wonder briefly, how *swallows* fly north? The Great Soul must be great indeed. But then, if a heart can flutter, maybe a swallow can fly?

The husband snatches back his hand, as if from an electric orb, staring at it in apparent wonderment. Finally, he emerges from his short fugue, and regards me for several moments. "Sruti dhara, apart from one thing," he pauses and tilts his head, "my name!" He laughs softly. "I think I quite like you calling me 'Husband'."

I laugh too. Is that the first time I have? It sounds strange. I don't even know my own laugh. I stop quickly. "Alright… um… Husband, where shall we start?"

Husband says we're like archaeologists trying to piece my life together from the evidence. If I'm to find out who I am, I need the artefacts of my previous life. He has to explain the meaning of archaeologist and artefact, just as he has to explain so many other things. He seems to enjoy it though, a bit like Sammie. However, because I'm sruti dhara, he only has to tell me once.

We go into a tiny bedroom with no beds, (confusing!). This room is utilised for studying, among other things. It was overlooked in yesterday's re-membering tour. Husband mutters something about Prof, which I do not hear and therefore do not remember.

Squashed into the small room (even smaller, even more cramped than the living room, this must surely be the dying room) is a large cupboard, an ugly black chair, a not so ugly tree chair, and a table, also tree. The table is strewn with parchment, books and an ominous metal object I can hardly bear to contemplate.

Husband sits down on the ugly chair, scraping the tree one back for me, with a terrible screech, which he seems not to notice.

He tells me that he's studying anthropology for his masters. I ask him who his masters are and he laughs. He says we both like to study. I ask what we study and he says anthropology, which is the study of human culture and society. I ask him if I'm studying human culture for *my* masters. Inside a small synapse grumbles, why would I want to do anything for any masters? and I feel somewhat rebellious. But I say nothing.

No, Husband tells me that I'm not doing anything for my masters (which is a relief) because we have two young boys and they need their mother. We decided that Husband would carry on his study, while I would take the role of mother, which is natural. We both believe in this.

Do we? I think. But now Husband has launched into a new subject, explaining how we're also both teachers. In fact I used to be a fulltime teacher at Mattie's school. But again, I have given this up to look after the sons, although I do go in from time to time and teach a bit of drama, while Husband does the odd bit of relieving to make us some money. I wonder why I'd need to give up teaching to look after the sons? But somehow the opportunity to ask doesn't arise.

A soft whispering emanates from the cupboard, the proposed site of our excavation, where forlorn looking red books moan softly.

"They're your journals," says Husband. "You'll find out about yourself, what you were thinking." We might even find out what was going on with you that made you run away." He pulls out the top book and stares at it, as if willing it to speak. "It wasn't that bad was it?" He says to the book. Then tosses the red artefact onto the table "I don't know if I should read it. Journals are supposed to be… confidential… You'll have to read it."

With some trepidation, I lift its red cover to reveal white parchment covered in a spider trail of writing. I feel faint. The journal burns on my lap. I don't read it. I can't. A sensation engulfs my mind. I see myself standing by the metal sink with my arms in water, gazing out at the rain and wind. I must be in the kitchen room but it feels like the dying room. I see Sammie and Mattie fighting in the living room; Mattie is hurting Sammie, but I don't care.

"I think I'll leave the journals for now," I whisper.

"Sure… Look, I know this must be really hard. Maybe I'm being a bit callous. You used to say that I was… sometimes," says Husband awkwardly. "What would you like to do? Shall we stop for a bit? I just thought… you know…"

"No we should carry on. I need to know. We all need to know."

"Yeah sure." He looks doubtful. "But maybe not the journals… They might be a bit too, er, confronting." He gets up and leafs through some other artefacts on the shelves. "Look here's your passport."

"What's a passport?" I take the small book in my hand.

"It's an identity document. They don't let you get into other countries without one."

All at once I see a street with many conveyances, small black topped yellow conveyances like bees, buzzing all over the place; multitudes of people milling and calling to each other. The sky is full of dust and the sun is orange. Pieces of parchment swirl and eddy.

"It's crazy. If you're a boat person, no one wants you, but if you have an American passport, you can go anywhere. It doesn't... are you listening? Hello, Am?"

"Oh... yes... I just suddenly had all these... pictures in my mind."

"Wow. Maybe this is working, excavating your past. What pictures?"

I tell him. He thinks it could be India. We've been there apparently.

He points to a piece of parchment with green lettering. "See, there's the visa and the stamp."

I flick through the rest of the passport and suddenly, there's a hideous picture of a very miserable woman. Even worse than the woman in the mirror.

"Oh yeah, passport pictures are always terrible. You should see mine!" laughs Husband.

Beside the picture are words. With my finger I trace the letters of one word, Amalia. Immediately my heart clenches in pain. But when I trace the outline of the word next to it, I feel a powerful surge through my body. "Is this my name too? Is this my identity too?"

"That's your second name. Nani gave you that one, to

recognise your Indian heritage. Prof gave you the first one after some scientist's wife. We call you Ama for short. You know that means mother. But Nani wanted…"

I don't know what a scientist is but I don't want his wife's name. "I want to be called this name, Kali. You must call me this name from now on."

Now we're back on the orange couch, having a cup of coffee. At least Husband is having coffee. I take two sips and feel sad, even with the milk and sugar. I decide I'll just have water.

"This is a bit like an anthropological study, with you like this," says Husband. "I mean it's a bummer. It must be hell for you and it is for me too. Of course it is. But it's sort of like… well, a first encounter."

"What do you mean?"

"Well, when you first meet someone, and you're finding out all about each other."

He looks at me with shiny eyes and I feel a small thrill in my stomach. Outside the windows, the long fingered plants wave in the wind. Somehow, I don't feel the urge to be out there with them. The sun comes out from behind the cloud and shines softly, making the dull floor (sanded and oiled by *me*!) gleam. The drab curtains glimmer in the light and the elephants wink down at us. I ask Husband if he can see the elephants winking.

"They do look a bit like that don't they? But at least it means you know what an elephant is!" He grins at me. "That's something else I've found out about you. Now you ask me a question."

"Hmm… have you got any other wives?"

"No… no… of course… Now why would you ask me that?" He laughs and frowns at the same time. "No…" He looks away and back at me a couple of times, then gazes out of the window where the car creature basks in the sun. "Okay, now my turn… um… how about this. D'you think you could remember how to drive?"

"A car? I don't know I might. I'd have to try. I feel as though I could. I seem to know things by feeling them."

"Uhuh. Yeah well. There's lots of ways of knowing things." Husband nods thoughtfully. "I thought you wouldn't forget how to drive. That's second nature."

"My turn. Do you know how to fly?"

"You mean fly a plane? No way. Do you know the extent of a plane's carbon footprint?"

"No not an aeroplane. I mean just fly, by yourself."

Husband smiles at me with what appears to be tenderness. "You're funny." He lifts a strand of hair away from my face. "You're different."

"Do you like me better?"

He studies me for a moment. "Okay I've got one. Do you know how to do this?" My Husband leans forward and kisses me.

I seem to know how to do this. I feel as if I've done it before. But maybe not with him. He puts his arms around me and draws me close.

The sun is poised on the hill overlooking my little brown home when Prof and Nani arrive with the sons. They've brought food for us all. Prof shoves open the transparent sand door, the wide brim of his headdress casting his face into shadow. Marching into the kitchen, he bangs open drawers and excavates a long knife, as if about to go to war.

"I have brought you some of my home made bread, Beti, can you smell? Nothing more evocative isn't it? If that does not recall your memory back... not like that shop bought rubbish served up yesterday... no surprises you did not eat." He starts to wield the knife upon a brown-topped object, which does indeed smell flavoursome.

Nani steps tidily into the house, laden down with bags. Wisps of grey hair have escaped around her face. Her soft grey garment swirls around her calves. She drops her bags, glancing over her shoulder at my sons who are sliding down a hillock on the fronds of the waving plants.

"How are you my angel?" She comes and takes me in her arms. "You seem to have some colour at least. Have you two had a good day?" She regards me with her gentle eyes. "Are you remembering anything?"

"Um, yes, I do seem to be."

Husband and I exchange glances. He raises his eyebrows.

"We're not going to stay. We'll let you all have an early night." She perches on the edge of the red chair, like a little bird. "We'll have lots to do this week, what with doctors and trying to get things back to normal. What are your thoughts?" She turns to Husband and pulls out a large black book from one of the scattered bags.

"I think we'll just take it one day at a time for now," replies Husband.

Nani has her pen poised over a black book. I wonder if it's

her journal? I wonder if it makes her feel sad?

"We have to have a plan, don't we?" She looks around helplessly. "What about Mattie's school and your studies and who's going to look after Sammie and…"

"She must see a psychiatrist as soon as possible," adds Prof from the kitchen.

Husband raises his hands. "Mattie doesn't need to go to school…"

From the kitchen, "Mattie must not miss school, even it is not very good school…"

From the red chair, "How will you manage? She needs to learn how to look after the boys and…"

"… And as for psychiatrists…"

At this moment, Mattie and Sammie come leaping in through the door, which bangs and clangs in the wind. They're both yelling, "I want to watch something. I haven't watched anything all day…" "I'm hungry. I'm starving…"

Husband puts his hand on his hips and raises his voice even louder than theirs, "How much have you watched already Sammie? I bet you spent…"

"Following our trip to the museum, we read from the encyclopaedia in the subject of black holes, isn't it Mattie?" Prof's voice comes even more loudly from the kitchen, accompanied by wild knife waving.

I make for the door.

As I touch the handle however, another discordant, ear piercing voice shouts even louder, "I told you, you can't run away when you've got *kids*." I make to cover my ears but then realise it's that firing synapse again.

Nani jumps up. "Where are you going?"

Taking my arm, Husband leads me back to the couch, telling everyone to calm down and stop arguing.

Prof puts down his knife. "Not to worry Mattie, there is sufficient food to feed whole army. Not as if Nani has not fed you every two minutes today."

Later, Husband says, "You seemed so much better today. Apart from running out at the end. But that could be a great way of keeping Prof in check! Brilliant!"

The kids are in Mattie's top bunk and Husband tells me we need to say goodnight to them.

"How would you like to read the boys a story? I think we need to get things back to normal as far as possible for them. We usually take it in turns to tell them a story." He shows me a pile of books on a table in my sons' room. "These are all the books. You can choose. It might help you a bit with the memory."

There's a whirring sound as I run my hand down the pile of books and suddenly I experience a jolt. I pull out a small book on the front of which is written, *The History of Dhruva Maharaja*, while inside is inscribed, in wobbly letters, 'ThIs BoOK BElonGs To MaTTiE hARRiSON'.

Two little heads, one golden and one dark peer over the side of the top bunk.

"That's my book," says Mattie.

"It's got lions in it," adds Sammie.

I climb up the wooden stairs on the side of the bunk beds, which Mattie and Sammie tell me they don't need and *never* use, and we snuggle together, my two sons and me, on the aeroplane cover with its faintly musty smell. I look round the room at Mattie's pictures of robots and Sammie's smudges of paint decorating the walls and then settle down to read, as *The History of Dhruva Maharaja* tingles and whirs gently in my lap.

Re-membering. Day Two:

I started out to record them in one of the red journals from the cupboard. Not a new one, as advised by Husband, in the effort to save paper and thusly trees, (here I was mindful of the wood-wrought surroundings and obliged to wonder...) and reduce the carbon footprint.

Apparently, it can help, in cases of fugue or memory loss, to keep a journal. Husband noted that my penmanship is far more elegant now than the spider's trails of before. He winked at me, adding that that wasn't the only thing to have improved.

Firstly, however, the book infuses me with untold sadness and second I have no need to record, being sruti dhara. So I'm not sure whether this will become a regular habit.

Herewith and with no especial ordering: museum, quality time, hole in the ozone layer (turning the sun into a fearsome enemy as opposed to a gentle warming friend), study, desk, pen, paper, exercise book, note book, journal, cupboard, computer, bag, masters, teacher, 'to' sand (different meaning to 'sand'), to polish, organic oil, archaeology, archaeological excavation, archaeological artefact, swallow (bird), toothpaste, toothbrush, natural toothpaste, robot, paint, the role of mother, passport, boat person, country, door handle, America, India, auto rickshaw, visa, stamp, scientist, (who Husband says is someone who searches for the truth as long as it doesn't interfere with his or her theories), encyclopaedia, black holes, anthropology, anthropological study, carbon footprint, kama sutra, tantric sex, wristwatch, bread (home made versus shop bought), salt, ladder, sweat  (very deeply shocking), library books, robot, back to normal, wink, goodnight.

# Chapter Four

# The Worst Thing

I'm dressed in soft silk the colours of a rainbow. Tantalising harmonies thrill my senses as we anticipate the arrival of the dancing girls gliding onto the diamond floor. Everyone is smiling and laughing, except one person who seems lost and confused.

She says, "I miss my children."

"Ah, Mattie and Sammie?"

She looks at me yearningly. "Yes, do you know them?"

"Yes, of course. I'm their mother," I reply, laughing.

The lost woman scowls at me. "No you're not. I am."

Then a handsome man, with a flashing coral complexion, takes her hand and they disappear into the throng.

Suddenly, thud! The ground trembles; the light is blinding. A small face with a maniacal grin stares down at me, snakes writhing above its eyes. I leap up to find yet another face staring at me. The person is not wearing soft rainbow colours but a shapeless tunic of sludgy pink.

A dull complexioned man intones, "Mattie, let Mama sleep. You know she's not very well."

Husband is wearing black trousers and his dark locks curl over the top of a white t-shirt. He shrugs and tells me this is what pretty much everyone wears, even though it's very boring and runs counter to his ethos of ethnic variety. I am similarly entombed in a variation upon this theme: trousers of dismal green, t-shirt of dreary purple. The brightest of garments in the cupboard of quiet but sad apparel, hang heavy on my limbs.

"Do I have to wear clothes?" I say, sounding like Mattie. At least my clothes don't whine.

Husband laughs as he takes my hand and leads me back to the study, for 'further archaeological research'. I'm a little afraid of the study with its cupboard of pain and other lands. However, Husband feels that if I can face the pain, we may find some answers.

I gasp as Husband reaches for the metal object in the centre of the desk.

"What?" He puts his arm around me, eyes flashing. "Nothing to be afraid of... it's just the computer... Do you... do you remember it?"

He draws the top of the object upwards to reveal something a bit like the machine that Mattie and Sammie were using, when was it? The bottom half is encrusted with white letters and symbols inscribed each on its own small black square, so many teeth in the mouth of a monster. I have a sinking sense it might devour me.

"You were pretty anti-technology before too... We both are. I can't remember you being afraid of it though. You sort of have to use it these days. Everything's on line. I thought we could check out your emails, your Facebook, see if there's anything there?" He gives me a squeeze. "It'll be one of those things, like riding a bike and driving, you won't have forgotten it. Look I'll show you." He presses one of the back molars of the monster and it starts to growl and whine. "That's the start button. It's just booting up."

Suddenly the man with a snake around his neck and a moon on his head appears. One of the images from the ugly furniture in the living room. I hear the faint beat of a drum. Ta-dum dha dhin dhin dha.

"Ah the same man as you have in the ugly furniture..."

"Ugly? What d'you mean?" Husband frowns at me. "That's our altar... it's not..."

"Um, who is he...? Do you know him?" I say quickly.

"Oh... well... he's Lord Shiva, the destroyer." Husband seems to cheer up a bit at this. "I'd like to know him. I suppose I do in a sense. But he's not a close mate if that's what you mean. Why," he stares at me, "do you know him?"

"He looks... familiar." I wonder why he's in the mouth of the monster, but I say nothing.

"Oh... well... great! That means your memory's coming back I guess. But the altar's not..."

But I don't find out what the altar's not because all at once Husband appears transfixed, gazing into the monster's mouth. A few moments later, he returns from his short fugue.

"Now you use the mouse to move this," he tells me, propelling a small black creature across the table. "You see this arrow on the screen there? That's the cursor. You move the mouse like this to get the cursor to go where you want it. See that symbol there?" He points, or rather the little white arrow points, to a small white square with a trident beside it. "That's the internet connection. We don't use Wi-Fi if we can help it. It's not good for the children."

"What's Wi-Fi?" I feel a growing sense of panic.

"It's these electromagnetic waves. They're like, all round us in the atmosphere. It's a nightmare. Who knows how much they're fucking us up? Especially the kids." He settles back in his chair, rubbing his nose. "They did this experiment on beans. One lot grew. The other lot, next to the Wi-Fi, was completely stunted. Scary. Prof loves it though. Of course. The wonders of science. Anyway, where were we?"

The mouse scuttles back and forth, a plastic smile fixed to its poor face, while the monster chews upon its long tail.

"Okay, so now we're on line. Let's check out your email, and then we could look at some pictures if you want. Here, why don't you have a try?"

The monster hisses. Husband clamps his hand over mine, urging the mouse on. Lord Shiva vanishes. Words, pictures spring up in the monster's mouth. The mouse hurls the arrow at a picture. Suddenly, I'm surrounded by piles of grey rock. Long metal ropes hang from blocks of stone, precariously piled, one upon another. Dust swirls, creating clouds, blocking the sun. A man appears, clambering over the rock, loosening great jagged pieces. He's wailing, his hair coated in thick red liquid. Over his shoulder, a small sack... No. It has legs... it's a child! A sharp rock hurtles towards me like an arrow. I lunge away, screaming.

"Ama! What the hell? Are you okay? What's happening?"

In my sideward leap, I have inadvertently shot the arrow again. Now a lady with grey curly hair and a lemon yellow garment peers down at me through glasses, as if from a great height. She wriggles her foot in and out of a pointed yellow shoe. I sit on the floor at her feet on a soft carpet while a miniature person and a long furry animal bear down upon me.

Somebody whispers, "Don't talk to her unless she talks to you. You should curtsey now."

There's more whispering, then I feel myself being dragged away.

"Let me go! Let me go!" I cry, thrashing my arms.

"Ama! What's going on?" Husband's bewildered face appears.

"Tell them to let me go!" I look round wildly. The monster grins. It's about to swallow me up. I slam its jaw down on to its teeth with a grinding crash.

"Am! Stop! What the fuck? You'll break it!" Husband goes to open the monster's mouth.

"No! Please! Not now... it... they..."

"No one's doing anything to you. You're here. What the hell was that all about?"

"I think it was hell."

"Maybe we should give the internet a little break for now." Husband squeezes his nose, shaking his head. He lets out a groan. "I just need to check you didn't break it. We need it. We can't really afford another one."

I look out of the window as the sun emerges from behind the cloud.

Across the grass, next to the long-tentacled plant, a tiny house rests atop a platform on four wooden poles. Sammie, Mattie and another small person climb upon the platform, leap onto a great white metal box behind it (a large fridge?) and swoop down their tentacle slide.

Placing a bowl of wrinkled fruits on the top step outside the sand door, Husband calls out, "Do you want some snacks?"

At this, the three small people come scampering across the meadow.

"This is Barney, the boys' friend from next door," Husband tells me, indicating the third small person.

"You know me, don't you?" Barney takes a handful of the small red fruits. "Mmmm, I love goji berries." He grins at me, his eyes and teeth white against the brown substance with which he's besmeared.

"You're pretty muddy, Barney, where've you been?" asks Husband.

"I'm muddy too," chimes in Sammie.

Barney regards me with dark eyes. "You look different, Ama. Have you lost your memory?"

"I'd actually like you to call me Kali now."

"Oh." Barney looks thoughtful.

"What's memwy?" says Sammie.

"I can't remember," Barney replies and he and Mattie laugh and laugh.

Husband is opening a small door underneath the house. "We have to try and help Mattie and Sammie's Mama to get her memory back."

"I know," Barney grabs another fistful of fruits and stuffs them in his mouth, "we can pretend you're an alien from another planet and we're showing you round like that story, remember?"

"I can't remember," says Mattie, wiggling his eyebrows.

"Ha ha. Not funny." Barney lunges at Mattie.

"No it's not funny," echoes Sammie, joining in the fray.

Meanwhile, Husband has been crawling under the house through the little door and now emerges with some black shiny shoes with high sides, which he suggests I put on.

"They're gum boots," explains Barney, disentangling himself from Mattie and Sammie. "They stop your feet getting wet."

"What about your feet?" I look down at his muddy feet.

"Oh I don't need those," he scoffs, moving onto more important matters. "Okay, now that," he points to the massive fridge box, "is a spaceship and you just landed in it."

"No it's not," says Mattie, looking at Barney in amazement, "it's a container."

"And those are poggles," declares Barney pointing to some small grey creatures jumping around near the spaceship container.

"Those are poggoos," affirms Sammie waving a small branch he's just picked up.

"No they're not, they're rabbits. They live under the container," says Mattie, glaring at Barney.

Husband goes into the house to make lunch, while the rest of us follow the leader, Barney, up the pathway. On the way, we pass two massive creatures with glossy copper pelts, waving mighty arched horns at us. I think they are bulls but they have four legs, and remembering the one legged COW in the hopsital, I realise I may be mistaken.

"These are our bullocks, Fidel and Che or Massey and Ferguson. They get called both, depending on how my Granddad feels," Barney tells me. So they are bulls, I think.

I give Fidel or Massey a scratch and he raises his head to the sky in pleasure. "They don't really like being enclosed in this small space," I say.

Barney regards me through narrowed eyes. "How do you know?"

"I think I must be getting my memory back.

"We'll see," sneers Barney looking down at my gum boots.

"Ow!" Suddenly something attacks my leg, sending an enormous jolt through my body.
All the boys laugh.

Barney casually steps over the innocent looking white ribbon stretched in a square around the bullocks. "That's a hot wire... it's got electricity running through it. You didn't remember that did you, Kali?"

Question: How does electricity heat? And light? *And* cool? And hurl thunder bolts through ribbons?

The air is crisp and a few clouds wheel in the sky. The birds' discordant chatter is tolerable today and there's a faint hum from above. I look up to see a shiny silver metallic-looking bird flying way up high in the sky. From here, we can see the ocean, which looks almost white, and that little island popping up through the water. This roadway is very narrow compared to the ones we were on a couple of days ago. On one side is the meadow surrounding our house and on the other, a large meadow with many black and white creatures, huddled together. They look like cow creatures though again they have four legs. But, no, they have short stumps instead of tails so I may be wrong. Up ahead, either side of the road, the meadows give way to the forest. Arriving at a door made of wooden bars, Barney swings himself over, with Mattie and Sammie close behind.

Sammie turns and opens the door for me. "Woll, you don't know how to open a gate, do you, Mama?"

The boys run towards what appears to be a small house, surrounded by bars made of trees. Inside the bars, a man sits on a very small three legged chair, his hands pulling at the teats, milking (not sure how I know this, but I do) a brown and white creature who must surely be a cow. But then she has a lovely long plumed tail, which she is swishing about. And four legs.

The man turns to greet me with a cheery, "Hello, Ama. How are you?" Blue eyes shine out from a nut coloured face; his skin is as wrinkled as the fruits we were just eating.

I don't remember him, however, and I'm not sure what to reply.

"She's not called Ama now," says Barney. "She's called Kali, and she's an alien from another planet. She just arrived in her spaceship, which is..." he points to the white metal box, "over there."

The man straightens up, wiping his hands on a cloth. He seems about the same age as Prof, and has a kind face. He wears a grey garment spattered with little flecks of colour and possibly mud, which covers him up completely. He grins and his blue eyes sparkle. "Is that right? In that case, I'm delighted to meet you, Kali."

The cow is glossy like the bullocks, with short sharp horns. She pulls intently at a bag of grass. I reach out to her and the man looks surprised.

"You can't touch Katy!" warns Barney.

"But she wants me to," I tell him and sure enough, the cow stops her eating to offer her neck for a scratch.

"Well that has to be a first!" The man opens his eyes wide. "You're brave!" He bends down. "Here," he says, presenting me with a container of warm, frothy liquid, "why don't you take some milk."

On the way back, I ask Barney if that's his father. He looks at me with big wide eyes and lifts the corner of his lip. He says I must have *really* lost it. That's his *grandfather*. The cow, he tells me, is called alternately Joan or Katy B, which is short for Kick The Bucket.

Apparently, when you're doing practical work, as Barney's grandfather does, you wear overalls. That's the name for the top and trousers all together garment he was wearing. And that's why the overalls were covered in spatters of different colours because they're to protect you from getting dirty.

"Yeah, men in overalls," laughs Husband. "It's probably

not the most important thing for you to know right now."

But somehow the name sticks.

It seems Husband doesn't own any overalls, although he'll wear an apron occasionally, to cover himself up in the kitchen. He very much appreciates the milk, however, and places it reverently in the small white fridge box to keep it cool. "Other things are more important than people's dress," he tells me, taking off his apron, "for example getting you reacquainted with the kitchen."

"Okay, yeah I guess," Husband says into his phone, rushing between the kitchen and the study.

The phone is another thing I'm yet to be reacquainted with, but Husband says, "All in good time."

We're not going to have much time today, however, because he's been called to teach at a school, at the 'last minute'. It's what he does sometimes, to make money while he studies. If a teacher's 'not well', he goes in and teaches the class for the day.

Even though I'm 'not well', money is important, so Husband doesn't want to turn down work. It's decided that Nani can look after me today and take me to visit Doctor Ganesh. So I won't have much time to get reacquainted with the kitchen, but all in good time.

Mattie and Sammie are outside on the 'monkey bars', while I hover in the living room watching Husband gather up a bag, his computer, and outer garment.

He tells me my reacquaintance with the kitchen will have to be a 'crash course'. "But the boys will help you… they can probably manage by themselves. In India, they'd be running their own tea stall by Mattie's age. I need to run." Husband opens the door and calls out, "Mattie, get your teeth done and give your backpack to Mama..."

Mattie shouts back, "I don't want to go to school. Do I have to go to school, Mama?"

I look at Husband helplessly.

Husband says, "No I guess you don't have to... It'll be a good excuse for you to stay at home and help Mama."

Mattie jumps up and down on the bar, yelling, "Yay!"

Husband turns to me. "I mean we only sent him to school because you were having a hard time with the home-schooling. I've got to go." Husband pulls on his green garment, gives me a quick kiss and rushes down the steps. "Mattie and Sammie, you'll have to help Mama get breakfast okay?"

Time for my crash course in the kitchen! I look round wondering where to start. I open up a cupboard full of shiny bowls. I'm sure I've seen husband using these on the stove. Choosing six different sized ones I place one on each of the black iron racks on the stove. That should be enough. Then I think, maybe we should use the woodstove? It's quite cool today and it would warm us up. I open the little door and pull out the tray of grey dust at the bottom. I know I have to do something with this, but I'm not sure what. I have to set the wood on fire somehow. But first, I'll see what's in the fridge. I'm already reacquainted with the kitchen! It's easy! I open the bottom of the fridge where the lovely cold ice is. I can't resist touching my cheek to it just once. Ouch! It's too cold. What will we need from here? I pull out different coloured packages. One has small green spheres on the plastic bag; another is decorated with something like Mattie's Lego. I get out several white plastic boxes too. I'm not sure which we'll need, so maybe I should just get them all out. I put some of the packages into the shiny pots on the stove, some on top of the woodstove for when I light it, and some inside the stove. Now what else? Things from the top of the fridge. Oh, there's the milk from Katy B we could definitely use that. What's this yellow block? It might be needed too. Ah and Prof's bread. When I've emptied the fridge, I realise we're going to need spoons and maybe knives. I pull all the drawers out. I'm sure they're in here somewhere. There's a drawer full of cloths. I think I've seen Husband using cloths in the kitchen so I get them out. There might be an apron in there too. Yes. I better put that on. That's what you're supposed to do. Here are the spoons. They seem to be very large. But what do I know? The knives are also huge and very sharp, good for cutting the bread. I could put the bread pieces into that silver machine with the black gaping mouths. I think that's where they go.

The front door bangs.

Mattie calls out, "You have to give this to the school. You have to sign it."

I walk into the living room, wielding a knife. "Sign it?"

"That means put your name on it." Mattie shows me a piece of paper covered with writing.

"Silly Mama," pipes up Sammie, who's now climbing onto the couch and jumping off it.

"It's about vaccinations," adds Mattie.

"What are vaccinations?" I ask, but get no reply.

Mattie is striding into the kitchen. "I'm starving. I'm going to make breakfast."

"I'll help. I'm good at cooking." Sammie leaps off the couch.

"What's happening in here?" demands Mattie when he sees the kitchen.

Sammie stares, open-mouthed.

"I'm making breakfast," I explain.

"Woll..." Sammie looks doubtful.

"You can help if you really want to," I tell them.

"We don't need you... you can just go and relax, cos you're not well. Right, Sammie?" says Mattie, opening a tall cupboard in the corner and dragging a chair up to it with an ear-paining screech.

I dither in the doorway with a sense of deflation, the great knife hanging uselessly by my side. Just then, there's a noxious stench and grey smoke emanates forth from the black mouthed silver machine. Prof's bread! I raise the knife and plunge it into the machine's mouth to rescue it. There's a loud crack and a flash, and the knife clatters to the floor.

Sammie clambers up onto the wooden shelf where the machine seems to have died.

"Silleeee Mama..."

Mattie leaps down from the cupboard. "Mama! That's *electric*!" He shakes his head. "That's very naughty. You could have electrocuted yourself! I think you should go and sit on the thinking chair and think about what you've done." He examines the blackened silver machine, then he turns on the light switch, looking up anxiously, but nothing happens. "Now you've really blown a fuse! Just wait till I tell Dada."

A rather plaintive little synapse within me demands, "Who is this child to be ordering me?" And I remain stubbornly in the kitchen. "Don't we need to use the stove?" I say. "Or the woodstove?"

By now, the grey dust from the woodstove has flown all over the kitchen, settling on the shiny bowls on the stove, the packages, and the big knives and spoons.

Mattie glowers at me and places his hands on his hips. "You'll have to do time out. One minute for every year. How old are you?"

Good question. I'm not sure.

"I'm starving. I don't have time for your nonsense." The dark son sighs and clambers back up to the cupboard, from whence issues loud rustling noises followed by a cylinder wrapped in red shiny paper and a golden package. "Catch, Sammie!"

Both items fall through Sammie's outstretched hands and land on the floor. ("Sam*mie!*"). I continue to stand ineffectually by, while the fair son picks up the shiny items and piles them on three small plates, together with three knives, forks and spoons, all small. Walking with great concentration into the living room he carefully lowers his burden onto the table.

Reaching back into the cupboard the dark son drags out a large glass container full of brown sugar crystals for our coffee. But I don't smell any coffee.

Meanwhile Sammie opens the bottom half of the fridge. "Where's the ice cweam?" he cries, jumping up and looking all over the kitchen. "Are you doing a tweasure hunt, Mama?" He goes into the hallway. "Is it in the bedwoom?"

Mattie jumps off the chair. "I'll find it. She's not allowed. Her time isn't up yet." He opens up the woodstove and there it is.

"But I wanted the chocolate one," whines Sammie.

They finally find the chocolate ice cream in the oven. Then we sit down to a breakfast of chocolate biscuits, chocolate, and chocolate and vanilla ice cream, coated with liberal helpings of sugar and fine grey dust. ("You shouldn't be allowed," grumbles Mattie but then grudgingly allows me a small helping.) We have to eat the chocolate and the biscuits with our knives and small tridents or 'forks' according to Sammie, but he will permit us to use our spoons for the ice cream. I use the big spoon and knife from the other drawer. However, as soon as I put the ice cream in my mouth I hear a cow crying for her calf. I see the calf being dragged away and having its bones broken as it's hurled into a monstrous conveyance. I take another mouthful, but the cow continues to cry, so I attempt to eat the biscuit with the knife and fork. But it breaks and the pieces scatter all over the floor. At that moment, the door grinds open and in steps Nani, hair flying and amulets jangling.

"Would you like some breakfast, Nani?" says Mattie.

Abundant spiders' webs cling to lights and every single corner of the wooden platform outside Doctor Ganesh's glass door. Mattie and Sammie launch themselves into a grassy area behind the house and begin to upturn square red rocks.

"They always do that when we come here," Nani tells me, delicately stepping out of her little black shoes with one tiny jewel on each toe and placing them neatly, side by side at the door. "They're looking for creatures under the bricks."

Always?

"A centipede!"

"Ants!"

Inside, the room is full of squashy brown plastic chairs and metal framed chairs with flowery cushions. A table in the middle is strewn with shiny books covered with words, (Our Lives on Mars! Killer Dentist! Living Green! Secrets Hospitals Won't Tell You!) and smiling women resembling toads.

A slightly built man in a grey jacket appears at an inner door, smiling warmly. "Good morning, Amalia."

"Oh, er... good morning. Are you Doctor Ganesh?"

Nani sniffs and wipes her eye.

Doctor Ganesh ushers me into a room lined with thick books which rustle softly.

Bending to his computer behind a vast expanse of table, Doctor Ganesh taps away at the white lettered squares. My sense of foreboding is assuaged only by the gentle concern in his eyes.

Through the window, I see Nani, Mattie and Sammie bent over an upturned brick.

"Your mother tells me you have had a fugue episode. Would you like to tell me about it?" I sigh, staring down at my brown hands while the books continue their whispering, then start to recount the tale of my life from as far back as I can remember. It is a short tale.

"Yes," says Doctor Ganesh nodding and tapping. "Appetite? Any particular food you crave? Any you dislike?"

I think back to the broccoli. Every time I stabbed it with my small trident, I heard its screams as it was torn from the plant. The potatoes look at me with their baleful eyes. The non fairtradeorganics fill me with horrors of being beaten if I don't work harder. The cheese, similar experience to ice cream. I've been living on fairtradeorganics mostly. We had to go to Save World to get more.

"Yes." Nod. Tap. "And sweat?"

Ah! Sweat! That was indeed a horrifying discovery on a par with...

"Bowel motions?"

"Yes, I have bowel motions, every day! It's terrible!"

Doctor Ganesh smiles faintly, asks if I prefer to be outside or inside? Like listening to music or quiet?

I tell him outside. Outside! And... there is no music is there?

"Fears?"

"Apart from the internet? I'm getting better... But the Save World! That World... "

In my inward eye, I recall the scorched and barren plain which unfolded before us outside the doors of Save World. It was strewn with the corpses of dead animals and trees, while emaciated brown men dressed in rags wandered forlornly. I could barely cross the threshold, despite Nani and Husband's encouragement, as more and more animals stampeded out of the doors collapsing in agony. Nani and Husband had to hold my arms very tightly.

"And dreams?"

Dreams? I thought maybe this was the dream, whereas...

The books rustle and whisper.

"Fugue is usually precipitated by trauma," continues Doctor Ganesh, peering into the screen of his computer where who knows what untold traumas lie.

"You probably don't recall but I was treating you for depression previously. That could have brought it on... " He looks at me and we sit for a moment. "Post partum depression can last for several years... and of course it can be very challenging with Mattie..."

"Mattie was very angry with me this morning..."

The books seem to sigh.

"I didn't know what to write on his vaccinations paper. And then..."

"Vaccinations?" Doctor Ganesh, hefting a groaning book from a shelf, stops abruptly. "Something at Mattie's school..."

"Vaccinations are very bad for children with autism. You know, until they started vaccinating in China they had no autism. Especially since Mattie is already affected by the birth chemicals. It could aggravate the symptoms."

No, I don't know. China? Birth chemicals? Autism? I lean on the table with my head in my hands. "I don't know anything!" I look up to find the small man gazing down at me with deep concern in his eyes. "Can you do anything for me, Doctor Ganesh? Can you give me my memory back?" I clutch the edge of the table. "Please! You see the worst thing is... "

The door bangs open and Mattie walks in on his hands, followed by Sammie.

"The worst thing is... "

Nani stands in the doorway, her brow furrowed. "Sorry.

We didn't mean to interrupt. Come on boys…"

"It's alright," says Doctor Ganesh.

"The worst thing is… I don't even know…"

Sammie picks up a small clay statue of a man's head, which is sitting in the middle of the desk. "Hanuman!" he murmurs happily.

The kindly man of medicine smiles fondly at Sammie. "He always calls him Hanuman," he says, knowing my son better than I do. "It's actually Hahnemann, the founder of the homeopathic system of medicine. These ancient systems of medicine are all there, if we know how to listen…"

The books rustle and murmur their approval.

"The worst thing is…" I say as the books, Dr Ganesh and my sons all seem to hold their breath and listen, "I don't even know my own…"

Here little Sammie climbs up on my lap and looks into my face and I am unable to continue. But Doctor Ganesh knows what I was going to say. So do the books.

Then my fair son slithers off my lap, joining my dark son crawling around on the floor, picking up tiny white balls and making them into piles.

"That's alright, just don't eat them." Doctor Ganesh gets up. "I will prepare your remedy."

"They always do that too," comments Nani, also knowing my own children better than I do. "They're the spilled pills. They taste like sweets." She enters the room as the books resume their whispering. "Can I have a quick word while we're here, about Sammie's teeth and Mattie…"

Nani breathes in deeply. "Mmm the ocean air. I knew it would be good for us all to come here. It's the best place for healing. So good for the children. Maybe it will do something for your memory. Who knows? It was a similar place where you... where you ... you know." She looks out over the ocean into the distance.

I follow her gaze. There's that small island again, the one that we can see from our road at home, sticking out of the water, looking like a giant tortoise against the sky. Tortoise? There seems to be no telling what I know. And don't know. I grip the small glass phial in my hand. I will start my 'remedy' tomorrow. And then...

We're standing on a tall cliff overlooking the shore. Three other cliffs of black rock jut out into the ocean and water rushes into a cave at the foot of the nearest cliff. A breeze blows the spiky grasses lining the path down to the shore, where two figures are drawing a big circle in the brown sand. Two other figures entirely in black carry long objects under their arms. Boats?

We look down on it all, like eagles from above. I know about eagles too. Eagles, boats, tortoises. Well that should be useful.

"Those are surfers," says Nani. "See the men with the boards? Do you remember that?" She watches me closely.

"Yes, sure," I say. I'm a little afraid of her sad smile. I'm also a bit tired of being told things. It makes me feel... small and... stupid.

"You do? That's wonderful!" Her whole face lights up like the sun. "I knew it was a good idea to come here... it could be taking you back to that day… Do you remember… anything?"

"You mean apart from the sufferers?"

"Sufferers?" The light seems to go out.

We're making our way down the side of the cliff, along the pathway between rocks and springy grasses. It's good to feel the warm sand between my toes. The boys have already reached the bottom and race across the sand. I run to catch up with them. The ocean!

Mattie gets a stick and starts purposefully digging holes in the sand until he reaches water, then starts digging another hole.

Sammie draws a line in the sand. "This is where the sea meets the beach." But he keeps having to redraw his line, as the foamy edge of the water washes it away.

Nani and I stand by the water while the sun shimmers on the sea in swathes of silver. The sand glints darkly. I bend down to scoop some water into my palms and drink it.

"Eeyuck!" It's terrible! I spit and spit, trying to get rid of the salty taste, the shock. A passing sea sufferer laughs.

"Silly Mama," says Sammie.

The sun is dipping behind the trees outside Nani and Prof's white house, but still lights up the wooden floor with its last rays. Almost four traverses of the sun since the beginning. I'm four days old.

"This is my favourite spot in the house." Nani sits in a soft blue velvet chair in the centre of the pool of sunshine, her grey dress tucked tidily about her legs.

We're having a cup of tea, lemon balm from the garden.

I'm tolerating it well. My mind is devoid of horrible pictures of squealing cows, gelatinous red liquid or other things...

On the way from the ocean, on Mattie's pleading, although Nani was not in favour after the Save World episode, we stopped at a shop where everything is priced at two dollars. At first, all I could hear was a moaning and a sighing but then I was shocked to see thick black treacle oozing out of the doorway and spreading far and wide, while birds tried in vain to walk amongst it and sea creatures writhed and floundered, struggling to break free. As Mattie and Sammie charged into the shop, I cried out to them to stop, they would get stuck too. Who knew what was within and from whence the slime emanated? Nani appeared quite fraught holding onto me near the doorway and letting my sons enter into that realm alone.

Fortunately, they both escaped unscathed, triumphantly bearing their spoils. Though at what cost they had them, I cannot tell.

Now Mattie is absorbed at the large mahogany tree table in the dining room (different from the living room), doing an archaeological excavation of the dinosaur's egg he acquired with who knows what endeavour from the treacle shop, to find the baby dinosaur inside. I'm unfamiliar with dinosaurs despite knowing other animals. I tell Nani what Husband said about us being archaeologists uncovering my life and am rewarded with the sad smile.

She stands up and straightens her dress. "Well, I better get cooking if we're going to eat anything today."

Meanwhile, Sammie, charging through a wide glass window, leaving grey curtains flapping, leaps onto a black cloth table. I glean through observation of Sammie and to a certain extent Mattie, that many furnitures have the purpose of being jumped on. And off. But a table?

"Come and jump on my twamp, Mama!" yells Sammie, bouncing up and down on the table.

"Oh are we supposed to jump on it?"

"Not you," says Nani grabbing firm hold of my hand. "We do not want any further incidents."

I follow her into the white kitchen room, where she removes various vessels and packages from white cupboards and drawers. Time for me to become reacquainted with this kitchen too, I suppose. I ask Nani if she would like me to help. A very sad smile crosses her face and she declines.

Prof is not pleased with pasta and broccoli, he calls it 'kids' food', declaring that children should learn to eat what the adults eat and not be pandered to. He adds his homemade pickle liberally. Mattie asks for some.

"It's very spicy, Mattie," warns Husband.

But Mattie insists. Sammie only eats cheese. I won't say too much about what I eat. Pasta fills my mind with dead insects and cheese as I mentioned, populates my synapses with pictures that seem to have usurped the place of the rightful occupants. I don't know where they come from.

Mattie, his mouth full of pickle, pipes up, "What's vaccinations?"

Prof puts his knife and trident carefully on his plate and sits up very straight in his chair. "Huge scientific miracle breakthrough, Mattie, which has reduced diseases throughout the whole world to almost nil. Should be compulsory I b'lieve. Highly irresponsible those who don't vaccinate." He casts a stern look around the table. "I will explain you in the encyclopaedia after."

"Doctor Ganesh told me they could be dangerous." I push my broccoli around the plate.

Glaring at me from under his deep brows, Prof's face is like a dark cloud against the startling white of his crisp tunic.

"But what do I know."

"Yeah, now people have other diseases like autism and blindness. That friend of…" says Husband leaning forward.

Prof glowers at us through his slanted glasses. "No scientific connection. Data was completely falsified as I understand."

"Right, and the peer reviews from scientists are not at all skewed by their connections with big pharma." Husband retorts, waving the broccoli on his small trident dangerously.

The plates rattle as Prof's fist lands on the table.

Nani quickly interjects, "We got some remedies for all of them today from Doctor Ganesh."

"Placebos." Prof's voice gets louder and bits of pasta fly everywhere. "When you are taking her to see a proper psychiatrist?"

"What did he say?" asks Husband, ignoring Prof.

"He doesn't think it needs to take six months… With this remedy memories should gradually start returning quite soon…"

This is interrupted by the painful screech of Prof's chair and the crashing of plate upon plate.

But then Nani suddenly leaps up too. "What are you doing?"

We all follow her horrified gaze to the white kitchen floor where two small boys crouch, spoons in hands and pink rimmed mouths, an almost empty box of what looks like ice cream between them.

Husband's chair gives a screech as he bears down on his sons. "You're not allowed, Sammie! We have to be careful with your teeth, you know that."

Some mumbling containing the words "proper dentist" emanates from Prof.

Sammie looks up, defiance in his eyes. "Woll, we had ice cweam for bweakfast with Mama."

"Oh yes," murmurs Nani faintly, "I was going to mention that…"

## Chapter Five

## Magic Remedy I

The sun rises over the horizon, gilding the edge of the spaceship, pouring gentle gold upon the trees in the endless forest. I hold the glass phial reverently in my hand. My remedy, *anacardium 1M.* Containing the potency of one thousand cycles of dilution, one thousand cycles of succussion. The paradox of the less the substance, the greater the potency, as proclaimed by Doctor Ganesh. Five tiny white spheres like miniscule planets, once early in the morning for five mornings.

Allowing the spheres to dissolve under my tongue, I feel a little thrill of anticipation. Who knows what powers might be contained within such microcosms? What worlds might open up to me? Then, as Doctor Ganesh instructs, "Wait and observe".

"I don't want go to school," moans Mattie as he shows me

to his classroom.

Maybe he's afraid of a monster hurtling across a meadow, roaring and spewing green spray. Or maybe he's afraid of the many coloured serpent creatures lurking beyond. Murmuring houses wrought of dead trees squat like a village of ogresses round a courtyard (whose black stones must surely prick Mattie's tender palms with every step). I wonder if he fears being swallowed in the houses' cavernous depths or whether he quails under the sightless gaze of their windows. Or possibly he yearns to be out in the fragrant smell paradoxically emanating from the monster.

Suddenly I'm speaking to a pair of muddy shoes. "I think you have to go to school, Mattie."

"Dada doesn't make me."

I try to explain as best I can with my infantile store of knowledge and reason, "Who's going to look after you while Dada's at the university, or at work?"

"I don't need anyone to look after me. I can look after myself. I'm six and a quarter."

However, Husband, Nani and Prof do not agree. Therefore, the six year old and the five day old are both at Mattie's school for the day. Nani is writing a book and can't be expected to supervise me all the time, Sammie is playing with a friend and Prof is at his vital job supervising the animals. Husband is at the university studying social anthropology for his masters, who seem to be very demanding, but will, if he serves them well, grant him a more academic career, rather than messing around teaching kids. I'm back at school, starting all over again.

Catherine, Mattie's teacher, (who, apparently, is a close

friend of mine), has said I can come in and help for the day. It's a small school, more like a family. That's why we chose it for Mattie, explained Husband, while Prof muttered something about a 'proper school' and 'lack of facilities'.

Mattie walks a few more heroic steps on his hands before collapsing in the doorway to what I assume must be the classroom. The classroom! Dangling lanterns wink at us from the ceiling and the walls are covered from top to bottom in writing; it's noisier than the roads or the hospital mansion. 'Our Literacy Working Wall, We are learning to write interesting sentences`, 'I am learning to understand why we need to learn handwriting`, 'Our numeracy working wall', `Our work groups'. A paper tree called Reading Questions grows out of one wall with all its fruits and flowers labelled: 'Can you think of a different way to say...?' `Why do you think...?' 'What do you know about...?` 'What do you think will happen next...?` On another wall, a big white bear is surrounded by words: I wonder how anyone can hear themselves think with the walls being so raucous. Then I notice several small people seated on small circles on the floor, in complete silence and stillness, gazing at us out of pale, golden and nut-brown faces. A woman seated before the children rises. Can this be my friend Catherine? She's about the same height as me, with rabbit hued hair pulled back tightly from her fair parchment skin.

"Sit down, Mattie," she instructs my son, indicating for him to join the children on the floor. Coming over to where I'm hovering in the doorway, hands clamped over my ears, she gives me a brief hug. "How are you, Ama?"

I quickly remove my hands and attempt a smile. "Oh. Getting better every day. Re-membering more and more…"

"Okay. I'm sure you'll be fine." She smoothes her tidy hair absently. "It's great for me to have a spare pair of hands, especially at this time of the year; the new ones can hardly sit still for a moment." She glances sternly at the group of children sitting like statues on the carpet. One boy moves his arm. "Sit still, Rudr!"

"I can still read," I say hopefully.

"Oh, right. You can take some children for reading practice."

I hear Mattie's loud voice, "Sit up and behave, Rudr!"

Catherine looks anxious. "I'll send Sofie and Akul out to you. Just find a spot outside. Rudr and Mattie, go and sit on the thinking chairs. Five minutes… both of you."

Mattie dives under a table, which soon begins to sway and talk. "I'm a tortoise!"

But the erstwhile tortoise suddenly darts out of the classroom, heading for the lurking serpents. Danger! I run out to stop him, but Catherine has seen it too.

"Mattie! Come back to the classroom, now!" she orders.

I have to confess, despite my aversion to orders, it is a relief to have someone else in charge. Otherwise, I too might have darted somewhere. But then, to which somewhere would I dart? And more, what dangers may lurk? Serpents, computers, electricity, monsters spewing green matter. But let me not become overwhelmed. My powerful remedy… it could be working already.

With renewed hope, I wander outside and 'find a spot'

under a small tree.

Closing my eyes, I lean against the trunk, soaking up the sun's warm rays and absorbing the tree's vital force. Peace. Gradually, a picture starts to form upon my inner eye. I'm sitting outside, under a tree... somewhere. It's a huge tree... where? Oh, now I see... I'm outside the palace! Yes, I'm waiting for my sisters... Oh, and we're going for a picnic in the forest. Yes! I remember! I'm playing a trick on them – so funny – by becoming invisible! A memory! Oh you wonderful little remedy! I look round eagerly. I have to tell someone! I am *remembering*!

Just then, two small people wearing little blue trousers and tunics, come skipping over to my tree spot, clutching books. Sofie and Akul. Looking straight at me, they suddenly stop, appearing to be searching for something. Then they turn and run back.

"Mrs Brodie! Mrs Brodie! We can't find Mrs Harrison."

Catherine appears in the doorway and looks over at the tree. "She can't have gone far, I don't understand it."

I wonder who they're talking about? Maybe I should help them search. After all, I am supposed to be helping. Then I realise they're talking about me.

After the whole class had put their shoes on and children were streaming over the black stone courtyard towards the meadow (witnessed by the sightless ogresses), Catherine sounded a shrill blast on a small silver instrument in her mouth. Immediately, the children halted, remaining rooted to the spot. At that moment, I stood up and waved diffidently from behind the narrow tree.

When Catherine finally noticed me, she slapped her hand against her lightly etched forehead. "There you are. I was terrified you'd run off. Aren't you supposed to be better?" Here she sighed. "I don't know if I can cope with another Mattie."

She had some hesitation about leaving me outside after that; she thought I might like to sit in the thinking chair for a while instead, but I insisted I had been there all the time, it was just a misunderstanding.

So, back under my little tree with fair Sofie and dark Akul.

Sofie snuggles up to me. "Why don't you ever come and play with us any more? You used to do dress ups with your sparkly dresses."

"Did I?"

Akul says nothing; he simply smiles and opens his book.

"Do Akul's book first," says Sofie, "because he can't speak much English. Look, you put the pen on the word and it speaks." She touches a blue rod to the image of a cow.

All of a sudden, the cow starts talking, "I'm not very happy here. There are so many of us jammed in together. They cut off our tails. We stand in the paddock up to our knees in mud for three days without water. The electric wires move us on relentlessly. We spend most of the day frightened. One day, number one hundred and eight got the smart idea to lift the metal bar, by our feeding troughs in the milking shed. We pulled our heads out. There was a stampede. I don't know what became of one hundred and eight after that, but we never saw her again."

Sofie looks at me, wide eyed.

"Does the book usually say that, Sofie?"

"No, it usually just says, *The cow lives in the field.*"

Akul moves the pen on to the pig, slowly reading the words. "*The... pig... lives... in... a... sty.*"

"Chance'd be a fine thing," grunts the pig. "I've never even seen mud."

Sofie gives a little start and smiles up at me uncertainly.

"I've never seen the sky or clouds. I haven't moved for how long? Yes we hear about clouds; the birds fly in and tell us about life on the outside. The two-legged animals can't stop them. We have our own language, which they don't speak. We're jealous of the cows wallowing up to their knees in mud. I can't even move to scratch. Imagine living your whole life with an itch? A seven year itch if you're lucky. We don't usually last that long. As we go into the truck, we say to them, 'Next life you'll be the pig and I'll be the butcher.' Ha, ha, snort."

Sofie looks puzzled. "Why don't they see clouds ever? Do you speak pig language?"

Akul is crying. Maybe he understands pig language.

We return to the classroom. My eyes take a few moments to adjust after being in the sun. Catherine is sitting on her chair surrounded by paper and words while the children sit on their miniature chairs, painstakingly inscribing words in small books.

Sofie says, "Mrs Brodie, the book talked."

"Shh, Sofie, classroom voice. Come up and talk to me quietly. Remember how we practised?" She bends down and collects several pieces of paper from the floor. "I know the book talks... it's a talking book." She looks at me. "You may remember I'm not such a fan of technology, not for the little ones, still… how did they go?"

"But the cow really talked, Mrs Brodie, and the pig…" Sofie jumps up and down in excitement, her hair popping out from its pink ribbon.

"Shh, dear, it's not respectful to interrupt when the teacher is talking. Now you go and do your writing. Here's your work. Off you go. Good girl."

I say, "The books at home and Doctor Ganesh's whisper, but not quite that clearly."

She looks a bit distracted. "I know they're amazing, aren't they? You just put the pen on the word and it says the word. So helpful for the ESOL children." She bends down and inserts papers full of words into cupboards. "You know they listen without saying a word for months. Then suddenly they can speak. It's extraordinary…"

"Yes, Akul seemed to really understand the pig…"

But she's not listening. "Mattie leave Sansita alone… go and sit in the chair for six minutes and think about what you've done."

People who go into the city to work can spend far more than six minutes in chairs, it seems. I suppose they may use that time for thinking or not. I don't know what the throng of people in their cars are thinking as they crawl very slowly along the roadway. I have no need to hold on tight when we go fast round corners as I did the first time in Husband's car, because most of the time we're not moving at all.

The road is bound by small white walls, beyond which

are great hills covered in bushes and grey fronded plants like the ones at home. And beyond these are houses made of dead trees, surrounded by living trees. Towering metal giants stride across the land holding long grey ropes in their hands, while huge green boards covered with white writing, kindly explain where you're going and when to turn onto a different road. It seems, unlike me, not everyone is sruti dhara. Conversely, like me, many people have problems remembering things. Where they are going for example. Or even where they are now.

It's hard to believe I used to drive. All in good time. For now, I'm relearning about time. Good Time, Quality Time and now, Short on Time. In a small aperture on the 'dashboard' of Husband's car, there are digits, which show the hours and the minutes, whereas the clock we have in the kitchen at home has hands going round from a central point. The long hand shows the minutes, the short hand shows the hours. The time on the dashboard clock now shows 08.36, which means we've already spent twenty-three minutes in our seats, going very slowly and thinking.

Husband is tapping the wheel. He tells me he's thinking we're Running Out of Time and he's going to be late for his classes at the university. I'm thinking about the car in front which says 'Bugger Off', and another that says, 'Baby on Board'. Then an immense car draws up alongside and I lose sight of the baby. Pressing a little black button on the car door (causing the window to magically disappear), I'm suddenly assailed by a noxious odour, worse than bowel motions and sweat, and I find myself face to face with an endless cloud of white birds staring at me with scared, accusing eyes. How many birds I can't count, all squashed inside yellow plastic boxes one on top of another. Husband tells me there are probably about six thousand chickens, poor buggers.

"What are they all doing in that huge car, did it eat them? But then why are they still looking at me?" I turn away from them. I can't take their staring eyes.

Husband says, "They haven't been eaten… yet."

I have an image then of men shoving birds into crates, together with the crunch of snapping legs and wings. Like the pictures in Mattie and Sammie's little tablet machine, the images follow in quick succession: birds' throats being cut open, birds being dropped into tanks of scalding water. Oh no! They're still alive! They can feel the pain. And now, an angry man breaks birds' heads off while they're still alive and stamps on them. I jerk open my eyes in shock to find not only the birds but now the beady eyes of the face in the monstrous conveyance staring down upon me. Its beaky nose protrudes from an egg shaped head attached directly to shoulders, with no intervening neck. The face sneers at me. But then all the small cars start crawling forward, so the monster turns its egg head to the road and ploughs on with its cloud of birds.

"Chickens have a hard life," says Husband.

I'm being taken care of by Husband today. Although he has to go to the university for his classes, I can just sit there and not say anything, while he keeps an eye on me. Mattie's at school and Sammie has gone to his friend's house.

Last night Nani said, "There'll be a limit on how many times Sammie goes there, maybe you should think of getting extra days at kindy."

I suggested we take him with us to the university. But everyone laughed at that. I'm not sure why.

Husband, Nani and Prof have decided that it's fair if they take turns looking after me, just until I'm well enough to look after myself, and of course, my sons. I was so excited to tell them about my returning memory outside the classroom yesterday but they didn't seem happy. Husband's eyes bore into me even more intensely, Nani's sad smile was replaced by clenched teeth, while Prof disappeared even further under his craggy brows. They insist I don't have any sisters, nor for that matter have we ever lived in a palace. What's more, my 'vanishing act' seems to have given Catherine quite a shock, and as a result narrowed our options for day care.

Now all the cars are going a bit faster. The chicken monster is far behind us. A green board overhead says 'City Centre' and we go off the motorway onto a smaller road, which goes underneath a great rock arch made of white stone. Husband tells me it's called concrete and there's lots of it in the city. We come out of the arch to daylight and the cars all stop for another creature possessed of red, yellow and green winking eyes, one atop the other.

"It's not alive, Am," explains Husband. "It runs on electricity."

Over the wall next to the road, are a mass of bushes and trees, which is a relief because they just grow and live and don't run on electricity. But then amongst that oasis of green is a mysterious creature with red tentacles. Husband tells me it's a sculpture. As we await the winking electricity creature's permission we are confronted by a massive black board set against the grey sky proclaiming 'Styx. For the quiet life.' under a huge black tower with STYX emblazoned thereupon. I assume this is the label for the city where many such towers shoot into grey clouds. The promise of a quiet life beyond the relentless thundering and hissing of the roads is appealing.

"It'll be a relief to get to Styx and have a quiet life," I say.

Husband's eyebrows squeeze together. "Yeah, I guess it is a lot quieter out in the sticks. Funny, you used to say it was too quiet…"

We enter into a terrain of looming grey buildings and scurrying people in black trousers who at times pause their scurrying to obey the winking creature or stare into the buildings' wide windows full of statues and words. The road becomes narrower, turning round and round on itself as we descend to a massive white concrete rock tomb where, I'm informed, the cars lurk while their owners are disgorged into the city above. Our voices echo as we run up stone steps to daylight and a continuous roar punctuated by voices and footsteps running, cars squealing and a gong chiming.

Quiet it is not.

Looking up at a rather ornate white building where a large clock is showing nine o'clock, Husband grabs my hand. He says shit we have to hurry because he's going to be late. We run along white stone pathways, past a building with many tables and chairs outside on the pathway and people sitting drinking out of white cups. There's a chink of cups and utensils, the odd peal of laughter and the same bitter nutty smell as Prof's coffee. A woman with a red shawl rustles past clutching a tall black cup, sipping from it and shouting to herself. We wait by a winking creature while its eyes change colour and a small green person in a box across the road starts marching but not going anywhere. We don't march, we run across the road while the cars wait, snarling impatiently and breathing out smoke.

Husband leads me to a wide bluish window doorway where a man with scraggly hair sucks on a white fiery tube. Smoke billows around him. It's a different smoky smell from the cars. Then he stamps on the tube. But I don't have time to see more as Husband is rushing me through the door which appears to glide open by itself. Other people swarm in with us, carrying black bags and phones.

University reminds me a bit of the hospital building. There are many shades of grey. In the moving grey lift many people are squashed in tight. Everyone is peering intently down into phones or at the floor. I look down, but can't see anything at first, except the dull grey floor. In a second, however, the floor transforms into the white feathered back of a swan and I see myself rising up off the ground, in a vehicle made entirely of flowers, surrounded by flashing people clad in iridescent cloth. But just as I detect the delicate aroma of parijata blossom, my arm is yanked and I find myself ejected from the lift onto grey carpet.

"Come on, Am, we're late." Husband propels me past grey walls and doors, which open on to who knows what grey interiors, and through the specific grey door we seek. Inside, several colourless people and one rather beautiful man with a kind face, look up as we enter.

There's a murmur of "Hi's" from the five men and thirteen women. One of the women looks especially interested.

The beautiful kind man says, "Hello Jay and Amalia. Everyone, this is Jay's wife who's honouring us with her presence today."

The other people nod and murmur, "Hi."

I say, "Actually, it's Kali, not Amalia."

Husband's eyes flash.

"Ah, Kali!" Beautiful Kind raises his eyebrows and smiles. "We're delighted to welcome you, Kali into our circle today. Let us begin."

Husband and I take our places with the colourless people around grey tables. While Beautiful Kind moves a small grey mouse in his hand and writing appears on a white cloth before us.

"You're all aware of the cliché about Eskimos having many words for snow," says Beautiful Kind. "It has been debated, of course. But did you know in Sanskrit there are many words for love? While in English we use the same word for loving ice cream as we do for the rapture of the soul in its pure form of love..."

The men and women sit around the tables, tapping on their computers or writing busily in notebooks as Beautiful Kind talks and moves the little grey mouse, which seems to make the writing on the white cloth change, but brings up no agonising images of blood.

Beautiful Kind reads from the white cloth, "*The question now before us is, when it is in our power to teach the English language, we shall teach languages in which there are no books on any subject which deserve to be compared to our own, whether, when we can patronize sound philosophy and true history, we shall countenance medical doctrines which would disgrace an English farrier, astronomy which would move laughter in girls at an English boarding school, history abounding with kings thirty feet high and reigns thirty thousand years long, and geography made up of seas of milk and treacle and rivers of butter...* This was the attitude of colonial Britain towards Sanskrit and its historical texts."

I'm not exactly sure what this last bit means, but I suddenly feel the urge to speak, "Yes, there are rivers of mango juice too. It's wonderful to frolic in them. And drinking from their waters makes our bodies smell so fragrant. The fragrance carries for many yojanas." I feel elated. My memories are returning! My magic remedy...

The five men and thirteen women stop tapping and writing and look at me enquiringly.

"Am! I thought we agreed you weren't going to say anything," Husband hisses in my ear. "Sorry. She's... well... she's lost her memory a bit," he explains, looking round nervously.

The flaxen haired woman, who had seemed interested before, now appears fascinated.

Beautiful Kind smiles widely. "She seems to be recalling something rather wonderful."

"It's probably stuff she studied before," mutters Husband.

"Possibly." The man regards me thoughtfully.

People are quickly putting books and pens in colourful embroidered bags or bags with little mirrors on or stuffing computers into black bags. They rush out of the classroom saying, "See you at the Korean..." or "No, I need to go and work in the library..."

Beautiful Kind and the fascinated woman are still here. I'm not sure what's beautiful about the man. He has the usual lines etched in the usual places on his face. Although I don't remember faces with etching. It's almost as though the skin gets carved into a happy face or a sad one, or a beautiful one or an interested one, like the ocean erodes the mountains on the shore and creates the face of a land. The beautiful man's lines are carved by kindness. He is gently picking up leaves of paper.

The fascinated woman is hovering.

Husband turns to me. "Am... I mean... oh anyway, do you remember Fern? She's doing her degree in social work. She has a son the same age as Sammie. They play together sometimes."

"Yes. Frank. Do you remember?"

"You probably don't, do you Am? I mean Kali. No, I can't call you that. It makes it seem like you're a different person."

Fern's golden hair is twisted down her back, and her skin looks almost white against the green of her flowery gown. She gazes upon us with wide, sky-blue eyes. "So what happened?"

"Well, we don't really know," says Husband. "You just found yourself on a beach, didn't you? The car was gone and it's never been found. She had no money, nothing. Just the clothes she stood up in, or rather was lying down in..."

"I'm getting some memories now though..."

"...and absolutely no memory of how she got there. It's a nightmare. We don't even know why. It's called a fugue. It's supposed to be a response to trauma, but we can't really work it out. Have you heard of it?"

"When we were in the lift and..."

"Oh no that's terrible! You poor things! Why didn't you tell me? I'd like to help, really! How did it happen?" Fern puts a pale arm around me. "I can't imagine what that must be like. How are the boys taking it?"

"Sammie says..." I start.

Husband makes a hollow sound, which could be a laugh. "They're enjoying chocolate for breakfast. And... oh yeah narrowly escaping electrocution by the toaster. It's a fucking nightmare."

Fern gazes at me. "Wow!" Then seems to collect herself. "Was your life really that bad, Am? You know, Frank's getting a bit like Mattie, hitting kids all the time. I see how it must have been so isolating for you socially. You feel anxious about going to things where there are other kids, don't you? Sometimes *I* feel like running away!" She makes a sound that could also be a laugh, but it's hard to understand why people laugh, when they actually want to cry. "At least you're so lucky to have a lovely husband like Jay." She rubs Husband's arm, giving him a wide-eyed smile. "What are you guys doing about it then?"

"We're trying our best," replies Husband. "We're doing homeopathy. If you try too many things at once, you don't know what's working. One thing at a time. Then we'd like to see Aelfraed too."

But Fern is suddenly enthralled by her phone. "Hey I'd better be going. I've got to pick Frank up from kindy. Look... let's get together. Maybe you can bring the boys over to play? Over the holidays? Oh no, what am I saying? I'm going to be on practicum." She leans in and gives me a kiss on the cheek. "Take care. Let me know if I can do anything, won't you?" She gives

Husband a quick hug and dashes out.

Beautiful Kind has not rushed off.

Husband says to him, "That was a great talk. Thanks." He scratches the back of his head. "I really hate this, reintroducing her to people she already knows. It's like some sort of game." He turns to me. "Like one of the drama improv games you used to do at school."

Beautiful Kind waits and listens in silence.

"Anyway, Am, this is Aelfraed, the Dean of our faculty. I think he might be able to help us." Time seems to slow down. "Do you think you could?"

The Beautiful Kind Dean looks into my eyes. Noises of talking outside the room recede into the distance. The greyness of the room seems to soften and take on its own life.

He bows his head. "I would be deeply honoured to participate in Kali's journey."

# Chapter Six

# Magic Remedy II

During the nightly discussion on where tomorrow's journey will take me, Prof wonders whether Sammie's friend's mother could have me too.

Nani thinks that's a ridiculous idea. "It's hard enough dealing with her two plus Sammie all going in different directions. One of them needs their bottom wiping. When you get back, another one's hit the third and run off down the garden path. Imagine adding an adult, who's likely to disappear as soon as your back's turned, into that mix."

I gather this is a reference to me.

"And I am not going to put my book aside again. I finally get to do something *I* want to do for a change. Something always comes up that's more important. It's not fair."

"You do not have responsible job as I do," points out Prof

glaring through slanted spectacles. "Now if you were Indian wife…"

"I took my turn yesterday," says Husband. "I have to study some time, I've got loads to catch up on now. She'll just sit there. You won't have to do anything. She was quite good today. It's not like looking after kids."

"I'm taking my turn on Friday," says Nani, crossing her legs and pointing her little grey shoe with its tiny bow at Prof. "That's fair."

"You will need to sit, very well behaved, just like Indian school girl ha Beti? It may be little boring for you, but what can we do?" My guardian for today swivels his head towards me from the confines of his stiff white shirt collar. His working clothes, apparently.

Although of course people's dress is not the most important thing for me to know, I do know that Prof's work shirts are ironed by him, because Nani told me she doesn't do his ironing, or any ironing at all if she can possibly help it. His trousers are similarly pressed, with a crease up the middle and his shoes are shining and creased too as he applies them to the car pedals.

Far more importantly, "I cannot risk en-nee problem with the animals." Prof shakes his head in apparent despair. "Other family members have no idea the sensitivity of my work."

He takes out his handkerchief, removes his spectacles and begins to polish them with some energy. The cars around us creep forward. A sharp squealing sound pierces the air.

"Oh you will just have to wait. Nonsense people. No

patience," shouts Prof, looking over his shoulder.

As we alternate between crawling along and stopping completely, white feathers gently swirl in front of the car and land on the windscreen. Prof tells me that there was an accident on this road yesterday, in which a chicken truck overturned and all the chickens fell out. He doesn't know what happened to the chickens but the driver was quite badly hurt. He heard it on the news. I ask him what the news are? However, he has more pressing matters on his mind. Consulting the small clock on his wrist, he says we'll need to hurry to be on time for the animals.

Out of the car tomb, we race up stone steps leading to towering trees with spreading roots and branches, then walk briskly through gardens, which vaguely recall to mind other gardens... the pleasure gardens of Nandana-kanana... Except the sweet smell of grass and sap of the trees in this garden are mixed with belching smoke.

There are no flowers in the lift today. Nor in the small room where I am to sit like an Indian school girl. Several chairs, a table, a clock, a sink, a silver and black machine and a few words on the wall inquiring politely, 'If we stop animal research, who'll stop the real killers?' comprise the sum of the room's contents. A sharp smell catches in my throat, but at least the walls are not noisy, or bossy. Just inquisitive. A door on the opposite side of the room is a different matter, however.

We are in the seminar room/ kitchen space of the research lab. My only exit is through the door we came in, which allows access to the toilet and the lift. The door on the opposite side, leading to the research labs (which are apparently not noisy either today as the university is on break), is forbidden to non-university personnel like me and lets me know in no uncertain terms: "KEEP OUT! AUTHORISED PERSONNEL ONLY."

The animals are one step further removed, in another area, which Prof tells me is fully sealed off from unauthorised outsiders. I think Prof must be speaking his language, as his words are mostly incomprehensible. What is a research lab? What is an unauthorised outsider? I enquire politely whether 'fully sealed off from unauthorised outsiders' is the Hindi way of saying a meadow or forest? For where else would the animals be?

Prof glares at me. "Not Hindi for meadow, Beti." And no further explanation is given. "I will come out and make sure you are alright from time to time." He opens the forbidden doorway. "There is coffee here. You can make yourself a coffee… if you remember how. I have to go immediately to my work, but I will help you later if you are not remembering." The forbidden door swings back and forth behind him, coming to a halt with an officious little click.

I look round at the four grey walls, relieved only by the clock going very slowly and the short questioning book, and sigh. The classroom might have been noisy, but at least there was something to do.

I add a few more re-memberings to my list: motorway, car park, concrete, shops, café, classroom, principal of a school (not like the school I can remember, where we sat rapt in meditation on the sandy bank of a river), teacher, playground, slide, chicken monster, university, digger, plastic bags, clock, minutes, hours, bank, debit card. (The last I am waiting to receive in the 'post' – because I had nothing with me on that ocean shore where I first remember being me. What I'd done with it, I don't know. I had to show the bank lady my passport because my signature seems to have changed. I won't go into the experience in the bank. Suffice to say that money, as many other things, seems to talk.), research lab, fully sealed off from unauthorised outsiders.

I look up at the clock. Only two minutes have passed.

How long will I have to sit, waiting patiently while other people live their lives? But then I remember my magic remedy and cheer up a little. After all, it seems to be working already. As Dr Ganesh predicted, memories are gradually returning. Indeed, who can tell what exciting developments might occur today, as the third tiny sphere releases its power?

At that moment, however, someone comes striding through the forbidden door. A bizarre creature! Is it from another planet? Or could it be a type of dinosaur? The creature is totally enveloped in white, with a white face, slanted eye masks, blue plastic bags for feet, blue plastic hands and a voluminous plastic bag head. A pendant around its neck is labelled, 'Daksh Prajapati'.

The creature speaks! "I thought you may be wanting something to read. Keep you out of mischief. You can still read isn't it? Make use of your time." It sounds remarkably like Prof.

The creature hands me a magazine, graced with no toad-like woman, but an actual toad, and whisks off through the forbidden door. I turn the pages of the magazine dutifully. More useful information to add to my list. But then I realise it's in a different language. Maybe the creature's language?

*Rodents were found to have improved memories after treatment by focused beams of ultrasound which stimulate microglial cells, which form part of the brain's immune system, to engulf and absorb amyloid plaques.*

*Without animal research, millions of dogs, cats, birds, and farm animals would be dead from more than 200 diseases, including anthrax, distemper, rabies, feline leukaemia, and canine parvo virus.*

*This year's Three Rs Award goes to Dr Timothy Woods, a senior research fellow at the Liddle Institute. Enrichment strategies for biological systems have resulted in improved welfare and suitability for experimentation, providing for such natural behaviours as exercise, opportunities for group interactions, nesting and foraging to replace more stressful traditional housing paradigms...*

Three more minutes have passed. Maybe I should go to the toilet? Even though it's possibly the least agreeable of all my re-memberings, I suppose it's one way of making use of my time. It might keep me out of mischief.

Leaving through the permitted doorway, en route to that most miserable of locations, however, I am saved from its vileness by the appearance of something extraordinary. An unexpected vision. A vision as incompatible with toilet and its attendant horrors as it is possible to be. Yes! A vision of such celestial splendour... That window, was it there when we arrived? How could my eyes have failed to see?

Before me, through the window of this grey, grey building, the city spreads, appearing just like Indra's capital, Indraprastha, temporarily burnished as it is by the capricious sun. Giant towers of emerald and silver soar into the heavens, like so many peaks of a glorious mountain. Further off, one building tapers into a sharp spear, while another bears a glistening blue shield, of a completely different order to the Microshield in the hospital. I feel a tingling in my arms. Enraptured, my eyes drink in the scene as a thirsty man in the desert of Save World, while the fickle sun plays its rays upon the spear and shield garnishing them with flashing gems.

Spear? Shield?

The tingling in my arms gets stronger. They start to burn and quiver. My inward eye all at once sees many arms. Arms and weapons. Arms wielding weapons. *My* arms wielding weapons! Brandishing a spear and a shield... And more. A silver sword, a bow, fire, conch shell and whirling discus. Ha! In my eighth hand, I clasp the hair of a decapitated human head, blood pouring from its neck. In an instant, I am no longer behaving myself like a good Indian schoolgirl, no! I'm perched atop the emerald tower building, the city spread out at my feet. I can see for many yojanas. The wind whistles through my hair. I have a desire to kill, to avenge; my tongue craves blood, as I look down at the tiny people, rushing hither and thither in their black trousers, like ants under the bricks of Doctor Ganesh.

"Where did you go?"

What? How? All of a sudden, the creature is standing over me! And I'm curled up on the cold, grey, plastic floor outside the toilet, next to a small window through which grey buildings rear their sorry heads into an iron sky, which seems intent on squashing them back into the sorry earth.

"Oh. Er... I was outside on that building. You see the one with the emerald... um grey shield on it?"

"What are you talking? You must stay seated in the room only. Remember, I was saying, Beti? Like a good girl. I cannot be running after you, here there. Toilet is okay of course. Is that where you were? Only, you were long. Don't go frightening me, eh? You wait patiently and we can have our tiffin together in few minutes."

Then before my sorry eyes, the creature whips off its hands, its face and then... its head!

It turns out not to be a creature at all.

Before I can say anything however, Prof is disappearing through the forbidden door, with promises to be back very shortly to make me some coffee, he has one task to complete... "Few minutes only... be patient now, Beti."

And maybe it's as well I didn't say anything. Just when I think they'll be pleased with me recalling my memories back, they don't seem to be.

Another five minutes pass, but unfortunately no more visions appear. So, now, how to keep myself out of mischief? Maybe I should try to make some coffee? I dither around the coffee machine. Recalling the reaction to my becoming reacquainted with the kitchen, I'm trying to reconcile Prof's offer to make coffee with his edict to be a good patient girl. But then something catches my eye and I forget all about coffee. A flashing silver amulet! Did Prof leave it there, on top of the coffee machine? Maybe it's the amulet for his car? I wonder why I didn't notice it before? It doesn't look like Prof's car amulet, it's too small. I wonder what it's for? I've never used an amulet, at least not for the last seven days, and it's a little exciting. Marginally more exciting, that is, than sitting in a chair. Now, I need a matching hole. Casting without much hope around the empty room, I'm encouraged by an interesting shaped hole in the forbidden door. My excitement grows. And lo and behold, as I insert the amulet, the door swings open!

A small synapse says, "Don't do it. You know what Prof said!" But then a far louder synapse shouts, "Go on! You need to explore the world and discover things for yourself otherwise how are you ever going to relearn?"

The one that shouts the loudest wins and I go through the door

It opens on to a hallway with several more doors and, at the end an even more tyrannical door than the one I just came through, roaring, "STRICTLY NO UNAUTHORISED ADMITTANCE BEYOND THIS POINT". The amulet seems to throb in my hand and my feet seem to float by themselves towards the far door in which another small aperture perfectly accommodates the winking amulet.

There are no windows, only violent light pouring down from intermittent squares in the ceiling. On each door is a paper label in a metal frame. The first says *Rhesus Surrogate*. No amulet is required for this door and I enter a square room illumined by two merciless squares of light, brighter than day, and colder than night. In each corner is a box made of strips of metal. In between, and halfway up the fronts of the boxes are walls of black plastic, such that each box stands in isolation.

Then I recoil in horror. Inside each box, cowers a tiny furry baby with a miniature human face and round, terrified eyes. As I approach, one baby clutches a wooden block covered with sharp spikes, screams, then retreats to the far corner of his box. In the next box, the baby runs to clutch a merciless wire form. The third box contains nothing, apart from the little baby who scurries as far as he can go, whimpering and quivering. The fourth box contains a metal shape, which the baby tries to hug. She screams as some force jolts her away from the form, then huddles, crying, in a corner. I feel my arms starting to tingle and expand. I want blood! This can't be right! Prof wouldn't want to risk en-nee problems with these babies, surely? I will cut the boxes open with my sharp sword! I look down. I have no sword. Ah, but I do have the little silver amulet.

"Come my little darlings, I will take you to play in the meadows with my Mattie and my Sammie." I unlock each box and coax out the shivering baby inside. "It's alright I'm not going to harm you."

The label on the next door says, *Rape Rack*. The four babies follow me warily inside, where we discover another four small boxes. Within each, a large creature is screaming at, beating, biting or throwing a small baby. Prof would be furious. These babies are at risk! I must do something. Unlocking each box, I remove the baby and place my hand on the mother creature's head. For that is who they are. As soon as I touch their heads, I know. I also know they are the grown versions of the little babies cowering at my feet. I can't let them out yet, although my hand has calmed them for now. They're too dangerous; they cannot help but express the pain within them.

I approach the next door with eight babies trembling at my feet. I'm also trembling as I read the label – *Pit of Despair*. Inside there is no cold light, all is in darkness. I can hear crying and rattling. A thick black metal box sits in the centre of the room. As soon as I place the key in the lock, I experience a jolt of agony far worse than the electric ribbon. All the babies are crying and jumping around my feet. I'm not sure whether to open the box. Nevertheless, I must.

The baby inside the box, which has no windows or light, is rocking back and forth, clutching himself, tearing at his skin and hair. I gently place my hands under him, lift him out and hug him close, feeling his quivering terror. "Poor little darling. You're going to need a lot of love." He gradually stills in my arms. The other babies look up anxiously.

I hear the outer door sigh and all the babies scamper to the back of the room. Footsteps sound and then stop. There's the sound of a sharp inhalation, more footsteps, a door banging and some muttering noises. A shadow looms in the doorway and a figure appears.

It's a relief to be outside in the sun. We're sitting on soft grass in the park we walked through earlier, beneath the gaze of a lady in a long gown and a man with a wide hat. Behind us, massive weapons are aimed in our direction. I'm trying to eat homemade bread and potatoes in a fiery sauce (all cooked by Prof because Nani is not an Indian wife) out of round metal bowls, Prof's tiffin carrier. The potatoes are not happy. Prof is not happy. Waving bread and pickles at me, he fires off words, along with a volley of crumb missiles.

"My professor! Important research! Eminent scientist! Sensitive experiments! Breakthrough of mankind! Ruined! Wrecked! My position! Trust! Broken! So many years! Faithful service!" He stops briefly to swallow. "One thing I cannot understand," the fiery potato clasped in his finger tips is aimed accusingly, "is how you got in there in the first place? That door is secured. The cages also."

Cowering like a baby monkey before this onslaught, I whisper, "You must have left the amulet. It was on the coffee machine."

"Amulet? What are you talking, amulet? It needs a special code to access. You need a plastic swiping card. Plus the cages. It is alarmed! I set it myself..." A shadow crosses his brow. "Did I not set? Maybe with my mind worrying about you and all? But it would be the first time in twenty five years. No... it cannot be." He cringes before the lady in the dress.

Prof later informs the family that he refuses to look after me again. I am more trouble than a whole lab of rats. Which leaves Husband and Nani.

It's hard for me to fathom why we (the children, the animals and I) require such serious and constant constraint, but my tentative suggestions along these lines are met at best with derision, at worst ignored.

Instead, "Thank god it's Friday," bleats Husband, as he rushes around preparing backpacks, 'lunch boxes', sandwiches and 'muesli bars' and putting small brown bricks in bowls, to the chorus of, "I want cornflakes!" "I want Weetbix!" "You've got Weetbix!" "But I wanted cornflakes!"

The other day, after Sofie reminded me of my sparkly dresses, Husband showed me where I keep my drama costumes. I was delighted to discover several shimmering cloths, which I immediately appropriated for daily wear.

It takes me a while this morning in front of the mirror.

"You used to make healthy cereal every day," whines Husband. "I don't know what's going to happen to Sammie's teeth at this rate."

"Yuck, healthy ceweal," grumbles Sammie.

But the pink shawl is not sitting quite right. Maybe I should wear the purple?

"I can't be expected to make healthy cereal, *and* get ready in time," I protest, gazing into the wooden framed mirror. I'm getting used to my face. It's only relatively toad-like. The paper retains at least a modicum of sheen, the lattice not too deeply etched. The eyes are relatively wide and dark, I mean compared to others I've witnessed in this last week. Besides, what choice do I have?

Soon Nani arrives as agreed, and I have to leave my shawl as it is. She looks me up and down, sighs a little then turns firmly to Sammie.

Every day so far this week Sammie has asked me if it's kindy day today. I've asked Husband and he's said no. However, today when Sammie asks me, the answer is yes and Sammie is not very happy. Finally, Nani persuades him into her grey car as long as I do his buckoos. And I do! Husband tells us not to forget to take the boys' library books back if we're going to the library, so Mattie staggers down the steps with a big pile of books.

Nani tells me Sammie loves kindy once he gets there. "He'll be fine, you just wait and see. Remember what I told you about the clinging?"

We drop Mattie off to school first, brooking no protestations. Then it's Sammie's turn.

Kindy is guarded by a black gate with a tube coming out of the top, so big people can pull it up and get in, but little people can't escape. Sammie grabs my legs.

"In we go, Sammie," says Nani in a cheery, definite voice.

Inside the kindy's black gate, there are pathways and flowers. I recognise a slide, a playhouse and climbing ladders, all made of dead trees not plastic as they are at school. Not serpents but play equipment. So now I know. And actually there's nothing to be afraid of at school. Or for that matter, kindy.

Across a dead tree platform is a sandy area. I wonder if there is a flowing river, but no. Now Sammy is wailing and clinging to me and I fear that all my efforts in the mirror may have been wasted. I can't work out whether to put my hands over my ears or to keep my wrap in place. However, Nani firmly removes my son, kicking and flailing, and deposits him in the sand.

"Look, Sammie," she says picking up a miniature chicken monster truck.

A slender lady with dancing eyes and bouncing hair emerges from a house building. "Hi, Ama! How are you?"

"That's Georgina who runs the kindy," whispers Nani. "She doesn't know… about you."

The lady, Georgina, joins us, "I wanted to let you know we

have space for Sammie to come all day. He's no trouble at all. He's a darling. He's settled in so well. Remember when he used to cry and cry and cling to you? As soon as you left, he'd be as good as gold."

"I don't really remember that, no," I say.

"Oh. I suppose it was a while ago."

"Just now actually," says Nani. "But there might be a reason for that."

Sammie is back, holding my legs. Georgina puts a hand on his back and he buries his head fiercely into my thigh.

Nani gets out her big black book. "I think we should pencil him in for every day just for now, mornings and afternoons."

"What? All of them?" Georgina looks at me.

Nani frowns. Sammie leads me by the hand to a small table to show me a round piece of hard paper with three holes in it, covered with blobs of green, purple and silver.

"What is it?" I pick it up and some green slime drops on my hand.

"It's a mask of course. I made it."

"Oh."

"You have to leave it to dwy. Silly Mama."

I wipe my hand on my beautiful pink shawl and leave a trail of green. Nani is still talking with Georgina and they look over in our direction.

"Come *on*, Mama," insists Sammie, dragging me into a house building, where he darts off through a doorway, leaving me next to a large cage labelled 'Guinea Pig'. Oh no, here too?

But the cage's furry occupant peers at me through onyx eyes. "No worries. I'm happy. Just sometimes, when the little people squeeze too hard..."

On a nearby wall is written, 'Responsibility', 'Respect', 'Caring', 'Honesty' in large letters, on another, 'Colours'... and then there is a rainbow of all the colours except grey. A basket is marked 'Puppets', a shelf is marked 'Books', then there's 'Play Dough Area' and 'Play Area' where a hint of bossiness creeps in – 'Stay!' 'Play!' 'Talk!' and over there 'Stop!'

In Mattie's classroom, I had conjectured that that's where the children must start learning their labels. However, coming here I realise no, they start learning them even younger. Fancy that! The walls here are much shorter books than in Mattie's classroom though; they are altogether quieter and more melodious. I can hear myself think. One wall tells me very gently, "I am at Preschool, I was not built to sit still, keep my hands to myself, take turns, be patient, stand in line or keep quiet all the time."

At that moment, Sammie appears in the doorway, wielding a sword and looking like the god of death. Ah, my son!

"Can we go home now, Mama?" he says.


"Kindy day is necessary for our mental health, whether Sammie likes it or not." Nani rests her great bag full of library books on a silver wooden bench outside the library.

I settle myself next to it. The bench is warm from the sun. "What's mental health?"

Nani wipes her eye and looks away. "Well let's just say, we might not be in this quandary, if you, or maybe I should say we, had looked after your mental health more."

I follow her gaze over the rooftops to the city in the

distance, where I can vaguely make out the spear and the shield through the hazy cloud.

"Your father says it's all very well having principles, but not when you have to sacrifice your health." She hefts her voluminous bag onto her shoulder. "I think for once, I'd have to agree with him." Rising from the bench, she pats down her skirt. "Why don't you come in with me and get a few books? You love reading. You used to like the self-help section. It might keep you out of trouble." She sighs. "It might even help the… you know. We could get on with what we have to do, without worrying what you're up to all the time." She looks close to tears.

I thought I was helping Prof yesterday. It just seems to have made things worse. He doesn't want to look after me again and there was a bit of a row about that.

"I'd like to sit outside for a little while, in the sun," I say. What I don't say is, otherwise I start feeling like those monkeys in their cages.

Nani looks anxious. "I can't leave you out here…" Her beady eyes flick back and forth, possibly checking for potential escape routes. "Although I suppose I could sit just on the other side of that window, where I can keep an eye…" She appears to consider this for a moment and then satisfied, totters off into the library.

As soon as she's gone, a small bird hops up to the bench, cocking his head and eyeing me beadily like a miniature feathered Nani. "Have you got any food for us?"

That's nice, I like birds. But didn't they used to be more colourful – flashing emerald, ruby, coral? I wonder what happened.

"Er... no, I'm sorry."

"Oh, just like me, I like to travel light too." He does a little hopping dance. "That's alright, sometimes when people sit on this bench they have food." He cocks his little head the other way, listening. "Ah, there's a picnic happening in the park... "

He sails off across the grass, a lacklustre whir of brown and grey feathers. Simultaneously a miserly cloud sails across the sky and the sun does his disappearing act. Everything becomes dull. I may as well go inside. Who knows, I might find some answers in the library books. Nani might be right. It can't do any harm. I wave at Nani through the window and wander inside.

No sooner have the glass doors closed behind me, however, than I'm deafened by a barrage of wild screeching. I didn't realise a library was a jungle full of discordant birds, I wonder what colours they are? But wait. It's not birds but trees! The parents of the books, all talking at once. Of course! I forgot to mention that the books at home have been getting louder by the day since... Wednesday... remedy day. So I could have expected this, but at the same time, so many books... it's a bit overwhelming. Some rustle like leaves, others murmur tolerantly, some whine, some sigh, some creak, others rage as though in a gale. On top of the cacophony of the trees are the unlimited voices of the books' writers: some strident and argumentative, some beseeching, some authoritarian, some cackling. Each voice is trying to make itself heard over the others.

I shout to Nani, "Where did you say I should get a book?"

How can she possibly concentrate on her writing in here?

Nani jumps up. "Shh! There's no need to shout. You're supposed to be quiet in the library." Taking my arm, she propels me to what she calls the self-help section. "Look," she says, indicating a row of books all gently chanting, 'I love myself, I really love myself', "You might find something here. I'll be right over there if you need me." And with that she trots off to her seat.

The beautiful chanting is all at once drowned by an intense screeching from a nearby shelf. Two inhabitants, *The Science Delusion* and *The God Delusion*, are painfully squeezed next door to each other. A woman with a long, silvery plait approaches, pushing a wire cage full of books, which she proceeds to cram between the already overcrowded residents.

"I can't live like this! Cheek by jowl with sentimentalists!" exclaims *The God Delusion*.

"I try to be inclusive, I try to be reasonable but he just doesn't want to know!" cries *The Science Delusion*.

The plaited woman ignores them as she continues to overpopulate the shelf. "Hard to choose, isn't it? There are so many religions!"

I don't know what religion is, but the unhappy squealing is more than I can bear. Extricating the two books I wander off to find them more congenial neighbourhoods.

When I return, another book is grumbling because they say the Dewey Decimal system has allotted two-hundred-and-twenty to two-hundred-and-ninety to Christianity, and only two-hundred-and-ninety for all the other religions of the whole world and it's not fair. I try to help by evening up the numbers. Then I hear books on other shelves complaining loudly about *their* neighbours: *Go Paleo* can't stand being next to *Veganism: A Diet for the Twenty First Century. Dare to Discipline* feels offended by the very presence of *How to Talk so Kids will Listen and Listen so Kids will Talk.* And so it goes on. I spend a very busy time in the library trying to rearrange all the books to their satisfaction, including several ESOL books who worry that if they always wiv same ranguage they no rearn Engrish. The trees still rustle and sigh, but it's too late to do anything about them.

At one point the lady with the plait says, "It's great to have people volunteering their time in the library!"

I'm feeling some sense of accomplishment at a job well done, when I hear a plaintive cry, "Read me!" emanating from a book called *Children Are People Too,* (which *Dare to Discipline* had insisted on relegating to a distant place). It says kindly, "Listen very carefully to children — there may be abuse or they may just not feel comfortable because they feel misunderstood."

In my inner eye, I see Sammie clinging to my legs and Mattie sitting in the thinking chair. I sense the book would like to make further acquaintance. "Anything else I should know?"

At that moment, Nani materialises at my side, "We have to go and pick up Sammie." Her bird eyes dart all around. "Who were you talking to?"

When I explain about the book, she clenches her teeth.

As we're leaving, I hear a slant eyed man say to the plait lady, "I no find any book I looking for. No book on shelf..."

We go out into the sunshine.

"At least you can't do much damage in the library," says
Nani.

"At least you can't do much damage in the library," says
Nani.

Chapter Seven

# Special Time

When I am roughly seven days old, no one in particular is required to look after me because the week has come to its end and it's *Family Time*, a sub category (I believe) of Quality Time.

A hut, involving all the furniture from Prof and Nani's living room is under construction. Mahogany tree chairs are draped with blankets, the carpet is an ocean, only to be crossed by cushion stepping-stones.

"You children, do one thing. You go outside for playing," says Prof. "We cannot have any sort of a meeting with such racket going on." He shakes his head at the upturned chairs. "My father would never have tol'rated."

Husband tips back the single remaining chair, slurping down his cup of tea. "Just as well he's not here then."

Prof ignores him. "Beti, I have something to do first in my

workshop. Shall you come with me?"

"She doesn't want to see that old thing," protests Nani.

"Now it is the only place where she has not seen, isn't it? That is not fair. The sense of smell is very evocative I understand. Assists the synaptic connections. In addition, it is beneficial for her to see how... other husbands spend their time."

Husband has gone into the living room. Nani is intent arranging a book, a notebook and a pen precisely on the mahogany tree table. I'm not sure what to reply. I feel a little anxious. I wonder what the workshop might be. And yet, since I have caused him 'untold harm' it might behove me to please him.

I follow Prof out amongst the tall trees, down a white concrete pathway. A black bird with a puff of white at its throat clucks and cheeps while a heavy green and white bird pecks at red berries, bending a branch under its weight. At the far end of the path, a small wooden house building sits innocently. Prof jangles his heavy load of amulets, and the door swings wide.

He breathes in deeply as we enter the darkness. "Ah! First class! The aroma of oil. It is I b'lieve next only to the alcohol in the lab."

He 'ons' the light and instantly the room is illumined by a dull electric orb dangling from the roof. Prof looks around in satisfaction. There's a black implement attached to a thick table, and a wall covered in metallic weapons. In a corner are a metal staircase and a small boat with a wheel.

"My tools." Prof caresses a wooden weapon topped by a metal crescent.

I wonder at its purpose.

He wields it up over his head. "For hitting things!" He whacks it down on the thick table. There's a glimmering beneath the brows.

I make for the door.

"No, no nothing to worry… Come. You used to like my workshop when you were a small, small girl."

He shows me thick black lines etched around each weapon holding them in place until they are called for… and many glass pots under a wooden shelf.

"These jam pots. I recycled them. In India we never wasted." He twists one pot and it comes off in his hand. "You see you stick the lid to the bottom of the shelf. Magic! And then you put inside your all screws, nails, small hinges and what all." He undoes several more to show me. "Very organised. I learned that from our neighbour Mark Anderson. He has a bloody big workshop. I wanted to learn how to be a real western man you see, Beti. What else was I coming to this country for?" As he twists the pots up into their lids, he eyes me through slanted spectacles. "And then you wedded that man. And now this. I could have exactly predicted. A man with no tools as far as I know."

I don't remember seeing any weapons surrounded by black lines at home, even in the wooden shed building next to the house. Only spiders' webs. "He doesn't believe in weapons, at least not nuclear ones. Or guns."

"Weapons? What are you telling?" Prof looks at me in disgust.

It's a bit scary. I look round me, grasping at something to

ease the mood. I was trying to be cooperative by coming out here. But somehow I'm getting it wrong. "I certainly haven't seen one of these," I say desperately, pointing to the metal staircase, "and I know he doesn't have any overalls."

Prof's eyebrows shoot up. "No overalls? And not even a ladder you say?" He looks pained. "You could come and stay with us, Beti. The boys too. We could look after you. Teach you all some discipline. The right ways. Not letting animals out of cages and all, being wild, wild."

Feeling a bit like an animal in a cage I cast around me for some way out. Prof's great collection of amulets sits benignly on the thick table. Beyond the table, a silver amulet hole glimmers dully in the yellow light. "What's in there?" I ask. No doubt, Prof will be proud to show me the inner recesses of his workshop. I hear a faint rustling noise and a moan.

Prof adjusts his spectacles and glares at me under lowering brows. A moment passes. He shakes his head. "No ladder! Dear me."

Taking one last inhale of oil, he tenderly realigns a weapon edged with razor sharp teeth then reluctantly turns to the door. "We will go inside now. Nani will be awaiting us." He sighs. "Between you and myself and this doorpost, I think maybe it is waste of time. But wife is always knowing best, eh? Come."

Nani puts her glasses on and picks up a book inscribed *Peaceful Parents, Happy Kids.* The big people are seated around the mahogany tree table. My sons' small house has been dismantled, the chairs replaced in their positions and the blankets and sheets folded away into a cupboard.

The book whispers, "It must be hard to have lost your memory…"

I think I might cry, but at that moment, Mattie and Sammie run in from the garden.

"We found some rats in the compost heap!"

"Where?" Prof rushes out. A few minutes later, by the many-coloured clock on the kitchen wall, he comes back looking very satisfied.

"Are you ready?" asks Nani. "I suppose no one read anything since our last meeting?" Nani looks around the table hopefully. "Don't you think we should carry on? I mean we can't put things on hold forever. The boys need some sense of normality. And consistency. We all need to be on the same page."

No one says anything. Prof gazes out of the window.

Finally, Husband says, "No I'm up for it. Let's get Am on board again." He turns to me, "You were the one spearheading this originally. Funny isn't it?"

"Hilarious." Nani peers beadily at Husband.

"Me?" I sigh. "Yes, yes. I need to know about this, don't I? If I'm going to look after… the… my… sons." I look round at the assembled expectant eyes, some of which are filling with tears. "And the book has such a kind voice. Not controlling at all. Not like those books in the library, what to speak of other people…"

Prof coughs. Husband raises his eyebrows.

Nani's mouth is a tight line as she presses open the book. "Right, let's start… We got up to empathic communication. Remember? Coaching not controlling. As er Am has rightly mentioned… Oh! Maybe you're getting your memory back. That's what's happening. The remedy's working. They can be very quick you know." Nani beams around the room. "What d'you all think?"

Husband nods slowly. "Possibly…"

Prof jigs his foot muttering, "Wishful thinking. That is not how it works. It is not by hearing voices and attributing them to books. Now when you get to see a proper doctor…"

"Look, let's just get on shall we? I think she would have wanted us to," says Nani.

"Who?"

"Well… I mean you. Of course. *You* would have wanted us too. When you were you." Nani decisively pulls her glasses down from their perch atop her head and appears riveted to the grey words. "Now here we are. Let's recap a bit. Who can remember what we've done so far?" She smoothes down the pages. "Shall we take turns reading as we usually do? I'll start. *You have to feel happy and peaceful yourself to be able to deal with children with love. You have to love yourself.*"

Prof takes off his glasses, wiping them painstakingly with his handkerchief and holding them up to the light.

"*And how do you do that? You need to deal with your stuff.*" She eyes Prof over the top of her glasses. "*You might have to go and see a counsellor, or at least talk to a good friend who will listen.*"

Upon my inward eye, a picture of a small child locked in a cupboard in the dark, for a long time. A memory? I shift in my chair and clear my throat. "I…"

"We got a good hiding where it hurt. It did me no harm,"

comments Prof. "I think I am alright. Better disciplined than those boys of yours."

Maybe I won't say anything.

"And what about special time? We must remember to organise that with the kids this week."

Special Time.

"Yeah everything's been really all over the show," agrees Husband.

"Well my life has not been. When you're having a serious job like mine, you cannot afford just to follow the flow with all of this wishy-washy business."

"There was a bit of wishy-washy business on Thursday though, wasn't there?" Husband grins.

Prof fixes his shadowed glance on the rainbow clock. What time is it? Waste of Time?

"Maybe you'd like to read this bit, Jay?" says Nani quickly.

"Okay. Oh great. *Why you shouldn't ever hit your kids and why 'time-out' doesn't work.*" He raises an eyebrow and smirks at Prof.

"I thought you said we *should* organise the time-out?" Prof puts his glasses back on.

"No that's *special* time," replies Nani. "Are you even listening?"

I'm trying to listen, but I'm distracted by Mattie and Sammie climbing up the walls in the hallway. Mattie puts one foot on each wall and shuffles his way up. Sammie tries and tries to follow Mattie, stretching his little legs as wide as they will go but they are too short. Not a happy kid.

"I'll help you, Sammie," I cry, as peacefully as I can, and

before you can say Special Time, I'm as light as a moonbeam and swooping Sammie up in my arms. Together we glide upwards like clouds in the heavens. Nani and Husband are staring up at us, while Prof rubs his glasses so hard I think he might break them. After a moment, we gently float down, coming to a soft landing on the green ocean-carpet.

Prof jumps to his feet, upending his chair. "I will let you all get on with this. I have things to do with my time at the weekend. *I* do not have the luxury of being idle while somebody else works hard. I am going now outside to tend my zucchinis." With that, he marches out.

My Time.

Nani has her face in her hands. Husband is scratching his nose.

"I want to watch something," whines Sammie.

Four minutes later, according to rainbow clock time, the boys are sent for time-out*side*, or is it special time? To play for ten minutes, while we, minus Prof, finish off our meeting in peace.

"*So you have to maintain the relationship. Relationship is what it's all about. If you have a loving relationship, they'll want to cooperate.*" reads Husband.

But then Prof storms back in, a howling boy in each hand. "Plucking my zucchinis! This one hitting, this one throwing soil. I will let you deal with them." He shoves Mattie. "That boy needs to be taken in hand and if you are not willing to do it..."

"You didn't smack them..." Husband leaps up.

"Someone has to discipline these children." Prof raises his hand in a chopping motion, like one of his weapons. He strides out, slamming the door.

Nani places her hands flat on the table, her head bowed for several seconds. The clock hands mark time-out. Husband has one unhappy child howling on his lap. I have the other. No one is peaceful. Finally, paper, scissors and glue are introduced and a tentative peace (adults) and happiness (children) is resumed.

Husband continues, "*When they don't cooperate, you know they have stuff in their emotional backpack that they're carrying around, and they're due for a melt down... which you support by setting limits with empathy.*"

*Emotional* backpack?

The Special Time of peace and happiness continues unabated for at least three minutes, (tick, tick), until Mattie reappears, spreading a fan of delicate golden leaves on the table.

"Can I use these?"

Nani takes a deep breath. "Well... er... no..."

Mattie waggles his eyebrows, his lips droop. "I really want them. I *have* to have them!"

"I know you really want them, Mattie, but I was keeping them for another time."

Another Time.

"I *must* have them!" wails Mattie, grabbing for the leaves.

But Nani gets them first and scoots out of the room.

Mattie charges after her. "Where did you put them? You have to tell me!" Mattie searches wildly through a cupboard, tossing clothes on the floor, and pulling out shelves. "Where are they?"

"You *really* want them. You're feeling really angry," croons Nani.

"Don't talk to me," shouts Mattie.

Now Husband holds him in his arms, while his sobs gradually diminish. "I really," sob, "want," sob, "them."

Sammie crawls on to my lap, watching wide-eyed.

Prof comes back in and observing the path of chaos left in Mattie's wake, storms after him. "Did you do this?" Grabbing his grandson by the arm, he opens the door. "Out!"

"Okay," says Husband, "I've had enough of this."

In no time, we're all in the car, hurtling out of the driveway.

Husband is hunched over the steering wheel. "So much for it takes a village to raise a child. Bloody hell!"

Mattie, happy again, despite a dearth of peaceful parents, pipes up, "My tooth came out!"

"What?" I gasp. "Oh no, what are we going to say to Prof?"

"Who the fuck cares?" mutters Husband through gritted teeth as the car skids around a corner. "Anyway, it's normal for kids to lose their teeth."

Mattie asks if the tooth fairy will come and whether she'll bring him some money for his *Mindstorm*.

"If she's got any cash, Mattie."

I asked whether Mattie remembered to bring his emotional backpack from Nani and Prof's. In the rush I worried he may have left it behind. Husband hopes he did. In an attempt at being responsible, I suggest we'll have to pick it up *Another* Time. Husband laughs. He reckons we'll leave it for Prof. He seems peaceful again. Only the car may not be, as it rattles up the rocky road home.

And me.

Losing teeth is normal, Mattie. (Peaceful parent, happy kid). Losing teeth is not normal! Sammie. (Anxious parent, unhappy kid). How do I negotiate the world of tooth loss? How do I negotiate the world?

And floating up to the ceiling, is that normal?

In bed, I put the question to Husband.

"Oh yeah, that was weird. We couldn't see the chair at first and it looked like you were suspended in mid air!"

"I thought I was."

"Yeah? I'm sure everything must feel a bit strange for you. Poor old Am."

Then he puts his arms around me and we don't mention it again.

I tell Mattie and Sammie to hold on tightly, we're going to see the tooth fairy. We arrive on the beach and the beautiful people are here, just about to frolic in the water and take their milk baths. The last glow of the setting sun casts its amber light over the water. Men and women with varied complexions: coral, rain cloud sapphire, lightning, emerald, set out utensils for the evening feast. Some using their four arms, others two. Delicate garments shimmer, feet barely skim the ground. The women's ankle bells tinkle, golden cups chink against golden plates. Mellifluous voices ring out, communicating in harmonious melodies. All around, the fragrance of uguru swirls, intoxicating the senses.

Suddenly, the lost woman I saw last time appears,

accompanied by two diamond complexioned men and hastens toward us, arms outstretched, hugging Mattie and Sammie to her bosom. Through crystal tears she tells them she loves them. Mattie gives her his tooth and she clutches it to her as though it's a valuable gem. Even though she's surrounded by jewels, the perfect tooth with its tiny root, is more precious. She folds it into her golden wrap and presents Mattie with a jewel from the ocean, a gleaming sapphire.

"Are you the tooth-fairy, Mama?" he asks her.

"We must go now," I say.

The woman seems to understand and reluctantly lets my sons go. Holding Mattie in one hand and Sammie in the other, we fly home.

Husband leaps out of bed. "Damn, I forgot to put any money under Mattie's pillow. He'll flip. Let's do it now, quick."

But by the time we get to the boys' bedroom, Mattie is sitting on his bunk clutching a huge blue sapphire.

"You said you'd give me money for my *Mindstorm*," he grumbles, waggling his eyebrows at me. "We went with you to see our other Mama and she gave me this, but I wanted some money." He chucks the sapphire onto the floor and kicks it under the bunk.

Husband scratches the back of his head, wondering where it came from, but at that moment, a raucous jangling emanates from the living room. We don't keep the phone in the bedroom due to the dangerous electromagnetic fields. We obediently rush along the hallway to answer the summons.

Nani's voice comes through the speaker phone. "Prof

wants to apologise. For yesterday. Here he is."

A distant voice crackles over the phone, "No, you can say for me."

"You should speak for yourself."

Prof's voice is louder this time, "Jay. I apologise."

"No, I'm sorry too," Husband replies into the phone. "I'll come round and fix that cupboard."

"That will not be necessary; no you stick to your books. I have the tools."

Husband closes his eyes and I can see him counting under his breath. I think that might have been mentioned in yesterday's book.

"Okay... then at least let me pay for it."

"That I would appreciate."

Nani's voice issues forth once again, "That's just about as much as he can cope with on the phone."

But in the background Prof's voice comes in fragments, "come to us... dentist... doctor... discipline."

"You can speak to them yourself. I'm not your mouthpiece," comes Nani's muffled voice, then more clearly, "Don't take any notice of him. All well?"

Mattie's voice rings out, "My tooth fell out. We went to see Mama and she gave me a sapphire."

Mattie's making a video using Husband's phone. He speaks into the bottom of the phone.

"Hello, my name is Mattie. I am putting on my shoes. My grippy shoes. Look." He shows the phone the underside of his shoes." We are not allowed lace-ups, because they're too hard to take off and put on. And we have to take them off and put them on, um, when we go into the classroom. I drew a picture last night and it was of a school in the forest. We wouldn't have to take our shoes off at all. We would climb trees too. Or the school could be up the tree. Not in a classroom."

"Come on, we're going to be late," says Husband.

"I like the look of my shoes. And I have matching socks. The bits at the top." He shows the socks to the phone. "Maybe I'll take my picture in today for show and tell. Is it show and tell today? I don't think Mrs Brodie could climb to the top of a tree though."

"Come on!" calls Husband.

"Can I take my picture in?" He looks into the phone. "My shoes are good for climbing trees because they are grippy." Mattie shows the shoes to the phone and puts the phone down on the carpet, along with the Lego. "I think we have to take them off um, morning tea break and play break and lunch and then the bell goes. And then put them back on. And Akul has to ask Mrs Brodie for help. I don't."

"Come on!" yells Husband.

"And when the bell goes sometimes I have to stay in if I hit Rudr, and do my writing. I don't like writing. I wonder how many times I put my shoes on and take them off in a week?"

"Here's your backpack."

"Have I got my picture of...?"

"Yes! Now. Get. In. The. Car!"

"Prof still has to take his turn. He can't use that as an excuse for ever. It's insane," Husband shouts at his phone. "You could. You're not doing anything import..."

I hear a squealing sound coming through the phone. It's Nani on the other end.

Today we don't have to crawl very slowly having lots of time to think and sit next to chicken monsters, because the school we're going to is in a different area.

Husband has his arm leaning out of the window, his phone to his ear. He presses the screen. "Same old story. It's my responsibility. If I had looked after you better and didn't have such airy fairy principles... blah blah blah." He puts the phone away. "If it wasn't a school where I regularly go, there's no way I could take you along. They don't seem to realise."

At this, something within (a synapse?) seems about to explode and I cry, "Well then why don't you just leave me at home? I didn't ask to come with you."

"Yeah, right." Husband turns withering eyes upon me.

Whereupon images of chocolate biscuits covered with ash, an exploding toaster and melting peas instantly quell the synaptic explosion.

"Look. The whole reason you were depressed was because you were at home all the time. You said you needed to get out more. So. Now you are."

He doesn't say anything else for at least seven minutes according to the dashboard clock.

Remembering the events of that particular breakfast, however, brings to mind Mattie's vaccinations paper, which in all the recent happenings seems to have been forgotten. I suppose I'd better mention it to Husband, prove that I can be responsible, I *can* look after myself and my sons.

"What?!" Our car swerves and almost hits the car rushing the other way. There's a loud screeching. "That means he might have had his vaccinations at school?! I thought they didn't believe in them. Bloody ministry, there's no fucking escape."

I say nothing.

"That could make him so much worse. Fuck! I'm phoning the school right now!"

We aren't too late when we arrive at a much bigger wooden building than Mattie's school, with a high pointed archway over the door. The sound of what must be hordes of children reverberates from one side of the building. It's louder than the library. Inside, however, all is calm. Soft music plays and walls the colour of doves' wings are dotted with wobbly pictures. A giant leafed plant sends out a single pink flower.

A large lady with fiery hair and a billowing tunic sails towards us, her lips stretched in a wide, red smile. "Hi, Jay!" she says cheerily. "It's fine you brought your wife with you. Amalia is it? Unusual name."

Husband glares at me.

The lady pats my arm. "You can help out. You still have your registration, haven't you? You can still read? What about maths?"

"Umm..." I try not to show my ignorance. I still have my registration! Whatever that is.

"Numbers, that sort of thing," explains the lady, as though I'm a child in her classroom.

"Oh, like on clocks? Yes I can tell the time."

"I'm sure the year eights will be over the moon!" She

laughs and her belly jiggles.

"Room eight A is it Denise?" says Husband briskly.

"Tony's left work for you. Just sing out if you need anything. Assembly's at eleven."

Turning to me, she adds with a wink, "You'll be able to let him know the time if he can't work it out by himself."

We march along a hallway, lined with more squiggly images, a bit like Mattie's robot pictures, while Husband informs me that he only does this for the money.

"I don't really agree with kids being stuck in schools all day. If I had my way they'd all be outside having school under a tree, along with Mattie and Sammie."

In my inward eye, I see the sand leading down to the river, beside which a massive tree spreads its canopy. From long branches hang other branches and roots, just like the trees in the park near Prof's workplace, but more vast.

We turn into the classroom where Husband has been many times before. It's not like the colourful chaos of Mattie's classroom. Chairs are arranged around bare tables; the surfaces of the cupboards are similarly devoid of games, baskets of beads, animals, and blocks. Husband tells me these are older kids; it's different from the younger kids' classrooms. The walls however, are not bare. A line runs right the way around the room, accompanied by long strings of numbers (maths?) which are unintelligible to me (Denise will be disappointed), followed by the words, 'years ago'. At one end of the line, is a red and orange ball of fire, then a small wiggly shape, followed by a very terrifying fish with huge fangs. The next fish like creature along the line, is half in, half out of the ocean. Next in line come frog- and lizard-like creatures. After that, I recognise the dinosaurs of Mattie's excavation. Further strange creatures follow each other around the room, until finally there are monkey-like creatures in various positions from walking on all fours to standing upright. At the end of the line are figures of a girl and boy, both dressed in the same clothes.

At that moment, another line appears, this time of people who are larger than Mattie but not as tall as Husband, all wearing the same clothes as in the picture – the older kids. Filing into the classroom, they drag out chairs with a huge clattering and sit down.

A woman with severe hair and glasses stands before the older kids chanting, "All eyes upon me!"

The older kids intone dully, "All eyes upon you", and stare absently forwards.

"Class eight A, Mr. Harrison will be teaching you today while Mr Hardcastle is away."

Several older kids seem to come to life and exchange mischievous grins.

"I trust you will behave yourselves," she says, fixing the group with glittering eyes, "especially you, Connor Jones!" She eyes one boy with particular ferocity, then clutching her coffee to her bosom, strides out.

I sit very quietly at the back of the classroom, while Husband flips through a large book and surveys the creatures lining the walls.

"Well, we won't be doing any of this crap," he announces. "Let's go outside and play some games."

There's a loud "hurray!" as the older kids erupt into the

hallway.

As we go, I ask Husband what the number is at the beginning of the line.

"Ten trillion years ago." He dismisses the line with a shrug. "Don't worry about that stuff. Come on, let's have some fun."

Twenty-nine of us emerge, blinking at first in the sunshine. However, as our eyes adjust to the light, a great landscape spreads forth before us. A familiar landscape, is it not? And yet... Do my memories return? Is my precious remedy effecting its cure? Wait, observe...

Yes, observe! On the far side of the playground, a river sparkles by a sandy bank under the shade of a huge tree, whose branches spread as far as the eye can see. The sounds of gurgling water, chorusing birds and lowing cows are floating towards us, their ancient melodies a restorative balm to my long suffering ears. And what is that aroma that fills my nostrils with its sweetness? Can it be the parijata flowers exuding their scent into the soft breeze? Ah, what a vision!

I wonder if the older kids are relishing the scene as much as I am. Then suddenly, one older kid breaks away from the herd and emitting a whooping cry, hurtles towards the river. It's Connor Jones.

The rest of the older kids appear transfixed, gazing around with astonishment. A few seconds later, another boy cautiously wanders after Connor Jones, looking back over his shoulder. Then a third, then a fourth follow the leader, who is now diving into the water, splashing and swimming. Many coloured cows graze, while iridescent fish glide in the clear water and rabbits and monkeys scamper along the bank. Flashing rainbow-coloured birds swoop by. There are no half-men, half-monkeys crouching by fires, nor half-fish partially submerged in the river. Nor do I espy any fish with fangs. Eventually all the older kids have dispersed, some to the river and others amongst the branches and roots of the great tree.

Husband stands scratching his head, but gradually enters into the mood, starting a game of tracking and hiding amongst the branches of the tree. After some time, (*Some* Time, which feels like No Time or Endless Time), the game flags and the divers and swimmers emerge from the water. No sooner have the older kids flopped down one by one on the sand, than a sparkling white cow appears, along with many beautifully dressed men and women, bearing trays of cakes, sherbets and all varieties of sweetmeats. Husband squats down beside me and with a happy grin, picks out a golden delicacy, and pops it in my mouth. Although my tongue is relishing the exquisite taste, I yet steel myself against the onslaught of painful images. But no. Nothing appears in my mind, except pure pleasure.

As Husband's arm brushes against me, however, I notice his wrist watch.

It is three minutes past eleven.

## Chapter Eight

## The Last Straw

The metal counters beside the sink are littered with dishes, pans and utensils, but no ash. Husband is contemplating the lower shelves of the large cupboard, while I very slowly scrape the middle-sized pan with metal wool and Mattie and Sammie lie on the blue carpet contemplating their magical screen.

Husband finally takes out a plastic container full of light brown powder. "Thank god it's the holidays!" he says, "No rushing off every morning, no having to steamroll Mattie into going to school. I don't have to feel guilty for taking time off work... because there is no work! We can spend time together as a family and look after you." He leans over and plucks the middle-sized pan from my hand. "And we have time to make healthy cereal for Sammie."

Spend Time…

"I want cornflakes!" A pathetic bleat sounds from the living room, followed by the appearance of Sammie.

"Let's have a look at your teeth." Husband opens Sammie's mouth and looks at his little front teeth. "I think Katy B's milk is helping. That hole is not getting worse, at least."

We don't have to say, "Come on, Mattie, get in the car!" five times, or even once. Both boys are in the car with their buckoos done up before we can say "Easter Show".

"You can do your buckoos up all by yourself, Sammie," I say.

Sammie looks scornful. "I can do them for wages and ages."

Mattie has even sacrificed his front seat for his grandmother, while I'm squeezed into the narrow gap between the sons' two small seats.

"We need a bigger car," declares Husband.

The Easter Show is in a huge building. I have a sudden memory of another massive building, a vast aerial mansion created out of the mind of a great yogi, Kardama Muni, which I believe could travel at his will. It didn't use petrol. Yes, now I remember. The mansion was seven storeys high and from what I recall could supply whatever one's heart desired. Its paraphernalia would *expand* over time. Just imagine! Not only that, but it was pleasing in all seasons, bedecked with flags, wreaths of fragrant flowers and tapestries of silk. Yes and I think I'm correct in saying that the floor was emerald and coral and the domes crowned with gold. I see it quite clearly in my inner eye. Oh, and at night, rubies gleamed… almost like eyes, spreading light, I think without even using electricity. The yogi's wife was a bit discouraged at the sight of the mansion as she was all bedraggled after doing austerities in the forest, but…

Mattie and Sammie are jumping around in the car park. "Come *on*, Mama!"

Husband is strapping on a backpack, I don't know if it's an emotional one. "Wait for us, boys!"

Hoisting a large brown bag over her shoulder, Nani peers in at me. "Are you alright?"

"Oh… er yes, I was just remembering something." Shall I tell them? I clamber out from my middle spot on the back seat. "I'm so looking forward to experiencing the wonders of this mansion…"

Nani and Husband exchange glances.

No, perhaps better not to say anything.

The colossal edifice is not quite what I had anticipated. However, my initial disappointment is somewhat diverted by the array of stalls, like a bazaar, all jostling for attention, and everything labelled as always, in case people don't know or might forget. Even the eco, which I thought was echo, but yes the height of the roof lends itself to ecos. Ecobags, ecoshopping, ecoflo, ecodeals, ecosmart. Or we have to be told what colour it is and only one colour allowed, green: green paper, green home, green living, green funerals, green ideas. This last is a little confusing, but as my inner eye sees things in colour, I can sort of understand, but why only green ideas?

Also, what are funerals? Oh and there is Go Paleo battling it out with Veganism: Diet for the 21st Century as usual. It's almost as fraught as the library.

"The Green Expo's about the only thing worth going to here," says Husband, grabbing a disappearing Mattie. "You have to hold my hand, Mattie, or you might get lost."

"I want to go on the dodgems." Mattie says, trying to escape.

"We'll just have a quick look in here first."

"A-a-a-h," moans Mattie.

"I could take them over there while you look round here if you want," suggests Nani. She puts her bag down by a sleek black car, with its doors wide open.

I wonder what it's doing inside the palace?

A tall woman approaches, smiling widely. "This is the new Tesla. There are only two in the whole country! It's environmentally friendly. Doesn't use petrol. You just charge it up. Would you like to get in and see how it feels?"

Mattie forgets about the dodgems, whatever they are, and he and Sammie clamber in, followed by Nani and Husband in the back, while I sink into the squashy comfort of the driver's seat. It smells of plastic and power.

"It fits seven or even eight people. Wonderful for growing families," continues the smiling woman. "Very cheap to run too. So much cheaper than petrol!"

"That would suit Prof," mutters Husband.

"He'll never allow himself to spend money on a new car. You know him," laughs Nani.

"When are we going to the dodgems?" Mattie wriggles

out of the car.

"Come *on,* Nani!" cries Sammie.

Husband slides out reluctantly. "It might be a while before we can afford this. One day... when I become head of department!"

"We'll just have to think positively. The law of attraction! Who knows?" Nani collects up her baggage. "Ready boys? We'll meet you in an hour, Jay?"

"I won't be that long. I'll come and find you. I just want to check out a couple of stalls..." He gives us a little wave as he approaches a stall called Fair Green EcoTrade.

There's so much to see at the Easter Show that Mattie seems to have forgotten about the dodgems. We're watching men on motorbikes do huge flips in the air, from one ramp to another. The whole bike does a somersault. Sammie informs us he can do a somersault and rolls over on the grass. Mattie scoffs that that's easy and he couldn't fly like that on a bike. I mention that Sammie and I have gone flying, although as Mattie points out it wasn't very high.

"But we flew to see our other Mama," declares Sammie coming up from his somersault.

"Would you like to go flying, Sammie? Up with the bikes?" I ask him.

Nani's jaw gets that tight look as she picks up her bag, and Mattie states that he *needs* to go to the dodgem cars right now. "Come *on!*" On the way, however, we get distracted again. Mattie spots a stall with big plastic red and blue versions of Prof's weapons, hanging all over the back wall, where a man of wide girth his trousers falling around his hips, aims some type of weapon. Mattie decides he wants a go so he can win a hammer. But Nani dismisses the hammers as junk and Mattie starts to cry.

Nani looks worried, "Let's go and see the animals," she says enthusiastically. "There's an ice rink too!"

This distracts Mattie enough to avert impending pandemonium and I've forgotten ice rinks, so I'm intrigued. A fact I refrain from mentioning. A bored looking man gives us small gumboots with knives on the bottom and Nani tells Mattie to get the socks out of the backpack. However, before he can find the socks, he lets out a piercing shriek and pulls out not socks, nor even emotions but... a big red plastic hammer!

Nani claps her hands to her mouth. "Mattie! What...? We'll have to take it back, Mattie. You can't just take other people's things."

"Might it be the law of attraction?" I venture.

Nani's lips are a thin line as she sizes up the milling crowd. "It'll take forever to get all of us there and back. What to do?" She sighs. "If Mattie and I go back and return this thing, can I trust you two to stay here? God, I don't know." Then she brightens a little. "Look, you can go in with the animals." She picks up the bags and guides Sammie and me to a large fenced area. "You can both stay in here. Now you mustn't go anywhere else, alright?" She looks round anxiously, cocking her head to one side and then the other. "I don't know if I'm doing the right thing here... but we'll be really quick..."

Mattie starts to cry. "I didn't take it!"

Depositing us within the safety of the fence, Nani takes

firm hold of Mattie in one hand and the big red hammer in the other. "Better not tell your Granddad about this." I hear her warning as they're swallowed up by the throng. "When he was a boy, if he took something that didn't belong to him, his mother would burn his palm with a hot iron."

Pigs, sheep and cows wander around the grass-strewn arena. Where does the pig live? A small enclosure contains tiny fluffy yellow chickens. Sammie picks one up in delight. Has a quick chat then pops it back with its brothers and sisters. Then he has a ride on a fat, woolly sheep with me holding him tightly. Happy kid! But not so happy when he finds himself face to face with a black calf. He backs away nervously. Not all cows are like Katy B I assure him. He asks me how I know and I tell him you just have to listen. So he has a good listen to the calf. After a moment he tells me she seems quite fwendly, and he reaches up to give her a scratch. I sit by, idly wondering how that might feel, when suddenly I find myself down on four legs, *my* outstretched neck being scratched by little fingers. And it feels... tickly, soothing. I raise my long head to the sky, only there isn't any sky. Where does the cow live? My legs feel a bit wobbly though.

Sammie looks round anxiously. "Mama?"

I nudge him with my broad nose. "I'm here, Sammie, I'm right here." I say, but all that emerges is a low bellowing.

With a terrified cry, Sammie topples back in the grass, bleating, "Mama! Mama!"

A large woman approaches. "Have you lost your mummy?" Although she looks all around, she fails to see me and plucks the small boy from the grass (bits of grass sticking in his straw hair), while he beats tiny fists against her expansive bosom, yelling, "I want my Mama!"

Doesn't he recognise me? I totter after him, barging into people and animals until I finally catch up and butt his feet with my head.

"Sammie, it's me!" I snort.

The large woman tightens her grasp. "Watch out for this one!" she warns a younger woman in green. "You should probably tie it up." Then she strides off with my son still screaming in her arms.

The woman in green has her name on a shiny pendant around her neck, which is helpful.

I bellow at her, "Tania, I have to get my son!"

However, Tania takes no notice and despite my bucking and lunging, ties me securely to the fence. If I could only undo my buckoos... Time for a fugue! But how? Come *on* synapses. Come *on* Great Soul. Okay... as soon as we connected with the animals I felt... what? A little voice between my floppy calf ears, or is it in my calf heart? whispers, "Peaceful." Peaceful? Of course, *peaceful* parent. That's it. My spindly legs collapse under me and I lay, head on hooves, breathing deeply and counting to ten as the kind book suggested.

A small girl with slanted eyes reaches out to pat me, but in a flash, I'm standing on two legs. The girl screams. My fingers fumble, trying to undo the rope round my neck. Tania is coming! Peaceful... Breathe... Count... Immediately, I'm tiny and hidden beneath the straw, enormous human and bovine legs towering above. If I could just reach the chicken enclosure, I might avoid getting crushed like an ant. But where is it?

Breathe. Count. One, two, three. A huge shoe throws a shadow over me. Four, five, six. I'm sprouting out of the straw, seven, rearing up to my human form, eight. The huge shoe is tossed in the air. Nine. I must find Sammie. Ten. Leaping over a portly gentleman, supine in the straw—everyone seems to relax with the animals!—I flee from the wooden enclosure, leaving Tania holding an empty rope. But I'm too late. The throng closes around me. Sammie is nowhere to be seen.

If I could just get some height, like the motorbikes, I could see further. Now I find myself rising off the ground. People start gathering to watch. I scan the multitude of people, but finding neither Sammie nor the woman, float back down. The crowd cheers. A man in black spectacles, looking like a fly, asks me how I did it. Maybe he thinks I'm part of the show, along with the motorbikes, flying through the air and turning somersaults. The answer is, I don't know. I don't know how I'm doing any of these things. They just seem to happen. A synapse whispers that it was ever since I took my remedy...

But no time to think about that now.

A friendly looking woman on a nearby stall offers me a trial taster of green liquid.

I grab her hands, knocking the green liquid flying. "Have you seen a woman carrying a small fair boy? Or another woman and a dark haired boy?"

The friendly smile fades. "Which ones did you mean exactly?"

Suddenly there's a movement in the crowd. Two large men both adorned in exactly the same sky blue shirts and night black trousers stride over, followed by Nani.

"That's her! Oh thank god! We thought you'd gone off again. Did you? Do you know who I am?"

They escort me to a table, at one end of the arena where the large woman, looking a bit frazzled, still clasps a screaming Sammie to her bosom. A woebegone Mattie sits at her side.

"Mama!" Sammie struggles out of the woman's grasp and hurls himself at me. "Why did you turn into a calf?" he sobs.

Mattie is crying too. "Why did you let Nani take me to the stall? I didn't take that hammer, you did!"

Nani is thanking the men in blue and the large lady and apologising profusely. She turns on me, her face bright red. "We're going home."

"Nooo," cries Mattie, flailing his arms, "I want to go on the dodgems."

Sammie wails, "I want candy floss!"

Mattie is thrashing about on the ground as Nani desperately fumbles with her purse. A minute later, both boys are peacefully absorbed behind massive pink clouds.

"I'm sorry, I'm not feeling like a very peaceful grandparent right now. Let's get that husband of yours and go to the car."

I follow obediently.

"Candy floss?" splutters Husband when we're all safely enclosed in the car. "Why did you give them candy floss? You know it's bad for Sammie's teeth. And it gets Mattie all riled up, too."

In my inner eye, I see one troop of evil soldiers entering Sammie's tender gums and establishing fortresses and another marching round Mattie's brain. My teeth start to tingle, lights explode in my head. I sit, squeezed in my gap between the children's seats, watching the back and forth going on in the front.

"For heaven's sake, Jay, that's the absolute least of our problems right now. If you'd been there to help…"

"Not if he has to have a general anaesthetic, you saw that test they did about young children. And I was only gone five minutes."

It's a quiet journey home. Nobody seems very happy. Or peaceful. Is that what holidays are about? After a little while, Sammie drops off to sleep and Mattie asks if he can use the phone to make a video.

When we arrive at Nani's house, she gathers up her bags with apparent relief. All of a sudden, she gives a little cry. "That's strange," she says, pointing to a gleaming black car lurking on the road outside her house. "It must be the law of attraction… as soon as you become conscious of something, you see it where you never noticed it before."

Husband agrees that it is indeed strange, especially since there are only two in the whole country. Still, he concedes, it's that sort of area. Nani points out that it wasn't that sort of area when she and Prof bought their house here all those years ago. In those days, it was considered *cheap*. She kisses us all goodbye, now looking a little more cheery, then patters up her pathway between the towering trees.

However, when we arrive at our house, we find yet *another* sleek black Tesla car sitting by the flax bushes.

"Now that really *is* strange. I thought that woman said there were only two in the whole country. Now we're seeing them everywhere." Husband rubs his nose, thoughtfully. "Who do we know who'd drive one of these?"

Three of us get out of our jaded old car to examine this young powerful one.

"I wonder if anyone's here? It can't be next door's," says Husband.

He extricates a floppy Sammie from his buckoos and we all traipse up the steps to the house. But there's no one here.

The car is still sitting there the next morning. It's not gleaming quite so much. When it's windy, dust from the road blows over and coats everything in a gentle layer of grey. The wind is buffeting the flax fronds today. The sky is also grey and the grey rabbits idly nibble the grass near the spaceship. It's one of those nothing sort of days, Husband tells me. The boys are restless; Barney has gone out, so they say they have no one to play with. The strangest thing about the black Tesla though, according to Husband, is that the key is in the ignition. I say doesn't he mean the amulet? And he gives me a Barney "You must have really lost it" look. Then his face changes, just like the moving clouds and the look is replaced with disappointment.

"I guess if someone doesn't claim it soon we'll have to tell the police."

Trying to be helpful, I suggest we could keep it. "It would be so useful for a growing family!"

"God," groans Husband, "it's hard enough dealing with the size family we've got."

Sammie howls that he wants to watch something, but Husband refuses and tells him to go outside to play. Mattie is sitting for one minute because he's just hit Sammie.

"It's not a time-out," explains Husband, "but 'if you hit you sit'." He understands that I might find it a bit confusing; he finds it hard enough himself being consistent.

Suddenly my arms tingle. I feel the sword and the spear in my hands and I sweep Sammie into my powerful arms. How many arms? I'm not sure. His small arms circle my neck. I smell the top of his little head, breathing in the apple smell of him, his hair like pieces of corn, tickling my nose. I stroke his delicate bird-like limbs. Tears hang on his eyelashes like diamonds. A wave of protectiveness engulfs me. I wield my sword and spear with two arms, while another two clasp my son fiercely to my breast. I will destroy anyone who harms this small person, this small boy who drinks my milk and calls me Mama.

Mattie sits obediently on the orange couch, waiting to be liberated from his consequences. I see the back of his head with his brown hair, curling over his checked shirt, like a mini Husband, and his hunched up little man shoulders. His legs stick out of his too short trousers and he twists his muddy feet from side to side. Like me, he's not too keen on shoes, apart from his grippy ones.

He catches me watching him, grins and growls, "Meeeiaoow," in his throat like a cat.

I sit down with Sammie and circle Mattie with another arm, stroking his cheek. "You've finished your time out, my darling. Let's have some Special Time together."

He snuggles up to me, purring as I scratch him under the chin. Husband says that when Mattie was younger, he used to be a different animal, insect or machine every day. But now he's settled on being a pussy cat and that seems to be it.

Sammie jumps off my lap purposefully and trots off to get some books, just like on that first day so many moons ago. "This is how we do it," he tells me, getting on my knee and pretending it's a horse, while we read the books. He opens the first page. *Where does the horse live?*

We always used to do this apparently, before school, kindy and all those interferences came along. I wish I could remember.

A grey car pulls into the driveway, followed by Prof's old blue one. Good. My parents will no doubt be encouraged to see me mothering my boys, just how I used to. Husband comes out of the study. My friend Catherine emerges from the grey car, carrying a big plant. Mattie, Sammie and I continue reading our books while Husband goes down the wooden steps to meet everyone. They stand around the greying Tesla, examining it, looking inside it, discussing. Then they all come inside. Nani looks happy to see our little tableau. Mattie jumps up and does a handstand in Catherine's face.

She throws her hands in the air in pretend horror, then comes over to give me a hug, handing me a small tree in an earthen pot. "Just a little something. Sorry I haven't been more in touch, but you know how it is with school."

Prof and Nani are here to discuss the 'situation' with Husband. It's the only day Prof will take off from the animals, and even that was a challenge. He says he needs to work all the hours he can to re-establish his trustworthiness. Nani tells Catherine that she and I should have a good walk. At least an hour.

"That won't be a problem," Catherine laughs. "I need a good walk after a term in the classroom."

We follow the stony pathway onto the road between the forest on one side and the cow field on the other. In the distance, the sea looks silver, the island shrouded in a misty haze. Catherine asks how I'm feeling. I tell her that my remedy seems to be working, but no one seems very happy about it.

"You can't blame them, Ama, I mean it was really scary the other day at school when you just disappeared." My friend stops, turning concerned grey eyes upon me. "They're worried about you. They hoped you'd get your memory back. That they'd get their daughter back. There've been a few dodgy incidents." She walks gently on, sidestepping the holes and rocks in the road. "But the Easter Show was the last straw. Now they don't feel they can let you out of their sight for a moment." She looks out towards the island.

The sun hides behind a massive cloud, which seems to have suddenly taken over the sky. The trees on the forest side start rustling. A tailless cow wanders over.

"You've got to do something, Am, for the kids' sakes. Mattie's getting worse in school. He's hitting kids every day. I've been like a lion with him. I have to put him out. Jay's not going to be able to cope much longer. You have to get yourself back to normal. Anyway, I'm here for you if there's anything I can do. But," she gazes at my sparkly, yellow wrap, "I don't really feel I know you any more."

I stop and face her. "Well, what *is* normal? What am I

*really* like? Tell me!"

Catherine looks down and sighs. "You were always a bit of a dark horse I suppose. You appeared to be quite easy going, but underneath... who knows what was going on? You know how you have to be to teach, a bit of a sergeant major sometimes. You can't let them walk all over you. And look at the way you've dealt with those boys. You had your whole family doing that child rearing stuff."

"You mean I was doing that?"

"You started it... But you know, I think you just got tired. Tired of looking after the boys. Mattie's not easy. And supporting Jay... he can be... well... Maybe it's better you don't remember too much." She gives me a searching look. "Perhaps we should talk about something else... I've been down to see Zoe for the Easter weekend..."

"Who's Zoe?"

"Oh Am!"

The black cloud has moved off to the horizon and sits behind the island. Clouds float like white cotton in the blue dome. A bird floats too, a bee wobbles into a flower and a bright orange butterfly rests in the air. I suddenly feel lighter than candy floss and the wind bears me upwards into the sky.

"Am? Am?"

"I'm here." I land lightly by her. I don't think she noticed.

"I think we'd better be heading back... School's going quite well..."

That lonely feeling creeps over me. If I'm not me, who am I? If I don't remember the things Catherine is talking about, how can I be normal and have friends?

"Come on in, have a cup of tea." Nani welcomes us in.

"Okay, why not, it's the holidays, after all," replies Catherine walking up the wooden steps.

Later, Husband tells me they've decided not to delay seeing Aelfraed, the Dean. Prof is not satisfied but Husband is not willing to go to a psychiatrist who will just give me chemicals. Also, he has called the police about the Tesla. Apparently it was stolen. How it got up here, no one knows. The police will come and take it away.

"That's a shame," I reply, but the lonely feeling continues to haunt me, together with little whispering synapses in my mind, which seem to be trying to warn me of something.

The visitors have departed after a brief lunch (which I made!) and so has the Tesla, but Barney's back from wherever he went. He and Mattie are climbing on the monkey bars. This afternoon they're space pirates. Sammie is delving into some mud with a stick. In the distance, a huge cloud approaches at some speed, finally revealing a metallic red car which zooms past our house to Barney's place, coating the flax bushes with a fine layer of white dust.

Husband shoots out, gritting his teeth and slamming the door, which bangs in the wind. "Those hoons! Don't they know we have kids living here?"

Barney, the dishevelled space pirate, climbs onto the playhouse to be 'look out', as the red car returns and screeches to a halt by the flax bushes. It's covered in dust.

But then our car is always covered in dust. Husband says it's the price you pay for living away from the continuous lawn mowers of suburbia.

A familiar slender figure in a floaty skirt appears from one door. From the other side, a small dumpy figure in crumpled black trousers and a shapeless black t-shirt emerges in a cloud of smoke. A pendant glints ominously around her neck. The slender figure sees Husband and I and starts gesticulating behind the dumpy one's back, putting her finger to her lips, mouthing something like, "Pretend you don't know me!" It's Fern.

The boys are now intent on digging something. I think they're trying to create an underground tunnel. Sammie looks up and sees Fern, who then starts gesticulating and mouthing to him, as he runs over to greet her. Dumpy appears to be oblivious to all this, intent on crossing the hillocky meadow to the house. She looks grumpy and flustered. Her mien does not bode well. Fern bends down to talk to Sammie, who runs off to impart something Very Important to Mattie and Barney.

Dumpy stands at the foot of the wooden steps leading up to the house, drawing herself up to her full height.

"Irene Stoddard, Child, Youth and Family Services," she announces, holding up her glinting pendant. I wonder why, useful though it may be, people need to wear pendants stating who they are? Did she also forget who she was once? If I'd had a pendant, would we have avoided the situation we're in now?

"Oh?" snarls Husband from the doorway, "and what do you want, Irene Stoddard?"

I take his arm. That doesn't sound like my Husband. Poor woman, she is obviously already fraught. Behind her, Fern shakes her head and her hands in a little dance, mouthing, "No."

Observing this charade is an audience of three bedraggled pirates, coated in earthy grime: Barney, his long hair hanging down his back, Mattie, his face hidden by wild curls and Sammie with his twig-filled nest of straw. Various toothless grins, some normal and one not, welcome our stout visitor.

"We have been notified that there are some children at risk living in your care. My colleague and I would like to ask a few questions, if you'll kindly allow us access." With some effort and heavy breathing, Irene Stoddard, Child, Youth and Family Services places an ample foot upon the bottom step and begins her ascent.

Husband is standing legs apart, hands on hips. Fern is covering her face with her hands.

"Of course, please do come in, you're welcome. We're delighted." I attempt to edge Husband out of the way and lean down to give her a hand.

Husband is unyielding. "Who notified you?"

Irene Stoddard doesn't answer until she reaches the summit, where she stands face to face with Husband. "My informant prefers to remain anonymous."

We manoeuvre around Husband and I offer the Dumpy One a seat. Losing her balance on a Lego brick, she lands uncomfortably on the orange sofa, puffing and wiping her forehead. Fern lowers herself onto the dull yellow cushion, folding her slender legs beneath her, also uncomfortable, but in a different way.

The three pirates file in, mischief in their eyes. Barney whispers something to his cronies and they hurl themselves across the sea of Lego bricks and scoot down the hallway.

"Was it her father?" Husband is relentless.

"Can I offer you something to drink? Some tea?" I attempt to welcome Irene Stoddard.

"Come and sit down, Am. They don't need tea. Who was it? It was him, wasn't it?" persists Husband.

Nevertheless, I've already put the kettle on, which I now know how to do without electrocuting anyone! I don't understand my usually hospitable husband, who considers it a sin not to offer a guest a little refreshment. He tells me it's part of our culture, especially if it's made with love and devotion. The consciousness of the receiver is uplifted. Judging by Dumpy's scowl, I think we could all do with some upliftment. Moreover, I'd like to be a good wife and make up for all the bother I seem to be causing.

"I'm not at liberty to say. I told you already, the person prefers us not to divulge that information."

Dumpy glances with suspicion at my little metal tray with its chipped china cups. At least the cup I give her has a handle and I've given her the last liquorice tea bag even though they're Mattie's favourite. She sniffs at the soaked barley biscuits, wrinkles her nose and shoves the lot to one side, replacing it with a large piece of folded paper and pen. Fern, stranded on her little island amidst bricks and blue carpet, nibbles miserably at the soaked barley offering, saying nothing.

"For god's sake, Am, will you just sit down," barks Husband.

I sit on the floor. Husband, however, remains standing.

"So what's all this about?"

"We've received some complaints regarding your children," she glances down at her paper, "Matthew and Samuel." Peering around the room, her small eyes rest briefly on the picture of the cosmos, (YOU ARE HERE!), and then the sacred altar with its deities.

"We understand you have been unwell, Mrs. Harrison. Loss of memory? Depression?"

"My wife is fine…"

"I did forget some things… but it's like ESOL, suddenly it's all coming back!"

Dumpy looks at my sparkly cloth, adjusted just so. I imagine it's hard for her.

Just then the boys rush in. "Who wants to find some hidden treasure?"

Irene Stoddard does not leap at the offer.

Sammie says to Fern, "Where's Fwank?"

Fern looks out of the window without replying. All the while Dumpy is scribbling on her paper.

Mattie studies her. "You're very fat."

She studies him back and a glint comes into her eye. "Any interventions for this young man's *Asperger's,* Mr Harrison?"

Mattie's face seems to collapse in on itself, his lips quiver and he clenches his fists.

Husband clenches his fists too. "We prefer not to put

labels on our kids."

Yes, they don't need pendants to remember who they are.

"Hmmmph." The Pendanted One writes several words then looks over her glasses at Husband. "He hasn't had his vaccinations either I gather. Any reason for no vacs?" She looks at the altar and the picture of the cosmos. "Is it a... religious principle?"

"Look, our spiritual beliefs are our business... what is this, some totalitarian state or something?"

"I'll take that as a 'yes'," says Irene Stoddard adding further words to her list. I wonder if she's ESOL too? Then she catches hold of a staring Sammie. "Is this the one who's not having his teeth seen to? Come here, let's take a look."

Sammie keeps his mouth firmly clenched, like a locked treasure chest.

"Yes, he never opens his mouth, he doesn't eat anything except chocolate and ice cream," I explain.

She regards Sammie's slender form. "Hmm."

"Am, what did you...?" stutters Husband. "Anyway, we've got nothing to hide. We're doing it our way. Naturally. But you wouldn't know about that, would you?"

Fern shakes her head anxiously.

"I'm just doing my job, Mr Harrison. If children aren't being looked after properly, being neglected, I have to do my duty and make sure they get looked after by someone who is capable of it." She turns to me. "And you. Do you think you are well enough to look after your sons?"

"Oh...um...as I said, I'm remembering lots of things. And

I've learned to make healthy cereal for breakfast, although Sammie doesn't eat it. And coaching not controlling, and in theory not smacking them. Time-out doesn't work either. And as I said, that Sammie eats only chocolate, ice cream and Mama's milk. But he also drinks Katy B's raw milk and that's helping his teeth like anything. And Mattie knows all about black holes and Panzerkampfwagens and sometimes he hits Sammie, but it's not his fault and we're working on that with peaceful parenting and I think the raw milk is helping that too and then also having school under a tree. That was lovely."

"Oh for fuck's sake, Am." Husband has his head in his hands.

"What sort of help did you say you were getting for your wife?"

"I didn't…"

Irene Stoddard flicks her glasses down, writes, then pushes them back onto her head. "And how old is Sammie?"

"I'm ten. Amn't I?" Sammie climbs on my lap. "I want Mama's milk."

More words on the paper. "Do you go to school, Matthew?"

"I don't like school."

Irene Stoddard suddenly finds herself face to face with a pair of very muddy feet. Her glasses go flying. She looks as though she might like to smack Mattie. But that is not allowed.

"Sometimes it helps if you breathe… and count," I offer, but my suggestion is not met with much enthusiasm… by anyone.

"I'd like to have a look around," says the Dumpy One,

heaving herself up off the sofa. "Get a feel of where the children are living. It gives us a more complete picture."

"Be my guest. Make yourself right at home," snaps Husband.

The glasses go up and down as the room is inspected and words upon words are added to the page. It reminds me of when I arrived home after my fugue although I wasn't writing anything down then. I wonder if we will have to restrain her from escaping?

The altar and the cosmos picture come under scrutiny, but her eyes don't fill with tears. She picks up a small glass bowl of green leaves and sniffs suspiciously. "What's this?"

"That's Tulasi, a sacred plant from India," replies Husband, as though she should surely know that.

"She's a goddess," I add helpfully.

Husband rolls his eyes up to the ceiling. I follow his gaze but see nothing particular. Oh yes, there's a cobweb with a spider in it. Oh and a poor fly caught in it.

"Hmmph," grunts Irene Stoddard, Child, Youth and Family Services.

Down the hallway – I wonder if she knows what a hallway is? She might need to add it to her list. I'm about to make that helpful suggestion, after all it was very helpful for me when my family reacquainted me with the household layout and paraphernalia. But just then we arrive at the bedroom and all other thoughts are forgotten.

The three grimy pirates gleefully circle the bed yelling "Ooh aaar!"

Barney says, "You're getting very waaarrrm!"

Mattie shouts, "You're boiling you arrre!"

Sammie jumps up and down on the bed itself and whips back the cover.

Mattie says, "Sam*mie*! You shouldn't show…"

But he doesn't get to say what Sammie shouldn't show, because everyone is struck dumb as the hidden pirate treasure is revealed in all its glory: a flashing sword, a razor sharp scimitar inlaid with diamonds and rubies, a bow, a golden shield, a spear, a disc and a pair of gumboots.

Irene gasps and forgets to write anything at all for at least ten seconds. She hobbles back down the hallway, muttering, "Very realistic," with Fern trailing helplessly behind.

She doesn't seem to want to find out about the bathroom. Maybe she's afraid of mirrors. Not surprising really, considering…

In the living room, she turns. "And what do you do, Mr Harrison?"

"I'm studying."

"So, not working then." She adds several more words, then inserts her pen in the sagging pocket of her black trousers. She turns to the transparent sand door. "Alright, that'll do for now."

Ah, this is where she flees. I know how she feels. We must restrain her!

"Thank you, Mrs Harrison," she says, going through the door. "You've been most helpful. We'll be in touch as soon as we've made our decision."

Husband doesn't seem keen to obstruct her, however, and, catching one foot up with the other on each stair, she descends the steps unhindered and waddles with dignity to her conveyance.

Fern follows, mouthing, "I'll do my best. I'll phone you." She mimes putting a phone to her ear, just as Dumpy turns round.

Sammie calls out, "Bye, Fern."

"*Sammie!* We're not supposed to know her," yells Mattie, pushing Sammie over.

"That went well," says Husband as the dusty red car shoots off with a screech, trailing a cloud of dust.

Watching the dust cloud recede into the distance, I'm suddenly very small and light. I find myself sitting on the back seat of the red car amidst crumpled papers, an apple core, old pens, a towel, a smelly shoe and an empty can, which says V. I think maybe I've died and gone to hell. The whole car is full of smoke as Irene Stoddard draws deeply on a fiery white tube, then flicks it out of the window.

"Situation is a no-brainer. The upliftment of humanity." She laughs deep in her chest.

I'd like to stay and hear what she means, but the fumes are asphyxiating. I cough loudly.

Irene Stoddard turns round. "What the hell was that?"

Meditating on fresh air, I find myself back on the edge of the forest, where it looks as though Husband and the boys are playing a game of hide and seek.

"Am? Where are you? Stop messing around," shouts Husband searching frantically behind the flax bushes and the spaceship.

"I'm here." I land softly beside him on the grass.

"Where were you?"

"I went to hear what she said."

"Look, you've got to stop messing around, Am. This bloody crazy society. Do you hear what I'm saying?" His face is working strangely. His eyes fill with tears. "We don't want to lose our boys."

Chapter Nine

# Red Flags

Frank is joining Mattie and Sammie in the game of pirates from outer space, standing legs akimbo, aboard their container spaceship. His mother, Fern, is sitting on the grass by the wooden steps sipping a lemon balm and pomegranate tea, watching him just in case he hits anyone, or anyone hits him. She counts on her fingers, "Medical neglect, teeth, vacs, Asperger's, mother's incapacity. That's enough red flags to..."

"But I gave her soaked barley biscuits! I made them myself."

"Taking them to the doctor is medical neglect," growls Husband.

"They didn't have shoes on." Fern turns her wide eyes upon us. "I mean what kid wants to wear shoes? It's just...

they looked, you know, *scruffy*. It all adds up to a picture, you know?" She frowns. "We went next door by mistake. It's a bit of a shantytown. Old cars everywhere, spilling their guts out…"

"But that's not us. They're just neighbours!" protests Husband.

Fern's wide eyes take in the landscape, the meadow, short in places where Massey and Ferguson have mown it down, and the endless green of the forest at the bottom of the hill. "Yeah, but you're all stuck way out here. They're part of your community or 'commune', according to Irene. We had a case like this recently, family from a religious cult and we were a bit laissez-faire, didn't do anything. The mother died. She was eight months pregnant. So did the kid. The media had a field day. We can't risk it." She takes a delicate sip of her tea. "You know next door had the police up about a stash of unlicensed firearms?"

"How come you came with her anyway?" Husband turns burning eyes upon poor Fern who seems very intent on balancing her cup in a clump of grass.

"Um… pure coincidence. I happened to be at the site. I'm on placement there, you know? Suddenly I heard your names. I asked if I could come." She looks at us earnestly. "Real bummer. Especially getting Irene. She's notorious. They're not all like that. Specially us new breed. But she's been around like forever. Real old school. You know. This stuff," she waves a vague hand at our house, our world, "is way outside her paradigm. So my advice to you guys, for what it's worth, is to start dealing with the flags. You better get some help, Amalia. I mean not alternative help, you know. Something more mainstream that people can relate to. And you'll have to take Sammie to a real dentist."

"There's no way they can take kids away from people like us." Husband angrily yanks up a fistful of grass. "What are we living in, some fascist regime or something? God, it's worse than I thought. I don't see why we should do anything. Cave in to their demands. Then the Prof's won, hasn't he?"

Frank is waving a large stick at Sammie, Fern looks worried. Then Sammie grabs his own stick.

"If it is him. You don't know."

"Course it's him. You must know Fern. Why are you holding out on us?"

"No, I really don't. She keeps things very confidential, Irene. And she doesn't miss a trick. I don't know what she picked up on with... well, Sammie and Mattie yesterday."

"I tell you what, we're not going to change anything. It's just blackmail!"

"I can't believe a father would do that," I say, looking from Fern to Husband for confirmation.

Husband finishes his tea with a gulp, and laughs. "Oh fathers are capable of many things, believe me."

Fern nods. "Yeah, there was this guy the other day..."

Husband slaps his thigh. "That's the last he sees of his grandkids. Two can play at his little game."

"Look, I wouldn't do anything to make the situation worse." Fern turns pleading eyes on Husband. "It doesn't look good cutting yourselves off from relatives, not with the overall picture of... well... religious isolation and you know... weirdness. Really, one more thing and it could mean she'll uplift the kids. I know she wants to. I'm sorry." She wipes her eye. "I better go. I'm supposed to be on site. But I had to tell you guys. Just be careful. I'll be thinking of you. I'll do my best, but I'm just on placement, you know? They're not exactly going to listen to me are they?" She brushes herself off as she strides over to her car, then looks over her shoulder. "And that's another thing. Why do you guys wanna live so far out here? You practically tick all the boxes." Shaking her head, she opens the car door, calling Frank to come *on*.

Husband climbs the steps watching her car disappear in a cloud along the road. "Look, we'll take Sammie to that natural dentist. That's okay, but we're not doing vacs or getting interventions. They'll just stick him on *Ritalin*." He pounds his fist into his hand. "At the end of it all, after a million and one complicated observations and assessments, and a PhD and fifty years experience, and three months to get the appointment blah blah blah. The final result? Bloody *Ritalin*. Fucking brilliant. Oh what a surprise! We never thought you'd put him on *Ritalin*. That must have taken so much deep thought and wisdom and knowledge on your part. It's all a big, big have. And I won't be had!" He's delivering his tirade from the small platform outside the door, arms waving and eyes burning, while the alien pirates observe from their ship. "Big pharma's got us all in the palm of their latex gloved hands." The flax fronds nod. The grass waves in agreement, where it has not been downtrodden by Irene Stoddard's solid feet. "Birth, ooh failure to proceed. Ah, the amazing intelligence that created this wonderful being, whose every intricate cell is more complex than a whole fucking city, could not possibly manage to get that even more intricate organisation of cells out into the world. Oh no! We have to fill them full of *Pitocin,* because that is what *we* have created and patented and we do no harm! Huh! Pharm… P harm, d'you get it?"

The forest backdrop tacitly acknowledges his truth. There's the sound of clapping. Barney's Granddad, Overalls, appears around the side of the house, in dark blue overalls and strong boots, carrying a ladder.

"Just going up to check on the water tank. Haven't had much rain lately. Overheard your speech." He puts down his ladder. "Well I couldn't agree more, mate. They came to ours first, you know. I soon told them where to go. Don't trust them as far as you can throw 'em." He pulls out a small, green pouch from his pocket. "They had a bit of a snoop. I told 'em none of the washing machines work. I've got about ten in my workshop waiting to be fixed. Never get around to it." He chuckles, his blue eyes twinkling. Next moment, the twinkle dies and he says gravely, "Have you heard of the Illuminati…?"

But Husband's not listening; his eyes are ablaze as he grabs my shoulders. "And you're not to do anything. Do you understand? Just get better and get back to normal, so that we can get on with our lives as we were. We were okay before. I mean, not perfect, we could've got more help for you. Now this. What a mess. I mean it, Ama, one more thing! You heard what Fern said. We could lose our boys."

The pirates are scampering down the hill towards the forest, their little backs brave and trusting. But how can they know? They're only children. It might be dangerous in the forest.

Who knows what ferocious animals may lurk there? I look round desperately but Husband is nowhere in sight. My arms tingle. We could lose our boys! I must protect them!

I run after them. "Wait, I'm coming with you!"

We slip and scramble down the hill, past the prickly bushes covered in yellow flowers, over the ditch and down a winding muddy path, to where the earth is black and swampy. Long, needle-like stalks grow in clumps. Leaping from clump to clump, we reach a silver, dead, tree gate hung with silvery jade fronds, and climb over into the forest. I listen carefully for signs of danger as I follow my pirate sons. Creeping under vines and over rotting logs, we come across a cluster of blue fungi shining fluorescent in the gloom.

"Look! Here's some more mushwooms," announces Sammie, discovering another cluster further on.

Following the trail of blue mushrooms all at once we stumble upon a clearing where the sun pierces through the trees, dappling soft emerald grass. Grass being appreciated by someone...

Someone black and white, who lifts her head from her grazing as we approach and regards us with gentle brown eyes. Immediately I know. It's cow number one hundred and eight.

"How on earth are we going to look after her?" demands Husband, striding up and down, crushing the grass beneath his feet. "I told you, Am, one more thing... I'm having a hard enough time coping with everything as it is."

Mattie alternates between offering our new family

member a piece of grass and chewing one himself, while Sammie sprawls with his head on her stomach, as she gently chews her cud.

"Maybe she's going to look after us?" I suggest.

"Every time I leave you for five minutes, Am. It's no joke."

"But you weren't here. I had to protect our sons!"

"I was here!"

"But the ferocious wild animals in the forest…"

Husband puts his face in his hands.

"Well what can we do with her?" I ask him.

"There's nothing we can do with her, we'll have to keep her, otherwise they'll send her to the works. Although it's weird. Usually they're sent after they dry up. Why would they have sent her? She's got loads of milk!"

"She escaped. We saw her in the book at Mattie's school."


Sammie has decided he likes One Hundred and Eight's milk straight out of the udder.

"We can't call her One Hundred and Eight. What sort of a name is that?" says Husband.

"I think we should call her 'Lucky'," says Mattie, "cos she was lucky to escape."

"And we're lucky to have her too," bleats Sammie, coming up for air.

Overalls has given us some hay for her. He offered to teach us how to milk her too. But somehow I think I already know.


"I've had so many memories since I started my remedy."

"They're not *memories*, Am... they're not *real*. It's like you're tripping or something. You're like a fly in a fucking web. Every step takes you further into the shit." Shoving open a black iron gate, Husband storms up the pathway, oblivious to the small shrubs spilling onto the path, offering up their delicate aromas as we pass, unaware of the luscious vine rambling over the house's yellow bricks. He yanks on a handle by the doorway and stands grimly, hands in pockets, as a gentle ringing echoes within.

A moment later, a bearded young man appears at the door. He bids us enter and be seated upon two rather elegant velvet chairs. Husband gives a curt grunt before perching on the edge of his assigned seat and I follow suit. Thus we sit, each isolated in our misery. What does it mean that my memories aren't real?

Around us, the windows twinkle, their rainbow glass dappling myriad colours like gems over the warm floor. The silence stretches out. Even the books here are silent.

After what seems like a yuga, Husband leans back into his soft cushions, heaving a great sigh. "Phew! I feel a massive weight falling off my shoulders just coming into this place." He reaches for my hand. "This whole thing's getting to me a bit... But we don't need to let it." He manages a timorous smile. "It's going to be okay. Aelfraed'll sort us out."

The bearded young man returns bearing fragrant tea made from the garden shrubs.

"Wow, smells divine." Husband accepts his vessel with reverence, breathing in the soothing aroma. "How long are you staying, Tobias?"

"I return to Germany in sree veeks." The young man replies, stroking his beard. "I hev been for few months here, helping Aelfraed with the garden and so." He smiles graciously. "I hev learned much." With that, he bows his head and goes out.

"One of Aelfraed's disciples," whispers Husband, winking at me.

A molten gold figure, set in an alcove by a small fountain contemplates us benignly, a wise smile on his face.

Husband follows my gaze. "Ah, Buddha's watching us."

Buddha sits in a cross-legged position, feet over ankles, peacefully gazing out at us from half closed eyes, hands resting in his lap. His rotund belly rises and falls as he gently inhales and exhales.

Something within me stirs. "The lotus position, padmasana."

"You remember that?"

"It's probably just a hallucination..."

"Hey, hey, don't be upset..."

A dark wooden clock with a swaying golden disc sounds a deep note and a beautiful figure appears next to the Buddha. It's the Dean.

Taking my hands in his, he looks gently into my eyes "Kali. So good to see you." He places a caring hand on Husband's shoulder. "Jay, how are you?" His voice is as rich and warm as the wood of the floor. "Thank you for bringing Kali... I wondered when I would see you."

"Yeah, we're not letting her drive at the moment. It's a bit risky. We're just trying to... get by, you know," explains Husband, scratching the back of his head.

"You've experienced a challenging ordeal," acknowledges the Dean.

Husband breathes out as though he's been holding his breath for far too long. "Thank God we have you to come to."

Silence.

Buddha breathes in. And out.

"Come on in, Kali." The Dean smiles kindly, guiding me into his sanctuary.

There are no ticking clocks here. All is silent. The walls are the deep pink of a lotus. The window opens out into a small garden with a pond and lotus leaves, where another Buddha sits, grave like a stone, contemplating the reflection of an overhanging tree in the water. Rain starts to fall softly.

The Dean sits peacefully, his hands resting in his lap, as the silence embraces us. Eventually he asks, "So, what's going on for you? Would you like to tell me?"

I look out at the Buddha and the weeping sky. The silence extends a few moments. "I keep getting things wrong... I'm trying to help but I seem to make things worse."

The Dean is silent. The Buddha is silent. The only sound is the gentle patter of rain.

"I *am* getting memories. Beautiful memories. But no one wants to know about them. Or believe them. They just want things the way they were before. But I can't remember how that was. Plus I wasn't very happy then, so why do they want me to go back to that?"

"No one accepts your beautiful experiences; they don't care if you're miserable, as long as everything goes back to normal. That must be hurtful." The Dean's gaze is full of compassion.

So is that of the Buddha, whose eyes flow with rain tears.

"They're always so anxious. When we were seven minutes late for assembly at Husband's school there was an uproar."

"Assembly?"

"Yes we were having school under a tree, it was so much fun! And we were a tiny bit late getting back. Honestly!"

"So exacting! You wish they'd all just relax." He nods.

"Everything has to be so… so… *tidy*. Monkeys all have to be tidied away in cages and chickens in boxes, and children in their seats! And me in mine!"

"Sounds like torture."

"Yes! And when I fly or become a calf or hear books speaking or something, they just completely ignore me. Or sigh or clench their teeth or glare from under craggy brows as though I'm trying to be difficult."

"They don't recognise your unique powers. You feel unappreciated, unaccepted…"

"I do. I used to be so proud of my powers…" I glimpse my brown parchment hands in my lap. "At least… I think I did."

"You're starting to doubt yourself."

"Yes… yes, that's right, I am. And… and now they're threatening to take away Mattie and Sammie…" A sob bubbles up in my throat, I can barely talk. "All… because of *me*."

"It sounds as though you feel the whole world's against you." Concern furrows the Dean's brow.

"I feel so… so… alone."

Silence.

The rain streams down the Buddha's face.

Hot tears stream down mine.

Silence.

"I'd like to tell you everything. I'd like to tell you about jewels and palaces and about Sammie, the way his hands are tiny, his fingers so delicate and tender. How he clasps onto me like a baby monkey but wields a sword like the god of death! And Mattie's treasure maps and complicated machines and when he cuddles up to me like a pussycat..."

"Yes." The Dean sits forward, listening intently, his peaceful eyes looking into mine.

"But maybe that's not important."

"What is important?"

"I'd like to be better, so I can keep my boys. Can you make me better?"

"That all depends," he smiles serenely, "on whether you think there's something wrong with you in the first place."

At this, there is a very long silence, which seems to lengthen into a night of Brahma. Then listening, listening, I finally hear a small voice in the silence. It could be a synapse whispering in my heart and somehow I know the answer.

And I know what to do. "I'd like to give you something." I say and stretch out my palm. A moment later, I'm holding a plump, golden mango. I offer it to my generous confessor. "See the drop of water?" I tell him. "It's dew. It's early where I picked it, the best time to pick them."

The Dean smiles and nods in acknowledgement.

"It's from the eastern side of the tree, with the sun's first blush on it. Smell it…"

"Mmmm. Thank you!" The Dean accepts the gift reverently, his eyes crinkling in delight.

Silence. The rain has stopped and the Buddha is smiling.

"Shall I show you something?" The heaviness of my limbs drops away as I rise upwards, weightless like the great planets in the cosmos, like Lord Brahma on the lotus at the time of creation. For a moment, the lotus room seems to unfurl into a vast universe.

"The eight yogic perfections," murmurs the Dean as I float gently down like a leaf. The great tree above the Buddha murmurs also, nodding its boughs in quiet affirmation.

A skinny black cat has adopted us. She's been drinking Lucky's milk. Lucky doesn't seem to mind. She's so full of milk; it leaks out of her teats and the cat licks it up. Then the cat sits on the step outside the house, washing her paws, her green eyes flashing in the sun. She carries herself with fierce dignity, her tail erect like a spear.

As a kitten, she tells us, she lived on the other side of the forest with her humans, a mother and two young children who used to swing her round by her tail. The mother didn't have the money for cat food; she could hardly afford to pay for the kids' food. I enquire whether CYFS were called? She's not sure about that, but finally she decided to run away. I tell her I know how she feels.

Mattie is pleading to keep her, though Husband is reluctant. "Where's it going to end?" But she seems determined to keep *us*. She says she was a bit wary of children, but feels perfectly comfortable with Mattie. He seems to know just what she likes, scratching her under the chin and rubbing the corner of his mouth against the corner of hers. As for Sammie, she says no one could be afraid of such a gentleman. She climbs onto Husband's lap and butts his chin with her little nose. Flashing eyes look into burning ones.

Husband sighs. "Well... I suppose she can look after herself... and black cats *are* supposed to be lucky. Maybe all these animals turning up out of the blue is a good omen?" He gives a soft chuckle. "You're lucky you came after our visit to Aelfraed, that's all I can say."

"But we've already got Lucky," says Mattie, "so what will we call her?"

Husband thinks for a moment. "I think we'll call you Shakti," he says, stroking the determined creature from the top of her head to the tip of her flicking tail.

Mattie does a whole cartwheel, while Sammie establishes respective rights on Lucky's teats.

So now in our abode we have both luck and power, and as husband says, we're going to need them. Although at this point, none of us can possibly realise to what extent.

Mattie climbs onto my lap and says into the phone, "Nani, we got a cow. She came out of the bush. We called her Lucky."

"Goodness! We were wondering how you all are... we haven't heard from you for a while."

"I wonder why?" calls Husband from the kitchen where he's making rice and dahl.

"What was that?" says Nani. "Is that you, Jay?"

Husband comes into the living room wiping his hand on a towel. "No, it's the boyfriend. Jay's left and I'm the third uncle the kids have had since Monday. I just beat the youngest against the wall, and threw your daughter out the window headfirst. That noise of bubbling you can hear in the background is the P lab I set up in the kitchen. First thing I did when I moved in. Great situation here, so far off the beaten track."

Mattie stares in amazement at his father, wondering what fathers are capable of.

"I want some ice cweam." Sammie comes in from digging his tunnel, trailing mud behind him.

"You'll get a slap around the ears, boy, if you whine like that. You'll eat what you're given and like it! And get that mud out of here right now! D'you hear me?"

"What's going on?" Nani sounds bewildered.

"I could ask you the same question, Nani dearest."

"I just called to say hello and see how you all were. That is you, isn't it, Jay? What's got into you?"

"Ditto."

"Maybe I better call back. Or you can call me. Maybe it's not a good time."

Husband grabs the phone. "Does the acronym CYFS ring any bells?"

"CYFS? What are you talking about?" Nani's voice comes quivering over the phone.

Mattie and Sammie sit on my lap gazing wide-eyed at their father.

"Someone called CYFS on us." Husband strides back and forth, forging dark tracks across the blue carpet. "It was Prof, wasn't it? It's a no-brainer. He's wanted to get these kids away from me since day one."

"Prof? Call CYFS? What…?" splutters Nani. "That man probably doesn't even know they exist."

"Yeah, he's only been in the country what, thirty years? He couldn't be expected to know anything like that. That sounds very reasonable."

"You sound pretty upset, Jay…"

"Me? Upset? Oh no, not at all. We're only about to have the kids taken away from us, that's all."

"Are the children there?"

"Children? They're on the fast spin in the washing machine as we speak."

"Look I think we better talk another time. I'll have a word with Prof. But I'm absolutely… Well, I'm in shock. I'll call you back later. But please don't talk about it in front of the kids. It's not their fault. Whatever's going on."

Husband thrusts the phone at me and storms back into the kitchen.

"Nani, we also got a cat… Oh, Nani's gone." Mattie is left talking to the phone. He slithers off my lap and lands on the carpet, not knowing quite what to do with himself.

"She can't resist a final parting dig, can she?" yells Husband from the kitchen.

"She didn't do it, Husband," I blurt out, then clamp my lips together, feigning serious interest in the bubbling pots.

Husband is pulling small jars of spices out of the big cupboard, slamming them onto the wooden counter. "How do you know, *Wife*?"

Can I tell him? I picture the Dean's gentle eyes full of encouragement. "I... I... looked inside her mind."

He stops his slamming and stares at me. "Right. And what about Prof? What's going on in his mind then? Can you see that too?"

I hear moaning. Confusion enters my mind along with a blurry image of huge eyes peering out of the dark. "I... I'm not sure."

There's a sudden hiss. "Oh shit, the dahl..."

The P lab smells good. I'm getting used to food, although there are limits. Sometimes I'm like Sammie and I only want milk from Lucky, or nectar from the flowers.


*"Forget about drilling, filling, and the inevitable billing. Your teeth can heal naturally because they were never designed to decay in the first place!"* Husband is reading to me from my Kindle, from a book called *Cure Tooth Decay*, while I do the dishes.

Doing dishes doesn't feel so familiar to me. I thought we used to throw away our glistening golden dishes after eating. But Husband says no. He explains that it would be very wasteful to throw things away after using them once. Thus I find myself with my hands up to my elbows in warm water, scrubbing the skin off my fingers, almost on a daily basis. The picture of me standing at the sink gleaned from my journals appears to be accurate and proves that some memories are returning despite their inconsistent nature. It seems sometimes I used to wash the dishes and sometimes I used to throw them away. But Husband assures me I never threw them away unless they were plastic, which was a terrible thing because they'd then sit in a landfill and not biodegrade for hundreds of years. Better, when we occasionally have to use throwaway plates, he tells me, that they are made out of potatoes.

I tried to do the reading and let Husband do the dishes, but I had to shout at the top of my voice to be able to hear. With all the books I have on my *Kindle,* it was almost as noisy as being in the library. I could hardly hear myself. I can still hear them murmuring, but they aren't quite as loud when Husband is holding the machine.

*"They were designed to remain strong and healthy for your entire life. But the false promises of conventional dentistry have led us down the wrong path, leading to invasive surgical treatments that include fillings, crowns, root canals and dental implants."* Husband continues at something above normal voice level, but not too loudly, as the boys are in bed. *"Now there is a natural way to take control of your dental health by changing the food that you eat."*

I get the tangle of scratchy steel and apply myself vigorously to the gunk on the middle-sized pan, in which the remains of Sammie's healthy cereal have congealed. We all quite enjoyed it, made as it was from fairtradeorganic and Lucky's milk. All, that is, except Sammie, who refused to open his mouth.

*"Dr. Price's program has proved to be 90–95% or more effective in remineralizing tooth cavities utilizing only nutritional improvements in the diet."*

"What are cavities?"

"It's when you get holes in your teeth. Dentists used to fill them with mercury."

"Mercury?"

I seem to remember Mercury as a brilliant planet where we used to go for pleasure excursions. I gaze out of the sand window at the stars shining bright against the dark night, but say nothing.

Husband enthusiastically reads on. "*Thousands of people have learned how to remineralize teeth, eliminate tooth pain or sensitivity, avoid root canals, stop cavities – sometimes instantaneously, re-grow secondary dentin, form new tooth enamel, avoid or minimize gum loss, heal and repair tooth infections.*"

"You mean all that can happen just in your mouth?" I'm so amazed that I stop scrubbing and milky water drips from the metal tangle onto the oiled-by-me dead tree floor.

"It's a fraught business living in this world, that's for sure," declares Husband bitterly. He continues, "*Cure Tooth Decay highlights include: The power of butter to heal teeth, how to find a good, minimally invasive, dentist, how to heal children's cavities, and find peace.*"

I remove the plug from the sink and grey water full of particles of healthy cereal and other healthy food, none of which Sammie has touched, go rushing down the hole with a loud snort as though a giant pig is just waiting below, to eat all the healthy particles, have cavity free teeth and find peace.

Valerie, the minimally invasive dentist, appears to be in her middle years. Despite this, few etched lines of anxiety crease her placid face. Her plumpish arms look as though they might provide a safe haven and motherly cuddles for some fortunate child. No doubt Irene Stoddard would approve. Valerie, in her knee length skirt and blue glasses, doesn't look like a person who forgets her children, is late for assembly, ticks boxes or waves red flags.

We sit down to wait on comfortable chairs of soft green cloth, with carved wooden arms, which feel somewhat familiar, while Sammie and Mattie explore the box of toys kindly provided for them. Sammie pulls out some small wooden blocks with what look like partial pieces of animals' bodies on each side. How confusing.

"Silly Mama, I can do it." Sammie grabs the block I'm examining and demonstrates how the different animal parts fit together to create a whole. Magic!

Mattie turns up his nose at the toys on offer, and starts fiddling with a cylindrical container full of water with interesting looking taps and levers.

"Probably better not to pull that apart, Mattie," warns Husband.

"I'm just trying to see how it works," Mattie reassures him.

Fortunately, at that moment we're called in. We don't have to be empathic or anything else with Mattie. However, inside Valerie's room there are allurements far more fascinating than the water container. Mattie heads straight for an intriguing tray of weapons, a miniature version of Prof's workshop, with tiny scissors, pinching implements and instruments with very sharp points like a jeweller's tools for working on Sammie's delicate pearls. Mattie puts a determined hand out for the most tempting weapon. Yes, I would go for that one too, Mattie. It has a delightful curly sharp point, a veritable weapon of torture. Mattie could experiment how that might feel on Sammie's arm for example.

However, Valerie restrains him with a firm hand and a definite "No".

Mattie scowls, clenching his mouth and fists. Instantly, before possible disaster can occur, an exquisite tray of dental implements arrives in my hands. After all, it's so much easier to give up temptation when one has something more thrilling on offer. I present them to an excited Mattie, who grabs them without even doing a handstand.

"Where did you get that?" Valerie seems surprised.

"A little trip to Pakistan, a place called, um, Karachi, have you heard of it?"

The implements, delicately wrought from silver or brass, each have their specially shaped place in a tray of maroon velvet, within the burnished wooden box.

"Oh, is that where your family's from?" Valerie laughs. "I didn't see you come in with them. It gave me a bit of a shock. They're very beautiful pieces. Very precise workmanship. Maybe I could just take a little look at them afterwards?" She has a gleam in her eye.

Husband doesn't seem so delighted. In fact, he has assumed his 'facing up to CYFS' expression. It seems to be becoming more and more frequent these days despite me trying so hard.

"Why don't you wait outside with Mattie, Am?" he says through a small gap between his lips.

"Mama," squeals Sammie, reaching out for me.

"Okay, *okay*, Sammie. *I'll* go out with Mattie. You stay here, Ama. But please…"

"Dada," Mattie, exulting in his tray of dental weaponry, trots after his father, "I could use these to do experiments in your P lab."

# Chapter Ten

# One More False Move

Husband is sitting at the desk in the study, the dreaded computer monster open before him. The opportunity for me to explore it hasn't arisen again. We've been so busy since those early days after coming back from the hospital. Two short days of being cosseted, then everything had to go back to 'normal' and rushing out of the house for something or other that we're going to be late for. Maybe today we could try the internet again? After all, it is the holidays and as Husband says, we don't have to rush off for things. I might even be able to do something called checking my emails. Husband says I probably have hundreds waiting for me.

"Okay, we did the dentist and we did a session for you with the Dean." With obvious effort, Husband unglues his eyes from the screen and briefly turns to me. "We're not doing vacs or interventions. We're still working with Dr Ganesh. So we've done our bit. That's it. Now I need to get on with some serious study."

The monster screen snatches back his eyes and I am left talking to the back of his head.

"But I thought... it's the holidays." I sit down in the tree chair, avoiding the screen.

"Yeah, holidays translates to: we have the kids to look after as well as you and now Lucky *and* Shakti." He remains transfixed. "It may be holidays for some people, but I have assignments overdue and my presentation to prepare. They were being a bit lenient with... our situation, you know..."

Lenient? The masters seem quite exacting to me. I wonder if I'll ever meet them?

"... but I have to get back to normal now and catch up on some serious study." Husband sighs. He moves the little mouse creature back and forth. Finally, he turns to face me. "I feel a bit stuck. I don't really want you going out with your parents, but I don't see we have any choice right now. Otherwise, I'll fail this degree. Then we'll never get ahead. And you heard what Fern said. We shouldn't cut off from them, even though I'd love to."

"Come *on*, Nani!" urges Sammie pulling Nani by the hand through the glass French doors into the big wooden shed next to the house.

Apparently, before all these events befell us, we were in the process of converting the shed building into a living area, which is why it has a metal firebox and the 'French' doors on one side. Fortunately, there is still a garage door on the other side, wide enough for Lucky.

In the small area not strewn with boxes, Lucky and Shakti lie companionably on a fresh bed of straw. A very ancient lawnmower, which Husband assures me he has never used, and various dust coated metal implements, lie abandoned in one corner. In another, two broken chairs are piled on top of each other. In between lurks a strange looking wooden insect on metallic springs, while above us, wooden beams provide a haven for spiders.

Sammie lies down next to his two friends and starts sucking on his designated teat. "I have milk too, see?" he tells Nani, milk dribbling down his chin.

"He can't do that. Can he?" enquires Nani. But then she seems to wither. "What would you know?" She sighs. "For goodness sake, a cow... and now a cat too. But where did they come from? Haven't you both got enough on your plates without this? Surely Dan next door could look after the cow?" She bends down and offers Shakti a tentative pat. "Your cat is very fat. I'd say you're probably going to have a few more people to look after quite soon. Oh, darling! What are we going to do with you all?" She takes a step back. "Looks like a nativity scene."

"Yes, doesn't it," I say.

"Do you know what that is?" Nani says doubtfully.

"Sure," I say.

"Well. If you're *sure*, that would be the first *normal* thing you've remembered."

It's hard to keep pretending. If Mattie was out here, he would no doubt ask what a nativity scene is and no one would mind, but he's intent on setting up a P lab with his dental weapons and hopes his Granddad will help him.

Sammie can't be depended on to ask. Whenever *he* asks a question, he gets comments like, "Sam*mie*, don't you know what black holes are? Sam*mie* you should know that. Sam*mie* you don't know anything." So he may have given up trying.

Husband appears at the French doors. "Oh yeah, what's she remembering now?"

Nani says flatly, "She *says* she knows what a nativity scene is."

Where are you Mattie when I need you?

Husband rubs his nose. "I guess we shouldn't underestimate the power of raw milk. It was known as liquid intelligence. I'm just studying about that. In past civilisations the great thinkers used to live on the stuff."

Nani grunts. "Better not tell your father about that." She turns to me. "He was just telling me how some kid in Australia died from drinking raw milk."

"No, we'd rather not tell the esteemed Prof anything, ever again," says Husband, bending down to give Lucky a scratch.

"Look, I know that must have been terrible for you that... the other day. But I didn't want to mention it in front of... you know."

"The cat? The cow?"

Mattie now enters the nativity scene upside down and collapses on top of Sammie.

"Hey! Dada! Mattie just landed on me!" Sammie crawls out of the hay and stamps off, pouting.

"Maybe we can have a conversation about it. I mean, of

course it's important. We need to talk about it. I'm not just sweeping it under the carpet. I can't believe someone did that. I mean what motive could they possibly have?"

Husband glares at poor Nani.

"I don't believe it was Prof," she says, intently brushing a few strands of hay back and forth with her pointed toe.

"Did you ask him?" Husband stands over her, hands on hips.

Nani wilts a little. "I couldn't even suggest it to him."

"Yeah, it might give him ideas."

Meanwhile, Sammie comes in brandishing a long stick, which he hands to his father, "This is a good weapon, Dada."

His father accepts the stick weapon, launching into a silent assault on the hay.

"They'd never take them away from you. Of course they wouldn't. They couldn't. Could they?" says Nani, vigorously stroking the swollen cat.

Shakti, sitting on Lucky, is tolerant. She's used to far worse, she tells me.

"Well, this certainly is a nice nativity scene isn't it?" I say, clapping my hands.

"What's a nativity scene?" demands Mattie.

Ah! Thank goodness for childish curiosity which hasn't been beaten out of him yet by school, as Husband predicts it will be. So far so good. However, now Nani and Husband are both glaring at *me*. What did I do wrong now?

It seems to me that life is very confusing. It's not surprising children lose their curiosity.

It's not the first time he and Nani have glared at me as

though shooting arrows with their eyes. Oh no. And I'm never quite sure what I've done wrong. It's not clearly explained, and if I ask questions, they shoot different weapons, of pain and disappointment.

Other things I find confusing are when Husband tells me, "No more funny business, Ama. One more false move out of you and we're finished."

And when people make a great fuss about being seven minutes late for an assembly, but they don't mind if children are imprisoned in grey walls for thirteen years and never see the sunshine and animals get cooped up in plastic boxes and electrocuted. I don't feel I have any basis for making decisions. I'm just expected to do some things, or not do others.

For example, when we ended up at the beach with Nani today, the boys were playing in the sand and Nani was just sitting watching them. I lay down for a few minutes to feel the warm sun on me. It was so beautiful after all those grey rooms. I don't know if I fell asleep or not. I was thinking about Irene Stoddard, registered social worker, when suddenly I found myself sitting opposite her in a truly dreadful grey room.

I was about to make a quick exit back to the sun, the holidays will be over soon enough, when I heard, "One more red flag on this case out in the wop-wops and I could uplift the kids. I'll give them to the grandparents." She was tapping the keys on her computer and staring fixedly at the screen as people do. Then she looked up, straight at me.

I ducked down. I didn't want her to see me. I didn't know if it would be one more false move or one more red flag, but I wasn't taking any chances.

"Shirl," she called to an equally large woman sitting behind a computer, "Did you see something? Or am I going mad?"

"Hell, *you* better not go mad, Irene, you've got your record to maintain. You must be the longest serving front line officer who hasn't gone fucking nuts."

"Sometimes I think I'm the only sane one in this place. 'part from you of course. I need a smoko. Coming kiddo?" She rose heavily from a nasty grey chair with spongy stuff spilling over the edge of it, leaving a large bottom imprint.

The two hefty matrons squeezed out of the door, puffing and panting, so I crept over for a listen.

It wasn't hard to hear Irene's booming voice, "Yeah, one of those daffy hippy types. Woman's completely crazy, wearing this ridiculous sequinned thing during the day, as though she's off to a ball. Unless she gets proper help there's not much hope for them keeping their kids. He's one of these intellectual types, all talk. Bet he beats her up and snorts coke." There was a long sucking sound and then a breath out. "It would give me great pleasure to uplift those kids. She wouldn't care anyway. You know? One of those. Don't bloody deserve to have kids. There must be more we can get on them. She's loony and he is too if you ask me."

I peeped round the edge of the door.

"No smoking thing's such a drag eh?" grumbled Shirl grinding out her white smoking tube with the thick heel of her shoe.

"Back to work."

"Or shall we just have another one?"

"Why the fuck not?"

Then Nani joined in, "It's not that I mind you going off for a walk or something, but considering all we've been through, and your history, if you would just tell me where you're going and what you're doing before you disappear, it would really ease my mind."

I couldn't see her until I opened my eyes and there she was, hands on hips, staring arrows down at me. I looked around and realised I was lying on the beach again.

"Was I asleep?" I said sitting up. "I've had a really weird dream."

"If you were asleep you must've been sleep walking, because I've been looking all over the place for you."

Very confusing.

The kittens have been born. It must have been some time in the night. We went out to milk Lucky and there they were! Shakti was looking very proud of herself, and rightly so. She says it was hard, but even though it's her first time, she knew just what to do. She knew how to bite off the umbilical chord and lick the amniotic fluid from their tiny bodies. Then when the placentas emerged, she knew that eating them would give her the nourishment she needed to feed the five tiny, tiny fur bundles blindly groping their way to her nipples.

"How did you know what to do?" I bend down and whisper to her.

"My body just knows what to do. The Great Soul tells me," she purrs.

"'s natural, isn't it? She didn't need *Pitocin*, a pin in the head, straps around the stomach to measure the heart beat and five people yelling, 'Push!' She managed just fine, all by herself. Funny that," says Husband, sitting on a bale of hay, flicking pieces of straw.

One kitten is tortoiseshell, two are black and two grey, all marked like tigers. Lucky gazes benevolently at her little family, while Sammie and Mattie watch in fascination.

"They're having Mama's milk!" chirps Sammie.

"Imagine having so many to feed at once," I say lowering myself into the hay next to them.

"Bit like you used to do with both boys, tandem feeding," says Husband through the straw in his mouth.

"Did I?" I ask wonderingly.

"It got a bit much. Mattie used to take all Sammie's milk. That's why you stopped. But it was so rich when Sammie was first born. Mattie went right back to it after he'd given up."

"I don't want to go out," moans Mattie.

"I don't want to go out too," whines Sammie.

"No, you'd like to stay with the kittens all day, wouldn't you?" I know how they feel. I'd like to stay here too, witnessing this miracle.

"And I don't want you guys to go out with Granddad," grumbles Husband.

Prof seems to have had a change of heart and is taking us out for the day, as it's his day off.

As Husband told me yesterday, we're in a bit of a quandary, as he doesn't trust him. "Why the hell would he offer to take *you* out after last time? What's his motive?"

But he's supposed to be taking us to an underwater world

with sharks and dolphins, so what could be the harm?

Husband gets up from his bale. "Sounds like the old jalopy now."

Prof appears, struggling with the French door, which grunts as it finally opens. "Could use some sanding on this door." Prof stands in the doorway rubbing the edge of the frame. "I can do for you. I will bring my sander the next time. And this handle is not well placed. It needs some adjustment." Prof fiddles with the door handle, turning it this way and that. He doesn't have on his noisy Do It Yesterday holiday clothes, but his crisply ironed white shirt, announcing that it's ready for work, which is strange. And his shiny shoes, with which he gingerly picks his way through the nativity scene of hay, dust and droppings.

"Alright Mattie, Sammie, you are ready to come?"

"Our cat has kittens! Come *on*, Gwanddad." Sammie takes Prof's hand and leads him towards the maternity area.

"Kittens? You have a cat? Oh! I was not knowing. A cat eh? Nani did not enlighten me in this. Since how long?"

"Woll, she came to live with us yesterday."

"No Sam*mie*, not yesterday. A week ago. That's seven days. Did you know that, Sammie?"

"Woll, tomowow, then."

"Sam*mie*." Mattie concedes defeat in the education of his younger brother and turns his attention to his Granddad. "Mama says I can bring my dental equipment. Can I work in your P lab?"

"What is this P lab?" Prof wrinkles his forehead.

"Dada and I are setting one up in the kitchen so I can do

my experiments. Can I do some experiments in your lab?"

Prof makes a forced coughing noise which could be laughter or choking.

"It's not a P lab, Mattie," Husband says with a mixture of annoyance and embarrassment. "I don't know where you got that idea."

"You said it on the phone to Nani. You said you'd just beaten Sammie against the wall and thrown Mama out of the window headfirst, after setting up a P lab in the kitchen."

"You silly billy, that was a joke," protests Husband, reddening.

Mattie starts puffing up his face, like the puffer fish in his encyclopaedia and glares through narrowed eyes. "Dada! I don't like being teased!" He launches himself at his father.

"Now, now, young lad that is quite sufficient with that carry on," says Prof, placing himself between them, and incurring the fist intended for Dada.

"Oof!" moans Prof bending over and clutching his stomach.

I go to assist him, but he waves me off with a hand and head shake.

"Okay, no problem. It is nothing. It is not paining. I am okay. You are becoming a strong man isn't it, Mattie?" He straightens up and breathes out. "Now let me see these kittens. And a cow also I b'lieve."

Mattie, sitting in front with his Granddad, has his tongue sticking out of the corner of his mouth as he carefully returns each implement to its correct place. I'm in the back of the old 'jalopy' with Sammie, who's steadily munching his way through the contents of his purple and orange lunch box: one yogurt suckie, one box of sultanas, one peanut butter and banana sandwich and three crackers with cheese sliced very thinly. I even remembered to put the scissors in Mattie's lunch box so that he can cut open both sides of the yoghurt suckie, not just the side that is perforated. I know how important this is to Mattie. I feel virtuous, proud, and dare I say, hopeful.

Prof is concentrating on driving, his smooth brown hands grasping the wheel. Earlier he enquired, "Where did you acquire this box of implements? It is reminding me my childhood in India. See, I have a golden tooth."

Mattie tells him we got it from the dentist, and I say nothing.

Now Mattie pipes up, "Granddad, did you know the sun is pulled in a chariot around the earth? And there are all these tiny people who sing songs in front of the chariot as it goes around?"

"Now where on earth are you getting that from?" snaps Prof, eyes glued to the road.

"Mama took us, me and Sammie, last night in our dreams."

Prof almost crashes into the car in front of us. "Well, Mattie, that is what primitive people who don't understand about things say. They have to find reasons for things, so they make up lovely stories like that one. The truth, I am sorry to say, is much less um fanciful. Equally wonderful though how it all just goes on by gravity and relativity and... equations."

"What's primitive?"

"People who aren't educated. Not so evolved as us. That's why you actually have to go to school, Mattie, young man. And if I was your father..."

"Boring learning!" Mattie looks out of the window.

"Now if you were at a decent school... but never mind, Mattie, we are working on that."

"What's equations?" Mattie's dental implements are now perfectly placed in their box.

"Oh, wonderful magical, well not magical, but mathematical formulae. Maths is the purest and most beautiful of the sciences."

Mattie says, "I like maths. I can count to a thousand in fifties. Fifty, a hundred, a hundred and fifty..."

"I knew my seventeen times table when I was your age..."

"Five million," offers Sammie.

"No, Sammie. Now I can't remember where I was..."

"We would carry minimum fifteen kay gee books to school in our satchel, plus tiffin carrier..."

"A thousand," chirps Sammie.

"Sam*mie*..."

"A gabillion he, he, he."

"Sammie don't *do* that!" Mattie starts to cry and struggles to reach Sammie.

"You boys behave," orders Prof loudly, "or no ice creams after!"

"The dentist said Sammie's not allowed," wails Mattie.

"Dentist?"

"I want an ice cweam now," bleats Sammie.

"I cannot drive with all this caterwauling," explodes Prof.

Mattie and Sammie continue to caterwaul, this time about who is going to press the button in the lift on the way up to Prof's lab, where, according to Prof, he's paying a 'flying visit' on the way to the dolphins. But of course we can't go with him, we must wait in the kitchen/seminar area like good Indian school girls.

Prof instructs the boys to take it in turns. "That is fair."

But Mattie, like me, probably doesn't understand what being a good Indian school girl involves. He may not speak Hindi. He declares loudly, "I'm doing it, Sammie, because I'm the oldest."

Then someone gets into the lift in a sort of mechanical looking conveyance with wheels.

Mattie gets quite excited. "He even brought his push chair!" he says gleefully, scrutinising the conveyance and eagerly opening up his toolbox to select the precise implement he requires, then plunging it into a perfectly corresponding aperture.

Prof pulls Mattie's arm away abruptly. "How dare you? That could be very dangerous! You immediately put back that implement." He turns to the man in the conveyance. "So sorry."

Meanwhile, Sammie, standing proprietorially in front of the buttons, has been controlling the opening and closing of the doors for four floors. Mattie is just preparing to insert the curly implement into Prof's leg, when he realises.

"It's not fair, Sammie, I didn't get to do any buttons!" Mattie gives Sammie a huge shove just as the lift doors start to close. I quickly lunge after Sammie, leaving us both marooned on the fourth floor, while the lift continues on its way.

"Woll, we just get the next one, Mama." Sammie doesn't seem too worried. "Come *on*, Mama," he says, taking my hand as another lift appears.

Soon we're sailing up to the seventh floor, arriving just in time to witness Prof dragging a screaming Mattie through the bossy KEEP OUT! AUTHORISED PERSONNEL ONLY door.

"Your son!" splutters Prof.

"Mama... Make him let me *go*!"

"This is my place of work. I cannot have this sort of performance and carry on here. You may not discipline him, but I must."

Before I can mention that with Mattie, you just have to know how to deal with him, force doesn't work, Prof has manoeuvred him to the forbidden territory beyond and Sammie and I are once more confronted by a closed door. What should I do? An inner synapse urges me to storm the fortress and rescue Mattie, but I'm wary. Listening to my inner impulses seems to get me in trouble and may be the 'one more false move'. I dither before the solid superior knowing of the door.

"Come on, Mama." Sammie takes charge, clambering onto a chair. "We can have stories sitting in this chair."

As I say, how do I know how to make decisions? After all, it's an opportunity to spend some time with little Sammie.

Maybe I should trust Prof? I sigh, resigning myself to following higher orders and sit down. Sammie pulls a book from his pink and orange backpack and we snuggle up together. The book turns out to be one of Mattie's reading books from school, which Husband says are 'uninspired' and 'lacking any sort of depth or creativity'. They're simply to get children to learn to read, not for the joy of finding out, or the wonder of the story. Another reason to have school under a tree.

Still, Sammie doesn't know it's part of an 'insidious, patriarchal, capitalist ideology designed specifically to destroy all that is good and original in children and ultimately people'. So I have to read it three times. The third time, Sammie wants Mama's milk simultaneously. Well, why not?

*"Once upon a time the sun and the wind were arguing.*

*The wind said, 'I am the strongest!'*

*And the sun said, 'No, I am the strongest!'*

*So they decided to have a little competition to see who was the strongest. A man just happened to be walking down the road wearing a big winter coat.*

*The wind said, 'We will see who can remove that coat from the man!'*

*The sun said politely, 'Alright you can go first.'*

*The wind started to blow and blow and blow and blow. And the more he blew, the more the man pulled his coat tightly about him.*

*Finally, the wind gave up, saying, 'It is impossible. Nobody could resist my force!'*

*Then it was the sun's turn. The sun began to shine as brightly as he could and the whole place felt like summer. The man stopped walking, wiped his brow and took off his coat because he was so hot.*

*'I have won,' said the sun.*

*'Ah but can you make him put his coat back on again?' said the wind."*

Just then, the forbidden door opens and out comes the creature, who is not really a creature, carrying a sleeping Mattie.

"I gave him a little something, to calm him down you know, Beti. I could not have him being a wild man here. Might be good you give him sometimes. It is a sedative we use on the animals. It is a kindness to put them out of their misery." Prof places Mattie's floppy little body gently down on two chairs adjoining ours. "Poor little boy. The doctor can help him too you know. I do not know why they are not doing anything at school?" He sighs deeply. "That school."

"I don't really know if you should have..."

"Oh no no, Beti, very, very mild effect. *Min*iscule dose." He shows me by pinching his blue thumb and forefinger together before his white face, the same way he does when he tells us his pickle is not spicy, "Little, little chilli." But then it's like a volcano. Although Mattie swallows it like a man.

"Why not use these scientific discoveries to our advantage eh, Beti?"

My little Mattie. I wonder if he's travelling on moon beams?

Then Prof whips off his other face to reveal him glaring in apparent disgust at Sammie suckling at my breast.

I follow his gaze and realise that Sammie is asleep too.

Prof turns into a driveway surrounded by trees. A large board on a stone wall shows a beautiful picture of what look like three large blue fish diving in a circle into the sea. We must have arrived! How unfortunate, Mattie and Sammie are still asleep.

The driveway, lined with very neat but sharp plants, opens onto a grey, dead tree house. I'm excited to be going to see the sharks and dolphins in their underwater world. Underneath the fish on the board it says 'Leakey Lane Clinic' in black writing.

"I thought we might pay a visit to a colleague, with the children sleeping and all," says Prof, pulling up by the house. He starts to get out of the car. "We will not be long. Better we leave the boys here to have their little sleep, then we can do in peace, isn't it?" He beckons me with his hand. "Come, Beti."

This doesn't feel right. "What if they wake up?"

"They will be fine." Prof's eyes seem to sink even further into the shadows and images of wide black eyes gradually shrinking to an impenetrable sliver, appear on my inner eye.

I hesitate. As I say, how do I know how to make decisions? It usually ends up being the wrong decision. One more false move... I follow him up stone stairs, glancing over my shoulder at every step.

As I touch a dead tree rail beside the stairs, and again as I pass through the dead tree door, I hear a whispering like the wind in the trees. "Two thoussand yearss. Just sstroke me and you will ssensse. Yess."

I look round to see if there are any books or writings on the wall. But no. There are four magazines placed very precisely on a low grey table. In the windows, severe black lines imprison small pieces of grey glass that send no colours to play on the floor like gems.

On one side of the room, a lady with all sorts of colours in her hair, a bit like our tortoiseshell kitten, sits behind a curved wall gazing into a slender computer. She looks up at us through red framed glasses and her multicolour hair swings this way and that. She's dressed entirely in black.

"Good morning, Renée." Prof greets the woman with an anxious lift of his lips.

"How are you, Daksh?" The woman gives us a wide red smile. Her teeth look sharp.

"Personally, I am well. Thank you. And your good self?"

"Never better!"

The lady, Renée, turns to me with a lift of her narrow eyebrows. "And this is your daughter, I presume?"

I go up to the wall and lean my hand on the top. Immediately, a clamour of voices start whispering urgently to me. I jerk my hand away as though from an electric toaster or ribbon and catch Renée observing me with apparent curiosity.

"I think it is my daughter." Prof watches me under hooded lids, a vulture waiting for its prey. "She looks somewhat like my daughter. But tell truth, she is behaving very out of character."

"She's had a fugue episode you say."

"That was diagnosed at the hospital when she was found. Doctor Chaturvedi. You are acquainted with her?"

"She surely advised further treatment?" Renée's thin

brows furrow in concern.

Prof leans his elbow on the grey wall, takes his glasses off and starts to clean them with his large handkerchief. "My daughter Amalia was married to a very irresponsible man. I blame him for whole episode."

"*Was* married?" Renée cocks one eyebrow.

"This person," he indicates me, "is still married to this irresponsible man. This is why she has not had proper treatment. They rely on snake oil, homeopathic placebos and some quack counsellor. She destroys scientific experiments. Big problem. And of course cannot look after the children properly." Prof returns his glasses to his nose. "Which is why I made an appointment with you. Someone must take responsibility, isn't it?"

Renée gets up. "Alright… Amalia is it?"

"I prefer to be known as Kali." I inform her, standing up very straight.

Renée looks me up and down. I'm wearing a marginally less sparkly shawl today after Irene's comments. Although I cannot be sure she was talking about me. Furthermore, it may have been a dream. Still, one more red flag… one more false move.

A small smile crosses Renée's lips. "Just take a seat for a moment. I'll be with you in five." She disappears through a grey door next to her area behind the low wall.

We perch on two uncomfortable square black couches, Prof leaning over to adjust the top magazine in the pile so it's perfectly in line with the other three, although it already is. We're enclosed in greyness; it's like being in a cloud. Grey carpet, grey ceiling, grey walls. The last relieved only by a single picture of a house wrought in many shades of grey.

Prof catches me looking at the picture. "Renée is quite the photographer in her spare times. The black and white mostly."

Suddenly, the picture of the house changes into a picture of a huge tall tree, with three very tiny men and eight tiny bulls pulling a cart next to it. It looks like the jambu tree at the top of Mount Meru.

The tree sighs, "I wass tall and sstrong, but the axss wass more sstrong."

The picture changes into a scene with a huge log being pulled in the cart by the bulls. I go over to it and press my face to the wall.

"Yess," whispers the tree, "yess."

I feel the grey house enfolding me in its embrace.

"Our ssisster will sshelter you, ssmall ssisster. Resst asssured. You will be ssafe."

I stroke the picture and the wall, experiencing a deep sense of peace.

"You see for yourself first hand. What normal person hugs walls? No daughter of mine."

Prof and Renée are both staring at me.

"I'm ready for you now, Amalia, if you'd like to come through." Renée is standing in the grey doorway behind the low wall.

I reluctantly leave the picture, which has resumed its form as a house, actually this house, and trudge after her. As I pass the low wall, I absentmindedly brush its wooden looking edge with my hand. Suddenly the voices start clamouring again, this time even more urgently. It's the trees, who've given their lives for this wall, been mashed into tiny pieces. They're not grumbling for themselves, as they are very humble and tolerant. However, they have an urgent message, which I *must* hear. I stop and listen. Renée watches me shrewdly, tapping a sharp red nail on the doorframe.

I put my hands over my ears. "It's so hard to hear you when you're all talking at once," I scream.

Out of the corner of my eye, I see Prof and Renée exchanging a glance. Beyond that, a tiny ray of sunlight, illuminating the grey picture, catches my eye. Something is there in the picture that wasn't there before. It's Prof's car in front of the house, parked by the sign of the three fishes.

I finally understand the trees' message.

The car door is open...

Chapter Eleven

# Underwater World

I'm running out of the door, hurtling down the stone steps before you can say dissociative fugue. Inside the car, Mattie's floppy body, head lolling, is still firmly buckood in his booster seat in the front. However, Sammie's buckoos are undone and his seat is empty.

I look round wildly, yelling, "Sammie! Sammie!"

He's nowhere in sight. Where could he have gone? I should never have left him. I shouldn't have listened to Prof. I should have listened to myself! My many arms are itching. I feel a sword slip into one of my hands. I must protect Sammie! But I can't leave Mattie. I don't have time to think, to wonder about the right decision, or whether this will be one more thing. I jump into the driver's seat. Where's the key? Sword, spear, bow, scimitar... Ah, here in a right hand is a key, the same key I found in the lab. I hear footsteps behind me and Prof calling. But it's not time to be a good Indian school girl, I tried that and look where it got us. I quickly turn the key and roar out of the driveway without a backward glance. Seems I haven't forgotten how to drive. From the Great Soul comes intelligence and remembrance and firing synapses...

It's a quiet street; there are no cars. Nor is there any sign of a three-year-old boy. Where could he be? Come *on* Great Soul... Come *on* synapses. We reach the end of the road. I have no idea where we are. I have no idea where Sammie is. But I'm not going back to Prof and Renée.

I lower the window, searching in every direction, calling Sammie's name. I turn left and drive very slowly up the road. Cars behind me start screeching their horns.

"Nonsense people! No patience!" I scream out of the window.

How far could a small boy have gone in the time Prof and I were in Renée's? Wouldn't he have known we were inside the house? Sammie's far too sensible to have gone off walking by himself, surely? Doubts assail me. Maybe I should go back to the house? Maybe he's behind the house? Or even up a tree? But then I see Prof in my inward eye. He's on the phone, looking very angry. I have a bad feeling. A little synapse whispers 'There's no time to lose'. I continue to drive slowly, combing both sides of the road with my eyes. He couldn't have come this far could he? All at once, I notice a big picture of a huge brown ice cream with a bite taken out of one corner, sitting on the pathway in front of a small shop. Could it be? I pull over and get out of the car, rushing into the shop, all the while looking over my shoulder like a frightened rabbit. I won't be long, Mattie.

Inside the shop, there is a little girl about Mattie's age, watching something on a screen. Sammie is not in sight.

"Where's your mother or father?" I yell.

A young man the same colour as me comes through a door looking frightened. "What you want? We don't have money… Barely we're making enough money to live…"

"Have you seen a small boy, golden, with straw for hair? Please… tell me you have!"

"No." He turns to the little girl. Despite his speaking in another tongue, I can somehow understand. "Did you see small boy? You didn't tell me we had customer…"

The girl turns reluctantly from her screen. "He asked me for ice cream, like that one," she says pointing to the one outside.

"Yes? Where did he go? Tell me… Quick!" I shout.

The girl looks fearful and remains silent.

"Please tell me!" I glance back at the car with Mattie's slumped body inside.

Finally, after what seems like a yuga, she leans up to her father and whispers in his ear.

"My daughter says he was crying for his mummy, because he has no money for ice cream. This man says he will take him to his mummy and paid for the ice cream."

"A man?" I'm almost out of the door. "Did she see which way they went?"

The man holds his hand in a chopping mudra similar to Prof's over the poor girl's head. She wordlessly points left, her eyes brimming with tears. Then, "They got into a car. I think… silver car."

I fly out of the door, a bell clanging behind me, and leap into the car. All my hands are trembling as I put the key into the ignition. I must think clearly. Come *on* synapses! I remember at the Easter show when I couldn't turn back into a human, I had to relax first. Peaceful parent, peaceful parent, one, two, three… But I can scarcely breathe, what to speak of relax, not knowing where Sammie is.

I've just managed to start the car, when I hear a thunderous pounding. What? I leap out of the car only to find Prof, panting and wildly thumping his fist on the roof.

"You crazy woman… tearing away like that. Where are you going in such mad rush?" He takes a deep breath. "I am almost having a heart attack trying to catch you. And not telling where you are going, interrupting Renée's precious time. I…"

I don't have time for this. "Sammie's gone. He's gone with a man… We have to find him…"

"Sammie… gone? What are you telling?"

"There's no time to lose. Get in or stay put, quick. I have to find him."

"Now let us not be rash." Prof places restraining hands on the edge of the door. "I have already called law enforcement when you took it into your head to go racing off in my car, like a banshee. They will be arriving shortly." He slowly pulls up his sleeve, lifts his glasses and examines his watch. "Better we wait for them. Then you can explain them what you have done with my grandson." He gazes into the distance, through lopsided glasses, presumably watching out for the law enforcement, while carefully repositioning his sleeve.

Just then, the worried face of the girl from the shop appears at the opposite window next to Mattie. She opens the door. "Hurry up! This is urgent! I can help…"

I glance at Prof. He now stands, arms crossed, surveying the traffic. He hasn't noticed. I beckon the girl to get in. She jumps in on top of Mattie, who finally stirs. We slam both doors and screech off into the road.

"Where are we going?" croaks a groggy Mattie. "Why are you sitting on me? Get off!"

The girl looks at me with huge brown eyes. "Black. We must go to Black. Step on the gas."

"Mama, what's happening? I said get off!" Mattie gives the girl a big shove. "I don't feel very well," he moans.

The girl topples into me, the steering wheel jerks and the car swerves. A monstrous truck coming towards us veers to the side, sounding its horn, followed by several other horns. I start to pull over.

But the girl pushes the wheel in the other direction. "No! We cannot lose even one second."

Mattie starts wailing and flailing his limbs. "Get her off me!" He's about to shove her again.

She turns huge eyes upon him, her hand held in the chopping mudra. "Don't be nonsense rascal. Your small, small brother is gone with a terrible man. We must find him or he may be hurt. You want that your brother is hurt?"

Mattie stops flailing and considers this for a moment. Finally, he concludes, "But you have to sit in the back, otherwise the policeman will come."

The girl doesn't move. "I must remain here only to tell you directions."

"But you have to…" Mattie's voice starts rising.

"Mattie," I say, "the policeman is coming anyway. I hope they will help us find Sammie. But I don't know which way to go and there's a roundabout ahead."

"I am telling you… Black…" says the girl in a firm voice.

Mattie clenches his fists and takes a huge breath in. "One… two…" he chants, fiddling with his seatbelt, "three… four…" he jumps up, "fivesixseveneightnineten." With renewed resolve, he opens a small cupboard in the dashboard and pulls out a book. "Black, Black…" he mutters, flicking through the pages then dragging his finger down rows of tiny writing.

Meanwhile we've reached the roundabout and I'm driving round and round.

Mattie holds his finger in one spot. "Black Road?" he asks the girl.

"Not road."

"Beach? Black Beach?"

"Correct. Black Beach."

Mattie carefully turns the pages of the book. "Page thirty-two, thirty-three… here it is." For a moment, he studies a colourful page, crisscrossed with red and orange lines.

We've now been round the roundabout ten times and I'm getting a little dizzy.

Just then, Mattie announces, "Take that turn off there." He points to the next road with a sign saying, 'North', and remains standing. "Well in India they don't have seatbelts anyway."

The girl agrees, "No, we would be eight on a scooter, my

all family plus baby."

Mattie looks at the girl with grudging respect. "What's your name anyway?"

"I'm Priya," she smiles at him, "and you are Mattie."

"How did you know?"

We're heading out of the city now; there are meadows with cows, horses and small stands of trees. The houses and cars are further apart.

Mattie is sobbing, "Sa-mm-ie. I don't want the terrible man to hurt Sa-mm-ie. Go faster, Mama."

"Yes, you must go fast. I don't know if we will be in time." Priya looks worried. "All my fault. That's why I had to help you only. I was too busy watching movie. I will never ever watch a movie ever again."

My heart is racing. All of a sudden, the car starts juddering, slows down and comes to a stand still.

Mattie leans over and looks at the black circles with white numbers and hands. "We've run out of petrol," he wails.

Priya looks at me, wide-eyed. "You must go by flying. Go. No problem for us, we will be all right. You will be quicker. Why I didn't think before?"

"But I can't leave you both here by yourselves. I know that much! What are we going to do?"

"I know, Mama," says Mattie, controlling his emotions manfully, "you could get a Tesla. They're good cars. Just make sure you get one that's charged up."

We jump out of Prof's car, which is stuck in the middle of the road.

Mattie tries to push it, but Priya grabs his arm, crying, "No! No time."

For at that moment our Tesla arrives, still covered in dust from before. In moments, we leap in and start the engine. I marvel at how the key from Prof's lab seems to fit every door and every car.

Priya cries, "Floor it."

Checking the black circles in front of the wheel, Mattie informs us that the car can go up to two hundred and forty nine kilometres per hour. "You can go fast, Mama. Or," he asks hopefully, "do you want me to drive?"

"That's breaking the law," says Priya.

Soon we're streaking along the road at two hundred and forty kilometres an hour. The white hand is right round the circle; the Tesla's wheels scarcely skim the ground.

"Will we be in time, Priya?"

"It's touch and go."

"Are we almost there, Mattie?"

Mattie is white faced. "Hurry, Mama, we still have to get to the end of this line."

A blue light appears in the distance and as it nears, we hear a wailing sound.

"It's the policeman!" cries Mattie. "Quick Priya, get your seatbelt on! We should've brought our car seats."

But Priya has other concerns. "They might stop us," warns Priya. "We cannot risk." She looks at me. "You must go flying only. We will be fine. Policemens will look after us."

Mattie looks a bit crestfallen. "You better take the map. Look we're here and you want to be..." he points to the end of the orange line where it meets some yellow then blue, "here."

"I could take you both…"

"We will be much too heavy. We will make you slow. You must not delay," cries Priya. "Now, go!"

All at once, I'm hovering over the road. The last thing I hear, is the voice of a small girl saying, "Mattie, do one thing, drive the car to the side of the road…"

It's almost full tide. The water is crashing over rocks and reaching far up the shore. I'm not yet sure why I'm here. Plummeting down on the air currents, I see shapes creating shadows on the silvery sea. What are they? Ah, now I'm closer I see… yes, they're fish, like the ones on Renée's sign. There appear to be three of them, leaping out of the water in great arcs near a cave. If I didn't have pressing business, I might stay and play, dear fish, you look so joyous. But wait. They seem to be showing me something. As I touch the water, I glimpse a flash of gold. Could it be…? Is it…? I swoop to the mouth of the cave. More flashes of gold.

Inside the cave, a man with a huge sweating neck and beak like nose stands, legs akimbo, wielding a massive glinting axe.

Before him, enchanted by the fish, his golden hair shooting out in all directions, a small person, hugging his tiny knees to his body.

The flashing blade of the axe is perfectly aimed… to coincide with the small person's tender neck…

In less than one lava, I grab the man by his hair. The axe flies out of his hand. My own sword carves the air in a perfect arc aimed at *his* neck. Soon I will drink the blood pouring from his neck and dance on his body. I laugh wildly.

However, in the truti between raising and wielding my sword, a white cloud surrounds the man, emitting a raucous cackling. I find myself being stabbed by small spears and my sword drops from my hand, landing just beside the axe. Engulfed by the white cloud, the man is borne away, high over the ocean. The cackling cloud disappears into the distance, leaving a sprinkling of white feathers drifting down onto the sandy floor.

I drop down beside the trembling golden boy, who turns to me, with a wobbly smile. "Mama? Where were you, Mama?"

"Sammie! Oh Sammie!" I clutch my precious little son to me in a fierce embrace, smothering him with tears and kisses. "We almost lost you my darling, darling Sammie!"

I clasp my golden one to me, rocking him back and forth in my lap, while the water swirls up the beach towards us. He buries his head in my breast and eventually his tense little body relaxes, is comforted and pacified, by drinking long and deeply of Mama's milk.

Who knows how long we sit thus, but after several laghus, my sunshine boy pulls away, gazing around in the gloom of the cave. For a while, he seems content to just sit, but then something irresistible catches his eye, enticing him from his refuge.

"Mama, look!" he cries, jumping up and bounding over to a huge object half buried in the sand. It looks like a giant stick. Sammie heaves and tugs, but to no avail. Digging around the artefact, he finally uncovers an immense axe. Then he spots another weapon, standing upright in the sand, flashing in the gloom. My sword! He plunges further into the cave to retrieve the hidden treasure, his voice echoing off the cave walls, "This was in your bed when we did do the tweasure hunt."

All at once, I feel water swishing around my calves. The tide is coming in fast. We need to get out. But wait, the water has blocked off the cave entrance. What are we to do? I wonder if we could wade out? The ocean is dashing against the rocks while Sammie strains to pick up the sword. We must fly away, quickly! I grab my boy in my arms and try to rise off the ground, but nothing happens.

"Sammie, put the sword down. We'll have to leave it."

"No, Mama. We need the sword for pwotection!"

"But unless we move, we're going to drown."

Reluctantly, he puts the sword down and I try again. Still nothing. I'm beginning to panic. Did we all risk our lives to save Sammie for us to both die anyway? Is the ocean going to reclaim me? Is this how it all started, with me coming out of the ocean, and now I'm going back? But not Sammie, my sunshine boy, with his whole life stretching before him, he mustn't die! Come *on...*

There's a clicking and whistling sound. All at once, three huge grey forms with smiling, bobbing faces, appear at the mouth of the cave. It's the grey fish! They whistle to us to climb on their backs.

"Can I bwing my sword?" Sammie asks the fish.

The sword and the axe have disappeared under the water, now lapping round my knees and Sammie's waist. It's too dark in the cave to see the weapons. I hear a wailing sound in the distance.

"The dolphin says we won't need it," says Sammie, clambering onto a great fish's back.

I get onto another dolphin and we hold on very tight, as the third dolphin leads the way, leaping and diving through the waves. The wailing sound gets louder. By the time we near the shore, the wailing sound is very loud and then abruptly stops. Suddenly, two small figures appear, racing down the beach. I jump off my dolphin, giving her a kiss and a thank you, just in time to see Mattie plunging into the water towards us. Priya hesitates for a moment at the water's edge, then jumps in too. The dolphins are still smiling and swimming around us. I'm vaguely aware of more figures racing down the beach, lights, the sound of loud voices.

My dolphin butts Mattie with her snout and whistles for him to come for a ride. The other one waits patiently by Priya who looks at me with wondering eyes. Soon all three children are clutching the dolphins and riding through the waves.

Now one very tall and one less tall figure appear at the water's edge, wearing glaring yellow school playground jackets, and dark blue trousers. One wades into the ocean and attempts to peel the children off the dolphins.

The other is speaking into a phone-like machine with a black rod attached. "We've located child and suspect. Bringing them in now."

"Your husband brought you some dry clothes. You might want to change out of those wet ones." The woman turns the key in the lock with a clanging sound and opens the door, which isn't really a door, but a series of thick metal bars.

I get up off the narrow bed and take the clothes from her. A toothbrush is wrapped inside the clothes, but nothing else. There's a small metal basin and toilet in the room. I suppose you could call it a bedbathroom. I feel like one of Prof's rhesus monkeys. I change my clothes very slowly. There are no sparkly cloths in the bundle. Then I lie down on the hard bed. Sleep does not come.

On the way back in the police car this evening, Sammie was sick. He explained that the man bought him a hundwed ice cweams and held up five fingers to show us. Mattie told him that was only five. But he used his kind voice. Sammie said when he woke up he didn't know where I was, but he saw the dolphin sign, so he knew we were at the dolphins. But it looked different from when we'd gone to the dolphins before, which wasn't in a house. He remembered that last time we'd parked the car and had to walk all the way down the street to get there. So he thought maybe that's what had happened this time. When he got to the end of the road, he saw the big ice cweam and realised he was hungry...

He told the man he wanted to go and find the dolphins, because that's where I was. He just didn't know it was quite so far away. And these dolphins weren't behind glass. Also there were no sharks. Woll, at least he didn't see any. One thing he couldn't understand though, was why I took so long to get there? Then the man flew up into the sky in a cloud of chickens. At this, Mattie opened his mouth as if to say something, but then seemed to think better of it and wiggled his finger in his nose instead. Also why did Mattie come with her? Here Sammie poked his finger in Priya's arm. And also why did they come in a police car? And also, does she, poking Priya's arm again, have any ice cweam with her? Actually, he's not sure if he weally wants any even if she does.

What is truth? Is there an absolute truth? Maybe the best the law enforcement can hope for is a gradation from the most to the least reliable version.

Article from this morning's *Daily Enquirer*:

A man was found dead, washed up in a cave on Black Beach at low tide yesterday evening. Who is he? And why was he there? To add to the mystery, his eye sockets were empty and he was covered all over with deep lacerations. Found nearby on the sand, were a priceless jewel encrusted sword, along with a sharp bladed axe. Whose weapons are these and how did they come to be lying near the victim? Do the answers reside with the woman who is currently helping police with their enquiries?

Initial psychiatric report, Renée Skinner:

"From my extremely brief observation of Amalia I believe we are dealing with a very sick young woman. She obviously hears voices loudly and overwhelmingly, which is one of the key indications of schizophrenia, in this case schizophrenia with paranoia. Moreover, she is acting on those voices and has very low impulse control. This could be extremely dangerous in terms of living life in the community, particularly in dealing with children. Furthermore, she exhibits elements of dissociative identity disorder, believing she is someone else. I would like to conduct a more comprehensive diagnosis of her symptoms, but all indications point to the presence of severe mental disorder as evidenced even at first glance."

Report by Police Officer Constable Richard Starling:
- Alerted thirteen hundred hours by Daksh Prajapati that Amalia Harrison, mentally unstable female, of mixed Indian/ European ethnicity, mid-thirties, average height, hair colour: brown, eye colour: tawny, glittery clothes, in possession of a stolen car, dark blue Toyota Sprinter nineteen ninety, registration number DIYGUY, making her way north on Leakey Lane. She has in the car her son Matthew Harrison aged six years six months and her son Samuel Harrison aged three years ten months.
- Further alert from Daksh Prajapati, thirteen seventeen approximately: possible missing person Samuel Harrison, possible but unconfirmed sighting in Anning Superette on Anning Road at unknown time. Priya Mistry, female Indian, aged five years seven months, daughter of Govind Mistry, superette owner. Possible abduction by Amalia Harrison. Car travelling north on Highway Seventeen.
- Alert, thirteen forty-five of stolen car: Tesla, Black, registration: NOGAS
- Alert, thirteen fifty, black vehicle sighted northbound on Coastal Highway exceeding speed limit.
Action Report:
- PC Richard Starling, accompanied by PC Penny Taylor, avoided

collision with stationary vehicle Toyota Sprinter abandoned northbound lane Coastal Highway. Traffic hazard reported to office.

- Pursued black Tesla, recorded top speed two hundred and forty. Tesla pulled over after three minute pursuit, driven by Matthew Harrison. Containing abducted Priya Mistry. No seat belts worn.

- Following repeated indication by Matthew and Priya of abduction of Samuel Harrison, abandoned Tesla on shoulder of highway after alerting office. Drove north on Coastal Highway to Black Beach.

- Arrived fourteen eighteen. Matthew and Priya exited police vehicle without communication, entered water, interacted with dolphins in potentially hazardous manner. Located Samuel also interacting with dolphin in similar manner. Located wanted female, Amalia, handcuffed and accompanied to car. Matthew, Priya, Samuel removed from water. Dolphins given warning.

- Children given severe warning, placed with firm hand into car. Put on siren en route back to head office to cheer up children and get home quicker. Emesis by Samuel Harrison on rear seat upholstery, car number two seven five. Request for car freshener.

- Overheard: talk of abduction by man/unusual disappearance of man. Conclude: collective childhood fantasy, fantasy of sick woman.

- Amalia Harrison remanded in custody pending psychiatric assessment.

- Statements taken. See attached.

Verbal statement, Daksh Prajapati (father):

"I was taking my family members to see the Underwater World, so my waste of space son-in-law could do his waste of time study. Family means, my daughter, who has had a personality transplant and my two grandsons who are both wild men, especially Mattie. But now it looks like also Sammie is following in his father's and now his mother's (if you are understanding my drift), footsteps and becoming wild man also. The two young scallywags fell asleep in the car before we were arriving at the Underwater World. I blame the father. Why two children fall asleep in the middle of the day if well cared for and stimulated in the intelligence? When I was a lad, I knew my seventeen times tables at Sammie's age. Thirty kilos books on my back walking to the school! We did not have such thing as holidays. When he is with me, Mattie reads the encyclopaedia, not all this rubbish video games.

This is some background informations to give more accurate understanding, so to speak. So as I was telling. Not worth to go to Underwater World when two young boys sleeping during the day. So I think why not to very, very quickly drop in on my colleague Renée, to arrange real appointment with real doctor? Some more background informations: my daughter is not well in the head. Personality transplantation I am already explaining you. Waste of space son-in-law has not taken her for any reputable treatment. Imagine!

We arrive to Renée's clinic, Leakey Lane Clinic, very posh posh place you may know. We race quickly into clinic, for one second. For less than one second. (Here there are accompanying hand gestures of the little, little chilli variety). All of a sudden, with no warning whatsoever, so-called daughter is screaming! Voices! I hear voices! And tearing off down the steps, into *my* car. Next thing is she is driving off at the speed of wind! Poor Renée was very shocked, as I also was. A madwoman for a daughter. Haaay. (Accompanied by shaking of the head and sighing). I immediately telephoned for law enforcement, which I believe was the most responsible action to take. You cannot have madwomans driving cars, at least not in this country, it could be dangerous. India is different thing. Then I went chasing after the car. I am not young man as you can see, but I manage to catch up with the car. By this time, she is telling she has misplaced one grandson! (He hits his forehead). Can you believe? Not only that, but when I caution her, wait for the police, they will be better equipped to find him, that is, if you have really lost him, she speeds off again in *my* car, this time abducting *another* man's child. Indian superette owner man too. Then as I understand it, she leaves my car in the middle of the road. Stuck out somewhere miles away. And me left without a car. Ran out of petrol! I do not like to put too much in at a time you know, someone may suck it all out. You never know and it could be wasted. But to think of leaving it there, in the middle of the road! I have had that car for twenty-three years and all. So dangerous. Then haring along in a Tesla as I understand. Stolen you say? I am not surprised. There was incident with a Tesla once before. Arey. You may draw your own conclusions."

Verbal statement, Govind Mistry (Anning Road Superette owner):

"I first heard a woman's voice. It should be about one

clock I b'lieve. She was sounding hysterical, screaming at my daughter. I was behind the shelf stocking the dry goods. I was afraid. I thought, 'Arey! Now we will all be murdered.' I came over to find a woman, maybe Indian woman, in shiny clothes. Indian women like shiny clothes. Then she asked have I seen her child? Boy? I say, 'No'. I asked Priya have you seen? Priya also said 'No'. Next thing, my back is turned one second, Priya is gone."

Verbal statement, Priya Mistry, aged five years and seven months.

"I was watching my favourite movie, Chota Chetan. I will never ever watch a movie again, I feel so bad! Small, small boy comes in I could not see him over the counter. He asked me for one ice cream. But he had no money. I didn't give. I wished I did give, but my father says we also have no money, and children stealing and all. Boy started crying, he says, 'I want my mummy at the dolphins. I want ice cream.' One man says, 'I will buy. I will take you to your mummy at the dolphins.' I thought that is good, it means we will get money. Father will be pleased. Man was looking horrible. Like a fat chicken. He was having no neck. When the lady comes in, I started feeling so bad. I ran after her. I told her I can help you and then we were driving so fast. I saw that small boy being carried to Black Beach in chicken man's car in my mind's eyes. So horrible man. He was going to do to Sammie even more bad than he does to chickens. That I have seen. I told Sammie's mummy to fly because the policemens were coming and we could not delay. I told her, policemens will look after us. So Sammie's mummy flew there and saved Sammie. But actually it was the chickens that saved him. Then policeman and policelady came and then we were riding on the dolphins and that was so fun and then we came home with siren so, so loud! Then my father growled me. But I deserved it. Whole episode my fault actually."

Verbal statement, Matthew Harrison, son, aged six years and six months.

"My Granddad gave me a drink and I can't remember anything else until Priya sat on me and I gave her a big push. I hated her sitting on me. But then Priya told me Sammie was lost and I was vey unhappy and frightened. So even though I had a very, very humungous volcano in my tummy, *much* bigger than any I've ever had before, because of Granddad's drink and I really, really wanted to push someone and hit someone, I stopped myself, because I knew it was Very Important and I did breathing like my teacher tells me at school and like my other Mama used to tell me, but I couldn't take Time Out because we were in the car and going Very Fast so we would be in time for Sammie. I got the map out and I found the Black Beach and I can read now even though I've only been in school not very long and I can read better than anyone in my class and I know about maps from doing space pirate treasure maps. And then the petrol ran out and then I told Mama to get a Tesla and so she did and we had to leave Granddad's silly old car in the road because of being quick to get Sammie. Then er... oh yes... I wanted to drive the Tesla but... did you know that the Tesla can go up to two hundred and forty nine kilometres per hour? And. That it can accelerate from zero to ninety seven kilometres per

hour in three point two seconds? Whereas Granddad's car...
and I did get to drive the Tesla and I had to stretch my legs to
the pedals because my other Mama used to let me drive and so
I know how. So when Mama went flying I pulled over because
the policemen came and I was worried because I didn't have
my car seat. But they didn't say anything about the car seat!
They just told me I was going a little bit too fast and where was
my mummy? So I told them and then we went to Black Beach
and rode on dolphins but the policemen said to the dolphins
they had to bring us back, then they laughed."

Verbal statement, Samuel Harrison, son, aged three years and
ten months.

"Woll, he was a vewy sad man and he telled me he puts
er... woll... a gabillion chickens in boxes in his twuck and he
weally likes picking them up by their feet and thwowing them
in and then he weally likes thin parts of people's bodies and
he just wants to bweak those parts like you snap a stick and
I telled him I like sticks and I like weapons too and he said
'woll... that's a shame then, because we think alike and if things
would of been diffwent...' He was looking at me eating my ice
cweams and I think he wanted an ice cweam too because when
the cweamy bit wunned down my neck he licked his lips. He
taked me to see the dolphins and then the chickens taked him
away. Woll... Mama wanted to kill him with her sharp sword
that was in the bed when we did do a tweasure hunt when the
fat lady comed and I wanted to take it and it was too heavy and
Mama couldn't fly with it, and so was the axe and then they was
under the water and we couldn't see them when the dolphins

comed, but my dolphin telled me we don't need it any more."

Verbal Statement, Amalia Harrison:

An inclusive rendition of the incident as previously described.

"Since I am sruti dhara this was not hard to do. Oh and I was also able to help the valiant policemen hugely with their inquiries by confirming the identity of the unknown man. He was none other than the monster from the chicken truck, otherwise known as the Chicken Monster."

# Chapter Twelve

# Tangerine Dreams

What do you mean, I can't come out?" I clutch the phone to my ear.

"Not for now, Am. It doesn't mean never. Just till you get back to normal, you know?"

"How do I do that? Haven't I been trying to do that all this time?"

"Yeah right. Sure you have." He pauses. "They'll have psychiatrists. I don't know how good they'll be. They might use other methods apart from drugs. I hope so. I could try and get Doctor Ganesh to see you or Aelfraed."

"I have to see my boys. How's little Sammie? He hasn't had his Mama's milk."

"He's alright, they're alright." Husband sounds weary. "They're tired."

"When can you bring them to see me? Today? This afternoon?"

"Thing is, Am… I don't think that's such a good idea right now. Not with things as they stand."

"So are you going to come and see me?"

"I need to look after the boys…"

I'm not going to waste too many words describing the psychiatric facility, since we only have a finite number of breaths and therefore, words. It doesn't merit extensive description, being indistinguishable from everywhere else. Regulation shades of grey with the addition of greyish cream. Routine bossy walls and doors: Fire Door, Keep Clear! No Exit! Mental Health is the Responsibility of All! No Male Service Users beyond this Point! Furnitures all made of the standard mishmash of murmuring crushed trees, as in Renée's low wall. Harsh lighting descends from the usual square and occasionally, circular, holes in the ceiling. As in the law enforcement facility, there are bedbathrooms, except here the bathroom component is surrounded by a wall. Surprisingly, the plastic mattresses on the beds are blue. Some people here wear brooches, reminding me of Hilary Brooch all those moons ago, and some wear bracelets. Although the labelling is understandable here since most of us have forgotten who we are.

The dining room consists of round mishmash tables and plastic chairs. There are several people in the dining room, two of whom wear brooches and are serving lunch from a small metal cart on wheels, stacked with small plastic trays, a bit like a metal plate Prof has at home, with compartments for the various food items. I think I've had similar gold versions in the past.

One man, without a brooch, is sitting on a chair, rocking back and forth, chanting, "Nothing works here. The medications don't work. I hate this place."

One of the brooched men hands him a tray and says, "Come on, Gordon, the lunch works, even if the medications don't."

Gordon takes no notice and continues to chant and rock.

A dark-skinned, unbrooched man starts laughing at me. I'm not sure why. He brandishes a large green cloth bag and announces, "I'm going to the library! I'm going to the library! I always go to the library on Wednesday." He looks at one of the brooched people, "Is it Wednesday today?"

The brooched person nods. "Yup, Stanley. All day."

The man breaks out into a little dance, laughing and punching the air. "All day? Wednesday all day? I'm going to the library!"

I sit down with my tray at a table with three other people, two men and a woman. I smile round at them, as I lift the cover off my tray, revealing several brown lumps in brown sauce and sixteen pasta shells. I pick up my knife and fork with some trepidation.

The young man sitting to my left suddenly looks up from his tray and puts his hands behind his back. "Which hand do you want? Pick a hand, any hand!" he tells me.

"You've got to choose," says the ancient man sitting opposite, pausing in his chewing. "He's got many hands like."

"Er... well... okay. That one," I say, pointing to his left side.

"But which one on that side?" insists the young man.

"Oh! Er... Hand number three?"

The young man opens out a hand, cocks an eyebrow and says very gravely, "Sword!"

The wizened man opposite cackles, showing a mouth full of half-chewed brown stuff and no teeth. "I've lost 'alf me teeth," he points to his mouth with his fork, "because of the medication like. Hee, hee, hee! Been on it for forty years now like." His whole face seems to be caved in on itself, sunken and yellow. "What's your name?" he asks me.

"Kali!" I reply, sitting up erectly.

"Ah... Amalia. That's a nice name." He chews a couple of mouthfuls and swallows, blowing out his cheeks.

The stocky young man stares solemnly into his untouched meal during this, then turns to me. "Which hand do you want, Amalia?"

"Oh... er... right?"

He waits.

"Number four?"

"One to three only."

"Alright, two then."

He produces his right hand, number two and shakes my hand vigorously. "Welcome to Hell's Café, Amalia!"

Toothless points to Stocky with his fork. "And Neville's fat 'cos of the medication, eh Nev?" He cackles.

Meanwhile the other member of our table, a young woman, sits contemplating something I can't see, over the other side of the room.

Toothless tilts his head at the young woman, lowering his voice. "Nevaeh's also a bit chubby due to meds like Amalia, but shh! Don't say anything. She gets hurt if you mention it." Nevaeh glances round the table at us, a gentle smile on her lips. Her eye lights on my lunch tray. All at once, she picks out a pasta shell from the front compartment and examines it in her fingers. Popping it into her mouth, she chews it thoughtfully for a moment, then smiles graciously upon me.

At some apparently unspoken signal, my three companions bow their heads in unison and push their trays together into the centre of the table. They all look up at me then back at the trays. Deducing that something is expected of me, I also push my completely untouched meal to join their untouched, except for three mouthfuls (Toothless) and one pasta shell (Nevaeh), meals.

"We like to give them a chance to play for a bit," explains Toothless.

"The sacrificial lamb," intones Neville. "It will be our turn next time round."

"Their turn to eat us. That's only fair like," says Toothless.

Four very small frisky black lambs unfold their legs from the food trays and frolic around the table, bleating for their mamas and flicking their tails.

"Next time you will kill us," whispers Neville to them gravely.

Nevaeh smiles upon them. Toothless cackles.

On another unspoken signal, the three of them stand and pick up their lunch trays. Neville marches quickly off to deposit his tray in a large black bin. Toothless dithers for a second, and then follows suit. Nevaeh, gazes at the floor, smiling. The bleating continues for several seconds then dies away.

Gordon continues to rock and chant, "Nothing works here. The medications don't work. I hate this place." His meal is untouched on the table.

Toothless turns to me. "Ciggie, Amalia?"

I follow him out through a glass doorway, (Ask About the Elephant, Smoking is Too Big to Ignore… No Smoking Anywhere on the Hospital Grounds!) into a courtyard open to the sky. I don't really know what a ciggie is, but no doubt I'll soon find out. The courtyard has plenty of concrete around the edges and a square of worn out grass in the centre. On one side there are two wooden benches joined to a grime-covered table. On the other side is a rough, solid bench, possibly hewn from the massive log in Renée's photo. Neville is already standing by the grimy table, swaying back and forth, as Toothless sits down.

"Pick a hand, any hand," Neville instructs me.

"Um… left. Um… number three?" I'm getting the hang of this. My quick learning abilities are standing me in good stead.

"Hmm." Neville reveals a small, red, plastic tube with a silver metal end.

Toothless cackles.

"Try again," orders Neville.

"Left, number two?"

"You can't have two lefts consecutively," Neville says reproachfully.

"Oh." I obviously didn't pick up the rules quite quick enough. "Hmm, right. Number one?"

Somberly, Neville produces a small golden box in a right hand, opens it with the same hand and takes out a white and brown tube for each of us. I look round, not sure what to do with the tube, even though I've seen Irene doing it from a distance. Toothless puts it in his mouth, squeezing his lips. So I do likewise. Neville presses the metal end of the red plastic object and holds a large flame to the end of my tube. I step back in shock.

Toothless cackles. "Of course. You're not from this hell are you? She's never smoked before, Nev, have you Amalia? They don't smoke where she comes from like. Watch…"

Neville holds the flame to Toothless's tube, Toothless sucks in ecstatically and the end of the little tube catches fire! I copy Toothless as Neville holds the fire to my tube again but the flames seem to shoot down my throat. I choke and splutter, while Neville watches me intently, producing another hand to pat me on the back. Toothless cackles wildly and continues to suck deeply on his tube. Neville has lit his own tube now and is sucking away in all seriousness. I leave my tube smouldering on the table. It was almost as bad as the internet. I cough a few more times then flop down onto the bench. Smoke swirls around us; blinding me, suffocating me. So this is what Irene and Shirl seemed to be enjoying so much, and those students outside the university. It's hard to understand. Maybe it's a form of austerity that people perform to gain power?

Neville takes another hand and knocks the end of my tube on the table. "We don't want to waste it now, Amalia."

"I think I might go and sit on that bench for a while,"

I splutter, looking at the smokeless side of the courtyard longingly. The other bench looks like paradise from here.

"Hee hee. You don't want to sit on that bench, Amalia. This is where we always sit. Isn't it, Neville? Though Neville doesn't sit down. He's too speedy."

"That bench is in another hellish planet. I wouldn't enter there again," says Neville. "There are lots of different hellish planets you know."

Toothless leans in confidentially. "I was a member of the third Reich in my last life like. That's why I'm in this particular hellish planet now, like, along with Neville." He takes the tube out of his mouth; it's much shorter now. "What are you in this hell for, Amalia?"

"Hell?"

"Didn't you know?" intones Neville.

"Before this, I used to live in the hell known as sheltered accommodation like Amalia," says Toothless.

I get an image of a room with bowls full of squashed up tube ends, a large picture of a man with a small moustache hanging on the wall, and an unmade bed with grimy sheets.

Toothless continues, "Then I could go to the head shop like. I'd get out of hell for a while."

Neville looks at him dubiously.

"Just temporarily like, Nev," Toothless reassures him. "I could buy my legal highs and my *Dodos*. I used to find roach ends on the street like and smoke 'em." He squashes the brown end of his tube onto the table. "But I didn't want to take my meds. They couldn't force me you see, Amalia." He stops. "Amalia? What sort of a name is that?" He cackles.

"Anyway, I hit the care worker like. She was hassling me like. Told me I had to come down at eight for my meds. So then I got committed you see, Amalia. They do blood checks on you here you know, for drugs like."

Neville gazes pensively into the distance. "There's a special hellish planet for someone who drinks alcohol." He inhales sternly. "They have molten metal poured down their throats for thousands of years."

"What about for people who smoke?" I ask.

"Ah," Neville closes his eyes briefly, then squashes his tube next to Toothless's, "we're already in hell. I think I told you that."

Toothless cackles. Neville sways back and forth. Of Nevaeh, there is no sign.

'Rachel Morton, Consultant Psychiatrist' announces the door. The lady by this name, dull haired and pale eyed, sits opposite me at a large table before a computer and a folder of paper. "We're just going to go through some details as a preliminary procedure. Dr. Skinner will be in tomorrow to do a more in-depth assessment." She peers at the screen, then at her notes, then her eyes scan back and forth across the screen. "Fugue state for about... six weeks now... No valid coherent memories surfacing yet. Believed to be a potential danger to others, particularly your children, and yourself. Under suspicion of harm and possible murder. Involuntary admission." She looks up at me anxiously. "Murder?"

"I wanted to kill him; I wanted to drink his blood. I would have killed him if the cloud hadn't taken him away.

He deserved it." My arms begin to tingle as I remember the axe poised above my Sammie's neck. My eyes widen. "An aggressor must be killed. That is the law of Manu! I had to protect my child!"

Rachel shifts in her seat uneasily and looks round. She gestures through a window to a man in a dark blue uniform outside the room, who stiffens to attention, eyeing me suspiciously.

"As I say, Dr. Skinner will be dealing with your case more thoroughly. But for now we're going to prescribe some medication and observe how you respond to that, until she comes in tomorrow." She taps something on her keyboard with very short jagged nails, unlike Renée's. They wouldn't be good for scratching someone's eyes out, for example.

I get a sudden image of a powerful man wielding a huge weapon with fierce jagged edges, leaping through massive trunked trees. Then an impression of a small girl dressed in white hiding in a cupboard.

She taps on the squares and looks up. "Do you have any questions?"

"I'm not completely sure where I am or what I'm doing here... When will I get to see Sammie and Mattie? Where did they go? I feel a bit lost. When can I go home?"

"You're here because you need to get better. We're going to try our best to help you. When you'll go home, I can't say. I don't want to give you false hopes. It depends how well you respond to treatment. Sammie and Mattie are your children? I'm not sure whether you'll be allowed..."

"What?" I sit forward on my seat.

Rachel glances at the man in the uniform. "Better you talk to Dr. Skiner about it tomorrow."

"I wanna get out of here!" yells a struggling woman with wild hair, whose clothes appear to be falling off.

Three brooched people are holding her by the arms, propelling her down the hallway. (Behind her the wall screams, Key Performance Indicators: Hand Hygiene, Length of Stay, Seclusion, Minimisation of Restraint). The lights continue to glare down at us. In a room off the hallway, behind a large half window-half wall partition, many brooched people mill about, sitting behind computers, shuffling pieces of paper and murmuring in a strange language, incomprehensible to me. I think it can't be ESOL, though maybe if I listen for long enough...

"Paranoid schizophrenic."

"Try him on *Ativan*."

"*Escitalopram?*"

"*Veralafaxine!* Or *Diazepam?*"

An unbrooched woman with glasses much more lopsided than Prof's, one side taped up with paper, stands in the hallway by the partition under a particularly unforgiving light. She's gesticulating and shouting, "People 'oo suffer from mental illness are sufferin' from pain and it's nuffin to laugh at and it's not funny."

At that moment, Stanley comes in waving his green bag and starts laughing at her.

She shouts, "It's not funny!" Maybe she has a big volcano in her tummy.

Then Stanley stops laughing and looks sad. He shows her his empty bag. "The library was closed."

The woman's face fills with consternation. "Closed?"

"Someone moved all the books all over the place and the librarians can't find any of them. They have to rearrange all the books." Stanley looks as though he might cry.

The one-eyed glasses lady puts her arm around him and they walk off down the hallway.

Toothless, Neville and Nevaeh appear from the opposite direction.

"Oh there you are, Amalia," says Toothless. "Coming to the sweetshop like, Amalia?"

Sweetshop? I follow them down the hallway to a small room. Sitting outside the room, Gordon is rocking back and forth, chanting, "I hate this place. The medications don't work. I hate this place."

Neville spreads two of his arms wide and announces, "Welcome to Hell's Sweetshop."

Inside the small room, (the wall shouts Zero Tolerance for Violence!), a brooched person with frizzy grey hair and glasses on the tip of her nose, is busy taking down plastic jars from shelves, undoing lids, checking her computer screen, and emptying out small colourful objects.

"That's Ruth," explains Toothless. "But we call her Bruth."

Bruth purses her lips and looks at him over the top of her spectacles. "I hope you boys are going to eat your sweets today like good boys."

Toothless looks offended. "We always eat our sweets!"

Neville appears to consider this, then takes a hand out and pats Bruth on the arm.

"Watch it, Neville! I had someone who wouldn't take their meds yesterday and ended up giving me a wallop," complains Bruth, clutching her arm in pain. She looks at me, "Now you know why they call me Bruth."

Nevaeh smiles sorrowfully at Bruth.

"And who's this?" continues Bruth.

"This is Kali… didn't you know?" says Toothless

Bruth checks her screen. "Don't seem to have any one of that name. Let's see your bracelet."

Our bracelets are plastic and very light weight, not nearly as heavy as the golden jewelled ones I seem to remember wearing before. I mean, *before* before.

Toothless points to various jars on the shelves. "I'll have a penny 'orth of rainbow drops, a hapny 'orth of raspberry and cream chews, and sixpence worth of cream soda sherbet bombs like." He turns to me. "Have you got your pocket money, Kali?" He looks from me to the jars on the shelves. "Kali? What sort of a name is Kali? That's a sort of crystallised sherbet!"

I may not be able to have any sweets. "Money? Oh no… they took my card away!" I wish I had some gems or pieces of gold, but all I had was plastic money, finally arrived from the bank. However, when I came here they said it was sharp, so I couldn't keep it.

"They don't do cards here like, Kali," Toothless cackles. "But it's alright I can lend you some for your first night or you can get it on credit." He grins at Bruth.

Bruth gives a sort of thin-lipped smile and rolls her eyes to the ceiling as Husband used to do, then hands two small white pots to Neville. "Alright, Neville, take it away."

Neville turns to me. "Which hand do you want?"

"Er... left number one."

Neville produces a small pot with two small orange and white beads.

Toothless peers into the pot. "Ooh tangerine dreams, Kali!" He gives a cackle.

"What do I do with these? Are they for my bracelet?"

Bruth says, "Neville will tell you…"

"Pick a hand… any hand!"

"Well, right hand this time, number three."

Neville produces another small white pot, this time it has clear liquid in it. "Put the sweets in your mouth and swallow them with the water," he orders.

"Eat the beads?" I ask in surprise.

"Kali doesn't know what to do like, they don't eat hell's sweets where she comes from," explains Toothless.

"It's your medication," Bruth informs me, busying herself getting other jars down from the shelf.

I put them in my mouth and start to chew. Toothless cackles.

"Stop!" Bruth puts down the jar in her hand. "You're supposed to swallow them, not chew them!"

Too late, I've already spat it out. It tastes like a sweet from hell.

So we have to go through the whole procedure again. Then we repeat it for the others. Toothless gets raspberry and cream, a red and white bead, which doesn't resemble what I imagine raspberries and cream might be. When we get to Nevaeh, she gets some beautiful lilac and lemon beads.

"It's not fair, hers are much nicer than mine," I say picking one out and putting it in my mouth.

"Stop!" Bruth puts down her jar and bats it out of my hand. "Good grief! Where've you been all your life? On another planet?" Then she gets out another pretty lilac and lemon bead for Nevaeh.

The thing is, I'm wearing a pretty lilac sparkly cloth today and I thought her beads matched rather nicely.

"Off you go," says Bruth, then starts murmuring in a foreign tongue, possibly some magical incantation, as she continues to organise her jars. "*Escitalopram, Trazodone, Ziprasidone, Aripoprazole, Olanzopine, Lorazepam.*"

We all shuffle out of Hell's Sweetshop. Gordon is still there.

Neville positions himself in front of him. "Which hand do you want?"

Gordon chants, "I hate this place!"

Neville produces two brilliant emerald beads in a pot and Gordon takes them.

"Which hand? Come on, we haven't got all day."

"The medications don't work here."

Neville puts out a left hand with a pot of water.

"Nothing works here!" chants Gordon swallowing his emerald beads.

My arms start to tingle. I feel a bit dizzy so I sit down next to

Gordon. (The wall opposite announces Occupational Therapy Programme, Crafts, Hearing Voices Group, Sensory Groups). I suddenly see many soldiers with upraised weapons attacking me. But they're very tiny. They're plundering the byways and pathways of the trillions of atomic citadel cells of my body, with spears, tridents, axes and swords, shooting arrows from tangerine and white bows. They carry shields too, so the minute soldiers on the defence, who weren't expecting this all out surprise assault, are hard pushed to fight back. The enemy soldiers are now swarming through my heart, challenging the Great Soul and the small soul living there, trying to route them out and occupy the whole territory. I can't sit down! I must fight!

I leap up onto my chair. "Which hand do you want, Neville?" I cry.

"Right, fourth." Neville doesn't flinch; he looks sober as the grave.

I whip out a javelin.

"Pick a hand, Gordon!"

"Nothing works here."

I wield a club. Then my limbs appear to take on a mind of their own and start trembling. My arms are jerking and I'm running down the hallway. I cannot be still. I must defend! I run back and forth, then halt, twitching and flailing in the doorway to Hell's Sweetshop. I roar out my battle cry! A bruise won't be all you have by the time I've finished with you, Bruth! But I cannot stand still. I turn and charge back along the hallway, weapons raised, ready to massacre and lay waste.

I screech to a halt to find myself standing in the bedbathroom. There lurks my blue plastic mattress in all its colourful glory. All at once I feel very drowsy, my arms fall limply by my sides. I drop my weapons out of my ten arms. I don't even hear them clatter on the floor, as I collapse on the blue mattress. I'm so tired.

I'm vaguely aware of Toothless's voice drifting across a huge abyss, "Tangerine dreams!" Then a distant cackling sound. "She'll get used to it. They don't have them where she comes from…"

# Chapter Thirteen

# Crossing Over

Wheyan cun I cm thome?"

"Ama, is that you?"

"Ee tharnt thlike ut heyuh. Thake muh thome."

"What's going on?"

"We might have to tweak your meds a bit today. You probably needed the sleep though, considering..." Renée Skinner, Consultant Psychiatrist, taps her reddened nails on the table and shifts her fruit emblazoned computer to one side. "So," she swivels her eyes from the screen to me, "that was quite some adventure you went on the other day. Would you like to tell me about it?"

"I feeel tyered. I whaant to go hooome."

The plastic chair under my legs is unforgiving. The square light pounds relentlessly on my eyes. I'd like to lie down in a mossy forest glade with the sun caressing me through a lattice of leaves and a brook gurgling nearby, instead of...

Renée swings her tortoiseshell hair and smiles her big red smile. "That's not going to happen for a while." Her smile is replaced by a frown. "What happened on Tuesday was a matter of grave concern. I wouldn't be taking my responsibility seriously either for your mental health, or for your family, or indeed the community, if we let you go prematurely."

"Wheen cn I gao?"

"That really depends on you and how far you're willing to cooperate in the treatment programme we plan." She tilts her head and looks at me questioningly.

As far as I'm able, I think about my boys. I picture Sammie's delicate tender neck and limbs and his manly determination to protect his Mama with a stick. My breasts prickle slightly, but my arms feel like lead. In my inward eye, Mattie, the great explorer, totters through the grass on his hands, tumbles over, then gently picks up a kitten. The scene changes and I see Husband trying to get both boys ready and out of the door this morning. Sammie's whimpering, Mattie's yelling and hitting Husband. Husband is red faced and yelling too.

"I'll doe anythung. Pwhatevuh I hev to."

"Mm." Renée looks at me, consideringly.

My hair is a tangled mass and my clothes are slipping off my shoulders. I'm not looking very sparkly. I didn't have any energy to do anything this morning. I wonder if this is better than I was before, one step closer to my normal life?

"Alright. I don't think you're up to much today. I'll get onto changing your meds. Tomorrow we can try another session.

Maybe you'll be more compos mentis. I have an idea where we can take it from here." She flicks her perfectly combed tortoiseshell mane.

If only I could be like her! She doesn't have to be here and leave her children to a red-faced husband and who knows what besides. A little speck of a thought nudges through the cloud, something about getting 'back to normal'.

Renée pulls the fruit computer towards her and gazes into it. "What are we calling you these days?"

"Umerleeyuh." My tongue feels like a big slug in my mouth.

"Good, good. That's a good sign." Renée starts tapping on the squares and chanting magical incantations to the computer. "*Acepromazine, Acetrophenazine, Benperidol, Bromperidol, Butaperazine, Carfenazine, Chlorproethazine, Dixyrazine, Fluanisone, Droperidol, Droleptan, Inapsone, Xomolix, Largactil.*" She looks up and appears surprised that I'm still there. "Oh you can go now. I'll see you tomorrow," she smiles through her bloody lips, "Amalia."


Stanley laughs as he skips down the corridor.

"It's not funny!" whines One-Eyed-Glasses, hovering outside the big room where the brooched people murmur in alien tongues. "It's nuffin to laugh at!"

"The library was open today!" declares Stanley. "What day is it?" he asks, opening his green bag to reveal a very large book.

A brooched man wheels a little metal cart down the corridor. "It's Thursday today, Stanley. All day!"

"All day!" laughs Stanley and skips off.

Toothless, Neville, Nevaeh and I are on our way to Hell's Sweetshop, where Gordon sits rocking back and forth. "I hate this place, nothing works here…"

I wonder what colour sweets Renée has arranged for today? I'm wearing a very dull maroon t-shirt. I didn't have the energy for sparkles and I don't really care if the beads, I mean sweets, match. I feel a bit less cloudy than I did this morning; my tongue feels more like one of the skinny slugs under Doctor Ganesh's bricks… Doctor Ganesh's bricks! My inner eye suddenly flashes on a rear view of Mattie and Sammie, little heads bent over an upturned brick. I experience an ache in my chest and see the soldiers still battering away at the fort of my heart. Oh no! I thought they'd gone.

I turn to Toothless and Neville. "I just want you to know that I have absolutely no money for sweets today. I want to make that absolutely clear."

Toothless cackles. "Well, Kali, it's alright lending you pocket money on your first day like, but two days in a row would be pushing protocol like. What d'you think, Nev?"

Neville shoves his hands firmly in his pockets. "No money, no sweets. That's the rule in Hell's Sweetshop."

Nevaeh smiles sweetly on us all.

With that understanding, we all proceed along the hellway, I mean hallway.

Bruth's hair looks even more frizzy today and is shooting out all over the place. It makes me feel a bit better about my own scattered tangle. Feel better? That seed of a thought puts out one tentative shoot, braving my inner cloud. Maybe I should… But another thought firmly crushes the shoot. No.

I'll get some pocket money tomorrow. I have other priorities today.

Bruth is busy as usual with her sweet jars. She looks at her computer. "Different sweets today for you, *Amalia.*"

Toothless cackles.

"Take it away then, Neville." She hands him a pot with two violet and indigo beads. A sorry match for the maroon.

"Ooh parma violets," murmurs Toothless, "not my favourites, like..."

"Now, now," says Bruth.

Neville takes the pot and puts it behind his back. Toothless stands in front of Bruth and appears to be very interested in the different pots on her table. We observe standard procedure and Neville hands me the pot. I tip it into my mouth, then take a sip of water and swallow conscientiously.

Bruth says, "Let's see inside your mouth."

I open my mouth.

"Okay," she says, then turns to Toothless. "Now what do you want today, young man?"

Neville cocks an eyebrow at me. I wonder what he did with my parma violets?

"Coming for a ciggie, Kali?"

"No, I've got things to do."

Neville looks at me uneasily. "How will you cross over?"

"You could try it from our bench like, Kali," suggests Toothless hopefully.

Neville jiggles his legs and scrunches up his lips.

Nevaeh has drifted off elsewhere.

"We could always say you were in the toilet like. You never can tell with parma violets."

So I join them at the bench. I'm not sure if I can do this, but in a moment Toothless's delighted cackle and Neville's knowing nod fade away in a shimmering haze. Simultaneously, the odours of smoke, disinfectant and the dead calves playing on our table at lunchtime, recede into the distance, to be replaced by the smell of dead trees.

I don't have to go in by the black door with the stopping-children-escaping tube. I'm already inside, in the wooden playhouse. I look out of the glassless window. There he is, sitting close to Georgina, looking shy, his straw hair standing up all over the place, a bit like mine today.

She's saying something to him, but I can't hear from here. Then they both walk towards the playhouse and go into the garden area. As they approach, their voices drift up to me.

Georgina says, "Shall we look in the garden and see what's there? There's not much at this time of the year, but there may be some zucchinis." She takes the small boy's reluctant hand.

"I don't like zucchinis," replies Sammie, turning away from her with the little frowning pout he does, his eyebrows scrunched over his eyes and his lips pressed together. Looking up, he notices me waving to him from the playhouse window.

"Mama!" he cries, charging towards me, leaving Georgina rifling through foliage, chatting to herself about zucchinis.

Just to be on the safe side, I duck down below the window. Although Georgina seems kind, I can't predict how people are going to react. It's a mystery. It seems I can't do anything without them getting anxious, sending me to hospital and threatening to take my children away. The only people who don't seem to be disturbed are children, animals, the unbrooched and, of course, the Dean.

Sammie climbs the ladder up the tree to the playhouse. "Mama, are you hiding?" A few stalks of straw appear over the edge of the doorframe, followed by a golden head, like the sun rising in the morning. My darling Sammie hurls himself at me, leaping into my lap with a satisfying thud. He takes hold of my face in his little hands, saying loudly, "Mama, where were you?"

"Sammie? Where are you?" Georgina's voice rings out.

I put my finger over my lips, "Shh!"

Georgina's voice gets louder, "S-a-mmie!"

Sammie and I freeze like statues in our hiding place.

Finally, Georgina's voice becomes quieter as it recedes into the distance.

Sammie whispers, "Why are you in hospital, Mama? Why aren't you at home with us?"

"I don't honestly know, my darling."

"Dada says it's because you're not vewy well. But you haven't got a cold. Your nose is not wunning." He thinks for a moment. "Have you got a sore tummy?" He pats my tummy sympathetically. "I have a sore tummy evewy day."

"Do you, my sweetheart? My poor Sammie! Why don't you come to see me with Dada?"

"Woll... he's too busy doing halfapology. And. Then we have to be with Fern. And. Fwank hits me. So does Mattie.

And. Then we go to Nani and Gwanddad's and they said the policeman won't let us. And..." The tummy patting seems to have risen a bit higher. "Can I have some Mama's milk?"

"Of course, my angel!" I cuddle him to me and drink in that sweet apple smell. He smells much better than a computer.

He drinks for a while, then sits up. "It hurts a bit." He pulls up his lip to reveal a very red, swollen gum. "It's a abscest."

"Oh no! Have you been eating too much ice cream?"

A shadow crosses his face, like a cloud covering the sun. "I don't like ice cweam any more."

Just then, we hear Georgina's enthusiastic voice, "Let's all find Sammie! He's playing hide and seek! We'll have to look everywhere for him! Off you go! See who can find him first!" Then the voice becomes less enthusiastic. "He can't have got out. Where the hell is he? Not Sammie. It would have to be Sammie..."

I wonder if she's talking to herself again?

But then another voice drifts up to us, "He can't have gone far. Don't worry. We'll find him."

Suddenly some midnight straw appears over the ledge of the doorway followed by a round moon like face which lights up when it sees us.

Sammie says, "Shh! It's a secwet! My Mama's here!"

A little slant-eyed girl clambers into the playhouse, crawls over and cuddles up without a sound.

Then some copper straw appears, followed by a freckly face.

The little girl whispers, "Shh! It's a secret! Sammie's Mama's here!"

A small boy with smiling blue eyes crawls in and snuggles up with us.

The little girl points at me. "I remember you. You were a calf at the Easter Show!"

Sammie says, "Shh!"

Then Georgina's voice comes very loudly, "Are you up there, Sammie? Come on everyone, it's mat time."

Oh no! She must be at the bottom of the tree. Even though I can't bear to leave, I can't risk staying. I must go.

"Goodbye, my darlings. Sammie's Mama has to leave now. I loved being with you!" I give them all a quick cuddle, squeezing Sammie as though I'll never let him go. "I love you, sweetheart! I miss you. I'll try to be home as soon as I can. I promise!"

He clings onto my leg as though he'll never let *me* go. But Georgina's voice is coming up the ladder. I see a faint halo of silver appear above the door ledge, followed by Georgina's face.

"Oh, thank god! There you are, Sammie!" She struggles into the playhouse. "Well done for finding him, Lulu and Frank."

As I leave, I hear Sammie wailing, "I don't want my Mama to go-o-o!"

"What's all this about Sammie?" asks Georgina. "You don't cry for Mama any more. You're a big boy now!"

Georgina tries to give him a cuddle but he turns his back on her and folds his arms.

"I'm afraid Mama won't be here for a while, Sammie," she says wearily. "Come on children, let's go to the mat."

"She was just here!" Sammie's eyebrows glower over his eyes.

"I know you must miss her, Sammie."

"She *was* here! I saw her!" insists Frank.

"So did I. And. She was a calf at the Easter Show too!" declares Lulu.

"But she said it's our secret!" says Frank.

I'm too far away to hear any more. Poor Sammie, having a sore tummy every day.

I'm just descending into the barren courtyard of the facility, when I realise it's the afternoon. And. It's not even Friday.


"Dora the Detective's been looking for you. Something about a social worker like."

"Dora the Detective?"

"You'll probably meet her one day." Toothless opens a little gold box, shakes it over the table. Nothing happens. He looks up expectantly.

Immediately Neville brings out two hands, box of ciggies in one and lighter in the other. They go through the procedure. I don't try to join in, despite my desire to gain whatever power might be derived therefrom.

"What did you tell her?"

"You were in the toilet for a long time like." Toothless waves his ciggie at me. "Problem is they checked."

Neville rocks back and forth meditatively. "There are

other ways to cross over..."

Despite not having any pocket money for sweets yesterday evening, I'm still lying in bed at nine o'clock the next morning and have refused all attempts to rouse me.

From time to time, I hear comments such as, "We'll have to get her meds changed again. It takes a while sometimes."

Or, "Ah just let her sleep, they're often like that. What else has she got to do anyway?"

What else indeed?

It's a slightly different experience today from yesterday and takes more concentration. It's like riding a bike though, you never forget it once you know. Having said that, I don't think I know how to ride a bike.

Even quicker than yesterday, in fact at the speed of the mind, I see the dangly lanterns winking at me from the ceiling, hear the walls demanding, What do you think will happen next? declaring, I am learning to understand why we need to learn handwriting, smell the faintly acrid smell of what is it? crayons? and feel the cold plastic of the tiny chair beneath my thighs. Luckily, the chair happens to be next to Mattie, who's sitting alone.

Catherine is saying, "Alright, everybody, now you can write your stories. You can finish your pictures afterwards. Remember, anyone who doesn't finish their writing will have to stay in at break."

I look over at Mattie's book. He's drawing a sort of machine person, which seems to be attached to an electrical gadget. On one side is a smallish figure with solid arms, circles for hands and lines for fingers. He doesn't stop to do his writing, but continues to draw something on the other side of the machine person. But there's not enough space, so he turns to the next page of the book, which is marked like this:

- - - - - Date

- - - - - -Title

- - - - - - - Writing

Across the whole page, he draws a larger figure a bit similar to the one on the previous page. The larger figure looks sad, as does the smaller figure.

When he's finished, he puts down his pencil. All of a sudden, he turns to me with a big grin. "Hello, Mama."

I want to give him a hug, but I'm a bit concerned. "Can you see me?" I whisper.

He looks at me scornfully. "Of course I can see you. You're here, aren't you?" He picks up his book. "Look, Mama."

But I'm distracted. Perhaps my alternative method didn't work.

Catherine is occupied with a small girl. "That's a lovely story, Sansita. Now you can finish your picture. Off you go." She looks up and scans the classroom. She doesn't seem to have noticed me. If she has, she says nothing. I wanted to be so careful this time. Especially as Mattie once told me that Mrs Brodie has eyes in the back of her head. Oh dear, now I see there's *another* lady sitting nearby and she's looking right at me! Or is she?

"I have to do my writing now." Mattie turns his book round this way and that and finally begins to write. He writes,

*I hav wun lego robot and too muthas.* Then he draws arrows to each of the figures he's drawn.

I sense he wants to say something else, but I suddenly experience pain. "Does it hurt to do your writing, Mattie?" I whisper. "I can do it if you want. What would you like to say?"

"My hand hurts when I do writing." He hands me his pencil and his book. "I want to say: *This is my mama who's here,*" He points to the big figure. "*Whereas my other mother is in a beautiful place.*" He points to the small figure. "*We've been there, but not very often. It's the place where the tooth fairy comes from.*" As he speaks, I write in my beautiful rounded script.

"*I wanted to go last night to get some money for my Mindstorm,*" He points to the machine person figure, "*but Dada said I had to go to sleep early because I might be bad for that intention lady, Barbara, and do asparagus.*"

He glances at the lady sitting nearby, who's still watching us. She smiles reassuringly.

Mattie continues, "*But then Dada had to take Sammie to hospital cos he almost died and Nani had to come and look after me to put me to bed and I wouldn't go to bed.*"

I drop the pencil mid word. "What do you mean, Sammie almost died?"

"He's still asleep in hospital. He couldn't speak properly and he couldn't move properly. His mouth looked funny. Then he went unconscious." He hands me back the pencil. "Can you write all that too?"

I have to go. "I'm sorry, Mattie, I won't be able to write that now. I must go and look after Sammie."

A screeching sound reverberates through the classroom.

"Who hasn't finished?" Catherine surveys the upturned faces. "You haven't, Mattie, you've been talking the whole time. Let me see." She comes over but completely ignores me.

As I leave, I hear Mattie saying, "My mother is here."

Before I can determine where Sammie is, I feel my arm being roughly shoved and prodded.

"Wake up, sleepy head!"

I reluctantly open my eyes to see a death-like face grinning down at me.

"Ha, you awake. I thought so."

Then I feel my back being forcefully levered off the blue mattress.

"Come on, up you get. Time to see your psychiatrist, she hasn't got all day."

I stare blearily at the wall.

"That's it. Splash cold water and you be wide awake."

"I have to see Sammie..."

"That's right, darlin'. Now up you get."

I swing my legs round on the bed and sit up. The death-faced person must have taken off her mask. She stands before me, hands on hips, regarding me through almond eyes.

"I don't know, yesterday toilet, today sleeping all day. What you running away from, girl?" She puts her arm around my shoulder and gently eases me up. "You have to join in with things. There's Art Therapy and all sorts to make you feel better." She walks me over to the bathroom behind the wall and stands me by the basin. "Come on! Splash cold water, then fine!"

"I have to see Sammie…"

"Yes that's right, we goin' to see Sammie just now darlin'."

As I dry my face before the mirror I catch sight of the woman's brooch, it says A-R-O-D. Then she whips the towel out of my hand and marches me off down the hellway.

I still haven't done my hair. The quick glimpse I had in the mirror while splashing cold water, revealed an even more tangled mass. I wonder what Renée is thinking as she inspects me through her shiny red spectacles.

"I have to see Sammie," I say. "He's in hospital."

"I see," she replies, looking into her fruity computer. "And Sammie is?"

"My son!"

"Oh yes," she continues to stare at the screen, "the one who you believed was kidnapped."

"He's dying in hospital. I have to see him!"

She regards me thoughtfully for a moment, then starts tapping away on fruity. "Do you often feel fearful about Sammie?"

"I have to go and see Sammie, I don't think you understand." I lunge for the door handle.

Renée stands up. "Amalia, unless you sit down and cooperate with me this minute, I will have to call for assistance to restrain you."

I hesitate. I'm not sure what she means. Is this about getting back some semblance of normality? Might running out of the room be a false move? But then Sammie…

Renée slowly approaches. Without taking her eyes off mine, she takes my arm.

"Come on. No one's going to harm Sammie. You have to trust me." She leads me back to the chair and firmly lowers me into it. She sits also, contemplating me for several moments. "All right," she says finally, "why don't we start off by discussing a little bit about your voices."

According to Renée, it's the voices in my head that are getting me into all this trouble. I tell her I can hear the trees in the table babbling softly as we speak. They aren't as loud and insistent as they were at the Leakey Lane clinic, but from time to time during our conversation they do speak up about Sammie being in hospital and needing me. And there's the little books in a shelf in the hellway which are not bossy at all but very empathic (Stressed Out? Having Suicidal Thoughts? Anxiety and How to Handle It) and of course the voices in my own mind which sometimes can't make decisions, like now. On one side, it's hard to sit down and cooperate. On the other, I don't like the sound of being restrained, so the voice telling me to sit down wins and I try to control myself.

She explains with a red-mouthed smile, that my visit to Mattie was all in my head, it didn't really happen. It's very common, she says, that the voices sound like members of one's family and they come across as very real. Then she asks me whether I heard voices telling me to go off after Sammie the other day? I reply that it was the mishmash trees in her low wall.

At that she starts murmuring incantations into fruity

and I assume it's time to leave.

"Paranoid schizophrenia, dissociative identity disorder, *Risperidone Risperdal Olanzapine Zyprexa Quetiaine Quetapel Seroquel Amisulpride Solian Aripiprazole Abilify Ziprasidone Zeldox Clozapine.*" She looks up, indicating the chair with a flick of tortoiseshell. "Are you trying to run away again? Sit down, we're not done yet."

As she lifts her shiny nails off the squares with a flourish, I'm reminded of musicians at the end of their concert. But where did that come from? Is it just the voices in my head?

"I'm going to recommend a course of medication," says Renée finally. "I want to suggest to you that these voices you hear in your head are the basis of all your troubles. It seems to me, looking at your history," she pauses and consults fruity, "that each time you have an episode, the common factor is the voices which prompt you to act in unhealthy, psychotic ways." She fixes me with a flinty red spectacled glare. "Episodes in which you put not only yourself, but others, particularly your children, in danger." She folds her hands in her lap and tilts her head slightly. "Would you agree?"

"But if I hadn't listened to the mishmash trees, Sammie would be dead now!" I object.

Renée shakes her head.

"And I didn't put Sammie in danger yesterday at kindy... he was so happy to see me! So were the other kids!"

Renée's expression remains blank. "This is my point. You think that you were at Sammie's kindy yesterday, even though, in actuality, you haven't gone beyond these four walls..."

"Well Toothless and Neville told Dora the Detective that I was in the toilet but…"

"I'm not convinced that you are understanding the severity of this situation, Amalia, and I'm at a bit of a loss quite how to communicate it to you." She pauses, leaning forward slightly. "I want you to listen to me very carefully." Taking a deep breath, she continues, "The medication will markedly reduce the impact of these illusory voices which masquerade as real experiences and sound so real." She points a red nail at me. "These voices are presenting you with misleading advice; advice which is *harming* people, in particular those dearest to you." She looks at me long and hard. "Are you following me, Amalia?"

I nod silently.

"If you cooperate and take your medication, there's a good chance the voices will stop influencing you to act in dangerous ways. A chance that you can get back to some semblance of a normal life." She shakes her head gently. "Isn't that what you want? For yourself? For your boys?"

"How did you know Sammie was in hospital?"

"Mattie told… um… well… I hear voices. I'm trying to not to listen to them. I'm going to get some medicine."

Arod walks past, smiling and sticking a thumb up.

"I didn't want to worry you. There's nothing you can do anyway."

The clock on the wall ticks relentlessly. A brooched man clatters the dinner cart along the hellway. The smell of pigs never seeing the light of day wafts through the atmosphere.

"Yeah, it's really weird. He was a mess… He could hardly speak and he was all floppy, but jittery at the same time." A strangled sobbing sound comes over the phone. "They did some tests. He had traces of antipsychotic drugs in his blood."

Stanley wanders past with his nose in a book.

"Georgina said he was hallucinating at kindy, saying you were there," continues Husband.

Gordon ambles by, chanting.

"It's in the water… The water gets treated but you can never get rid of that stuff. People chuck them down the toilet…" There's a sound of water running. "Although it's weird because we're on tank water." The clatter of a middle-sized pan. "I'm doing the dishes while I talk to you." The scratch of metal on metal. "They said the other way is for drugs to pass through breast milk. But of course, that's not possible at the moment. Hey, don't worry about Sammie, okay? He's going to be all right. He's going to be fine. Nani's with him now and we're going to pick him up soon."

Two brooched people with rubber tubes round their necks stride by, deep in conversation.

"I'd say *Thioxanthene, Tercian Esucos Droleptan.*"

"Or even *Dridol, Inapsine, Xomolix, Innovar Depixol, Fluanxol…*"

"So I still can't come in. I'm sorry. It's all a bit much. Irene was up again snooping around. I don't know why, cos Fern said she thought our case would go to the bottom of the pile now, they're so busy. Fingers crossed…" Silence. "Er… Fern's been helping me a bit."

"Oh. That's good. I suppose." I nod and smile into the

phone.

One-Eyed Glasses waves her finger at me. "It's not funny!"

"Hang on, Mattie wants to tell you something."

There's a scuffling sound.

"Mama! The kittens disappeared!"

In the background I hear, "Don't tell Mama that, we mustn't worry her... she's not very well. I told you, Mattie. Why don't you tell her about your writing?"

"A-ah... do I have to? Oh o-kay, if really have to..." There's a snorting sound. "Mama? Mrs Brodie said my writing was really good." There's a loud thud. "And the intention lady, Barbara, said I'm Gifted and Talented and I have to have Special Needs."

"Wow... er that's wonderful, isn't it?"

"No it's not... I told them *you* did the writing. But Barbara just said, 'You see he has a great imagination.' And Mrs Brodie told me to go outside to play." Another thud. "And the hospital said Sammie has to have his teeth out for the abscests... what?"

A clatter, then, "Mattie don't tell Mama that!"

# Chapter Fourteen

# Voices

How many psychiatrists does it take to change a light bulb?" Toothless demands, slurping his tea, while Neville jiggles a spoon, and surveys the small audience with a knowing air.

Gordon is sitting in Nevaeh's place this morning for some reason. He stares dolefully at his toast and cornflakes, saying nothing. Somewhere in the sludge of my mind, the thought hovers that Sammie would probably quite like to be here. I wonder if he's getting cornflakes in hospital? I wonder if he's still in hospital? Maybe he doesn't like cornflakes anymore. Who knows what's going on in Sammie's little mind. My own mind is cloudy enough today after last night. I stare dolefully at my cornflakes too.

The brooched man is closing the doors of his little cart. There's a quiet hum of talking and just the background hum of I'm not sure what, but it's always there. The chatter of mishmash? The walls murmuring? In the murky abyss of my mind, they hardly register. Which, if I could think at all, I might consider a good sign. The smell of cooked eggs and decaffeinated coffee are less overpowering, the pitiless lights dimmer.

I remember the lone light bulb hanging from a wire in Prof's workshop, casting shadows on all his weaponry. In those days, I hadn't long known what a light bulb was. Electricity was a mystery. It seems so long ago and so far off. I wonder if I'll ever see Prof's workshop again. My mind hurts even thinking about it and I don't even know if I care. The brief croaking, screeching and mewling which suddenly assail me, soon die away.

A thought dredges itself up from the quagmire. "Do light bulbs have to be changed?" I slur.

Toothless cackles. Neville frowns.

Gordon intones, "Only one." He finally looks up from his gloomy cornflake contemplation with the tiniest hint of a smile. "But the light bulb has to really *want* to change."

Toothless cackles uproariously. Neville jiggles his spoon faster and faster, gazing upon us triumphantly.

My cornflakes have changed beyond all recognition into a soggy mush, whether they wanted to or not. Sammie wouldn't eat them in this state. The thought seems to have some significance, but is swallowed up in mental quicksand.

At that moment, I become aware of a growing silence around me. I glance up and on cue Neville and Toothless start slowly pushing their trays into the centre of the table. Gordon hesitates. I give my tray a listless shove and he seems to get the idea. After a second or two, four black and white cows raise their heads and moo at us, before wandering off the table in search of grass. Toothless and Neville remain seated, although Neville's foot is dancing up and down. Gordon stares at the trays. Suddenly, out of the cornflakes, emerge several beetles with shiny brown backs. A brief vision of small boys and bricks, soon gets sucked under. In the beetles' wake come a flurry of various coloured butterflies, then a whole swarm of bees buzz through the dining room.

Toothless smiles. "We can't kill all the bees off can we?"

Neville says sadly, "There won't *be* a lifetime for them to come back and kill us."

Gordon whispers, "Nothing works here, the medications don't work here..."

Finally, some tiny blue and red flowers poke their heads up through the trays, slither along the table and disappear over the edge. Still Toothless and Neville remain seated. I'm vaguely expecting the cue to stand and dispose of our trays.

However, Toothless remains seated, looking from one to the other of us until he has our full attention, cloudy or otherwise. He coughs, then in a grave tone declares, "We'd like to officially welcome Gordon to our table!"

Neville jiggles. Gordon bows his head.

I look around in bewilderment. Something's not right. "But what happened to Nevaeh?"

"Ah," intones Neville, "Nevaeh crossed over into another hellish planet."

"The sheltered accommodation hellish planet like," adds

Toothless and does not cackle.

I hear the faint roar of wind accompanied by an image of a plumpish young woman... but I ignore it and she soon slips back into nothingness. Our newly formed group stands and makes for the black rubbish bin, with me shuffling at the rear.

"Coming for a ciggie, Amalia?"

But I have to go and lie down and this time I'm not pretending.

"Get up, girl!" Arod's face swims into view. "We going have to change them meds for you."

She puts her arm around me and heaves me upright. "Time to see the psychiatrist. That'll be a treat."

"I'm too tired," I groan.

She finally drags me off the bed and into the bathroom where we repeat the cold-water ritual from yesterday. Today it has little impact. I barely register my mane of wild hair in the mirror. But when we start off down the hellway I notice vaguely that Arod has changed her name to Dora overnight.

I experience the hellway as a huge mountain. My legs don't want to cooperate and Dora has to support me under my arms. Eventually we arrive at a door and she drags me in. From under a huge brick in my mind, a tiny slug of awareness that the person in the room is not Renée, but someone else I've seen before, starts to worm its way up to the surface, but then gives up. I flop into the seat facing this other person.

"Thanks, Dora," says the person, smiling first at Dora and then at me.

My head starts nodding. I don't even notice Dora leaving.

The woman opposite me gives me a gentle shake. "Do you remember me?"

"Vaguely," I mumble.

"I'm Rachel Morton. We had a brief session when you came in the other day." She smiles. "We're going to try a bit of hypnosis on you today to see if we can get any memories coming back about what happened on that day and also from your previous life before the fugue incident."

I start nodding again.

Rachel gives a little laugh. "It's not going to be hard getting you into a relaxed state!"

She explains that the deep state of relaxation helps in surfacing memories from before.

"If you don't remember your previous life how can you go back to it?"

Then she starts counting numbers. I know my numbers, at least I used to.

"Now we're going to go back in time to the day you went to the clinic and first met Renée. Can you tell me what happened from the time you left the clinic?"

I get up to the part where the Chicken Monster is just lifting his axe. I can't go on. I thrash around and start screaming.

Rachel murmurs in a very soothing voice, "It's alright. We're going to leave that time and go even further back in time."

"But Sammie needs me! I can't leave him," I yell.

"Sammie is going to be fine. Everything's going to be fine," she croons softly, "I'm going to count you down to another place, another time. The time before you found yourself on the shore by the ocean. Ten, nine, eight… seven… six… What is happening? Where are you?"

In no time, I see myself on a sandy beach. The sand is sparkling gold, covered in jewels. The white ocean glistens in the setting sun. The strain of sweet music comes to me from a distance along with voices and birds singing. I'm rolling on the sand now and crying. A man is looking down at me, telling me that it will not be for long, barely for the blink of an eye. His eyes are kind, but his expression is firm. I plead with him. He tells me that I will understand one day, that it has to be this way. Then he bends down and kisses me. I feel the sensation of his lips and a wail of anguish escapes me. I jerk upright in the chair, all my earlier fogginess dispelled.

Rachel hands me a cup of water looking concerned. "Maybe you were too affected by the meds to get a good result."

"Or it could have been when we were in India. Husband did say we'd been there…"

"Possibly." She looks at me doubtfully. "You know I think we won't give you any meds this evening. We might get a clearer picture tomorrow."

"Oh no you have to. Renée said. Otherwise I'll hear voices telling me to do things and I'll harm myself and my children and I'll never get back to normal… Please!"

"We'll see."

The fog descends once more.

I don't feel like going to the day room with the television. It reminds me of the internet. I might hear voices coming through it. I can't risk that if they're not going to give me meds today.

With yesterday's beginning to wear off, who knows what I might get up to? The television might tell me that Sammie is having a general anaesthetic for his abscests and it's all going wrong and will cause arrested development and I just have to do something and I can't trust anyone else to help him. Or else Mattie's having Special Needs and having intentions and special medications and vaccinations which will make his asparagus ten times worse and Prof will lock him in a cupboard and he'll be damaged for life. Or that Shakti's kittens are all locked up in cages in Prof's lab, with wire mothers. Or that Lucky has been taken away by the Chicken Monster in his truck. Or that the fate of all the bees in the whole world depends on me.

I've no idea what Art Therapy is, but I'm not going to risk that either. Besides, I only feel inclined to do one thing. I stumble down the hellway, keeping a watchful eye out for Dora, and with relief collapse onto the refuge of my blue mattress. Nevertheless, despite the lingering fuzziness from last night's *Blue Razz Jawbreakers*, oblivion doesn't immediately overpower me. In fact, the little tiny seed of a suggestion, which was nudging at the edge of my consciousness yesterday during Renée's session, has now blossomed into a fully-grown tree of invincible conviction. While today's session with Rachel seems to have sown an even quicker blooming seed of doubt intent on fighting to the death. Thus, supine on my blue mattress, I am witness to two increasingly strident voices warring in my head.

The first voice declares with absolute certainty, "You've just got to get back to normal."

The second voice scoffs with extreme scepticism, "How

can you go *back* to normal if you can't remember what normal is?"

Voice One counters this with, "You just take your meds and you'll get better as Renée told you!"

Voice Two retaliates, "Oh yeah? But if you do that, Rachel says you won't be able to be hypnotised and remember what's normal. *And* how can you go *back* to normal if you can't remember what normal *is*?"

This is rather worrying.

A *third* voice, somewhat bossy, then joins in with raised hands. "Hold it! Hold it! We're never going to get back to normal while you Voices are still around. So off you go! Shoo!"

Voice Two then turns on Voice Three, scoffing with extreme scepticism, "So tell me oh *wise* one, how can you get back to normal if you can't remember what normal *is*?" It cackles with glee, sounding eerily like Toothless.

It seems that I really need to get back on my medication.

Voice Two then challenges, "Oh yeah? But then you won't be able to be hypnotised and remember what normal is. *And* how can you go *back* to normal if you can't remember what normal *is*?"

What a quandary! But at least if the Voices are at war, I won't be able to act on them...

Voice One then pipes up with invincible conviction, "No you must act! You've got to get back to normal!"

I'm just about to get up and take refuge in Art Therapy, when Voice Three raises a hand for silence.

In modulated yet assertive tones, she suggests, "What we could try, if you're agreeable, instead of going *back* to normal, since we don't know what that is, is to go *forward* to normal."

Voices One and Two appear to be stunned into silence because soon after that I'm asleep.

At least I assume I'm asleep. I'm not hearing any Voices, which is a relief.

Apart from a faint Whisper, "You're not really asleep."

Then a counter Whisper hisses, "Of course you are, this is all a dream."

What's outside my head is fortunately interesting enough to quell these warring Whispers and they soon fall silent.

I appear to be wandering through a house, which looks at first glance like the image I had of Toothless's room in the sheltered accommodation. But don't think about imaginary things like that; that was just the visual equivalent of a Voice. Whereas, as Mattie would say, this is real.

"No it's not it's a dream," whispers Voice One.

"Now don't you start again," Voice Three I presume, says firmly.

The television is shrieking, just like in the facility, although there appears to be no one here except me. This could spell dangerous Voices. I try to block it out and focus on other things. Suddenly I notice there *is* someone here besides me – a cat. However, not a cat like Shakti or the kittens. He's a dull yellow brute of a cat with a squashed face and half an ear missing. His hackles rise and he walks stiff legged towards me, spitting. Something is following him, mewling pathetically – a little tortoiseshell bundle, stumbling along on tiny legs. The big cat hisses at the bundle and bats him with a giant paw. Oh poor little baby! I pick up the bundle and cradle it in my arms. Big Yellow leaps at me, yowling, claws unsheathed. I hold his eyes with mine for a moment. He lets out a small mew, then topples onto an armchair, where he starts washing furiously.

A little Whisper bleats, "That's not normal!"

I hurriedly move on, holding baby puss in my arms.

In the kitchen, a pan coated in orange and black slime lies abandoned in the sink. There is no metal skein in sight. Several boxes labelled *Hell's Pizza* are scattered over the counter. Mugs and cups containing varying amounts of brown sludge squat on the bench, the living room floor and a small table by the armchair where Big Yellow is still washing himself. A light bulb dangling on a wire reminds me of Prof's shed and this morning's breakfast.

Maybe the problem is that now I have *two* psychiatrists? I hear a vague Whisper and rapidly adjust my focus to a series of bowls overflowing with ciggie ends, many of which have spilled on to the floor. The little bundle purrs in the crook of my arm.

I wander through to the bathroom to find a bath half-full of grey water. A ripped towel is flung over the top of a shower door slick with grime. Another towel lies mouldering on the floor. On the edge of the basin sits a comb stuffed with grey hair. Maybe I could give my hair a quick do? I look in the mirror and get a double shock. Will I ever get used to being me? And. My *hair*!

A Whisper hisses, "That's not normal!" So I rush speedily on. Besides, I don't have a free hand.

Another room contains a bed with grey, wrinkled sheets

full of cat hair, crumbs and ash. Clothes are scattered over the floor. I note the predominance of black, an element of grey and a touch of dark blue amongst large stretchy trousers, t-shirts, vests and sleeved garments with hoods. Not a sparkle in sight. A thick layer of dust, a metal bendy lamp with a torn black plastic shade and two bowls of ciggie ends adorn a small cupboard by the bed. Curtains hang unevenly at the window.

Big Yellow is now mewling and stalking me round the house. Poor thing.

"It's okay, puss puss." I reach down to stroke him under the chin and receive a swipe of claws.

What a vivid dream.

"It wasn't a dream," whispers Voice Two.

I resolutely reset my awareness, but the crumpled bed and Big Yellow have disappeared. In their place is a familiar office with a heavy dark brown mishmash table with black metal legs, two mishmash desks and three metal chairs with spongy stuff spilling out.

A young slender woman with long flaxen hair jiggles a small baby wrapped in a grubby blanket.

A familiar voice says, "Better put him down. Don't want him to get shaken baby syndrome. Now that really wouldn't look good. Although it would add to the case."

Another familiar voice says, "Don't really need much to add to that case."

I wonder at first if they are *my* familiar Voices, or whether...

The baby's screams fill the office as the young woman, who looks just like Fern, places him gently in a drawer.

"Bloody hell! What a racket! Who would have one? Give me a cat any day, eh Shirl?" says the woman, who strongly resembles Irene.

The Fern looking person who actually is Fern, sighs. "What a day."

"No worse than any other day," growls the woman who actually *is* Irene. "If you're going to be part of this, you'd better get used to it. Develop some calluses. No good being sentimental."

"Do you want me to write it up?" Fern flops into a chair before a chunky, decidedly non-fruity, computer.

"Write it all up. Family group conference. Parents questioning CYFS taking away their children. What's next? Oh yeah, how could I forget?"

The baby continues to scream.

"Baby Todd uplifted from heroin addicted mother. Put the name in there. No caregivers available. Ditto three children under five in hospital waiting by bedside of mother thrown out of window and suffering head injury."

"Why do these women put up with it, eh Irene?"

"Fuck me, I don't know. And don't forget the court affidavits. We'll get that religious nutter's case rolling on through. Remember I told you, Shirl? That hippy dippy cult place me and Fern were at the other week? Filthy urchins, no shoes and crazy, probably stoner mother in a ball gown. Shit load of medical neglect. Out in the wop-wops? Well I talked to the dentist. Something about a P lab in the kitchen. You better add that to the list, Fern." She gets up. "Well that's me finished for the day."

"Drink?" asks Shirl.

"Hell, yeah."

"What about the baby?" Fern looks anxious.

"Supervisor'll have to deal with that. Just give her a yell. Unless you want to stay on?"

"I've got to pick up Frank."

Irene makes a grunt in her throat. She puts on a vest covered in yellow cat hair. "I don't have to pick up my cat, or even the new kitten." She slams a half-full cup on the table. "I just leave the TV on for them."

"Oh have you got a new kitten?" asks Fern patting Todd ineffectually. "That's funny cos so have I! My um... boyfriend gave it to me..."

"Talking of kittens," Irene puts her head on one side, "do you hear anything?"

In my arms, the tiny tortoiseshell bundle mews faintly and crawls deeper into the crook of my arm.

"Must have been my imagination."

"Come on, Irene, time we were outta here."

"Yeah, we can get a pizza on the way." Irene slams the door behind them.

Fern picks up the crying baby and walks round the room.

"Fern?"

"Who's that?"

"Me, Kali... you know... Ama."

"God, if I stay at this place, I'm going to go nuts like

everyone else. Anyway Todd it's between you and me. You won't tell anyone I'm hearing voices will you?"

When I wake up there's a small kitten cuddled against my chest. That's nice. She can play with all the other animals here. I'll have to ask Toothless and Neville where they all go after they leave the dining room.

"They don't stay here, Amalia. Anyway, like, Neville and I have got a bit of a proposal for you." He's tapping his hands on the table and his feet on the barren courtyard ground. He seems slightly agitated.

Neville sways back and forth, solemnly, arms firmly behind his back.

"I suggest you give the little pussy cat to Neville here for safe keeping like." Toothless fidgets in his pocket, pulls out a small gold box, opens it, closes it, sighs and puts it back. "Neville's good at secreting things away like." He sees my face. "Only temporarily like, Amalia, you can have her back tonight."

I sit down. Neville remains rocking where he is.

"Okay, here's the plan." Toothless and Neville exchange glances. Toothless looks a bit uncomfortable. "The thing is, Amalia. We've run out of ciggies, like, Neville and myself." He stops and they both look at me expectantly.

"Oh… well… I'm sorry but I don't have any. Otherwise I'd definitely give you some. No question."

It seems that's not exactly what they had in mind.

"I have got money for sweets," I say urgently.

We're getting closer to Hell's Sweetshop.

There are several Voices involved here. Voice One is being very vocal and insisting on sweets. Voice Two is reiterating that in order to go *back* to normal, I have to know what normal *is.* Voice Three is mediating and reminding us all that we had agreed that I would attempt to go *forward* to normal. Further information on what that involves has not been forthcoming. To complicate things, Toothless and Neville are insisting that I'm penniless and there's no possibility I can afford sweets tonight. Gordon takes his usual stance regarding the sweets here.

With all these Voices swirling around, it's hard to think coherently. I must confess my sympathies lie with Voice One. I'm afraid of the Voices and what they tell me to do. The only way to drown them out is to have no Voices at all.

"I must have money for sweets!" I plead, "I need to have money for sweets!" I'm clutching onto Toothless with one hand and gesticulating with the other. My hair is shooting out in all directions.

At that moment, Dora appears round the corner at the end of the hellway.

Toothless shakes me off. "Shh! Amalia, like."

"What's going on here? Everything all right?" Dora looks at us shrewdly.

Toothless adopts an expression of baffled innocence. Gordon stares at the ground.

Neville turns his back firmly to the hellway wall and smiles charmingly. He does a couple of rocks and then assumes a quizzical expression. "How do you cross over to see your family every day, Dora?"

She regards him suspiciously. "What are you after?"

Toothless appears hurt. "It's a genuine question, like, Dora. We're doing a bit of detective work." He gives an ingratiating cackle.

"Well… I either walk or take the bus." She eyes us warily, then proceeds slowly down the hellway, with several backward glances.

"You have to watch that one, like," whispers Toothless.

"Dora the Detective," adds Neville gravely. "She's got eyes in the back of her head."

The kitten gives a faint miaow.

"She'd take our ciggies away from us if it was up to her like, Kali," Toothless looks pained, "and give us nicotine patches."

"Nothing works here," moans Gordon.

We're now outside the Sweetshop.

"Okay, so you know the plan… you've got no money for sweets today have you, Kali?"

"But…" I look at them all helplessly.

"It's five votes to one, like, Kali. You're outnumbered."


I settle the sleeping kitten amongst my clothes in the green cloth bag in my cupboard. "You just stay there quietly, puss puss, until later. Then I can look after you. Alright?"

Next to the green bag is a small bowl of milk from the decaffeinated coffee making facility, and a plastic tray containing some chicken from dinner. Toothless apologised to the bird profusely, but explained that it was necessary. I've scarcely closed the cupboard, however, before a small bird-like figure with greyish hair appears in the doorway.

"Nani!"

Nani trips in, dropping several bags on the floor and embraces me tightly. "Amalia! My angel! What a terrible thing! I can hardly believe it!" She holds me for a long time. Finally, she pulls back and examines me, with tear-filled eyes. "It's all a horrible misunderstanding. It must be."

She keeps one arm around me as we sit down together on the bed, clasping my hands in her other hand.

"I'm so sorry I haven't been in before. The first couple of days they said best not to until they got you settled, then Jay said you were completely groggy… you could hardly talk!" She reaches up and strokes my face, looking searchingly into my eyes. "Oh my poor darling." She pauses. "Then of course there was the furore with Sammie and the hospital. I've been trying to keep the boys on an even keel. They're both upset. They've both been sort of hallucinating that they've seen you. It must have been so disturbing for them, this whole thing." She wipes her eyes roughly. "But I mustn't upset you. I wasn't going to burden you with all this. You just have to get better. Back to normal. It's no good worrying you." She gets up and fetches one of the bags. "I've brought you some clothes. They wouldn't let me bring in anything else. I'd made you a cake. I don't know what they thought I'd put in it. They said it was standard procedure. Or some such."

She looks at my hair. "Goodness, look at you!" She drags over another bag. "I tell you what, I've got a comb in here somewhere. How about I give your hair a good comb? At least

I can do that for you."

Voice One nods happily, while Voice Two hesitates. Voice Three has an idea.

Nani pats the chair. "Come and sit here. You look like a mad woman with it all over the place like that!" She laughs then stops suddenly. "I mean... well... anyway." She rummages intently in her voluminous bag and finally pulls out a clean, brown comb. "I'm sure if you look tidier you'll feel better..."

While she gets to work, we talk about what's been happening in the facility. I tell her about Renée, Rachel, Toothless and Neville. Some parts of my tale seem to elicit harder tugs than others. Despite this however, it's a nice feeling having someone take care of me. It reminds me of a former time in the far distant past. She tells me Prof doesn't want to come in because he's too upset and can't bear to see me like this. In fact, she says, he's probably the most upset of everyone. And here she gives an extra hard yank. She says the sooner I get back to normal the better.

Out of nowhere, Voice Two suddenly pipes up, "But can you tell me how to get back to normal? When I can't remember what normal is?"

Nani stops her ministrations to think for a moment. "I suppose... well... it's like children learn by modelling on adults around them, don't they?" She gives my hair a final pull. "That's a hard one... because you don't really have any... I'm sorry I don't mean to be... but the people here are ill and you need to find well people, normal people you know..."

Voice One then leaps into action, pointing with great eagerness to an image of a house with a Big Yellow cat and a bathroom basin whereon lies a comb full of hair.

Nani stands back and admires my new sleek hair, with a sad smile. "What shall I do with this?" she says showing me her comb stuffed full of my hair.

"Oh you can just leave it on the basin. That's fine. Thank you so much for doing my hair." I get up to look at myself in the bathroom mirror.

At that moment there's a mewing sound from the cupboard. Nani looks at me questioningly then opens the door. Out tumbles a sleepy little tortoiseshell bundle.

She gazes up at Nani with round eyes. "Miaow!"

"How did that get there?"

I look at her astonished face. And before I can say a word, Voice *Three* butts in with, "Oh no need to worry about that, there's a *perfectly* reasonable explanation!" and here I feel obliged to offer my most ingratiating smile and add extremely politely, "I heard the kittens had disappeared. Maybe you could take this one for the boys?"

Nani covers her eyes with a hand and shakes her head helplessly. When she removes her hand, I see she's crying again, but struggling not to. "I thought you'd be getting better. I thought it was all a big mistake. I started to forget how it's been... with you..." She roughly brushes away a tear. "But then every time I allow myself some little glimmer of hope, you... you... do something..." She presses her lips into a thin line and clenches her jaw. Her eyes shoot me that arrow glare. "And those poor boys..." She opens up her bag of endless artefacts. "Just put it in... I'll take it... but I don't really know how much more of this I can bear."

As I'm carefully placing the tiny ball of fluff into her bag, she grabs my hand.

"What's that?" She turns my arm over to examine three vicious looking welts on my wrist.

"Oh, it's just where a cat scratched me…" I say vaguely.

Nani looks from the tiny kitten to the angry lacerations on my wrist and back again with a furrowed brow and sighs deeply. "I better have a word with one of the nurses before I go."

As soon as I lie down on my blue mattress, they start. I knew I should have had some sweets.

Voice One mocks, "I told you so!"

Voice Two counters, "No. Not true. I'd say you're a bit closer to knowing what normal *is* now wouldn't you? Remember what Nani said?"

Voice Three holds up her hand for silence, "Voices! Voices! You can have your sweets tomorrow! Meanwhile since you didn't have them, you may as well make the best of it. You could use tonight to your advantage. Remember what Toothless said? And let's not forget! *Forward* to normal and all that…"

I remember Toothless mentioning earlier when we were discussing 'the plan', and here he looked me up and down, that a new outfit might help my case, like. But what did Nani say again?

Voice One sighs. "Hopeless."

Voice Two jumps up excitedly waving her hand in the air. "Ooh, I know! Pick me! She said you should find some normal people to model yourself on, so you can be just like other people, not the ones here of course, who aren't normal." She sits down smugly.

Voice One calls out, "No calling out!"

Voice Three commands, "All eyes upon me!"

We chorus, "All eyes upon you," and await instructions.

Voice Three draws herself up to her full height and surveys the sea of upturned faces. "Who are the most *normal* people you know?"

We bow our heads to the task of working this out. I'm still working on it when Voice Two starts waving her hand wildly. "Ooh, ooh, I know, pick me!" She is no doubt Gifted and Talented and Special Needs.

Voice One mutters, "Show off."

Voice Three tells Voice Two to wait and give the slower ones a chance to catch up, it's only fair. Soon we're all waving our hands in the air wildly.

Voice Three says, "Yes, Voice One?"

Voice One looks round condescendingly as she reels off the answers.

Voice Three smiles. "Well done, Voice One!"

So now it's on with the plan!

I have a full schedule, so although I would have liked to visit Shakti to return her kitten, I was also relieved that Nani saved me that errand. I can't work out if it's a good thing that the Voices are in agreement or not. At least when they weren't it prevented me from taking potentially dangerous actions.

"Oh just get on with it!" grumbles Voice One.

But where shall I go first? In response, the Voices start

shouting over each other, giving me directions. It's amazing I get anywhere. But when we finally do get somewhere, the Voices are struck dumb. Even Voice One is silenced. We find ourselves overwhelmed by a multitude of *other* Voices, *ESOL* voices. If I could only distinguish the words I might be able to understand, but everyone is yelling, muttering and complaining simultaneously.

"One dollar, just one dollar, whole day…"

"My mother burned to death in fire…"

"Twenty hours evly day, nefer efer get a blake…"

"I owe so much monay. I hev to do eet for the cheeldren…"

"One dollar a day…"

"One dollar? I only fifty cent… you lucky!"

I'm just about to add my voice to the din, lamenting that I didn't take my sweets, when Voice One finally finds her voice and tells me to get on with it, we haven't got the whole night. Then of course the three of them start, "Nani says if you look tidier, you'll feel better…" "Toothless says it'll help your case…" Voice One helpfully holds up pictures of Irene and Renée and points out salient aspects of their dress, stressing very heavily the complete absence of sparkle or ball gowns.

So, my task is to find black suits, black hooded garments, vests, t-shirts and trousers, with a few dark blue and grey garments thrown in, a sort of combination of Renée and Irene's attire. I gaze at the endless railings of clothes all squashed up together. I don't know where to begin. However, an unexpected cooperation starts to occur. No sooner do I picture what I want, than a Voice, which is not one of mine but, curiously, far more helpful and friendly, will stop shouting and grumbling, and indicate where to find it.

"Over here!"

I hasten to follow its bidding and find a smart black suit, which fits me perfectly.

"You know these things when you've made as many suits as I have," whispers the Voice kindly.

I'm starting to enjoy the experience. In fact, I've collected a great armful of clothes, when a deafening screech drowns out every Voice in the place far more effectively than sweets. And since I have no hand free to cover my ears, all I can do is flee.

Without the aid of any Voices, I now find myself in a softly lit room with endless shelves of packets, bottles and jars. There are soft mooing, crunching, and miaowing sounds. Again, I'm not sure where to start.

Voice One raises her eyes to the ceiling and yawns exaggeratedly, then points to an image of Renée's mouth. She folds her arms as if to say, "I give up."

Voice Two is jumping up and down, near a shelf with small cylindrical packages on it, shouting, "I've found them! Over here! Over here!"

Voice Three just stands back and watches tolerantly. I go over to Two's shelf to investigate but as soon as I reach for a strawberry coloured package, other Voices begin.

"Our eyes are hurting. They're hurting so much."

"They're propped open. The chemicals are dribbled in..."

"I died for that lipstick."

"My blood is in that lipstick..."

I open the cylinder and out comes a tiny unformed baby.

I whisper to him, "You can kill me next time..." Then he disappears.

So many Voices! If only I could have some quiet... And that's when I notice them. A series of miniature black towers lined up on the next shelf in complete silence. And behold! It's Styx. Aha! Of course I remember... the promised citadel of the quiet life! A promise that was heretofore never fulfilled. But now! I need them, I do! The stalwart little towers suffer being grabbed and stuffed into pockets of black jackets and trousers, without a murmur.

But alas, the quiet life is of short duration. Before I can say 'deodorant', all the Voices including my own are silenced by a fresh burst of screeching, which, like before, is not only unbearable, but drowns out all thought.

Immediately, I find myself in a new location, again without Vocal assistance. This time we are in a much vaster room, almost as big as the Easter Show palace. The lights are glaring down upon us and people wander between tall shelves, carrying little green baskets or pushing wire mesh carriages on wheels, full of boxes, metal tubes and plastic packages. One person all in green bears a small brooch inscribed: SAVE WORLD. SaveWorld? Is that where we are? Last time I was here I didn't manage to get through the door, with all the animals stampeding through it, hurtling to their deaths on the barren plain beyond.

Before I can confirm this possibility, however, the movements of the wandering inhabitants take on a more unified direction, as they all begin to converge on a vast, black, transparent sand window. They seem to be congregating to watch some sort of show with blue flashing lights, accompanied by a familiar wailing sound. In the distance, I can still hear that awful screeching.

My Voices are standing, arms folded, expressions grim. They appear to be unanimous in their opinion. We silently glide off into the night sky, discussing where to go next. The discussion rapidly degenerates into an argument between One and Two, while Three hopelessly calls out, "All eyes upon me!" Meanwhile, I look down and notice something familiar, a large ice cream with a corner bitten out of it. Without any help from the Voices, I gently come to land.

The voices this time come from a doorway at the back of the shop, where a man and woman eat their meal, watching colourful girls dancing and singing in a television, reminding me of something else, somewhere else. Beside them, a small girl sits, resolutely facing the opposite direction.

The man says, "Go get us some chocolates." At which the small resolute girl enters the shop, picking out a selection of shiny blue packages from a shelf. It's lovely to see her again.

"Priya!" I whisper.

She drops the chocolates with a clatter.

"What's going on in there?" The voice of Govind Mistry sounds from the back of the shop.

Priya looks at me with massive brown eyes. I tell my Voices to be quiet and point silently to a glass cupboard behind the counter. Priya looks terrified. Wasn't there something about them making no money and people stealing things? I don't want to get her into trouble... I would consult with my Voices but they seem to have gone. I reassure her that it's going to be alright and she gets down a tiny key from a shelf, opens the glass cupboard and hands me several golden boxes. Then my Voices appear, looking decidedly mischievous and delighted with themselves, jumping up and down, pointing in glee. There on the counter is a beautiful blue sapphire! Oh well, that should be adequate recompense. The Voices are just stuffing their pockets full of chocolates and curious looking coloured snakes, worms and slugs, when we hear footsteps.

"Why so long? Do I need to give you a reason to hurry? Hmm?"

But we have long departed for our last errand of the evening.

# Chapter Fifteen

# Better The Hell You Know

My room is beginning to look satisfyingly normal. The blue mattress peeps out of twisted, crumpled sheets. Black garments litter the ground and the bed. Several plastic beakers with varying amounts of cold decaffeinated coffee sit neglected on the floor and bedside table. I wanted to avoid certain people at breakfast, so it made sense to bring the drinks back to my room, which only enhanced the ambience of normality. I don't know about ciggie bowls inside the bedrooms; that might not be allowed. It's a shame I couldn't keep the kitten here too. However, Nani's hair filled comb has pride of place on the edge of the basin.

On a personal level, I'm wearing a very smart skirt and jacket, over a t-shirt, all in matching black, finished off with a good coating of blood red on my lips.

My Voices have shown little reticence during these

proceedings.

Voice One warns, "It's all very well being normal on the outside but it's the inside that counts."

Voice Two threatens, "You'll never really know what normal is. Call this lot normal?"

Voice Three watches anxiously, tapping her nails and reminding me that I didn't get anything for my nails.

I agree with One, which is why I avoided certain people at breakfast today. I can't risk not having sweet money any longer.

I'm just heading out of the door, when Dora appears. Her jaw drops and her eyebrows shoot up her forehead. "Wow, girl! You looking smart today!" She grins. "Your mother bought you those new clothes, huh? Very nice! Lipstick too!" Then she pauses, a shadow crosses her face. "I checked the bag... don't remember seeing no black clothes in there. Nor no lipstick." She peers over my shoulder then pushes past me into my normal room. "What's going on in here?" She shakes her head. "She only had a small bag..."

She grabs my arm and examines my wrist. "Your mother mentioned this." Then she spies my hair-filled comb in all its glory. "Uh oh. This is way too sharp." She puts the comb in her pocket. "Don't know how that got in here. Your mother bring it? Don't know what's good for her own daughter." She looks round again, sucking on her lips. "I'll have to report this lot. I don't know what we going to do with you, girl."

After she leaves, I flop down on my crumpled sheets. The Voices are going wild.

One seems to have been heavily affected by Dora and screams, "Get yo ass down to the Sweetshop right now, girl..."

Two nods sagely. "I told you, you might not be quite on track for normal."

Three says, "Well you tried your best and you're not finished yet, are you? Let's be reasonable."

In response, I make my way quickly, yet stealthily to the haven of Hell's Sweetshop.

Bruth is busy with her jars as usual. "No cronies today?" She looks me up and down, briefly raises an eyebrow, then indicates two pots on the table. "You'll have to manage by yourself then."

In one pot are two lilac and lemon sweets. I look down at my severe black attire with a twinge of regret.

"Just get on and take them, girl!" screams One.

"I told you..." Two folds her arms and looks the other way.

I pick up the little white pot. Instantly, Voice Three starts ringing a big bell in my ear and gesticulating wildly to an image of a young plumpish woman swaying in the wind.

Firmly ignoring Three, I quickly pick up the pot of water, tip the lilac and lemon sweets into my mouth, and with some difficulty, wash them down.

Bruth watches me. "You should be getting used to that by now."

"Yes, well I've only taken them twi... yes of course! I'm getting used to everything! Getting back to normal."

"I don't know. I quite liked your other outfits... Added a bit of colour to the place."

Now that I've safely achieved my sweets mission, I'm at liberty to do my next mission. Toothless and Neville are out at the benches looking a bit lost when I arrive, hands firmly behind my back.

"Which hand do you want?"

Toothless brightens, while Neville appears to be struggling with conflicting inner emotions.

"Go on! Pick a hand, any hand!" I urge.

Grudgingly, Neville points to my right hand.

"Which number?"

"Seven!" cackles Toothless.

I proudly present Neville with several golden boxes, at which he cheers up rocking back and forth.

"Better than nicotine patches like, eh Nev?" says Toothless.

Neville pulls the plastic off one golden box, extracting three white and golden ciggies. Soon he and Toothless are breathing in deeply.

"Looking good, Kali!" says Toothless happily.

Neville nods.

I'm not feeling so good though. I feel a bit light headed. Voice One is indicating bowls overflowing with ciggie ends and Irene and Shirl outside the door having a smoko. Voice Two suggests that I don't have to go that far forward to normal. Voice Three shrugs. I pick up a ciggie reluctantly. I'm not sure whether this counts as external normality or internal normality but by now my Voices are becoming very faint. Neville offers me a flame from his number three hand and I breathe in deeply.

I cough and splutter as usual and await the usual scoffs and jeers from One, but nothing. My Voices have finally deserted me. All at once, I feel a churning inside, like a volcano.

I want to get up and move but I can't. I jiggle my legs, but nothing happens. I look at the ciggie. I don't even know what to do with it. It drops from my hand. A big cloud seems to descend on me. Tears stream down my face. I see Toothless's concerned face through the fog, I'm vaguely aware of Neville rescuing my dropped ciggie. I have to move! I have to move! Suddenly I'm jerking over to the other bench, the rough-hewn trunk lurking across the courtyard. I flop down, unable to move, although within, the volcano rages on.

As though from a great distance, I see Neville and Toothless standing at the other benches watching anxiously.

"She crossed over."

"Hmm, lilac and lemon chews can do that, like."

"Better the hell you know than the hell you don't…"

The volcano is threatening to erupt. I feel surges of anger and frustration as I hack away at this bench, remembering the father who abused me. I'd love to be hacking away at *his* neck. Ah, whose memories are these? Oh no! It's the Chicken Monster! The Chicken Monster, who mercilessly hacked this bench out of the tall tree's log. The Chicken Monster… aaah. It's my fault he was suffering and now I've killed him. I killed him. I'm a demon! I deserve to be in this hell. I see him as a little boy with his brother, their two spindly little necks silhouetted in front of the television, terrified of that father who is going to come in any moment and beat them. He didn't deserve to be killed… his spindly neck…

Killed him as he was about to hack into Sammie's spindly neck. Sammie with his abscests, aaah! I can't give him my milk… He has to be in kindy… He may be having anaesthetic and never be the same again! Oh my Sammie... motherless little boy... I deprived him of his *mother*. All because I was so proud, so proud, I had to be taught a lesson, but why should he have to suffer?

The volcano is churning. Is this how Mattie feels in his little tummy? My poor Mattie, what have I done to you? All those drugs when you were born. That was my fault. The pin in your head was my fault. Because I wasn't there. I could have protected you. I had the power. But no! I was too busy enjoying myself somewhere else. And now you're suffering and you may never have friends or feel happy ever, *ever* because of my neglect aaaaaah... Brain damage harms you for *ever*...

Neglect. Husband is being told he can't teach any more because of the assembly and it's my fault and he's lonely and he's crying and he's struggling to do everything by himself and now, oh now! He's with Fern and they're laughing together and was that what happened before? Aaaargh! And. The other mother was lonely and she was by herself and that's why she went away but it was all my fault because I wasn't there for her, was I? Was I? Too busy having pleasure somewhere else! She was depressed and she wasn't a peaceful *wife*. Peaceful wife, happy husband. She didn't want to have sex any more ever again... And I didn't care... I didn't even know...

And Prof and Nani are sitting on the couch in their living room. Prof is saying they lost their daughter and Nani is crying and saying she doesn't know if she can bear it and Prof says I don't think it's her anyway it's not Ama it's someone else who's masquerading as her... it can't be her, we've lost her and Nani says one way or another we've lost her, and I'll never have the life I want and write my book, they're both crying and crying…

And now I see a young plumpish woman swinging in the wind and it's all my fault and I can't bear it but I have to because there's no escape. I wish I had my comb. I can't bear it…

"Come on, Amalia, like."

Neville and Toothless are crossing over to save me. I wish they wouldn't. It'll be my fault if they have to suffer. I don't want them to suffer. Not like this. They're each holding an arm, of which I only have two, dragging me inside, away from the unknown hell. But it doesn't make any difference. The hell is following me. Wherever I am is hell. We go past the big room behind the glass window, where brooched people babble in magical tongues, "*Neuroleptic dysphoria, tardive dyskinesia, akathisia, dystonia…*" and end up in the day room, where the television is chattering away. I don't care. Television holds no fear for me now. Nothing can be worse than this. The television makes no difference. Nothing makes a difference. The terrible images keep presenting themselves one after the other; it's all my fault and I can't escape.

Toothless and Neville lower me onto a chair.

I'm vaguely aware of Gordon sitting peacefully, chanting, "The medications *do* work here…"

Dora comes in and asks if I'm all right.

Toothless shrugs. "Lilac and lemon chews, like."

Then a man in the television says, "Was it a burglar or are all our alarms faulty? Several shop alarms went off around ten pm last night in the Westpark Shopping Centre.

Police arrived on the scene to find what looked to be a theft of lipstick. The manager of Westpark Pharmacy says it looks as though more items may have been taken. Likewise, the manager of *Gardener's* thinks many black garments may have been taken, but until they do a complete stock take it will be hard to tell how many. However, the owner of the Anning Road Superette affirms that there was definitely a loss of significant numbers of packets of *Benson and Hedges* cigarettes from behind a locked glass cabinet without any damage to the cabinet, plus practically his whole stock of fruit chews. But he found an item on the cash till to pay for it. The item is now being examined at the Victoria Museum, as it is estimated to be a priceless blue sapphire. Police are wondering if the incidences are related in some way? Or whether it's all a big coincidence? They're also very suspicious of such a valuable jewel turning up out of the blue, so to speak. The superette owner is helping police with their enquiries."

Dora is watching me suspiciously. Yes I did it! It was all my fault! I did it! See what further damage I've caused! I yell, but no sound comes out of my mouth.

Toothless and Neville are watching me too, but with more generous expressions.

Gordon laughs. Everyone stops watching me and looks at him in astonishment.

Then Bruth rushes in with two little white pots and hands them to me. Toothless nudges Neville and he picks them up, "Which hand do you want?"

"Oh no you don't!" Dora takes the pots out of Neville's hands. "Open!" she commands. She pops the lilac and lemon sweets in my mouth and hands me the pot of water.

I wake up late the next day, still feeling groggy. Life has continued apace in my absence. One-Eyed-Glasses passes me in the hellway, now with two-eyed glasses and a big smile. "Hello, Kali, how yer doin'?"

She knows my name!

She gives my arm a solicitous pat. "Yer know yer look just like I always used to feel. God! I feel so much better now. I'm gettin' out today, yeah!"

Well, that's encouraging. Voice One casts a superior look at Two, who assumes a just wait and see expression.

"I'd better get down to the Sweetshop and get my meds," I say as cheerily as I can muster.

"Sweetshop? Oh nice one! Yeah, cos they have started to taste a bit like sweets. I never thought of that before!"

We're standing outside the big room where the brooches move amongst papers and computers. For once, I can understand them.

Bruth says, "Here's a first, I didn't get walloped once yesterday! Things are looking up."

Another brooch pipes up with, "Gordon's better. Have you seen him?"

From across the room comes, "Everyone seems to be better!"

"Don't tell Renée! She'll be wanting to trial a whole new bunch of meds!"

Dora, fiddling with something behind the counter, adds, "Only that girl Amalia Harrison seems worse."

"Yeah. Better up her meds. Double the dosage."

Then they notice us standing outside and they revert to their other language. "Paranoid schizophrenia, suicidal ideation, dissociative identity disorder, Delusional Parasitosis…"

Before I make it to the Sweetshop though, I see Toothless and Neville coming down the hellway towards me. Without a word, they each take one of my arms and propel me out to the benches.

"I need to get my sweets!" I protest.

"I don't think you do, Amalia," says Toothless. "In fact, we'd suggest you may not have money for sweets today, Amalia. Just a suggestion like…"

Neville lights their ciggies in silence. They don't offer me one. Toothless sucks meditatively.

Neville takes a long pull on his cigarette and squints through the smoke. He stands motionless for several moments. Finally he speaks, "Nevaeh crossed over. Last night. She came in to bid us farewell."

"What?"

"They found her this morning." Toothless does not cackle. "While you were in your bed. In your own little private hell, like."

I see her body hanging from a strong tree, twisting and turning in the wind, the image tormenting my inner eye for two days now, the image which I've ignored.

"You could have stopped that, couldn't you, Amalia?"

At that moment, Dora comes out and announces an Art Therapy session. Toothless and Neville ignore her but then it starts to rain so they finish their ciggies and shuffle inside. I remain outside in the rain. What have I done? Or rather not done?

My Voices are clamouring. Three is most insistent, "I tried to warn you. You didn't listen."

I block my ears. "No! It can't be true! No! Nevaeh!" I wander unseeing across the courtyard, futilely beating my fists in the air against fate, some merciless master, a hostile universe, the Great Soul. Someone, anyone to blame for this cruel deed. Surely it was not my fault? Not like everything else? No!

But suddenly thud! My wild progress is all at once halted by a solid object. An immoveable object. The hellish planet of the rough-hewn bench looms massive and forbidding. The bench... and its single occupant. The bench... and its creator. Gazing out of hollow bloodied sockets.

Voice One shouts, "Quick! Get out of here! You need to go and take your..."

Two cuts her off, "Don't even think of it..."

Three sighs. "And create more suffering?"

The eyeless person shakes his head silently, sadly. The rain continues to fall on this hell and the other, while I remain frozen, in my inner hell. The capricious sun seems not to be aware of this, however. Suddenly, a radiant light penetrates the gloom, beaming through the rain and sprinkles the rough-hewn bench with diamonds. The silent person raises his mutilated eyeholes to the sky and we wonderingly follow his gaze.

There, encircled by a halo of light, a figure hovers in the

small patch of sky above the courtyard, gazing down with infinite compassion. It is Nevaeh.

The Voices quietly murmur, "How?" "Why?" "But I thought...?"

She beckons lovingly. The Voices are instantly silent, acquiescent, as amidst the soft drizzle, the gentle figure ascends into the sky. Chicken Monster smiles, maybe for the first time in his sorry life and nods to us to follow her. Hell gives us an encouraging shove.

"Wait, Nevaeh, I'm coming!" we cry as one.

I'm soon soaring over towering buildings, (the shield, the spear!), then roads lined with miniature houses, and eventually forest. In time, the forest gives way to a clearing containing a motley assortment of buildings and dying cypress trees. And there below... our house, its solid blue roof stalwart against the wind. I'm distracted. When I look up again, Nevaeh has gone.

I'm being called. I'm being pulled down. The Voices seem to have gone too.

Husband's car cowers in the driveway, next to a robust blue and white one. What's happening? Peering in through the window door (no longer shiny, no longer transparent), I witness Husband cringing before two massive men, one fair, one dark, in familiar sky blue shirts. I recognise Richard Starling from Black Beach and the other one too. Was he here about the misunderstanding with the Tesla, or did I meet him at the Easter Show? I draw nearer, the better to hear.

"We have reason to suspect that you may be involved in a series of break-ins and thefts in the local area." Richard

Starling is like a tiger in a cage, dwarfing our poky, (but dear!) living room. "We'd like to take you to the station to ask some questions."

Husband opens his mouth as if he wants to speak but no sound comes forth. His face is like the grey cloud above. I let out a small cry and the police officers look round suspiciously.

"What was that?" Richard Starling lunges into the hallway, opening each door, looking under the beds and in the cupboards as though on a pirate treasure hunt. "What the hell? I can't find anything."

They keep a wary eye on the hallway, while Richard Starling continues his onslaught. "It's also been brought to our attention that you have a P lab on the premises." Here he picks up the bowl of Tulasi leaves and gives them a sniff.

Husband finds his voice at last. "That's ridiculous. It was just a joke. This whole thing. I can explain..." But then he seems to think better of it.

"You can explain everything at the station. Mike, take him to the car. I'll check for meth."

Mike clips handcuffs round Husband's wrists, I know how that feels, and propels him through the door. I've never seen Husband like this. His very life sucked out of him. Lank hair, lank clothes, even his eyes are dull. Just like me these past days. Before I became normal that is. He seems to find it hard to walk and forgets to put his shoes on. Mike gives him a shove.

"Get a move on, mate."

He struggles, but fails to put on his shoes with his handcuffed hands, so I carefully manoeuvre them onto his feet and tie the strings.

"Fuck me!" Mike watches, blinking, as the shoes apparently put themselves on and do themselves up.

Richard Starling comes out of the kitchen with a bag of rock salt, matches, a bottle of vinegar, baking soda and batteries, ingredients no doubt of Mattie's volcano experiments.

"We've been up this neck of the woods before. Next door had a stash of illegal firearms."

He looks disdainfully at Husband, who shrinks even further, if that's possible.

"I'll just check out the shed. Ideal spot for a P lab, off the beaten track. They could be doing anything up here."

I follow him into the shed, where Lucky moos happily to see me. She comes over waving her regenerated horns, and when I give her a scratch, she raises her head in ecstasy.

Richard Starling backs out of the door. "Bloody great cow in there."

Husband stares out of hollow eyes. "I need to get someone to look after her... if I'm going to be... gone... I have to ask Dan..."

Without thinking I shout, "I'll do it. I'll talk to Overalls..."

Richard Starling and Mike look round. A hint of a smile plays on Husband's face.

"What the hell's going on? I feel like I've heard that voice before." Richard Starling fingers the black pouch on his belt, scanning the horizon. "Something weird going on here."

Mike looks uncomfortable but says nothing. Husband brightens very slightly.

"Don't mess with us. What's your game?" says Richard Starling pushing Husband into their superior vehicle, whose bulbous eyes gaze scornfully at Husband's dust covered one.

"Let's go."

Mike presses his foot down and the car squeals off sending small stones flying. A few rabbits pop up from Mattie and Sammie's tunnel to investigate.

I can't believe I'm here. It seems so long ago that I used to live here. It seems like a different lifetime. I want to nestle in and stay with Lucky forever.

"I've missed you," I whisper into her soft neck.

"It will be alright," she replies.

Shakti arrives, trailed by a tortoiseshell bundle who is now leaping at pieces of straw and her mother's tail. She wends around my legs. I wonder if my time in the facility has all been a dream? Maybe the kitten who is with Shakti now was always with her and never saw the inside of the facility, what to speak of Irene's house, and any minute Mattie and Sammie will rush in, hand standing and jumping on the hay bales.

Overalls doesn't seem in the least surprised to see me on his doorstep and agrees to look after Lucky and milk her until Husband gets back. He asks no questions.


I'm reluctant to leave, but I feel someone taking my hand. It's Nevaeh. Trailed submissively by the Voices. She says nothing, but I know I have to follow. She glides over the forest back towards the city. Soon I spy a chubby figure dressed in a dark blue hooded garment and grey trousers, grinding her shoe into the butt of her ciggie. A phone rings and she rushes inside.

Her voice sails up to me, "The father's been taken in? Perfect. About time. I'll get onto it..."

I want to hear more but Nevaeh is beckoning me with

some urgency. Retracing our steps, we come to another familiar building. Black stone walls rise ominously from concrete. Nevaeh smiles encouragingly. This time I must be careful not to make a sound.

And of course at that moment the Voices choose to spring to life.

One warns, "No good will come of this. You'd be better off going back to the facility and getting yourself back to normal the way everyone else does. You're just going from bad to worse. But I don't suppose you'll listen. I don't know why I bother... But you mark my words, there'll be hell to pay if you walk through those doors. You'll never make it out unscathed."

Voice Two looks down her nose at One, "Where's your sense of adventure? You're such a conservative narrow-minded bigot. Ever heard of torsion? Thought not."

Voice Three looks strained, "Maybe we could come to a win-win?"

I'd like to put them all on thinking chairs in the classroom of my head. Acting on higher orders from Nevaeh, however, I float undeterred up the stone steps, through the glass door into an entrance way, with several chairs, and a half wall partition, like the facility. It's not the facility however. The walls are very sober here: 'One in seven young people report being harmed on purpose at home`, 'Family violence investigation: one every five and a half minutes`, 'Three quarters of offences by family members are not reported to Police`, 'Nine children killed each year through family violence.

Nevaeh suddenly appears and gives me a very stern look. So I leave my empathic communion with the walls and make my way to a tiny room with silent walls containing three chairs, a table and a machine. A door opens and in comes Richard Starling filling half the room, followed by the shrunken version of Husband, still in handcuffs, who takes up no space at all. They both sit down. Richard Starling places a folder on the table. Luckily, the Voices and I take up no appreciable space either, for at that moment Mike enters, filling the other half of the room. He places three cups on the table.

"Penny's a very kind police officer," says Richard Starling with a faint lift of the lips. "She always insists on giving offenders a hot drink."

"Bit like your last meal on death row," adds Mike.

Husband bristles a bit at this. "Am I an offender? Isn't the policy innocent until proven guilty?"

Mike laughs, tipping his chair back and cradling a steaming cup in his huge paw. "Normally you'd just get water, if that, at this stage. So consider yourself lucky, mate."

Richard Starling looks through the folder, taking huge slurps from his cup. Draining the last of his coffee, he indicates the small machine fixed to the silent wall. "We're going to be videoing this interview. Are you agreeable to that?"

Husband gives a brief nod. Staring glumly into his coffee, he moves like one of Mattie's robots to pick it up.

All at once, the Voices are clamouring, like the screeching in the shops or the bell at Mattie's school.

Two is screaming, "I know what to do! Let me! Can I do it?"

One is screaming, "No... don't you dare!"

But Three is not holding Two back so that One can catch

up, or even considering a win-win. It seems that emergency measures are called for. Before I can choose which Voice to listen to, I've swooped down and knocked the cup straight out of Husband's hand. Brown liquid streams all over the folder, and drips off the table, onto Richard Starling's black-clad thighs and Mike's solid shoes.

"Jesus!" Richard Starling leaps up. "Go and get a cloth or something would you, Mike?"

One covers her face with her hands. "You fool! I told you! Just making everything worse as usual."

Mike goes out and returns with a bucket and cloth. "Sometimes we get drunks vomiting. You could say this is relatively minor in the course of a day's work." He starts mopping up the liquid. "But you're not getting another one!"

Richard Starling goes out to wipe off his trousers. Miraculously not a drop spilled on Husband, though he probably wouldn't have cared if it had. He sits slumped in the chair possibly wondering how this will make everything worse. I remain hovering. I'm not exactly sure what my purpose is here, but Nevaeh hasn't returned so I will wait and observe.

Finally, Richard Starling resumes his position at the table. "Okay, Mike turn on the DVD." He clutches a pen in his massive fingers. "Ready, Mike? Okay, my name is Constable Richard Starling. I'm speaking to you today concerning thefts and break-ins in the local area. Can you confirm that there's no one else in the room?"

"Um... er... yes. I think." Husband gazes round the small, full to the brim room anxiously.

"Well it's either yes or no...," says Richard Starling, pen

poised above his paper.

Mike smirks.

"Can you confirm your full name?"

"James Nathaniel Harrison."

Well! I didn't even know my own husband's name!

"Age?"

"Thirty-six."

"Okay, Mike. The stolen goods…"

Mike produces images on a diminutive screen, which he struggles to operate with his huge fingers, a beautiful blue sapphire, a black Tesla, several pairs of very normal black trousers, t-shirts, hooded garments and suits, four cylinders of lip reddener and a big golden box of ciggies.

"Do these pictures mean anything to you?"

Husband looks aghast and seems at a loss to say anything at all.

But then Mike drops the small screen to the floor with a clunk and Richard Starling lets the pen fall from his hand. They both appear equally aghast and at a loss for words.

Now Richard Starling just sits, staring blankly ahead of him, his hand poised inert. Two large tears form in his eyes, wend their way down his face and drip onto the folder. Meanwhile, the four legs of Mike's chair are now firmly on the floor and he sits, gazing into the distance, an expression of horror plastered on his face.

Meanwhile the DVD machine continues to whir and video the interview.

"Go on," urges Voice Three, "now's your chance."

Voice Two waves her hand enthusiastically. "I know what

to do! Let me!"

One looks as miserable as the two policemen.

"I'm here!" I say.

Husband's eyes dart from Richard Starling to Mike anxiously. "Am?"

Mike jerks a foot out, then Richard Starling lets out a wail, but other than that, they're motionless, unaffected by hearing disembodied voices. Although who can tell what's going on within?

I decide to manifest my form, supported by two votes to one from the Voices.

"Come on, let's go! We haven't got much time," I tell Husband.

"Ama! What are you doing here?"

In my pocket, I find the little silver key which has proven so useful for starting cars and opening doors. I deftly unlock Husband's handcuffs.

Meanwhile, Mike and Richard Starling, although looking increasingly panic stricken, remain glued to their chairs.

"Quick, let's get out of here."

"But we can't just go... it'll make things much worse in the long run. You know how these things are." He looks from one police officer to the other in bewilderment.

One nods smugly. The other Voices, however, are beside themselves with impatience.

"And how are we going to get out?" says Husband.

"Ask questions later... Come on!" I propel him out of the door and along to the entrance way.

Behind the partition, a policewoman, possibly Penny, sits

behind a computer, head in hands, rocking from side to side and moaning. We run through the glass door, down the stone steps and into the rain. Looking up, I see Nevaeh smiling upon us.

We take the first car we find, parked by the side of the road. The key works like magic. I explain that it doesn't matter, that I'll reimburse the owner later, but it's an emergency.

Husband looks resigned. "In for a penny, in for a pound... Where are we going?" He climbs into the driving seat. Although his wrists are a bit sore after the handcuffs, he still doesn't trust me behind the wheel. We head west.

I tell him, "The police have told Irene about you being brought in and she said she'd get onto it. I'm not exactly sure what that means, but it didn't sound good..."

"Yeah. Georgina, Catherine and Valerie have been telling tales too. That woman has her informers everywhere..."

"Eyes in the back of her head..."

"Too right..." and then the words tumble forth, "I let the boys stay with Prof and Nani for a while... I was trying to take all the work I could... before my registration runs out. Now, since that day you came in... we were late... it's a bit up in the air... It was too much for me, studying... looking after them... working. Sorry, Am. I didn't think you'd be in so long. I thought it would all get worked out... about that man on the beach and all that... They can't do stuff to the kids. I mean like vacs and teeth stuff. I thought it was just going to be for a little while... until you came home... It wasn't s'posed to be for long." He finally pauses. "Also Fern's been... um... helping out a bit... I think I told you that." He looks uncomfortable. "She told me things were hotting up with Irene... We have our informers too." He gives a hollow laugh. "Maybe Fern will give up on me now she knows about the arrest..."

We talk back and forth. Sometimes the Voices become insistent about one thing or another and I have to put them in their places. I reassure Husband that it's not *him* I'm telling to be quiet. Weighing everything up, we finally decide on a plan. I estimate we have less than twelve hours.

Our first stop is to get the boys from school and kindy before Nani arrives to pick them up. Then we rush home to pick up passports and pack a few belongings. I'm sorry not to be able to take my new black wardrobe, but we don't have time to fetch it, nor can we take the risk. Surely, they have black clothes elsewhere. Maybe I won't need to wear black clothes elsewhere. Husband runs over to Overalls and tells him we might be gone a while. We speed into town and replace the borrowed car in its original parking place, together with a ruby and diamond-encrusted scimitar, which I consider adequate recompense. Husband says to place it in the boot since it might be stolen if we leave it in full view. After that, we stop into a travel agent shop to buy our tickets. We're going to the UK where Husband's father lives. He didn't consult me as to where to go because I still don't know my way around the world.

Some of the people in the travel agent shop seem to be half-asleep in front of their computers. The woman who serves us says that's what happens when you drink too much coffee, you have a downer afterwards and she herself doesn't drink coffee, only freshly squeezed fruit juice. We thank her for the tickets and drive as fast as we can to the airport.

Husband remarks that the traffic is surprisingly light. Normally it's packed at this time. We seem to have a favourable wind behind us, which is surely a good omen. Despite this, every red light feels like a yuga. Husband glances at his watch.

The boys say, "Are we there yet?" every two minutes and bounce up and down on the back seat, unrestrained by their car seats, which are still in Nani's car. Mattie doesn't seem so worried about the policeman coming this time.

While we wait for the light to change, Husband and I remark how strange it was that when we arrived to get Mattie, Catherine was sitting in the thinking chair and didn't even say hello; in fact she seemed oblivious of the children milling around her. To be fair we were in a huge rush and we were probably a bit oblivious of her too.

Finally, we drive into the airport car park. I'm quite excited, as I haven't been on one of these sorts of aeroplanes before.

"I haven't either," says Sammie.

"I have," scoffs Mattie, sounding just like Voice One.

Husband and I each grab a bag and a boy's hand. The boys shoulder their backpacks. Mattie seems to know instinctively to walk on his feet.

Now we're inside the airport! I gaze up at the vast ceiling feeling as though I'm in a temple to freedom. I can breathe. There are all sorts of people milling around; some with huge strange looking packages. By a board with writing on it, which flicks and changes every few seconds, are a group of people wearing brightly coloured clothes, flower necklaces and flowers in their hair. I ask Husband if that's where I'm from and could we possibly go there? He tells me we've already bought our tickets and there are lots of interesting people in the UK.

We negotiate a maze of silver poles and white ribbons which are not full of electricity. We 'check in' our only case which goes wobbling off on a moving black pathway, looking somewhat lonely. Mattie wants to get on the pathway too.

"We could put you in a suitcase," I joke, then bite my lip.

But Mattie laughs along with the rest of us. Then we're up in an area where there are cafes, shops and even more people flowing up and down moving stairways. From time to time I notice people sitting in cafes looking very unhappy, staring into cups or glasses. At one point, a man runs past us screaming. Most people however, look happy and excited. No doubt we do too, although our excitement and happiness are tinged with trepidation.

Every step feels like a triumph. At 'security', the woman in a very small room scrutinises me long and hard and says, "are you the same person as on this photo?" She holds the photo next to me and looks back and forth. Finally, she seems to be satisfied that I am in fact the same person and we're allowed through.

Now we're sitting waiting for our plane at gate number eighteen. Almost there!

Husband says, "As soon as we take off on that plane, we're home and free. They can't get us then!"

The queue for boarding seems to take forever.

Every time there's a loud voice asking different people to

board, Sammie says, "Is that us?"

And Mattie says, "No Samm*ie*, we're row fifty-four!"

My Voices are noticeably reticent on this and all other subjects since Mattie and Sammie have arrived on the scene. After what seems like hours, we're standing at the back of a long snaking queue. From time to time, we see someone in a uniform and Husband goes very pale. We haven't told the boys anything of course. Mattie asked earlier why we're going on holiday and Husband explained that we all just need a break from school and kindy and… hospital. Both boys seemed to accept that as very reasonable.

Now Husband looks at his watch anxiously. "We're making good time… I hope."

"We'll be fine," I reassure him.

We go through a little gateway where we show our tickets to a woman in a beige jacket and trousers, who smiles kindly at us. Then we're in a sort of tunnel with carpet, waiting in another queue to get on to the aeroplane itself! Eventually we're stepping through a big metal portal and being greeted by a woman and a man in beige jackets and trousers, who tell us to go on the left side.

Now we're jostling down a very narrow hallway. I didn't think it would be like this! It's not as I remember flying… but still.

Mattie announces, "Here's row number fifty-four! I want to sit by the window!"

"No, I do!" wails Sammie.

"You can take it in turns!" says Husband, sounding altogether like Voice Three.

Finally, we're seated and none of us is by the window because we're in the middle section of seats.

"It's not fair!" whine Sammie, Mattie and vague echoes of Voices One and Two.

Soon that's all forgotten as we hear a loud voice telling us that there's been a delay, but not to worry, everything will be sorted as quickly as possible and then we will be preparing to take off. In the mean time, they will be bringing us a selection of beverages. Mattie and Sammie are in the 'aisle' seats and very carefully hand us in our drinks. Husband and the boys choose orange juice and apple juice, but I take a cup of tea.

Husband says, "They must really have some problems if they're giving out tea and coffee." He looks at his watch again. "How many hours have we got?"

A loud voice announces, "We apologise for the delay. We assure you we are making every attempt to rectify the situation and expect to be underway as soon as possible."

We notice that a woman in beige is sitting on a small seat at the front of the plane looking distraught. Suddenly I start to feel light headed. The Voices nudge each other and immediately spring into action.

Voice Three holds up an image of a man in a beige uniform slumped dejectedly over a panel of dials and levers, reminiscent of Husband's car, but on a grander scale.

He's muttering, "I just want to die, I just want to die..."

Voice One says, "I told you so... didn't I tell you so? I told you it would end in heart break."

A woman in beige with a beautiful red mouth approaches us with another tray of drinks. This time Husband chooses tea.

Voice Two shouts, "Don't drink it!" and I knock the drink from his hand for the second time today.

At that precise moment, two huge figures in sky blue shirts appear in the doorways at the head of the aisles, talking into black phones. The one on the left is then jostled to one side as another figure, shorter but still huge, resolutely pushes her way past.

All three then commence their inexorable procession down the aisles, heading as certainly as impending death towards their destination: The middle section of seats. Row: fifty-four.

Chapter Sixteen

# Mistress Of The Great Escape

When I finally awaken the next day, my head feels as though it's been shattered into a hundred concrete shards and my mouth as if I've been eating sand. Dragging myself up off my crumpled sheets, I stagger into the hellway. Everything seems hushed; I don't meet anyone until I reach the big room behind the window, and then instead of the usual bustle and foreign tongues, everything is silent. The few people occupying the room sit mutely gazing into screens or at the wall, with agonised expressions. I continue down the hellway to the Sweetshop, but Bruth is not there. In her place is a grim looking woman with iron coloured hair. She's taken all the jars off the shelves and appears to be refilling them with new sweets. She barely registers my presence.

"Where's Bruth?"

"Who on earth is Bruth?" She sweeps some strawberry creams into a jar. "Nurse in charge of medications is off sick. Seems the whole place is off sick today. They called me in as a last resort." She firmly screws the lid on. "I'm supposed to be retired."

"Where's everyone else?"

She finally looks at me. "Who?"

"Toothless, Neville... There doesn't seem to be anyone around."

She refocuses her attention on the jars. "I don't know anything about them. I do know there were a few moved on to sheltered accommodation yesterday and a couple sent home. Seems as though some patients have made unprecedented recoveries on this ward. Can't for the life of me understand how, the medications are all over the place." She screws down another lid, then looks at me dourly. "I hope you're not expecting any medications because I've had no instructions for anyone. Funny way to run a psychiatric ward, but there you are." She looks me up and down. "Though I could probably make a fairly good guess in your case."

"Go on, what would you give us?" Voice One perks up.

Two gets up blearily and rubs her eyes. "Ner, I don't trust her."

Three is still asleep.

I make a rapid exit, looking look left and right, I wonder where to go. Across the hellway, I notice Stanley sitting in the day room surrounded by a pile of books. He looks a bit forlorn, not his usual laughing self. The television is chattering in the background as usual but there's no one else in sight. I take the risk of going in, and sit down beside him.

He looks at me sadly. "They've gone and left me."

"Who's left you, Stanley?"

"My friends… But I'll never get to go." He looks mournfully over his pile of books. "And there's no one to take me to the library today." Then he cheers up a bit. "Do you want to see my books?"

Meanwhile a morose looking man in the television is saying something about a pilot committing suicide and things coming to a standstill all over the city.

"The books are still all over the place in the library. The lady told me. This," he says indicating a book called *The God Delusion*, "was next to this." Here he holds up a small colourful book labelled *The History of Dhruva Maharaja*. "They were having a good old chat. They said they were just about to find some common ground, so I couldn't break them up; I had to get them both. But look!" he exclaims, opening the cover of the small book. "The lady said it doesn't even belong to the library! So I can keep it!" He laughs in pure delight.

Inside the cover, it says in large squiggly letters, 'ThIs BoOK BElonGs To MaTTiE hARRiSON'.

It must have been in that pile of books Nani and I took back to the library. My heart is pounding as I ask Stanley if I can have a look. However, Stanley isn't keen. He doesn't want to separate the books. They're friends and it's not very nice to be separated from your friends. We both sit gloomily for a moment or two, meditating on how it's not very nice being separated from friends.

Finally, he says, "You'd have to take both of them together."

He thinks about that. "But you mustn't take them out of this room, because I have to take the bigger one back to the library."

I wonder if I'll be able to read the book with the television blaring, what to speak of my Voices, who are getting a bit restless and complaining they've been sitting here for hours. I agree to stay, though, because after all, it isn't nice to be separated from your friends, and I only want to feel the book really, to look at it, because it belongs to Mattie. I don't need to read it. I can understand what's in a book just by feeling it and besides, I already know the story. Who doesn't? Dhruva Maharaja is the Lord of the Pole Star and he's famous throughout the universe.

As soon as I pick up the book, however, my Voices sit down cross-legged on the mat, eager to listen to the story. Even the man in the television becomes quiet. I look up and he's just sitting there, dismally staring out of the screen. I'm able to focus my full attention on the small book before me, which contains such a huge story. I suppose too that it's a somewhat relevant story. As you no doubt well know, it's about a good mother and a bad one. The bad one deprives the young boy Dhruva, who's about Mattie's age, of his birthright. The good mother tells him the only way he can get his birthright and fulfil his heart's desire is by going to the forest to approach the Great Soul. Something stirs within me, a vague memory from before.

All at once however, the thought is banished by a shocked howl from Stanley. The man on the television has assumed an expression of total panic. I follow Stanley's eyes to see a translucent but furious figure hovering above the table in the middle of the day room. It's the woman from my dreams.

She points at me with a quivering finger. "Get up! Get out! Protect my sons! I have been allowed to come here once and once only, because you are too dense now to come to us." She advances on me, almost snarling with rage, "Your body is filled with noxious substances; you will become duller and more vacuous every day, until eventually, you will never escape. Soon you will eat the sacrificial lamb. I will not be able to come again. Do you understand? Very soon, Mattie and Sammie's little bodies will be filled up with noxious substances also, just like you and Nevaeh, Toothless and Neville. Their innocent bodies will never be the same. They will suffer." She grabs hold of my hands. "Nevaeh was drugged. She took her life. Do you want to follow in her footsteps and leave our boys to the mercies of the ignorant? Rouse yourself! You do not have much time. And nor have I. Don't become like Indra, content in his pigsty!" She releases my hands and her image begins to dissolve. I can hardly hear her final words, "I was made a promise that my sons would not suffer. Now it rests upon you to fulfil that vow!"

I hesitate when I see Stanley's crestfallen face. Although he is mollified somewhat by me leaving the Dhruva story with his friend *The God Delusion*.

He says wistfully, "My books are my friends too." He picks up *The God Delusion* and gives it a hug. "You have to go. Go on. Don't be like Indra."

But as I turn to go, I see a fat tear falling down his cheek. The man on the television is crying too.

When I get to my room, I start dithering all over again. I only have a small bag. Shall I take this hooded garment or shall

I take this suit? There again, should I take these trousers and leave this t-shirt? The Voices are no help and start jumping up and down on the bed saying they're not interested in clothes, who needs clothes? Boring! My brain still feels cloudy; it's so hard to think. Casting round in desperation at the litter of clothes, I notice that the Voices have stopped bouncing and are sitting very respectfully on the bed, just like good Indian schoolgirls, with their fingers over their lips, all eyes upon something, or should I say someone? Following their adoring gaze, I'm delighted to see Nevaeh hovering amongst us. She's shaking her head sadly.

Without warning, Two starts waving her arm wildly in the air, crying, "Ooh I know! Pick me!" and looking exultantly round at the others.

Without even waiting for One to catch up, Three joins the arm waving, leaping off the bed in eagerness and yelling, "No pick me!"

Voice One sits between the two waving arms, looking from one to the other uneasily.

Nevaeh smiles gently upon them, shakes her head and indicates me.

"Ah-ah!" grumbles Two. "O-kay, if I must." She shows me an image of a black and white cow using her tongue to unlatch a metal hook from a barred doorway, a cross between the entrance to Sammie's kindy and the gate to Katy B's enclosure. And of course the cow is none other than Lucky, the mistress of the great escape.

At that moment, who should walk in but Dora the Detective. The Voices all screech then put their fingers back over their lips, but the nurse doesn't seem to notice them, or the pile of clothes on the floor. Wading through the black sea, she sits down heavily on the bed, scattering Voices in all directions. She seems on the verge of tears.

"I been thinkin'." She looks up at me through puffy eyes. "I never sit and think. I don't have time. Last twenty-four hours seems like that's all I been able to do. Couldn't har'ly move." She catches her nose between her fingers. "I saw it all… flashing before me like the judgement day." Covering her face with her hands, she sighs deeply. After several moments she drags herself up off the bed with a huge effort, and hobbles out.

Two shouts, "Quick before she comes back!"

Three repeats the demonstration of just how you pull the iron bolt from the metal bars and does an impersonation of Lucky jumping off the truck and walking free into the forest. Then Nevaeh floats gracefully out through the closed window.

Heeding Three's sage advice, I manage to open the window wide simply by lifting out a bolt. Was it always that simple? I thought it was locked… I climb onto the sill. Meanwhile, Voice One cowers under the bed, muttering about danger at every step.

Two cries, "Come *on*! We haven't got all day…"

Three warns, "If you don't come right now, we're going without you!"

At the exact moment we jump out of the window, a voice behind us says flatly, "What's going on, girl? Jeez, I don't have the energy to clear up that mess."

Chapter Seventeen

# School Under A Tree

Following closely behind our guide Nevaeh, we retrace our previous flight path as she leads us over tall buildings, small buildings and back to the forest. The endless forest at the bottom of the hill by our house. We land gently in a mossy glade.

And now... here we are... roaming at our own sweet will, with no one ordering us around. After all that struggle and heartache, we just leaped out of the window to freedom. It was easy!

"No," pipes up One, who decided she didn't want to be left behind at the very last minute, "it wasn't exactly like that."

For once, Two agrees, "You couldn't have just walked out before because of the boys."

"You *had* to be good and do what you were told," says Three, "otherwise you might have lost them."

"But then you lost them anyway," sighs Two.

"And it was all your fault," accuses One.

"But now at least you've got nothing to lose," comforts Three.

"And you've still got us!" chirps Two.

We wander deep into the forest through tangled vines and gnarled trunks of trees, spotting the odd flash of a blue toadstool, until we come to a clearing from which a mighty tree, straight as an arrow, soars into the heavens, its boughs kissing the clouds. Standing at the base, we gaze up in awe.

Eventually, Voice Two whispers, "I'd like to climb that tree!"

Voice One whispers, "But it's got no branches."

Voice Three says, "Shh!"

I spread my arms round the magnificent trunk, circling barely a fraction of its circumference. Listening intently, which works for trees as well as animals, I realise, "It's you, isn't it? The sister tree!"

I hear, "Yess little ssisster. Sstay... you are ssafe now. Take sshelter with uss."

The Voices have sat down very respectfully at the sister tree's feet.

"Do you know that tree?" asks One.

"I met her brother once... a long time ago. Before you three were... born."

The Voices appear anxious.

"Was there a time before... us?" whispers Two.

I think back over my short lifetime, remembering how even from the beginning those little synapses used to fire their advice at me from time to time… and I wonder. "Maybe not… but you weren't quite so… *vocal* in those days…"

The Voices look at one other uncertainly.

"Or maybe I just wasn't listening before…"

At this they brighten a little. But still remain uncharacteristically silent. Suddenly an idea pops into my mind. Quite independent of the Voices. I suppose it's the first time I've been able to hear myself think for a while. "I know, why don't we all make ourselves comfortable here… then I could tell you a story!"

So as the evening darkens into night, we have our school under a tree… And gradually the Voices relax as I describe the rest of the history of Dhruva and his austerities in the forest.

"… After his good mother gives him the advice to go to the forest and meditate, he runs away from the palace until he comes to a great jungle, a bit like this one. Immediately, Narada Muni, the eternal spaceman arrives to guide him.

"First, however, he tests him, 'Go home and play little boy, you're just a child. What business do you have in this dangerous forest, where so many dangerous animals might injure your tender body?'

"However, Dhruva, his proud warrior heart bursting within him, cannot tolerate these words of submission. He is unswerving in his resolve. He is not afraid of ferocious animals. He is fixed in his purpose to obtain a kingdom greater than that of his grandfather, Lord Brahma, the Lord of the universe. Seeing his great resolve, the master gives the young boy a mantra, a hymn, like an affirmation, but billions of times more powerful and saturated with transcendent potency to harness the chanter to the Great Soul. Such that by its repetition, day after day, month after month and the accompanying austerities – the first month he eats only dry leaves, the next only water, the next he imbibes only air – he is able to press down upon the universe, and choke up the breathing of all living beings. Finally, the Great Soul appears before him ready to fulfil his heart's desire for a kingdom greater than Lord Brahma's. The boy is wrapt in such ecstasy, however, that he no longer has any ambition for lesser material objectives. Nevertheless, his desire must be fulfilled… he has asked and he must now receive."

The Voices wait expectantly. It's quite a turnaround. What do I do now?

"What are we going to do now?" asks Two. Good question.

"Well… er… maybe we could… let's see. We could chant the mantra like Dhruva?"

"Ah-ah! Boring!" grumbles One. "I don't believe in all that stuff. The Great Soul! Huh!"

"I suppose you think it's all down to *synapses*," sneers Two.

"Voices, Voices!" pleads Three. "How about a win-win?"

Phew and there was me thinking I was free… even in the forest they're at it. The idea of chanting the mantra is growing on me; maybe I'll get a little break.

Then I get *another* idea. "I know," this should satisfy everyone, "we could do it as a sort of scientific experiment…"

"Ooh, ooh, pick me!" says Two, waving her hand urgently.

"Boring," whines One with ear paining intensity. Seems you can't satisfy everyone.

"It might make us powerful," I tell her.

"*If* it works."

"Tell me, what else has worked?"

"Bigot," mutters Two,

"Maybe…" says Three.

"But why do we need to be powerful?" pesters One.

"So we can get the boys back for a start."

"But what if we don't want the boys back?" The whine continues. "We might not like them. Mattie might be mean to us."

"You might have some friends to play with," I say. "We have other aims to fulfil also." I sigh heavily. "We haven't been very successful so far."

One still looks doubtful. Two sits up very straight and attentive, her hands tidily in her lap, like an extremely well behaved ISG.

"Come on, you guys," says Three. "She's right. We may as well try it. At this stage, from where I'm sitting, we haven't got much to lose."

"Goody-goody," mutters One.

"You'll probably love it. I've done it before. It's a bit hard in the beginning, but in the end, the minds settles right down."

Two looks anxious. "Does that mean you'll forget about us?"

"Well… you may just drop off to sleep…"

The queen of the forest chuckles gently as her branches way up in the heavens rustle in the wind.

The birds are squawking their last goodnights to each other.

The sun disappears early, sinking all of a sudden behind a distant mountain like a huge golden plate dropping off the world. Behind me stretches the endless forest. I'm not afraid of the wild animals, their eyes glinting in the night. The only ferocious animal I fear stalks the forest by night with metal weapons.

As I predicted, the Voices have all nodded off, lulled to sleep by the song of the waterfall, safe under the protection of the mighty queen of the forest. If they get restless tomorrow they can play and climb trees, even search for blue mushwooms.

I see Nevaeh sitting on a nearby branch, her smile is strained, as if she's saying, "Don't delay..."

Thus, as the inky black of the forest closes around me, I begin to murmur Dhruva's magic incantation for the acquirement of the power of the universe.

"Om Namo Bhagavate Vasudevaya."

The hymn that Dhruva sung trillions of years ago.

"Om Namo Bhagavate Vasudevaya."

I hope it will work. Queen Tree silently acquiesces and she should know. She's lived for millennia. She's been the witness to countless happenings down through history.

"Om Namo Bhagavate Vasudevaya."

There's a rustling in the undergrowth. An owl cries.

"Om Namo Bhagavate Vasudevaya."

I hear far off voices, cracking twigs, a muffled shot.

"Om Namo Bhagavate Vasudevaya."

The waterfall sings through the night.

"Om Namo Bhagavate Vasudevaya."

I lean against Queen Tree, feeling the pulse of her heart

and her ancient wisdom. Her brothers and sisters have all gone. She was alone. But not any more. We're together now, the tree, the waterfall, the night.

"Om Namo Bhagavate Vasudevaya."

The moon comes up, a crescent, scarcely giving light. The stars take their places along the Milky Way like paint spattered by Sammie at kindy, or Lucky's milk splashed from its pail, spread thus by Lord Brahma the cosmic artist.

"Om Namo Bhagavate Vasudevaya."

Eventually, the sky lightens slightly but it's still practically dark when I go to the river. The Voices are fast asleep. I sip a few palmfuls of icy water, then plunge under the shower of the waterfall. The freezing cold shocks my body at first and the Voices open their eyes in bewilderment. But when I climb up the river bank, dripping water, a warmth radiates through me and the Voices nod off once more. The massive grey boulders sit peacefully within the water, unmoved by the cold or the water swirling around them. They're as still as the water is restless, like statues meditating waist deep. I sit on a rock while the water pools around me and the sun comes up over the canopy. The Voices rub their eyes blearily and start asking what's for breakfast? When they see that nothing is forthcoming, they decide to go off and explore. I don't know what Irene would say. Fortunately, she's not here. Or unfortunately? Maybe she would enjoy a little meditate in the forest?

"Om Namo Bhagavate Vasudevaya."

A twig attempts to pass between two rocks, propelled by the water. The rocks remain steadfast, like an elephant struck by a flower.

"Om Namo Bhagavate Vasudevaya."

As the sun climbs higher, I no longer see anything. Through half closed eyes, the water and rocks merge into one. I cease to notice the sun and its traverse through the heavens on its celestial chariot. I think the Voices have given up. Maybe they found some wild fruits?

"Om Namo Bhagavate Vasudevaya."

I am no longer aware of anything separate from me, outside or in, flies landing on me, an insect crawling up my leg, the water smarting as it dries, the wind passing through the ferns and tangle of vines.

"Om Namo Bhagavate Vasudevaya."

I've no idea where the Voices are, but I trust they're safe. Maybe they're hiding behind a rotten log or snoozing in the afternoon sun on a bank of moss.

"Om Namo Bhagavate Vasudevaya."

I trust that they're happy and cared for.

"Om Namo Bhagavate Vasudevaya."

The sun once more slips behind the mountain. In the gathering dusk, I wend my way back to Queen Tree, delighted to find my trust rewarded. Cuta, mango and panasa fruits hang swollen and glowing all on the same vine. I take a small taste. A few of the twig ends still have scraps of fruit flesh on them. The Voices must have roamed this way. Here they come now looking radiant and satisfied after a day in the wild. They snuggle up as I begin my night-time vigil. They're asleep before I can say, "Om Namo Bhagavate Vasudevaya."

I hear swishing and rustling. Sometimes I think I catch a glimpse of Nevaeh peeping through a tree or sitting on a log.

Her smile is no longer strained. The world goes round. The moon sails on her journey, slightly fuller tonight. The wind rises and falls like the breathing of the earth. In and out like the breathing Buddha.

"Om Namo Bhagavate Vasudevaya."

The world goes round. The world goes on. Who knows what my children are doing? Maybe they're sleeping or riding on moonbeams? But I mustn't allow my focus to waver.

"Om Namo Bhagavate Vasudevaya."

The sun rises, proceeds across the heavens and exchanges with the moon in a celestial relay. Stars accompany the moon. Trees bend and sway to the rhythm of the wind. The water flows incessantly. The rocks, however continue to stand their ground. Queen Tree moves very slightly. The wind cannot sway her; only her leaves rustle gently. Rain falls softly, then harder. Sometimes I catch sight of the Voices scampering past saying, "Shh! Don't let her see you!" In the evening, I follow them along a tangled path under a vine and over a fallen mossy log with tiny brown toadstools and discover vines hanging low with kovidara and jambu fruits, the colours vibrant against the darkening greens. The fruits don't taste like anything I've tasted since I've been here. They remind me of another time, another place. The trees give joyously and plentifully, like hosts at a banquet, "Have more!" But I just take a taste. Dhruva only ate leaves after all and I want to do this right.

Nevaeh appears briefly, as wispy as a skein of gauze, with a small smile of encouragement, while I crawl through the branches back to my sacred place at the feet of the towering

Queen. The Voices are already there, smiling in their sleep. Maybe they are riding on moonbeams? Maybe they're riding with Mattie and Sammie? They start to stir. Nevaeh gives me a stern look.

"Om Namo Bhagavate Vasudevaya."

I wander down to the river for my morning bath. The water is full of black and white patterns like the pelt of some wild animal. All of a sudden, there's a yowl and a black shape leaps through the air at me.

It's Shakti with her tortoiseshell kitten! We're overjoyed to see each other. I sit down while she wends back and forth, butting me with her forehead and purring. The kitten follows suit. Although we haven't known each other for very long, she probably remembers me from the facility. I stroke them both, digging my hands into their silky fur and scratching them under their chins. I welcome them and enquire how they are? Shakti tells me they're well, although they're missing the other four kittens.

I ask her how she knew I was here. She replies, the Great Soul, cats always know.

I tell her what I'm doing. I don't know where the Voices are, probably still asleep. But I will introduce them later when they awaken. Shakti looks worried and asks me what sort of Voices? Not the sort that swing cats round by the tail? I think about Voice One and experience a moment of doubt, but then remember all three of them playing happily together along the forest trails. I reassure her that they've been no trouble since we came to the forest and I'm sure they'll all get on fine. They'll especially love Kitten! They've met before anyway. Shakti licks her paw rapidly for a moment or two. Kitten follows suit.

We continue to the waterfall, Shakti leading the way through the undergrowth her tail tall, followed by Kitten with her miniature tail tall, like two little soldiers. I perform my morning ablutions while Shakti watches sympathetically, Kitten by her side. Shakti licks her paws, then Kitten licks her paws. After a while, Shakti steps delicately onto a rock at the edge of the river and takes two laps of water. Kitten steps delicately onto the rock and takes two laps of water too, but almost falls in. Then they both sit in the sun, blinking amiably, while I assume the lotus pose, padmasana, on a rock. Another day has begun.

"Om Namo Bhagavate Vasudevaya."

When I feel the chill coming down and the light lessens, I open my eyes. Shakti has gone. Kitten has gone. I make my way as usual to the place of my night-time vigil. En route are pomegranates full of ripe possibilities, kovidara, badari and aksa fruits. I recognise them all though I've never seen them in this world. I take only a very small taste to thank the trees and vines, which reminds me of Toothless and Neville. I wonder where they are now? I didn't even manage to say goodbye. Then I see Nevaeh up ahead, looking stern.

I arrive at the sanctuary of the Queen to find Shakti and Kitten have also brought an offering. The Voices are looking shyly at the two cats and Shakti is pushing the offering towards them with her nose. I decide to leave them to their own devices, and soon they're all curled up together in one lightly snoring tangle of fur and limbs. I resume my meditation, as the soul of the rat offering hovers over its body, meditating on the sacred syllables of the mantra, then drifts upwards and joins Nevaeh on a high branch.

"Om Namo Bhagavate Vasudevaya."

Wandering in the bush today, I find fresh sitaphala and abhaya fruits hanging full upon boughs. Abhaya means fearless and Sita is the goddess of the Earth. Tomorrow I will cease to eat. The Voices look panic-stricken. Nevertheless, I refuse to let them sway me from my resolve. One issues dark warnings of starvation. Two looks pale. Three grits her teeth and clenches her fists ready for the challenge. I tell them they're free to do what they want. I'm not forcing anyone, but I want to follow Dhruva's example. It's an emergency situation.

One mutters, "Goody-goody."

Two relaxes.

I resume my vigil accompanied by two sentries standing sentinel and Voice Three, who's determined to be strong. But as soon as One and Two scamper off into the bushes, Kitten goes bouncing after them and, after a moment of inner turmoil, so does Three. Shakti looks on indulgently, then engages in a brief spell of washing.

Settling down, I experience the great energy of Mother Earth surging through me. Today I'm standing, tree-like, harmonising with the hymn of the trees, the great hymn of the universe.

"Om Namo Bhagavate Vasudevaya."

I don't count the hours. Eyes half closed, I distantly register the rising of the sun, its arc across the heavens and its sudden descent into night. Shakti does her own meditation, eyes like slits glinting in the dark, tail flicking. The young ones have returned and are huddled together twitching and sighing in their sleep. Queen Tree does not sleep and nor do I.

Deer arrive at our peaceful sanctuary, pausing in their flight from the self-acclaimed king of the jungle. They delicately nibble moss from fallen trunks then silently glide into the night.

Rustling and snuffling, pigs, rats and possums pass through peacefully. The ferocious animal, who rules the jungle with his metal weapons, stays far away. Dhruva is not afraid of the ferocious animals, he is fixed in his vow. So let me follow in his footsteps. Nevaeh smiles. The Voices and Kitten variously grunt and mew. Number One is grumbling in her sleep. I'm half-aware of the parijata tree spreading her aroma through the forest. I'm not eating. I'm living on air. I do not move from my position. I'm like the stones being washed by the river.

"Om Namo Bhagavate Vasudevaya."

On the twelfth day, the world goes still, as still as before the Creation.

In a flash, the Great Soul explodes resplendent onto the lotus of my heart, dazzling brighter than fire.

The world and all that's in it recedes like the ebbing tide.

I need nothing else.

Tears of joy course down my face.

My heart expands to encompass the universe – all of time past, present and future, all creatures, all worlds.

And simultaneously melts. Is this love? Surely the

word falls short. Words. This world of *words* and *labels*. So inadequate.

I'm diving and floating in an ocean of nectar...

But what is this? Suddenly. You are gone! After knowing You, how can I bear Your absence? Are You to be as capricious as the sun?

No!

The world subsides into brown and grey. A scorched and barren SaveWorld plain encircled by jagged concrete shards.

No! My heart shrivels. The lonely feeling creeps into my belly.

Then I experience a Voice. Whose Voice?

"You will not see Me again for some time."

No!

"Because you came to Me with some purpose to fulfil..."

"No! I no longer care for that... All I want now is..."

"Your desire must be fulfilled. You have asked and you must now receive...

Silence. (The water pounds, a branch scrapes on another, a brown bird takes flight).

I bow my head.

I do not take orders. But this...

My arms tingle. Though I have foregone my sword and my scimitar, my other weapons remain. Though I have not yet sliced off heads and swung them in glee, I am willing. I stand under Queen Tree on one leg in the mudra of war. If that is to be my destiny, so be it. I am ready.

Ready to tilt the world on its axis.

# Chapter Eighteen

# Secret Intelligence

When I finally open my eyes, the light, falling like diamonds through the lattice of branches, reveals a world as fresh as the day it was born. I blink, marvelling at the crispness of every leaf, so many vaidurya and marakata gems hanging from each sharp-edged twig.

Suddenly, there's a great cracking of branches, as loud as thunder to my newly minted senses. The glimmering leaves tremble. A glint of amber, a flash of gold, a shimmer of opal and the foliage is torn asunder. What can it be? The full moon arising from the bush?

And lo!

Before me appears a magnificent creature.

Pure milk white, dazzling. Her horns and hooves shining like gold.

Is it? Could it be?

"Lucky?"

I move to embrace her beautiful moon like neck and she gently nudges me with her soft muzzle. Her reassuring form unfolds like an ocean of milk before me, the perfect solace.

For a while we stand thus. Then, an echoing crackle of twigs and rustling of dry leaves proclaims the arrival of further company. While the magnificent creature and I behold one another, two smaller, but nevertheless equally splendid creatures, burst into the clearing: Shakti and Kitten.

A long moment of silent communion and wonderment enfolds us all.

Eventually, the two cats make the first move, winding their way round Lucky's legs while she responds by licking them with her long tongue. In the time we've been in the forest, Kitten seems to have grown from an uncoordinated ball of fluff into a sleek and sinuous tiger, while Shakti with her sleek black pelt gleams like a panther.

It seems my aides de camps are ready. But where are my Voices?

Our eyes are lasers, blazing from our one pointed forest vigil. School under a tree has changed us. I take one last look over my shoulder for the Voices, as our cavalcade marches out of the forest, ready for battle, but they have vanished. Looking neither right nor left, we make our ascent, witnessed only by sky, birds, and the heavenly gods.

Further up the slope, Fidel and Che or Massey and Ferguson, half heartedly munching within their enclosures, lift their great heads to gape at our procession, strands of half chewed grass dangling from their lips. Then, as one, the two massive bullocks step with calm deliberation over their white electric ribbon and fall in behind us.

At the top of the hill, we find our homestead deserted – bereft of Husband, bereft of children laughing and jumping. Poor house! There's no one for you to cosset. You're like a raided tomb, echoing hollowly, a skull with its flesh devoured. Clothes spill out of drawers, dishes lie mouldering in the sink. Someone made a quick exit, packed a bag with only a few essentials, which even now might be circulating endlessly on some deserted moving black pathway in Birmingham airport.

However, we are not daunted. We may be a small army, but the Great Soul will help.

We decide to adjourn to the shed building. Here we stack a great pile of firewood and drag hay bales, abandoned wooden chairs and sagging cartons of forlornly chattering books into new formations, establishing our barracks and our headquarters. Massey and Ferguson apply their horns and bulk to the heavier tasks.

For now, the newly arranged shed will be our heart of operations. It may be rough but don't be deceived. From this nerve centre, we will tilt the axis of the world.

The world? The universe!

And since an army runs on its stomach, we have our *kamadhenu*, wish fulfilling cow, Lucky, to provide whatever our hearts desire. For now, however, the cats and I are satisfied to sip milk, and the bovine soldiers, to munch sweet hay. After all, it's unwise to overeat after fasting.

Chewing the cud following our light repast, we discuss possible tactics, manoeuvring pieces of straw with Sammie's abandoned stick weapon to illustrate our logic. We're just debating who's going to be 'intelligence', agreeing that Fidel, Che and Lucky might be too obvious, might stand out in the crowd, when there's a decisive rat-tat-tat on the glass French door. We exchange wary glances. Were we anticipating visitors? Shakti quickly rearranges the straw map laid out on the floor. Then we sit looking at each other anxiously.

It's most unorthodox for one in my position, but I finally relent. As Prof said, the door's a bit sticky and the handle is not well placed, and I am the only member of the troupe with an opposable thumb.

There, outside the shed, against a backdrop of waving grey flax fronds and the boys' spaceship, I witness three mysterious figures, their feet planted solidly on the stony path, their hands placed resolutely on their hips.

The six members of our battalion jostle for space in the doorway in a highly unregulated manner, while the strangers appraise us through blackened glasses reminiscent of ferocious eyes in the night. They remain motionless, their blood red lips unsmiling, their trim black clad figures seemingly coiled like springs.

We had not anticipated this. No one seems sure of the correct procedure. Are they friend or are they foe? How do we find out? We hesitate in the doorway for what seems like a night of Brahma, while the fronds wave and the strangers glare. Then, acting completely without sanction, Tiger Kitten all at once slinks over to the alien presence and winds herself around their legs, purring. In the face of this blatant overture of friendship, the strangers' gravitas slips just a fraction and it could be my imagination, but I get the feeling that the slightly mutinous, the eager and the somewhat bossy expressions I glimpse behind their masks are eerily familiar.

I turn my laser eyes upon the assembled battalion, who are by now fidgeting and muttering to themselves. They seem to know that all eyes are to be on me without a word exchanged and silence descends.

"I believe," my voice cuts through the stillness, "'intelligence' has just arrived."

I scarcely recognise them, so suave and mature. Tiger Kitten obviously wasn't the only one to grow up in the forest. School under a tree seems to have suited them. They've mastered survival skills, how to live off the ends of ferns, tracking, orientation, how to talk to animals, how to make animal sounds, the art of disguise, total self control, how to influence people, how to read minds, how to read different natural phenomena and all manner of jungle manoeuvres. It's been gruelling. Sometimes they were hungry. But they've become totally self reliant and equipped for life and they wouldn't trade their training for the world.

I can't take my eyes off them, *my* Voices! All grown up!

"You can't call us your Voices any more. Sorry," warns One.

"No," agrees Two, "you can't treat us like kids."

"So, what's the plan?" demands Three, hands on hips, surveying our nerve centre through black glass eyes.

We're instructed to call them Agent One, Two and Three, or better still, *Secret* Agent One, Two and Three. If we really must however, for example in the midst of battle, it's acceptable to refer to them as One, Two and Three.

Assignations are thus apportioned as follows:

Defence, heavy-duty artillery and tanks: Che and Fidel

Stealth and cunning: Shakti Panther and Tiger Kitten

Provisions: Lucky

Intelligence: As above

Weapons: Me

Now all we need is the plan.

The evening is drawing in as we deliberate on strategy. At one point, I light a fire in the firebox and we gather round. One of the Secret Agents' talents is to read natural phenomena as I mentioned and we all gaze into the flames as they point out fiery images that we might never otherwise have noticed.

We see Sammie not having any dinner because he's having his anaesthetic tomorrow. He's telling Nani he doesn't care because he doesn't want to eat it anyway. Then the Agents show us inside Sammie's mind. I think I could do that to some degree before they came along, but it was, I confess somewhat haphazard, far from the calculated finesse of the Agents. Sammie feels sad because he's gone off ice cweam and he's not getting Mama's milk, so he's often quite hungry. Chocolate biscuits are his only source of nourishment. Then we see everyone going into the living room and Sammie creeping out into the kitchen and clambering on a chair. Now he's pulling down a shiny red package resembling the one we had for breakfast all those moons ago. Maybe he can join the battalion later in the stealth department? However, that's part of a long-term strategy. For now, the short-term plan is to deal with tomorrow's situation.

I feel a bit guilty having breakfast the next day, especially the delicious breakfast offered by Lucky. However, an army runs on its stomach. Furthermore, not only have I been fasting for several days, but we have a long journey ahead.

Secret Agent One is coming with me, while Agents Two and Three will stay back to develop a more detailed plan of attack with the battalion. One, I mean Agent One, says she'll let Two and Three be deployed on Operation Mattie, but she'd like to be involved with Operation Sammie's Teeth.

Of course, it's not good to fly on too full a stomach, so we resist second helpings and shortly before seven thirty, we're cruising through the airways at low altitude. All the Agents can tell the time to the nearest second by the sun, which is extremely useful. It's lovely having a companion on the trip, a co-pilot as it were.

A single bowl of cereal sits neglected on the mahogany tree table.

Sammie goes into the kitchen where Nani is cutting up apples and putting pieces in Sammie's purple and orange lunch box. "It's not fair. I want chocolate biscuits."

Nani looks down at him. "You can't have anything before your operation. You know that. You can have some after, I promise." She looks in the big white cupboard, rustling through packages. "I'm sure I put a packet of biscuits in here yesterday."

Mattie walks slowly into the dining room.

"Mattie, you're not having an operation. Your Weetbix is on the table," says Nani.

Then Prof rushes into the kitchen, slurping coffee from a mug labelled 'Alpha Male'. "Come, Mattie. We do not want to be late on your first day. There may be jam in the traffic. Get your knapsack."

Mattie doesn't reply.

Agent One says, "Come on, it's not time for Operation Mattie yet."

Next stop is Valerie's. One and I have to wait a while in the comfy green chairs as we came by the direct route, as the eagle flies, while Nani and Sammie are probably stuck in jam. I show One the animal puzzle and she looks somewhat disdainful. Finally, in walks a small, straw headed boy. My heart leaps.

His little face lights up and he runs to me. "Mama!"

Nani looks around suspiciously. "Sammie, don't start that now."

Valerie looks around suspiciously too. One shows me inside Valerie's mind in the water container. She's half fearing the manifestation of a rare set of dental implements. She's had enough of that. It was harrowing being part of that inquiry. First, she had to give a statement to the police and then CYFS. She still doesn't know if she did the right thing. That poor family.

I put my finger over his little lips and whisper into my Sammie's heart, "Hush, my sweetheart. Don't worry my darling; I'll be with you. You have nothing to fear."

"Mama, I want chocolate biscuits. I want Mama's milk. When are you coming home? When can we go home?"

"Hush now, my baby, I'll take you where you can have the most beautiful chocolate biscuits. You'll see. We'll soon be home all together. Now you'll be going to sleep for a little while and we'll have a lovely dream together."

"Sorry about that," says Nani. "He hasn't done that for a while. It must be anxiety I suppose, about the anaesthetic and the operation. His parents filled him with such terrible tales about it." Nani laughs nervously, has one last surreptitious look around and hastily manoeuvres Sammie towards the chair. "It's alright, Sammie. You'll be fine."

"I want to watch something." Sammie's lower lip wobbles.

Valerie looks guilty. The water reveals to us that she's thinking if she hadn't told about the P lab, then maybe they wouldn't have lost their mother... and their father. But then Sammie wouldn't be getting his teeth seen to now. So maybe it's all for the best, his highest dental good.

Sammie sits in the chair looking very tiny, dwarfed by implements, lights and machines. His feet barely reach halfway down the seat. Valerie places a black mask over Sammie's star dusted nose.

Cries of "Mama! Mama!" fade as Sammie's little head droops.

The minimally invasive dentist then pierces the skin on the back of his little hand with a sharp needle. I wince as I remember a similar experience, many, many moons ago. But no time for that now.

"I'm still here, my darling. Take my hand, little Sammie. I'll take you with me while they're taking out your poor teeth. You want to watch something? I'll give you something fascinating to watch. We're going on a journey."

"Where are we going, Mama?"

"We'll travel to the planet of Dhanvantari, who attained the pot of nectar from the ocean of milk."

I cuddle him to me. I've missed his little body fitting snugly to mine.

"Look! We're riding on the moonbeams, my love. You see down there is your body and Valerie will try to take your teeth out, but we'll travel faster than light. We'll get back before you can say 'tooth decay'.

"See, there are others flying too. See the eagle who lays its eggs while flying between the planets. We won't visit the subterranean heavenly planets, where the serpents have jewels on their foreheads to light up their sunless worlds. Not today anyway."

Soon, in the wink of an eye, we are gliding down to land before a shining palace inlaid with jewels and gold. All around, trees oozing honey and laden with flowers and fruits, waft delectable fragrances on the breeze.

"This is the palace of Dhanvantari, little one. Here we'll meet the twin Ashvini Kumaras, the royal physicians to the gods, who know all the healing arts. They only require one glance to understand what you require."

Together we sit in the coral courtyard of the palace, while beautiful damsels serve us intoxicating elixirs, sherbets and mango flavoured nectar from the river of mango juice. Then there are delicate wafers covered in caramel and ice cream churned from the ocean of milk, which Sammie gladly devours despite his recent aversion, ("This is diffwent"). Finally, when Sammie is fuller than he has been for a long time and can't eat another mouthful, the twin Ashvini Kumaras emerge from the palace, one bearing a diamond goblet, the other a peacock feather. They are glowing so brightly we can hardly see them.

They stand before Sammie, radiant as the sun. One of them says, "Try and tell us apart. Then your teeth will be healed."

I feel a little anxious because they are identical twins, and we have to get back soon before…

Sammie pipes up, "Woll… you've got a cup and you've got a peacock feather."

The twin Ashvini Kumaras laugh melodiously, in tones simultaneously soothing yet unbearable to the ears. One of them gives Sammie a draught from the goblet and the other strokes him softly with the feather. Then they tell us they have to leave us because they control the reins of their father, the sun god's chariot. At dawn, they must be present at the first golden rays of the sun. They would offer us a ride, but they can't come so close to the Earth. They bid us farewell. They mustn't be late. And nor must we!

"Come, Sammie, let us cross the universe and return, faster than lightning, faster than an arrow from Cupid's bow. Let me have a look at your teeth as we fly."

Sammie opens his mouth wide.

"Oh, just look at those beautiful pearls! The tooth fairy will have to leave you rubies and emeralds for those!"

At that moment, we arrive back in Valerie's surgery where she is just preparing to remove Sammie's teeth. She checks her notes and then looks in Sammie's mouth. Of course, she hasn't seen inside his mouth for a while. Having an anaesthetic was the only way to open it. She watches in amazement as Sammie opens his eyes and climbs with aplomb off the dentist's chair. The small boy looks round confidently. If he were a cat, he would have his tail in the air.

He smiles kindly at Valerie. "I'm looking for my Nani."

Valerie can't quite believe what she's seen. "You woke up so quickly. I haven't even started. Let me see your mouth again."

Sammie opens his mouth wide for her to see, the boy who would only open his mouth under anaesthetic. She's stunned to behold a mouthful of shimmering pearls, each placed perfectly in their settings. She's never seen such beautiful teeth in twenty-four years of practising dentistry. That natural healing obviously works!

Nani takes off her glasses. She's been busy with her book for barely five minutes. She'd been hoping for a good morning's writing. But her hopes are dashed. Again. "Oh. Finished already?"

"There wasn't very much to do in the end, and Sammie's come round very quickly. Remarkably quickly. In fact, I've never known a child to come round so quickly."

Nani laughs nervously.

"I really must congratulate you on your application to the *Western Price* diet. The healing is miraculous!"

"Oh well… um… of course, yes."

"Nani!" says the new man.

"Sammie… let's have a look at your teeth."

Sammie opens his mouth proudly. "We went to the planet of Dhanvantawi and my teeth are pearls."

Nani looks as though she's going to faint.

"Oh, er well… I expect you'd um like those chocolate biscuits I promised you?"

"No thank you Nani, I alweady had ice cweam with Mama. It was soma wasa flavour, churned fwom the ocean of milk."

Nani collapses onto her chair. Sammie gives a laugh, which sounds like heavenly music. Pulling a peacock feather out of his pocket, he revives his grandmother with a few gentle strokes, while Valerie stares open-mouthed. Sammie seems to have learned well on our short visit to the heavenly physicians.

I look round for Agent One. She's sprawled in a green chair.

"You didn't come with us after all," I say, plopping down next to her. "I appreciate your diplomacy. It was a rare opportunity to have Sammie all to myself."

"What do you mean, I didn't come with you? I was with you all the way." She sits up. "If it hadn't been for me yelling out directions we might have got completely lost when we turned left after the moon. We might have ended up in one of the subterranean planets." She still has something of the grumbler about her. "And what about the time we almost bumped into that giant eagle? I don't know how you managed before I came on the scene."

"Is that right?" I look at her wonderingly. "I don't think

I did manage very well... which is probably why we're here today." I stare miserably at the animal puzzle for a couple of seconds.

Then Agent One says, "Cheer up. Got to live in the present. No good lamenting." She holds out her hand. "Here's to the successful completion of our first mission!"

We shake hands vigorously.

Operation Sammie's Teeth accomplished.

As we're passing over the meadow on the way back to HQ, we notice Massey and Ferguson behind their white electric ribbons once more and drop down to find out what happened.

"We didn't want to give away the location of the HQ," they whisper in unison through the corners of their mouths. They look round furtively in case spies are lurking behind the flax bushes. "We thought we'd better spend a bit of time out here. Otherwise, they might get suspicious. We'll come over later though."

Agent One and I are bursting to recount our adventure, but on arrival at twelve hundred hours precisely, we're greeted with stern faces all around. Agents Two and Three scrutinise bits of straw; Shakti and Tiger stalk round HQ, flicking their tails with an aura of supreme stealth; Lucky, meanwhile is fully deployed in the stomach department.

"We have to get the plan sorted for this afternoon," Agent Three mutters out of the corner of her mouth, swiping at areas of straw with Sammie's abandoned stick weapon.

Agent Two, using a pincer-like Lego contraption of Mattie's to pick up and reposition stalks of straw, mutters out of the opposite corner of her mouth, "This is the Professor, this is Mattie," "and this is the medical centre. And this," she positions a fat piece of straw, "is the nurse. And these," moving some tiny slivers of straw, "are the vaccinations."

They simultaneously drop their batons and march to the window, where they gaze up at the sun.

"ETA approximately fifteen thirty."

"Synchronise watches."

At precisely fifteen fifteen hours, I find myself deployed to the medical centre in the company of Agent Two, for whom Mattie holds no fears, she being his equal in the realm of the Gifted and the Talented. We arrive at fifteen twenty and thirty-seven seconds precisely and sit beside our quarry. Agent Two looks over Prof's shoulder to investigate the paper he's reading. *It is mandatory that your child has all his or her vaccinations up to date, we do not want disease spreading in the school. Please be responsible about this...*

Prof smiles to himself then inserts the paper into a sleek blue folder. Agent Two nods to a big glass tank containing yellow and black fish in which we can study Prof's mind. The folder and the letter appear to be reassuring him. They confirm his decision regarding Mattie's schooling. It's all very professional, not like that other rinky tinky school, where they're not even sure if they believe in vaccinations and even if they do they can't get it together to do anything about it.

He extracts the paper and peruses it once more.

"What else do we know about the mission?" I ask over the top of Prof and Mattie's heads. I'm surprised that Mattie can't see or even hear us.

Two mutters out of the corner of her mouth, "They're waiting for the practice nurse to administer the vacs, but Mattie's so behind in the vacs schedule, he's due for a whammy."

I stroke the crystal vessel in my lap. "Just as well I brought this from the heavenly physicians."

Mattie's not doing any handstands or climbing up the walls, he's sitting listlessly beside his grandfather, not doing anything at all. When he tries to move, Prof fixes a stern eye upon him and waggles a finger.

"We can read the encyclopaedia or learn your tables which one do you want? Or maybe you should do your homeworks. At least they give homeworks at your new school not like that wishy-washy school. Actually no, until you know your tables we will not read the encyclopaedia. I have decided." Prof raps Mattie on the knee. "Twelve twelves?"

Mattie stares into the distance. Why can't he see me?

"Mattie?" I say into his heart. But his heart is closed.

"What are twelve twelves? Answer me young man."

"I don't know," responds Mattie drearily.

Two is urgently muttering out of the corner of her mouth, "Can't you do something?"

I know she feels compassion for those with Special Needs. Alright. Here we go. And lo, a small white rat, with a grey patch over its left eye, like a space pirate, is crawling up Mattie's arm.

Quickly the rat crawls up to my boy's ear and whispers, "Wake up, Mattie my darling. Mama's here."

"Mama," says Mattie. He gently takes the rat from his shoulder and starts to stroke her. "Can we go home? I miss you and I miss Dada. I don't like my new school."

Prof is horrified. "Eh. What is happening? From where did you procure that rat?"

Mattie jumps up and runs to the door but Prof lunges after him, grabbing hold of his arm. He brooks no resistance. He's used to taking animals by force. Mattie sits back down and starts crying quietly.

"Mattie, you must grow up and learn to be a man. Now give me that rat."

"No!"

Prof seizes her and quickly walks to the door. But looking down, the rat has disappeared. A woman and her young child have been watching, fascinated, but Mattie just stares off into space. Just then, a nurse comes out of one of the doors. I'm happy to see her. I miss the nurses, Bruth and Dora and of course all my friends from whom I'm separated. However, no time for that now. Agent Two puts her finger over her lips and beckons me. We creep stealthily after Prof and Mattie into the nurse's room, where Two proceeds to reel off a whole screed of classified information out of the corner of her mouth. "Jessica Wilson aged twenty nine, loves her work, far cry from how she was raised, ardent believer in vaccination programme."

I notice the brooch on Jessica Wilson's bosom confirming her identity. She takes Mattie's six-year-old unvaccinated arm with reverential tenderness and prepares her needles. Little does she realise what she's injecting into his rich red blood.

Prof hovers deferentially. "I have a lot of respect for the work you do. I am working in a similar field." He steps forward eagerly. "I could even have a try at doing that myself…"

"That's alright, Mr Prajapati. I'm sure you would be very competent, but I couldn't allow it," replies Jessica Wilson. "Besides," she winks at him, "I rather enjoy doing it myself, especially on a virgin."

"Oh ha ha. Virgin eh? Ha ha I get it."

Prof watches in awe and satisfaction, fingering the letter in his pocket, as the golden liquid slides down the syringe and enters Mattie's little body.

All the while Agent Two divulges further top secrets counting off on her fingers, "Fact number one: Of statistical significance, that this area will produce above average children of outstanding genius. Single unifying denominator: whole cohort children vaccinated within three days. Fact number two: Same individuals will be very healthy and never succumb to measles, whooping cough etc. Fact number three: All individuals will live to a very ripe old age of over one hundred years. Fact number four: An investigative journalist will finally discover a causal link. Jessica the nurse will be confirmed in her life's work. Although by this time, she will be extremely old, living to a healthy age of one hundred and fifty years." Two finally draws breath, ready for a fresh onslaught.

I say a bit impatiently, "Do we really need to know all this?"

She laughs. "Not really, I'm just showing off."

I look at her cherry lips and chic suit, then think back to when she was still just a Voice. Maybe she hasn't changed so much after all, at least, not on the inside.

At that moment, Mattie performs a lengthy handstand and goes stalking out of the surgery on his hands. Prof frowns but Jessica Wilson claps her hands in delight. Quickly, Prof wipes the frown off his face and beams too. Two and I have a quick look in the fish tank, and observe Prof thinking, 'Aah what a woman! Top notch! She would have been a first class wife!' and then, 'I might have been a bit too hard on Mattie. After all, if this scientific jewel of a woman thinks he is okay walking on hands and what all, then maybe he is!'

Outside the surgery, Mattie turns to me and says, "I can stay up way longer than that, Mama." Then he does another handstand all the way to Prof's car. We creep stealthily after him, hiding behind cars and sneaking out when the coast is clear. Two sidles up to Mattie and suddenly pinches his nose with his *Lego* pincers. I hold my breath, but he laughs until tears stream down his face. I wonder what Prof is going to say about pincers coming out of thin air.

But Prof says, "Is that you, Renée? What are you doing here?"

Two assumes her most haughty expression and stalks off with an air of offended dignity.

"Oh. Excuse me, I though you were a colleague of mine. Very sim'lar. Really."

As we depart, I overhear Prof saying to Mattie, "Where did you get that from, Mattie?"

"It's my *pincer*kampfwagen!" giggles Mattie, pinching Prof's bulbous nose.

At which Prof roars with laughter, to such an extent that he has to resort to his white handkerchief. Wiping his eyes, he shakes his head in wonderment. "What an extraordinary afternoon!"

Operation Mattie's Vacs accomplished.

Che and Fidel are back with us in the shed as it's dark and no one will notice they're gone. We're sitting round the fire, satisfied after our excellent supper, debriefing on Operations Sammie's Teeth and Mattie's Vacs. Shakti and Tiger's ears prick up when we come to the pirate rat. A big tear rolls down Lucky's face on hearing about ice cream churned from the ocean of milk. Che and Fidel are fascinated by the *pincer*kampfwagen.

Of course we're only semi-relaxing. The debrief is vital for establishing our future strategies. We may need to tweak certain tactics going forward, depending on present outcomes. In addition, before the evening is over, we need to have our campaign well planned for tomorrow complete with salient procedures and manoeuvres.

The agenda is kept by Shakti who is this evening's chaircreature and will keep order should discussion get out of hand. We're not anticipating that that will be the case as we're all so grown up now and there's no wild waving of hands, jumping out of seats and cries of "Ooh, pick me!" Agent Three wanted to be chaircreature, but elders first, so she will take the minutes. There are four items on the agenda:

1. Debrief from today's Operations.

2. Che and Fidel: A secret point they don't wish to reveal until it's discussed fully.

3. Tomorrow's plan, including developing a campaign for a search and rescue operation for Husband.

4. Long term stratagem.

I raise my hand and Shakti nods briefly.

"Still under the umbrella of debriefing, I'd like to enquire from Agent Two exactly how you came by the classified information you divulged this afternoon?"

She looks at me sternly.

"You never know. It could come in useful to know these things..." I trail off lamely.

Her face is completely inscrutable as she mutters out of the corner of her mouth, "Better not to know too much."

Moving on to our second topic, Che and Fidel are bashful but keen. "We've decided to take on code names, aliases," they chorus, pointing their horns at each other. "He's going to be Panzer and he's going to be Kampf."

So we aren't really sure who is going to be who.

"Better not to know too much," they mutter darkly out of the corners of their mouths.

Shakti asks if their point has been covered to their full satisfaction and they both nod their great heads and horns. She calls for a vote on the motion and we all enthusiastically raise our hands. At this point, there is a bit of hand waving but it doesn't get too wild and then we're onto topic three.

Agent One makes the point that while it's crucial to put Operation Husband into effect, unlike Operations Mattie and Sammie, it's not necessarily time sensitive. Agent Three raises her left hand while she continues to jot down notes for the minutes and suggests we do a bit of reconnaissance before jumping to conclusions. So we all shuffle a bit closer to the fire while Three indicates cardinal details in the flames with Sammie's stick weapon. Two has a quick search but then remembers she's given the *pincer*kampfwagen to Mattie at which Che and Fidel, alias Panzer and Kampf stiffen to attention.

Agent Three points to a particularly multicoloured flame, with a base of blue and green shooting into reds and yellows and ending in white.

"He's at Aelfraed, the Dean's," declares Three.

We see a brief image in the flames of Husband down on his knees, violently tearing green plants from the ground next to the Buddha. Three makes a funny sound in her throat, then a green flame flickers and wipes out the picture.

"The Dean stood bail for him because he spent all his money on air tickets," continues Three with a sad little edge to her voice.

A blue flame, the colour of a police car light siren, now subsumes the green one.

"He'll probably get community service. He'll do it at The Dean's place."

I look at Three proudly. "How do you know all this?"

She gazes into the fire. "It's not enough to see the images… You have to know how to interpret them as well." She pokes the fire dreamily with the stick weapon. She has a strange expression on her face. Is it my imagination or is it softer? Less bossy?

Agent One speaks up, "Much as we'd like to get him back on side, so to speak, I vote we leave Husband be for now. He can't come to any harm at the Dean's and we need to focus on more urgent matters."

There are murmurs of "Here here" and "I agree" all around except for Three, who still has that slightly dreamy expression. She's overruled however, and we move onto the next topic, which is, if we're not going to do Operation Husband tomorrow, what are we going to do?

It's decided virtually unanimously, eight votes to one, that since our next manoeuvre will be quite complex and tricky it would be expedient to use tomorrow for training and preparation purposes and defer the actual engagement until the day after.

Tiger's is the only dissenting vote. She mews petulantly, "When am *I* going to see action?"

"Don't worry," Agent Two reassures her, "you're going to see plenty of action. In fact," says Two, wagging her pencil ominously at the eager kitten, "you're going to be one of the key players."

Tiger's eyes flick from side to side as she washes her paw in nervous anticipation.

Shakti surveys the assembly. "Anything else?"

Panzer and Kampf are also reassured of their part in the action, while Lucky is deputed to keep the home fires burning. I raise my hand and enquire whether Agent Three will be joining us this time since she hasn't seen any action yet either. She responds that she usually leaves the front line work to others. Her role is to crew the nerve centre and be the brains behind the operation. Someone has to maintain a vantage point to study the state of play and inform the front line contingent of any crucial developments which might affect tactical deployment on the ground.

She touches her heart and smiles at me sweetly. "I have to stay at the heart of the operation. Do you understand?"

One pipes up, "She doesn't want to get her hands dirty."

Two jeers, "She doesn't want to break her nails."

Three blushes demurely.

We quickly go over some pointers for tomorrow, then Shakti suggests that we defer topic four until the next confab. She calls the meeting to a close. Agent Three notes our finishing time, twenty one fifty three, in the minutes. Then we all start rustling in the straw barracks in preparation for some well-deserved slumber. The conversation gradually dies away. Soon the rest of the troop is snoring. Only the Agents, who still sleep huddled together, continue their urgent whispering into the night.

# Chapter Nineteen

# Operation Panzerkampfwagen

Today we're to be arrayed in full battle dress. The Agents are in charge. It involves giving me a total makeover, just another of the many skills they acquired in the jungle, although Three mutters about not asking too much. They dress me in a sheath of shimmering silk cloth, the like of which, they inform me, has never been seen in this world and is specifically designed to bewilder men's eyes. There are jewels for my hair, which they comb to a shine and twist down my back. The first time since Nani combed it. I feel a bit like Kardama Muni's wife after her austerities in the forest. There are golden bangles for my arms and sumptuous glittering unguents for lips and eyes. Perfume is unnecessary due to my natural fragrance of roses acquired in the forest. No need for Styx!

Eyeing me shrewdly (my momentary gloat withering

under her Renée-like glare), Three whips us all into a line for inspection. We stand there saluting, while she moves sternly down the parade, adjusting a fold here, brushing a speck of dust off there, patting down a stray hair. Not that anyone else has a hair out of place. Shakti and Tiger have been preening and primping since dawn and their sleek pelts glisten in the sun. But a few wisps insist on rebelling from my hitherto undisciplined mane. Three snaps her fingers at Tiger who jumps onto my shoulder and licks the strays into place.

"That should quell the revolt," she says.

Then it's time to inspect the arsenal. I've spent hours polishing my trident, shield, discus, mace, chalice of fire and bow and arrows. They wink and gleam in the sun. You have to squint to look at them. Three picks up each in turn, tutting and rubbing at invisible blemishes of dust. My sword and scimitar have been declared missing in action, but Three reassures me that they'll be back. I'll need them if I'm going to accumulate a decent garland of skulls.

"Are heads going to roll?" asks Tiger eagerly, as we troop out to examine 'transport', but the company is too stunned to reply. If I thought *my* weapons were gleaming! If we had to squint to look at *my* weapons! Well! The sight that meets our eyes is so utterly polished, so utterly incandescent, nay *phosphorescent*, that for a moment we're blinded.

We rush to the glorious vehicle and start patting it and emitting oohs and aahs. Panzer and Kampf flinch and dodge to avoid our attentions, grumbling as one that they've just polished themselves and we're going to leave dirty finger prints. I should explain at this point that while Lucky has her talents in the kitchen department as a *kamadhenu*, which means she can produce anything you desire instantly, the boys also have their hidden talents, which until yesterday, nobody was aware of; they can adapt themselves to almost any form of transportation, not just draught haulage. We discussed the pros and cons of different modes of transport. Bullock cart, the obvious option, was rejected as too slow, although P and K insisted they could go fast. Then there was the original Panzerkampfwagen, which was the clear favourite for the boys; they became very frisky – not easy in a limited barracks. However, the tank idea was rejected as it might draw unwanted attention, even if disguised by camouflage paint. In addition, as someone rightly pointed out, where are we going to get camouflage paint? Finally, we decided on a trusty Tesla. It's fast, it will blend in anywhere, plus it's sizeable – big enough to accommodate a growing family. We're going to need that.

I remember Nani's maxim that if you look tidier, you feel better. I think we all feel better this morning. Just to make sure though, Agent Three climbs up the steps to the house, to the platform where Husband issued his big pharma speech in what feels like a past lifetime. She stands tall, clears her throat and looks to the horizon. "We are at war! We'll fight them in the streets, we'll fight them in the forest, we'll fight them on the beaches! We will never, never, never give up in our battle to retrieve what is rightfully ours! To reclaim our lost territory! To liberate the prisoners, hostages and innocent casualties of this horrible war!"

Everyone cheers and the Tesla, alias Panzer and Kampf sounds a deep bellow with its horn. I cheer too. I don't wish to dampen anyone's enthusiasm, especially Three's, by confessing my doubts about things being rightfully ours. After all, this could well have been her finest hour.

Ten hundred hours. The official start of Operation Panzerkampfwagen. Agent One is our first driver and Shakti sits next to her in front as second in command for this segment of the campaign. Tiger is mewling about the unfairness and that she wants to sit in front, but she is silenced by Agent Two who reminds her of the complexity and gravity of this afternoon's operation which will depend entirely upon her stealth and cunning. She's going to need every ounce of energy and we need to be able to depend on her. I'm also part of the rear guard. In order to make rapid getaways, I need a driver who can pull away 'on a dime'.

I say 'driver', but it's not quite like driving a normal car. Agent One isn't going to have to floor it or slam on the brakes. It's more a question of issuing commands in clipped tones. Get Up for move forward, Easy for slow down, Whoa for stop, Gee for turn right, Haw for turn left and Back for reverse. In addition, there's Step In and Step Out for parking and Come Boss for recharging. Agent One simply has to turn the steering wheel and give lots of encouragement and Get Up's to go faster. Buckoos are not provided. Ditto car seats.

Operation Panzerkampfwagen or PKW for short is the overall code name for today's campaign. However, it consists of three parts, all classified top secret. To divulge even a whisper in advance would be to reveal far too much. For without exception, they all depend on the element of surprise.

Operation Panzer, OP:

Ten forty-five hours: The Panzerkampfwagen pulls up outside a wooden building, with a tall archway, with an "Easy" "Gee" "Step In" and "Whoa".

Ten forty-six hours: Two briefs me on the bare essentials.

Ten forty-seven hours: Colonel Kali (C.K.) enters wooden building; engine of PKW is running. Agent One, Panzer, Kampf and Shakti, the navigator, on red alert for C.K. return.

Ten forty-eight hours: C.K. locates corridor by green plant now with two flowers, leading to hall, secretes self in alcove off said corridor, presume unobserved.

Ten forty-nine hours: Female: Denise, orange curly hair, huge billowing scarlet top, sweeps up corridor. Destination: hall. Purpose: assembly, "before the rabble descend".

Ten fifty hours: In plenty of time for assembly, not like some people, male: Tony Hardcastle (T.H.) demoted to teach Year Two in the wake of near nervous breakdown precipitated by teaching Year Eight A, following late for assembly episode, in particular one Connor Jones, now being treated for ADHD. Happily T.H. doesn't have to deal with thorny issue of evolutionary theory with Year Two. Said male traverses corridor in vanguard of troop of thirty-one six-year-olds.

Ten fifty-two hours: Locate target, bringing up rearguard of troop, proceeding on hands.

Ten fifty-three hours: C.K. emerges from said alcove, finger on lips, murmuring, "All eyes upon me". Target reverts to foot propelled transportation, saying, "All eyes upon you", makes eye contact with C.K. proceeds in straight line towards

C.K. Apparently appreciating delicacy of situation, whispers, "Mama you look different. Have you got a rat?" Takes hand of C.K.

Ten fifty-five hours: Unnoticed by T.H., C.K. and target retrace steps along corridor.

Ten fifty-five hours thirty seconds: T.H. makes one hundred and eighty degree turn to rally troops in preparation for assembly. Sights target proceeding along corridor in counter direction to orders. Possible offensive manoeuvre averted by enchanting dress and fragrance which can bewilder men's minds. T.H. smiles, continues in line of duty, issuing orders for Year Two C to march single file into assembly, and "Halt" and "Eyes straight" and "All eyes upon me" etc.

Ten fifty-eight hours: C.K. and target exit wooden building; proceed to and enter rearguard of PKW. "It's not fair" "I always sit in front" etc. "Back" "Step Out" "Haw" "Get Up!" "Get Up!" etc.

Eleven hundred hours: Operation Panzer accomplished.

Operation Kampf, OK:

Eleven twenty-five hours: "Easy" "Haw" "Step In" "Whoa". PKW pulls in adjacent to black gate.

Eleven twenty-six hours: Agent Two briefs C.K., Shakti Panther (S.P.), Tiger Kitten (T.K.): bare essentials etc.

Eleven thirty hours: C.K. inquiry as to feasibility of releasing guinea pig. Receives eyes rolled to ceiling glares, code for 'Are you crazy?' from S.P., T.K. Can't release someone who doesn't want freedom. Or risk adding complexity to already water tight plans.

Eleven thirty-two hours: exit PKW, C.K. conceals self behind personal shield outside gate. S.P. and T.K. incursion over top of said gate, objective: use of stealth and espionage tactics as per training manoeuvres to approach target.

Eleven thirty-six hours: S.P. and T.K. attract attention of target, lure target to gate, whisper codeword: "Mama's milk".

Eleven thirty-eight hours: C.K. elevates tube on gate. S.P., T.K., target, exit via gate. C.K., T.K., target enter PKW in rearguard position. S.P. resumes vanguard position. "Not fair" etc. "Mama's milk", etc. "Back" "Step Out" "Gee" "Get Up!" "Get Up!" etc.

Eleven forty hours: Operation Kampf accomplished.

We have a reconnoitre in the park round the corner from Prof's work place, under the gaze of the rather dour lady and gentleman. Agent Two tells us, however, that the lady is Queen Victoria and she was expert in annexing whole territories that she felt were rightfully hers. As Two divulges this information, the Queen smiles graciously upon us and we all curtsey and bow.

Mattie is delighted to be reunited with Shakti and Tiger. After initial greetings of head butting and mouth rubbing, he trots around with them on all fours. They discover a very accommodating tree with a huge wide trunk full of entrances, exits, ramparts and well placed arrow slits. It seems an ideal spot for a temporary HQ. Although Mattie suggests that it's actually a pirate spaceship and this is his room and that is Sammie's, which adds a new flavour to the whole enterprise. Different members of the battalion situate themselves at various elevations on the ramparts of the pirate spaceship HQ to consume provisions issued by Lucky.

Agent Two is delighted with Sammie and reunites him with his abandoned stick weapon. Although he's secreted three more in his 'room' already. They discuss the merits of various kinds of weapons over lunch then go off to explore and scale the huge canon weapons standing on the hill, proudly defending Her Majesty along with all that is rightfully hers. Panzer and Kampf are of course, already there, checking out the heavy artillery and talking in low voices about calibre, range, mobility, rate of fire, angle of fire, and firepower, in between tearing up great hunks of grass to recharge their batteries. Well, we weren't going to leave them in that concrete tomb of a car park while we're all out here enjoying the sunshine. Agent One unyoked them and keeps commanding them to "Come Boss" but the two massive bullocks pay no attention, immersed as they are in the finer points of heavy artillery.

One finally gives up on vehicle duty – it's Two's turn to drive next anyway – and strides up and down a pathway under Her Majesty's watchful eye, in earnest discussion, apparently with herself. She terminates the discussion and comes over to me looking worried.

"That was Three. She wants to know why we're indulging in frivolity at this crucial juncture. According to her, we're behind schedule for Operation Wagon and we can't afford to rest on our laurels. Time is of the essence." She looks up anxiously at the sun, which has just gone behind a cloud. "Oh and by the way, she mentioned, that the Queen has forgiven you for not curtseying to her great-granddaughter the other day."

Oh, well that's a relief.

We quickly assemble the troop in the spaceship HQ to outline and recap on the strategy for the upcoming mission. After Tiger's successful completion of this morning's Operation Kampf, Two admits to having full confidence in entrusting this final assignment to her. However, she warns, it's not going to be a walk in the park. While the rest of the troop will be on full alert mode, Tiger is the brave comrade who's going to infiltrate enemy territory and risk her life.

What follows is an account of Operation Wagen delivered by Private Tiger. Being sruti dhara as you may or may not remember, I am able to replicate the account in its exactitude. My rationale being that it would be doing Tiger an injustice not to present her exploit in her own unique words, being the kitten on the ground, so to speak. Agent Three of course, from her vantage at the heart of operations witnessed all proceedings but she wasn't the one actually doing the dirty work and thus her version might lack a certain, how shall we say, immediacy.

Operation Wagen, OW, Verbatim Report of Report by Private Tiger:

"The sun is just past the middle of the sky when I begin my mission. I'm not going to give exact timings; cats don't operate like that. We operate on instinct. Besides, I never went to school and that sort of stuff's boring anyway.

"I start behind the tree designated as temporary HQ/ pirate spaceship and make my way stealthily to the closest tree. I continue a stealthy tree-to-tree prowl until I reach the street, blending seamlessly into the background. Now comes a tricky part. Looking both ways, I streak across the street. I'm not a great fan of street crossing. I don't have much experience and as any cat will confirm, it's a risky business. Even big toms have fallen by the roadside. However, I make it over in one piece, thanking the Great Soul for Her intervention and do a quick recce of the entrance to the building. Now comes the even more tricky part, where my hours of stealth training separate the tigers from the kittens. My tortoiseshell tiger skin coat provides me with a certain natural advantage as camouflage but it's not so helpful in a grey building, which is why humans wear black and other dark colours. Alongside stealth and cunning, I may need to switch on my weapons of artificial affection, cuteness and sheer chutzpah. If that fails, well I'm a tiger after all... I know Three instructed us not to spill blood if we can help it, but as I say, we cats operate on instinct.

I crouch behind a small wall near the entrance until a gaggle of humans, clucking and quacking, jostles its way through the door. Then I rapidly but stealthily leap into the fray and wind my way in, camouflaged between various legs. I'm in! I locate a blue door to the left and hide behind some legs until someone opens it. Quick as a flash, I'm through and on my way up the stairs, keeping a beady eye out for lurking humans. Action brief advised stairs as opposed to lift as less likelihood of encountering possible counter manoeuvres. On nearing the seventh floor, I flatten myself against the wall and slink with ultimate stealth toward the door. Fortunately, an oversize human (using the stairs instead of the lift in an effort to reduce size, honestly, humans!) exits at that moment, eyes front and due to my bewildering forest powers, fails to observe my instantaneous ingress. Even more fortunately, the door to the kitchen area is open and the room is devoid of human presence. The Great Soul is definitely helping! Although to be fair, we did plan the timings to a tee. However, the riskiest operations are yet to come.

Now I need to locate the key on top of the coffee machine. This is going almost too smoothly. I succeed in opening two doors with various markings on them, which might be words but I can't read them because I didn't go to school, pass three doors that give me the jitters, then arrive at another room containing several cages. Opening the one in the far corner, as instructed, I climb in. Bang on cue, in comes a male human with glasses, a white face and a plastic bag over his head. Bingo! I recognise him from the time he stole my brother and sisters. Secreting the key in my cheek, I utter a plaintive mew.

He approaches my cage first of course. Who could resist my charm? Studying a small machine in his paw, he pats it a few times then scratches the plastic bag. He peers at me through his glasses. Humans have such bad eyesight. They can't even see in daylight what to speak of the dark. I slink around my cage with my tail raised, rubbing myself against the bars, purring ingratiatingly and stopping every now and then to blink up at him with adoring eyes. He takes off his glasses, wipes them and puts them back on again, peering through the bars at me. My eyes reduce to black slits as I draw him into my mesmerising gaze and he stands helplessly, rooted to the spot. After some time, I miaow and pat the bar of the cage with a velvet paw, eyes wide in helpless appeal.

"You want to come out is it, little puss?" He drops his machine with a clatter.

"Miaow!" I say, which means yes please!

He fiddles in his pocket for an implement, not a key, with which he opens the cage and very tenderly lifts me out. He cuddles me to his bosom, stroking me completely the wrong way. The sacrifices we make in the name of duty! Then I spring lightly out of his hands and walk purposefully to another cage, looking over my shoulder with come-hither eyes.

"You are a really saucy kitten, isn't it?" says Plastic Bag Head. "What? You're wanting me to let that biological system out now, is it?" He looks at the tiny quivering mess inside the cage and suddenly his heart is smitten. We cats can read humans like a book. Not that I can read but still...

I won't go into all the details. I'm a cat after all, not a shaggy dog, and cats get bored easily. Suffice it to say, Plastic Bag, sorry Kali I know it's your father we're talking about, feels infinite remorse for these vulnerable creatures in his care who have never seen the daylight or smelled the fresh grass and decides, since it's a nice day, to give them all a treat.

"I tell you what, saucy pussycat, I will not just let that kitten out, I will let whole contingent out for some hell-thee fresh air and sunshine. Will do us all good, no? Will fit nicely under the umbrella of behavioural enrichment strategies."

This time, I go down in the lift with Plastic Bag and all the cages. He tells the man by the door to mind the remaining cages while he makes several trips back and forth to the park.

I lead the way, tail erect, no longer stealthy under the aegis of the esteemed Plastic Bag.

Fair play to Three, she may be a bit squeamish about bloodshed, but she was flawless in her timing, because I observe that Plastic Bag is starting to feel sleepy. As I mentioned, cats can always read humans, especially in regards to sleep. We are the ultimate authorities on sleep. Indian humans like a little siesta in the afternoon and with all the animals capering around the park, this one can hardly shoot off to get a coffee. What a dilemma. He stretches out for a little relax on the grass. Bees hum melodiously, the sun beams gently down. Soon, he's asleep. Queen Vic looks down her nose at him. You can never trust the natives.

Okay, time to round up the troops.

With Panzer and Kampf pawing the ground at the edge of the curb, I raise my tail and walk straight legged across the grass, looking seductively over my shoulder. Soon, nine baby rhesus monkeys, two mother rhesus monkeys, six kittens, eight rabbits and twenty rats are trotting scuttling and bouncing after me in single file. This is potentially the most hazardous leg of the operation. But with my charm offensive still switched to full, we reach the PKW without casualty. We turn and bob a quick curtsey to Her Majesty, pile into the PKW and roar away. I feel a twinge of disappointment at the absence of bloodshed, but I certainly saw some action!

Current position: getaway Tesla, chock full of escaped prisoners, on orders to RTB. I'm in the vanguard with Mattie and Sammie. Everyone's congratulating me on a successful mission as I make my report.

Then One says, as though she can read my mind, "Don't worry, Tiger, it's early days. Heads are definitely going to roll when the department finds out they've lost all their animals!"

Operation Wagen accomplished. End of report by Private Tiger.

It would be heavenly if we could all curl up happily together in our straw barracks but that is not to be. It wouldn't be safe to keep escaped prisoners in so obvious a situation. The arrangement is that Agents One and Two will take them into the forest and conceal them under Queen Tree using special tactics to keep intruders at bay and put them off the scent. It might do them all some good. It worked pretty well for us. The Agents can teach them survival skills and they could even do a spot of meditation. Agent Three naturally declines to join them.

Lucky will send provisions daily with an envoy, who might be any of us remaining comrades, apart from Panzer and Kampf who are too unwieldy for the tangle of the forest and might leave tracks. The escapees can also eat the fruits from the forest and of course learn to survive with just their wits.

Panzer and Kampf are reluctantly heaving themselves up to return to the white ribbon, when a shadow looms in the doorway.

It's Overalls. The two bullocks shuffle and hang their heads.

"So that's where you are. We thought you'd been abducted by the Chicken Monster." Overalls stands solidly in the doorway, arms folded across his chest. "You may as well stay there you ol' codgers. I'm glad to see you're still in one piece. As for you," he points to Lucky, "I'll thank you not to go AWOL on my watch again."

Panzer and Kampf sink back down gratefully. They've worked harder than anyone today.

"Police were round ours earlier," continues Overalls, pulling out a tangle of brown stuff and rolling it into a tiny piece of paper, "wanting to know where two young men are. Seems they're missing." He looks around. "They're obviously not here." He turns to go, then stops. "Let us know if you need help. We've got a few guns." He licks one side of the paper and smoothes it with his finger. "It's going to come to that one day. We'll have to defend ourselves." Casting a last ominous look at the gathered company, he sticks his creation behind his ear and retreats into the descending night.

The night! I hope that Sammie's all right in the forest. I sent an extra pot of milk for him with Shakti. I know Mattie will be fine; he's the same age as Dhruva after all. I try to relax over supper and have faith in One and Two.

Three however does not relax. Since Overall's visit, she's been pacing up and down. Suddenly she comes to an abrupt halt. "It's not safe for us to stay here. They're on our trail. We'll all have to disappear into the forest. We can't risk it." She looks anxiously at her nails. "And we need to go now!"

Panzer and Kampf sigh deeply.

"Not you two," continues Three. "You're too big. You'll leave too much evidence in your wake."

The bulls cheer up and return to their munching.

"No, you two will have to stay behind the white ribbon."

The two oxen regurgitate a huge bolus of cud, and sigh even more deeply.

"You'll be on surveillance patrol." Three resumes her pacing, pointing a red talon. "You'll be our ears and eyes. You have an excellent vantage point at the top of the hill here. It's perfect. You can be liaison and informants. You'll be our first line of defence. You can position your heavy artillery to cover all directions, land, sky, or ocean." She pauses. "It might come to that."

P and K brighten at this and begin chewing over such details as calibre, range, mobility, rate of fire, angle of fire, and firepower.

"You'll be there come rain or shine," warns Three, but the boys aren't listening.

We quickly douse the fire and make our exodus into the blackness. Tiger leads the way having the sharpest night vision, but half way down the hill stops without warning and we all tumble on top of one another. We soon understand why. Not just sharp night vision but also sharp hearing. At first the footsteps are very faint, in the distance, but then they rapidly get louder. The earth begins to tremble and then out of the night appears a raging bull, charging our way!

A raging bull which turns out not to be a bull at all, but Katy B, complete with a small passenger, clinging desperately to her back. She screeches to a halt just in time.

Turns out, she's eager to join us, feeling like she's missing out on the action. She gazes at us with pleading eyes.

Her passenger with mutinous ones.

"I'll do anything," moos Katy B.

"She could help you, Lucky," says Three.

"Hmmph," grunts Lucky doubtfully. "Can you do anything? Apart from kicking milk pails over? Can you produce meals instantly according to people's desires?"

"Well... no. But... I'm willing to learn!"

"You can train her up," says Three. She turns to the passenger who has given up trying to cling on to Katy B's back and now stands before us, arms folded, chin up.

"What about you? What can you do?"

"I can do heaps of things," scoffs the passenger. "I already know all your jungle skills."

"Leave him to me," mews Tiger, "I'll make a man out of him. He can be our scout."

A faint smile flickers across Barney's face.

By the time we get to our Queen Tree, Sammie is fast asleep. Two says he didn't miss me at all and she fed him milk by letting him suck her finger. Shakti is by the tree waiting for us. She's delighted at the prospect of more fresh cream, welcoming Katy B and enquiring what her role will be. Katy B shakes her horns proudly, replying that she will be involved with provisions. Lucky throws her a pained glance.

Queen Tree seems delighted to have so much company. She also seems relieved when she hears that Panzer and Kampf won't be coming.

"It wasn't their fault about your... you know... brothers and sisters," pipes up Katy B earnestly.

Lucky gives her a cautionary wave with her great horns and the young cow pipes down and gives a little curtsey.

Mattie is full of all he's been doing since he arrived in the forest. He eyes Barney speculatively and asks Two what *he's* doing here?

Barney draws himself to his full height, gaining at least half a head over Mattie. "I'm going to be the scout. I get to check out the lay of the land and deliver vital information. *And.* Do real spying! I'll probably be the most important person in the whole operation."

"Well! I was here first," retorts Mattie.

"Alright everybody, better settle down for the night," says Three, "we can establish the pecking order in the morning." She wields one of Sammie's new stick weapons ominously. "Along with our strategy."

I look round at the scene before me and sigh contentedly. I'm happy to be back in the forest, not only in the company of Queen Tree but especially with the boys! I couldn't have wished for a better outcome.

"Outcome?" Three laughs without humour. "We've only just begun." She gives a determined thwack of the stick weapon. "Okay, troop! Time to sleep." She frowns. "We're going to need it."

She surveys the comrades and released prisoners all curling up and bedding down for the night, rats and rabbits snuggled up to cats, monkeys and humans snuggled up to cows, One and Two a bit off to the side whispering intensely.

"Lights off in the barracks!" she barks. At which the half moon, whose soothing light is filtering through the trees, quickly hides its face behind a cloud.

Long into the night, while snores and snuffles mix with owls' screeches, I hear her pacing up and down, beating the stick weapon.

# Chapter Twenty

# Tilting The World

However, the next morning there's not much time for establishing pecking orders or even strategy. Barney makes an initial sortie well before dawn.

"It's not fair," grumbles Mattie. "Why can't I go?"

"Because you, young man," says One sternly, "are a wanted person. The policemen are on your trail and you have to stay in hiding." She gives him a glare that could freeze fire. "You're going to have to be *very* brave and *very* strong."

Mattie eyes her thoughtfully. "You mean like when I controlled my volcano and drove the Tesla?"

"Precisely," agrees One, shaking his hand solemnly. From that moment on, Agent and boy have what you'd call an understanding.

Understanding, but not peace. At that moment, Barney sprints back to base camp flushed, sweating, and spitting out his words. "Che and Fid... I mean Panzer and Kampf say the police have been up again checking out the whole property. They were just leaving the shed last night as the car arrived so they hid behind the spaceship and did some spying." He pauses and takes a huge breath. Sammie rushes to give him a cup of water, which he waves away.

"The police were looking through the shed, picking up stuff and taking fingerprints. They felt the fire. It was still warm." He bends double, gasping for breath. "They're coming back at first light to comb the whole forest with tracker dogs and helicopters."

The Agents immediately spring into action, barking orders and thwacking sticks. Rats stream everywhere getting under cows' feet, rabbits collide with kittens and the two rhesus monkey mothers start lashing out at everyone in sight.

All at once, a booming rumble rolls over us, "Peasse, my friendss, my ssubjectss!"

Everyone stops and looks up. It is our Queen! We quickly scramble to find a place at her feet and await her decree in silence. The pecking order has begun.

"You musst learn to cooperate. Many yearss ago, when my brotherss and ssisterss were taken we did not have that posssibility. You do. Don't throw it away. Everyone hass hiss or her unique talentss, which are necesssary for thiss to ssucceed. Your job iss to disscover and usse them to their besst advantage. I for exsample, have my height. I can ssee for miless. And I can interssept and sspy on helicopterss."

There's a short cheer at this.

The Queen nods her branches graciously. "I alsso have my

yearss of exsperiensse." Her branches rustle. "We are in a sstate of emergenssy. We are under sseige! There iss no room," here she drops a leaf on Mattie and another on Lucky, "for perssonal agendass or internal quarrelss. We musst unite!"

There's a louder cheer.

Our Queen continues, "I ssuggesst that Agent Two be in charge of Offenssive Tacticss, Agent One Defensse and Agent Three Desseption. The resst of you can disstribute yoursselvess according to where you ssee your talentss besst ssuited. All right that iss all. I hear the whine of a helicopter and the disstant yelping of dogss. We musst prepare oursselvess without delay."

In less than a minute, everyone is in their respective division, busily making plans and listening attentively to orders. Of course, the Agents are expert in jungle warfare. Soon we are at our posts ready for action.

The cats are to lead the dogs off the trail on a merry dance all over the jungle. The rabbits are to dig burrows all over the area for escape hatches. The monkeys are to take on an aerial bombing raid, leaping through the branches and bombarding the enemy with cones and whatever else they can find. The monkey mothers have permission to take out their aggression where they deem appropriate but blood should be shed only as a last resort. The rats are to trip the humans up and scurry away as quick as lightning. The cows and I are in the defence division, the girls with their terrifying horns, and me with my flashing weapons. Using my fire weapon, I will create a ring of fire that flares up if anyone comes within a certain radius of our Queen. Under her beneficent shelter, my sons will be concealed in an underground hideaway, which they're now excavating in total cooperation, not a single "it's not fair" between them.

The rabbits are a bit unsure about digging, having lived their whole lives in cages, but the rabbits from under the spaceship container have been draughted in to assist by our scout, Barney. The latter also has orders to go and warn P and K to be on the alert with their heavy artillery as the time is nigh. Barney scoffs that the bulls had it all set up ages ago, and then tells One that his granddad is keen to join in the offence if we'll have him. Of course, we're happy to have the extra help, though as we will discover, the more members you have, the more challenging it can become.

We've all been briefed by Three, Commander of Deception Special Division, that the enemy are not to know what's hit them and not to realise that anything is out of the ordinary. She gives Overalls a stern look. We don't want to attract more attention. We want them to be satisfied they've combed the whole area and not found anything. In that sense, the Deception Division is the most crucial. Here she gives her hair a little pat, checks her nails and asks us if we understand.

By the time we hear the *chop chop* of the helicopters and the baying of the dogs we're ready.

It's not the longest battle ever fought, but there are some supremely memorable manoeuvres. Manoeuvres that will no doubt go down in the annals of history. Tiger objects that she doesn't know nothing about history, but I have no doubt that she'll be telling the story to her kittens, and they'll be telling the story to their kittens, for many generations to come.

The Queen seems to be everywhere at once, intercepting the four helicopters and scanning the horizon for further aerial attacks. With great regularity, huge canon balls of cow dung land splat in the path of the opposition, causing them to slip over or even better, indelibly besmirching their glowing school playground jackets, or best of all hitting a bull's eye and blinding them completely. The cow dung assault is relentless and even strikes the helicopters and their pilots when they swoop within range.

Shakti, Tiger and their band of kittens are splaying the dogs out in all directions, peering over their shoulders with come-hither glances and then bounding off through the undergrowth in the opposite direction from our Queen, so that the dogs and their handlers believe they've covered every inch. Moreover, the animals of Agent Two's Offence Division are coated with Mattie and Sammie's smell, (first thing this morning, Mattie and even Sammie were rubbing mouths with the kittens, while the monkeys picked through their hair, the rats ran up and down their arms and the mother monkeys gave them affectionate biffs for practice. The rabbits, however, stayed well clear, as the last thing we wanted was the dogs sniffing out the escape tunnels).

Every time the opposing ranks come close to the Queen, they're butted by horns, which appear to be intransigent branches. Dogs are tossed, yelping in the air. Humans curse and try to find a new route. Or else they see flames shooting up and believing they've discovered a new geothermal area, beat a hasty retreat. Sometimes I use my shield and they experience an impenetrable thicket of vines.

Overalls wanders round with his gun, firing the odd shot into the air. When he encounters one of the opposition, he tells them innocently that he's been ordered by the council to cull the deer and he's only doing his duty. And no, he hasn't seen or heard anything and he's been in the forest all night.

Barney is our eyes, ears, and legs. He's up with Panzer and Kampf replenishing their canon fodder, liaising with the Agents, tracking the humans and the dogs and giving signals to the different divisions by means of prearranged birdcalls.

The Agents are everywhere too, providing water, urging us on, checking out the play, leading the charge, co-ordinating the action, in full-on camouflage mode at all times. Even Three pulls her sleeves up. They're in their element and the power is always on the side of those who are in their element, whereas the opposition are floundering around, muttering, "Bloody native bush, eh?" Although by the time it's over, Three's nails are in shreds.

We also have some unexpected but welcome help from other inhabitants. Initially, Three is worried because they haven't been briefed; but not only do they operate on the basis of inside tips from the Great Soul Herself, but also, because they're natives, they don't arouse any suspicion. Deer appear to be wandering peacefully through the forest, then with no warning leap through the air landing almost on top of a dog or a human, frightening them practically, but not quite, to death. The opposition will be going in one direction when all of a sudden a wild pig will charge them from the rear. The possums wake up and join with the monkeys. When someone looks up to see what's hit them, all they see is a possum fast asleep in a tree.

However, the biggest surprise assistance of all is the cloud. Agent Three tells us weather can be used to one's advantage in warfare and certainly, the weather must be on our side. While the Queen is dealing with two helicopters, two reinforcements come into view and they're out of canon firing range. Against the clear blue sky, a huge white cloud, appears, which looks vaguely familiar. It divides itself into two and swarms around the reinforcement helicopters, which are soon buzzing into the distance like angry wasps.

By twelve hundred hours, it's all over. The men and dogs retreat from the forest, hands in the air, tails between their legs. "I think the bush has beaten us this time..." "Native bush, eh..." "Didn't locate missing persons but there's no way they'd survive in that..." "Either they're dead or they're not there..." "Bloody jungle..."

As they depart, a rain of soft white feathers floats down from heaven, dusting the ground and gently adhering to their cow-dunged playground jackets.

When we all reconvene at the foot of our Queen, everyone is excitedly chattering about their exploits, "Did you see when I dropped an old nest on that guy?" "At one point I had five dogs on my tail!" "I got three dogs at once with my horns!" "Did you see that canon ball knock off the helicopter? That's some fire power!" This last from Panzer and Kampf who've been allowed into the forest, eyed warily by our Queen, on the basis that the whole place has been laid to waste anyway in this morning's skirmish. Moreover, although we don't expect an immediate return to this location, they must resume their posts smartly as soon as we've had our debrief. During all this, there's not a single "it's not fair" from Mattie and Sammie, who are in fact looking rather smug. While all the action has been going on above ground, they, in cooperation with the rabbits, have been busily tunnelling an underground labyrinth. They proudly take us for a guided tour of the subterranean pirate spaceship.

Surprisingly, the "it's not fairs" are coming from a different quarter. Our Queen recommends we have some sustenance before we do anything else and on this topic a dissension has arisen among the ranks, namely between the provisions officers and the feline members of the company. Lucky draws the line at catering non-veg diets, insisting that it's against her principles and the feline brigade can live on cream, or be responsible for their own karma, by catching their own.

Shakti and Tiger on the other hand, grumble that it's not fair; their needs should be catered for. They work as hard as anyone else does. They don't see why they should do extra work on top and besides, they need non-veg for their eyesight. They'll go blind without their taurine supply and then where will we be in the forest, depending on human eyes? At this, the other animals bristle slightly, but remembering our Queen's instructions, say nothing.

Fortunately, rather than grumbling behind backs, politicking amongst the divisions and stirring up general dissension, which could destroy all we have achieved so far, they have brought the debate to the feet of our Queen where it can be discussed in a productive manner.

The Queen mediates sympathetically, "Doess anyone have

any ssuggesstionss?"

Overalls raises his gun and offers to deal to that side of things.

A grey kitten then speaks up timidly, "I haven't had much practise at Catch Your Own and I'm just starting to get the hang of it. I'm getting quite a thirst for the thrill of the chase."

A couple of the other ex-prisoner felines nod in agreement. "We need it to hone our skills..." "It's our nature..."

Meanwhile the rats and the rabbits are looking very uneasy.

We haven't reached a final conclusion yet, because everyone is getting hungry. But after some back and forth, the suggestions on the table are that Lucky try her hand at providing veg dishes which contain taurine, possibly soy based; the cats can continue to CYO if they feel the urge, but strictly not on our own patch; and Overalls can do a little providing on the side, as long as he promises that his prey can kill him next time round. Katy B has a little glint in her eye but I'm not sure what that's about.

We finally sit down to a delicious rejuvenating repast of tender lettuce, dandelion leaves and rocket; cheese; fruits provided by the trees, including bananas; cream; soft, new grass and twigs; vegetables and curds fried in golden clarified butter and fresh bread; plus whatever else the cats add into the mix.

Before we're half way through however, Three stands up and bangs her spoon on her plate for attention, announcing that we will all reconvene at fourteen hundred hours to debrief and to shape our next plan of attack. Because, as she cautions us, "Don't think we're out of the woods yet."

After we've thrown away our golden utensils in the disposal area, we drift over to the boulders downstream from the waterfall where I came for my daily meditation. Three has informed us that we're going to debrief here. Our Queen can see everything from her vantage so she doesn't mind. Only P and K are grumbling because they've been ordered back on surveillance. We almost have another confrontation about this. "How can we be part of the plan if we don't know all the details..." "But then who's going to watch out above..." Finally, two of the rats offer to do a turn on sentry duty as the Great Soul will keep them informed and they can probably be more... ahem... discreet in their tracking of any possible alien approaches. One of them can streak down the hill like lightning if there's anything to report and it's not as though P and K have to maintain the pretence about the white ribbon any more. The seeds of further dissension seem about to sprout, however, as Barney senses his privileged position as chief scout being stolen from under him.

Tiger challenges him, "Are you a man or a mouse?"

The rats grin at each other. They have their own version of that, namely, are you a rat or a mouse? Barney looks doubtful but stops complaining.

However when we've all gathered on the boulders and the river bank he can't resist one further complaint. "We didn't take even one Prisoner of War." He eyes the deep water hole below the waterfall. "I wanted to make someone walk the gang plank."

Tiger pats him indulgently. "That's the man."

Then Three shouts, "Attention!"

Everyone becomes silent except for Mattie whose sole voice sings out, "All eyes upon you!" He clenches his fists and glowers at Sammie. One raises an eyebrow at him and he subsides.

Three struts back and forth on a huge boulder in front of us, thwacking her stick. The stone remains unmoved.

"We're going to watch a short action replay of this morning's engagement. Then we'll take any questions and comments." She scans her audience. "After that we'll have an update on the situation and plan out our next pre-emptive move."

The replay is going to be viewed in the cascading water of the waterfall. At first, there's only the sound of the water thundering into the water hole below, but then, to our delight, scenes from this morning begin to emerge along with the appropriate audio accompaniment. It's inspiring to see how valiantly everyone played their part. Afterwards there are no questions or comments as we sit in appreciative silence.

Before we can become too sentimental, however, or rest on our laurels, Three is smacking her stick on her palm and moving us on to the update of the situation. The scene in the waterfall transforms and a man's head appears. I'm sure I know him, but I can't quite place him. Then he starts speaking and I realise he's the dejected man from the facility television! At first, he's not looking quite as jaded as he was on that particular day, but as he talks, he becomes increasingly gloomy, along with his entire audience.

The scene first zooms in on a white house, surrounded by tall trees, where a couple, one dark and bespectacled and one petite and bird-like, sit huddled together on a green couch. The woman looks out at us, her face contorted with pain, tears streaming down her cheeks. The man takes his spectacles off and vigorously wipes his sunken eyes.

The man from the television asks them what's going on and the woman replies that they don't know where their grandsons are. Police have been out all night searching for them with dogs and helicopters and there's no sign.

The scene changes to a police officer, plastered in white feathers. "We combed every square inch using our best tracker dogs and not a sign. Now we have to widen the search. But of course every day that these boys, Matthew and Samuel Harrison are missing, the hope of finding them alive decreases. We urge anyone who has any information to come forward..."

The scene reverts to the distraught woman. "The worst thing is that it happened while they were in our care. I should never have grumbled about looking after them. We let them down, and their father, who refuses to talk to us," she swipes her eye with her hand, "and their mother. But she's also missing and presumed dead. We really don't know. She's believed to have been on that plane that went missing, or she committed suic..." Here she completely breaks down.

The man takes over. "And on top of that I lost my job and caused no end of problems in the department. Not that that is important, relatively speaking, but just letting you all know that on top of everything else it was the final straw, isn't it?" He blows his nose hard.

Trying to be jaunty, but failing miserably, the television man continues, "And where is Matthew and Samuel's father in all this? He is apparently on trial for a series of major and minor thefts. Why was he not looking after his sons and what does he have to say for himself?"

The scene zooms in on a pathetic bundle of rags shuffling along the road under pelting rain. I notice Three watching very attentively, her stick is still. The bundle of rags arrives at a black iron gate, opens it and goes up a brick pathway. The scene changes to the bedraggled bundle sitting on a velvet chair inside a peach coloured room, tears streaming down his face.

He looks out at us, despair etched on his haggard face and pleads, "If anyone knows anything about the whereabouts of my sons, please, please tell us. I've been out searching for them all night. If anything happens to them, I don't know what I'll do… I just lost my wife in that missing plane. That was my fault. I'll never forgive myself. The whole thing is my fault because I didn't look after her properly."

He buries his head in his hands. Mattie and Sammie are transfixed, tears streaming down their faces. They aren't the only ones.

The scene changes once more. The television man appears outside a wooden building with a high archway. "Matthew Harrison had recently started attending this school and it is from here that he went missing late yesterday morning. There are varying accounts of what happened."

Denise appears in voluminous black. "One minute he was with us and the next he was late for assembly. The whole assembly was interrupted. We're all most upset. Especially poor Tony."

Tony Hardcastle appears, speaking from the day room in the psychiatric facility, where we see a miniature television behind his head showing Tony Hardcastle speaking from the dayroom in the psychiatric facility. "Suddenly this man just grabbed Mattie and ran off, I didn't have a chance to stop him. At least I think that's what happened... or maybe Mattie ran out by himself? I know he wasn't very happy at school... we had that in common."

The television man says, "So what did happen? The children say something different..."

A six-year-old girl speaks confidently out of the waterfall, "It was a teacher who took him. I know, because she said, 'All eyes upon me!'"

Then another child blurts out, "No it was a witch..."

The scene shifts once more. This time we're outside a black gate. We go through it to find Georgina sitting at a low table covered with white circles daubed with green goo, tears streaming down her face. "It would have to be Sammie. It's the second time it's happened to him. Because everyone wants Sammie. We all love him so much and we really miss him. I feel so guilty. I don't know how he got out. When we found he was missing, the gate was securely locked. And he was such a happy little chap." She weeps softly. "Of course we want to do anything we can to help with the search."

Sammie's little mouth is quivering.

The scene moves on to the playground of Mattie's old school where Catherine, other teachers and the whole school of forty children appear grief stricken. Akul and Sofie are crying.

Catherine addresses us from the waterfall, "This is a small school. We're like a big family and we love all our children like our own, even after they've left us. We're all completely devastated, especially after one of our ex-teachers was lost on that plane. We're reeling. We're holding a twenty-four hour vigil and of course making ourselves available for whatever we can do."

The next scene shows Irene looking traumatised after being hauled over the coals by her supervisor. "You can't win as a social worker. Damned if you do, damned if you don't."

The media according to TV man is having a field day. "Should Irene Stoddard have taken these children away and put them in the care of their grandparents? Or have CYFS bungled it yet again?"

Then Fern appears, weeping quietly. "I've tried to explain to Jay but he won't talk to me..."

Three utters a low moan.

TV man ploughs relentlessly on, "So it seems Matthew and Samuel aren't the only members of the Harrison family to be missing. But where is their mother, Amalia Harrison? Another of life's mysteries. The airlines say she had checked in and boarded the missing flight ER 247. No one seems to have heard from her since."

"That was a very tough day for everyone. One pilot was suicidal and no one was coping. The plane should never have taken off," says a red-lipped woman in a beige suit.

"But," continues TV man, "one psychiatric nurse claims

she might have the answer."

The scene returns to the psychiatric facility day room where Tony sits in one chair and Dora in another and there's Stanley also, waving at us out of the waterfall.

"Things were down all over the city that day. I was late in. I'm never late in. I wasn't my usual self. I saw her just walk out of the window." Dora sighs and shakes her head. "I didn't have the energy to clear it up. It's the second suicide we've had in two weeks."

Then a huge face appears in the waterfall yelling at us that it's not funny and it's nothing to laugh at! The scene abruptly cuts to water then instantly transforms to a dingy room with a picture of a man with a small moustache on the wall. A gaunt figure sits on a grimy bed. On a table is a bowl, brimming over with squashed ciggie ends. The waterfall zooms in on his face and he's crying.

Then the scenes start shifting very rapidly – a miserable looking Priya with a bruised cheek; the families of the scientists whose work was ruined; the families of the people who committed suicide that fateful day, when the rate spiked randomly; the families of the passengers on the missing plane; the families of the search and rescue team who risk their lives to save children and are all suffering post jungle warfare trauma, what to speak of their dogs, and won't be available to save children whose lives really are in danger. Then it's just the waterfall, relentlessly thundering into the water hole below.

The whole assembly remains as motionless as the boulders. Three doesn't get up to rally us. There are no questions, comments, or pre-emptive plans. Our Queen sighs as the gloom of the night descends.

All at once, there's a rustling and crunching of twigs from the riverbank. A small shape leaps headlong into the water then crawls up onto Three's boulder, looking like a drowned rat. He turns to face the dismal crowd, gasping for breath. "An alien vehicle," puff pant, "stopped outside base HQ. Two men went inside." He pauses for breath and surveys our stunned expressions. No one moves. "What? Aren't you going to do anything? I did that whole rat race for nothing?"

Three listlessly picks up her stick then puts it down. The Queen says nothing. All that can be heard is the sound of Mattie and Sammie wailing over the roar of the waterfall, "I miss my Dada!" "Poor Nani!"

Barney puts his arms round their shoulders.

Then there's a much louder rustling and crunching of twigs and suddenly, in the growing gloom, two white feathers appear, phosphorescent against the night, and float gently over to Three's boulder.

Then a voice comes through the darkness, "Ah, I thought I smelled a rat." A pause. "A very natural smell I always say."

I'd know that voice anywhere.

I place my chalice of fire on a rock in the centre of the gathering, and in the golden flames we see the gentle smile of the Dean. In his hands, he bears aloft the two white feathers.

"We come in peace, comrades," he smiles round at the assembly. Then he turns slightly and bows low. "Your Majesty."

The rat is sitting on the rock with Three and the Dean

looking a bit puzzled. Then in the radiance of the fire, another figure hesitantly separates itself out of the shadows.

"Dada?"

The rat says, "I thought I smelled *two* aliens!"

Three smiles bashfully.

Then Mattie, Sammie and Dada are jumping over the boulders to clasp each other so tightly it looks as though they'll never let go again.

Our Queen calls for silence. "Welcome to our two emisssariess." She bows her top branches in benediction. "Now let uss hear their messsage."

Three is sitting close to Husband and the boys as the Dean rises to address the assembly. He closes his eyes for a minute as if to gather his thoughts. Then he delivers his message.

"I have the honour of being spokesperson this evening. I assure you I come as an ambassador of peace and goodwill. I would like to propose peace talks, a negotiation whereby we can resolve the present state of conflict, which is affecting many lives." He surveys the assembled company.

"What may I ask is your long term plan?" Here everyone shuffles uncomfortably. But he's not really talking to everyone. "Are you planning to continue tilting the world on its axis? To continue holding the world to ransom?" His eyes, hitherto so gentle, now bore into me.

"You could have received the benediction of the highest love it is possible to experience. You could have chosen the highest good for the world. You were given that opportunity. But no. What did you choose? You chose Power. You chose

Victory. You chose to fulfil your own personal agenda. You still haven't learned.

"No one is able to move on after the episode in the city; a plane is lost, lives are disrupted. There are ramifications. You've caused a lot of chaos, harmed many people. What are you adding to the sum of universal peace? Causing more conflict, more suffering. Is that what you came for?" His eyes flash with anger. "I expected better of you than this. Do you want to return to the scene of falling concrete and blood?"

A cold fear creeps over me. "What are you asking me? If I go back, they'll put me back in the facility, fill me full of sweets and take the boys away, not let them visit me... We'll be worse off than ever. I can't go back to that. I have to fight for my family. The other mother said..."

His eyes are gentle but firm. "You won't succeed by fighting Goddess. You'll have to find another way. You're not going about things," he smiles apologetically round at the Agents, "very intelligently, if you don't mind my saying so.

"You see..." He pauses for a moment. "Let's take vaccinations for example. They may indeed be wonderful; they do *indeed* cure many dangerous illnesses. But! They may bring a whole gamut of further problems in their wake. It's an endless cycle of cause and effect. If you try and avoid the effects at the same level they were caused, you'll never be free."

"I don't know if I understand what you're asking..." I begin.

"Just this: If you continue to use power to get your own way at other peoples' expense, your future doesn't look bright. I trust," his gaze includes the Agents, "you will all use your discrimination to work out what that means. But there must be no tinge of personal ambition, desire or agenda if you wish to escape the cycle."

I imagine a few of us are looking quite stricken. Why do things have to change? Why can't we just stay here forever with our Queen? We're so happy. Why does everything have to be spoiled? We're doing all right, aren't we?

"I thought you were on my side!" I cry out in anguish.

He shakes his head and smiles sadly. "It's not a question of sides, Goddess." He scans the assembly. "Even amongst you," His eyes fall on Lucky and Shakti, "chaos has started to infiltrate... dissensions amongst the ranks, which you can rest assured will manifest more and more. Conflict is inevitable. You have to find a way beyond it." He holds my eyes with his. "And it lies with you to resolve the chaos, to set the world back on its axis."

He remains standing in silence. An owl screeches overhead. The wind rustles in the branches. The waxing moon comes up and guilds the summit meeting in pale silver. No one dares to move. The Dean gazes around the chastened assembly with utmost gravity. "Thank you for allowing me to address you all this evening, it has been a privilege." He bows to us and to the Queen, then nods to Husband apparently signalling their departure.

I jump up and grab his arm. "What's going to happen now? You can't just leave like that. Are you going to tell them we're here? If you do that, we'll be finished!"

The rest of the company jostle forward, their fate in the hands of this man. Will the rats have to go back to their cages?

The rhesus monkey to the pit of despair?

"I told you I came in peace. I will honour my word. However, I feel it is only fair to put people out of their misery regarding the safety of the children and to call off the search. So what do you suggest?"

Everyone starts talking at once, "Maybe the boys should go with Jay?" "No, then Irene would take them away again." "Maybe we shouldn't tell anyone?"

Three starts thwacking her stick and shouting, "Attention!" But no one pays her any attention.

Mattie and Sammie are crying and clinging to Husband to prevent him leaving. Suddenly a loud shot blasts through the pandemonium, followed by instant silence, broken only by a whirring of wings and an indignant squawking overhead.

Overalls plants himself in front of the Dean, obdurate as the God of Death. He looks him squarely in the eye. "You can tell the grandparents they're safe, you can tell them to call off the search. But tell them this too… If anyone, and I mean anyone, comes snooping up here trying to find them, they'll never lay eyes on them again. Is that clear, Mr. Peace Envoy?"

There's a general grunting, squeaking and mewing of approval. Everyone turns to me. I look expectantly at the Agents but they're looking at me.

"Okay," I say finally. "I can't think of any other way. At least," I look at Three helplessly, "until we have our long term plan sorted."

The Dean seems disappointed. "That's your final verdict?"

There's a half hearted "yes", and he turns to make his way up the hill.

Husband is giving the boys a last hug. "You have to be strong Mattie and look after Sammie. We'll all be together soon."

Mattie scoffs, "I'm already strong. I can control my volcano."

Sammie pipes up, "I don't need looking after. I'm stwong too! I have my feather!"

Husband turns to me. "It was nice to be together tonight the four of us, wasn't it?" He takes my hand gently. "You seem very quiet, Am, are you alright?"

I glance up at him in disbelief. "I didn't spend much time with you at all. You were sitting next to Three the whole time."

"Who the hell's Three? We all sat together, don't you…? Oh, Am…" He takes me in his arms and whispers into my hair, "We've been through a lot, haven't we?"

"Can't you stay?"

"I want to, but I can't." He takes a step back, holding my hands. "I'm on bail conditions… because we tried to escape. I have to stay with the Dean until…" a shadow crosses his face, "the trial." He drops my hands and adds unconvincingly, "I'm sure it'll all work out."

The Dean is already striding off through the foliage.

"I have to go." Husband looks me up and down wistfully. "You're looking so good, Am, despite everything…" He turns to go and soon disappears into the night, leaving Mattie, Sammie and Three gazing after him.

And of course me, still arrayed in my battle dress.

# Chapter Twenty One

# Personal Ambition

**W**as the Dean's prophecy a curse? I don't know if even he could have predicted how rapidly the chaos would invade our ranks, like some insidious disease for which we have no vaccination.

Three has not been herself since last night. She keeps muttering, "We're not out of the woods yet" and swiping her stick forlornly at unseen objects. She's lost her pizzazz. She has several hairs out of place, her suit is rumpled, her nails are still in tatters and her skin has taken on a faint greenish tinge.

Lucky has declared all we're getting is porridge this morning, because she caught Katy B doing a black market deal to acquire taurine containing substances from some local wild boar, and she wants to ban her from the kitchen. They've reached a bit of a standoff. The cats have disappeared somewhere distant to satisfy their cravings. The rabbits have been arguing all night over who's going to have the best rooms in the underground palace and haven't surfaced yet.

Some rats are blaming the sentries for allowing two aliens to enter our midst. They could have done something. P and K would have. They must have ratted on them. "Rat fink!"

But other rats take the sentry rats' side. "Just cos you're a wimpy hood rat!" "Sack rat!" "You're like rats deserting a sinking ship!"

It's like civil war. The monkey mothers have reverted to conditioning and are biffing everyone in sight. The babies are cowering balls of misery.

Mattie and Barney have had a fight and the latter has gone up the hill to his granddad in tears.

Sammie is sitting in front of the waterfall wailing, "I want to watch something!"

Mattie turns on him, with clenched fists. "Sam*mie!*"

Panzer and Kampf have resumed sentry duty behind the white ribbon, out of frustration at the porridge austerities, although they never argue with each other since they are always of one mind.

One and Two however, are not.

"I told you from day one that she should have eaten her sweets! But no, you said..."

"Oh yeah? You bigoted old redneck, you think you're so clever you don't even know about conflict theory. If it was left to you we'd all still be in the bloody facility!"

Our Queen is very quiet. I sit under her shelter and try to focus my mind on my mantra. It's not easy. My heart hankers for the early days when it was just us. The Agents were still

Voices then and we were happy in the forest, depending on the trees to shelter and provide for us, satisfied with a little fruit and water. Above all, my mind was focused on the Great Soul and I was peaceful, swimming in an ocean of delight. Now we've grown so big, we're having opulent feasts on gold plates and squabbling over facilities. My mind is more shredded than Three's nails and incapable of focusing on the task entrusted to us, or should I say me?

But there's no time to lament. Without warning, there's a thunderous crack and two marching figures storm into the camp. It's Overalls followed by Private Barney carrying a smoking gun on his shoulder.

"And Halt!" orders Overalls. "And stand at ease!"

Barney lowers the gun so the butt is resting on the ground. His big brown eyes burn with fervour.

"I'm giving him some training. Reckon we're going to have to defend the place sooner or later, after last night," announces Overalls cheerfully. His cheery tones echo eerily around the forest. Then he observes the plastic throwaway plates full of half-eaten watery porridge, the deserted camp. "What the hell's going on around here?"

"We seem to be experiencing a bit of chaos," I tell him.

"I'll give you chaos. D'ya think we've got time for chaos?" he splutters.

Barney strokes the gun, a malevolent glint in his eye.

Overalls turns to Barney. "Round up the troops," he snarls. "Use the gun if you have to."

"Wait! That's not how the Dean said to do it. That's not going to work!"

"Oh no? And when Mr Peacenik tells everyone what's going down here, you think they're going to leave us in peace then, my pretty Goddess? Oh no! Then the shit is really going to hit the fan. Believe you me. I don't trust them as far as I can throw 'em. You'll be back in the nuthouse before you can say schizophrenia." He turns on Barney. "What are you waiting for, lad?"

Barney's off like a flash, rallying the troops with the odd bird whistle and animal cry accompanied by a barrage of gunshots. The rats saunter along in dribs and drabs with indignant "what's ups?", rabbits casually pop their heads out of holes to weigh up if they really need to bother, cats stroll indolently through the undergrowth and monkeys lackadaisically swing from branches and vines. One is smirking, Two is sneering. Three shuffles along, looking forlornly off into the distance. Mattie stumbles, glowering, at the end of Barney's rifle. Sammie strides to the tree, brandishing an extra big stick. Lucky and Katy B are waving their horns at everyone. Panzer and Kampf are barging their way blindly through the bush, leaving a trail of smashed trees and saplings in their wake. A bevy of possums have taken up positions on high branches and are placing bets, while a couple of wild bore hang around the perimeter of the camp in hopes of scoring a deal. The deer are nowhere in sight.

Barney stands before the troops scrutinising them through the barrel of his gun.

"Line up!" barks Overalls.

The troops start pushing, shoving and yelling at each other. It's chaos. Barney fires two shots into the air and we all move reluctantly into some sort of haphazard line, rolling our eyes to the sky and nudging each other.

Then Overalls strides up and down the line, putting his face into individuals' faces and poking them in the chest. "You snivelling little rat… Don't you monkey round with me… Stop pussy footing around… Who do you think you are – a sacred cow…? Are you a man or a mouse…? And you, wipe that grin off your face right now, you're no one special, you're just a number… You all better remember where you came from! You've no cause to be proud."

Then he steps in front of me, puts his nose right into my face and jeers, "As for you…"

I feel my arms tingle. "Stop! This isn't right! This isn't how we're going to rectify things!"

Overalls still has his nose right up to mine.

"Oh no? And who's going to stop me? You, my pretty angel?"

The volcano inside me starts to erupt. My arms are burning. "Yes I will stop you!" I roar.

Overalls gestures to Barney, who aims his gun. I whip out my bow and golden arrows and take aim. Suddenly, there's a flash and Tiger soars through the air, claws outstretched to protect her young protégée. In one truti, my arrow soars, and the kitten falls limp at Barney's feet. Shakti leaps into the arena howling and scratching, Barney drops the gun and collapses at Tiger's still twitching feet.

There's a deathly hush. Mattie hurls himself onto Tiger's little body, wailing. Shakti is washing her desperately as though that could revive her limp corpse. Sammie tentatively strokes her with his feather but she doesn't move.

Far, far above us, our Queen sighs. "I've sseen it all before, countlesss timess. I'm getting sso tired. Sso very tired." She sways ominously. "You may bury your brave little fellow warrior besside me and we will be together."

Her trunk creaks and groans. The troop looks up fearfully.

Three emits a hollow laugh. "FUBAR. We're FUBAR."

Everyone stares at the jaded soldier.

She turns glazed eyes upon us. "We're fucked up beyond all recognition."

"Ah," sighs the Queen. "Maybe not. Maybe not after all."

We look up and there shimmering above us is Nevaeh, smiling down with infinite sadness and compassion.

Immediately, the Agents stand to attention. The animals line up behind them, except Shakti who is keening along with Mattie, Barney and me, next to the body of her only remaining daughter. The animals are bewildered and shocked. They need someone to organise them and reassure them. There's a loud splash from the river but no one pays it any attention.

"Uhuh," says Three, eyes focused once more. "Yep. Okay will do."

One and Two are also nodding sagely at something. Sammie and the animals appear to be regaining some sense of purpose too. However, Panzer, Kampf and Katy B are shuffling anxiously. Next thing, all three are crashing through the few remaining trees to get to the waterfall. What now? This is beginning to turn into a hellish planet. The hell we witnessed in the waterfall has visited itself upon our band of hopeful warriors.

Three has picked up her stick and One and Two are urgently conferring with her, nodding and gesticulating.

"Attention, everyone," says Three in a very gentle un-Three-like voice. "It's time to get going." She looks round. "Where's Overalls?"

Barney looks worried. "I think I know where he might be." He rushes off in the direction of the waterfall.

"And where are Panzer and co?"

A minute goes by and we can stand the tension no longer. To a woman, child and animal, (minus Shakti and Tiger), we hasten to the waterfall, where we're met by an extraordinary sight. Panzer and Kampf are up to their necks in the waterhole beneath the falls, struggling to keep their balance on the stony riverbed. Beside them bubbles are coming up to the water's surface. The rats seem about to jump in followed by the other animals. I'm holding Sammie's hand, but Mattie is clambering onto the boulder by the water hole.

"I can swim," he says. "I'll save them!"

"No!" screams One, leaping after him, just in time to grab him.

Three stands up and I don't think I've ever seen her so powerful. "No animals or children are to jump in, I command you!" and with that she executes a perfect dive into the water, followed simultaneously by One and Two.

Soon Three surfaces with her arm around someone's neck and makes for the bank. Then One and Two emerge supporting someone else. Now Barney is coughing up water, but Overall's body appears to be lifeless.

Meanwhile the bulls are struggling to keep their heads above the surface. The monkey mothers start screeching and chattering and leaping into the vines. Soon they reappear dragging a long vine, which they place round P and K's necks. The young monkeys wind the other end of the vine around Lucky and Katy B's necks and the two cows strain together with the concerted effort of woman, child and creature, to pull the bulls out of the water. We toil and struggle until we reach our Queen, and loop the vine around her for a pulley. With a final vigorous tug, the bulls gain a foothold on the bank and heave themselves out of the water.

One has been administering the kiss of life to Overalls, but to no avail. Sammie rushes over, pulling out his feather and strokes Overall's chest gently. After a few moments, there's a slight rising and falling. We watch intently. Eventually there's a choking and spluttering and a great gush of water as he gasps his first shuddering breath.

The gun however, remains at the bottom of the river.


"Get up you old codger." Three pats Overalls affectionately on the back. "We haven't got time for personal agendas now okay? Don't worry, you're forgiven."

It seems as though we've received a crash course in how to get on and leave behind personal ambition. We're all chastened, none more so than Overalls, who hardly dares look any of us in the eye. He's haggard and bent as he silently follows Nevaeh's instructions to get his truck and bring it to the edge of the forest immediately, even though he's only just returned from the door of death.

We're going on a special reconnaissance mission and Mattie and Sammie are excited to be part of the action this time, along with a skeleton party. The soldiers who are staying back, maintain their composure magnificently without a whiff of "it's not fair". Besides, there's a lot to do at base camp. Keeping a look out remains crucial, because despite Overall's heavy-handed approach, he could well be right. Who knows if or when 'they' could be back? That's why time is of the essence. And just in case 'they' do come back there'll be a welcoming crew to greet them. But aside from this and executing the usual training manoeuvres, the crew at base camp have a special mission to help Panzer and Kampf with the development of some heavy duty machinery. Rabbits, flicking white tails darting everywhere, are already busy filling in the underground pirate spaceship. It only caused heartache in the end and unbeknownst to anyone has adversely impacted our Queen's root system. So much for personal agendas.

Katy B has promised something more than watery porridge for our meal. We need something to help us all with the shock. She'll be busy, as she hasn't mastered the instantaneous aspect of providing sustenance yet.

Shakti and Barney won't come either. They're maintaining vigil by the side of Tiger, watched over in turn by our ominously swaying Queen.

I ask the Agents if they're coming, but they look at me askance, asserting that they have tomorrow's whole strategy to plan. A feat that is going to be doubly, if not trebly complex and taxing if we're not permitted to use any force whatsoever. And better I don't ask too much.

Mattie and Sammie are already in the front of the truck by the time I reach the edge of the forest. Mattie is turning the pages of a small, familiar looking book; pages covered with green, crisscrossed with orange and red lines. Sammie has a small stick, which is not exactly a weapon, but could be useful for something. I open the door to get in the front too. But Overalls tells me he's already got four in the front, Mattie, Sammie, himself and their special *guest*. I'll have to sit up back with the animal delegates, Lucky, one kitten, one monkey mother, one monkey baby, one rabbit and one rat.

Soon we're bumping over the rocks and tussocks up the hill then right onto the stony road. We climb higher, passing through forest. After some time, we turn left again into a meadow. Now we're bouncing and lurching over a rough pitted track, like a roller coaster ride from the Easter Show. I wonder how Mattie and Sammie and the special guest are enjoying this in the front? The animals in the back are standing on their back legs looking over the top and the side of the truck, the wind blowing through their fur, pointing out sights and chatting to each other. Lucky stands her ground squarely, apparently enjoying the wind whistling through her horns, bringing all sorts of messages, a faint smile on her face. We're climbing, climbing. We suddenly lurch over a great gaping hole in the track and even Lucky has to adjust her stance. The rest of us are thrown into the air. We crash back onto the floor of the truck, but not before we've observed how the track ahead plummets down towards what looks like the edge of the world. We hold on as best we can with our various appendages and prepare for the downward plunge. Then we're zooming, bouncing and hurtling over the ground.

Bang! The truck stops dead. My heart lurches. I look round. But the animals appear as calm as if they'd just had a leisurely stroll in the pleasure gardens of Nandana-kanana. Overalls lowers the back of his truck and offers his arm to Lucky who steps daintily to the ground like a heavenly damsel dismounting from her flower aeroplane.

Our division gathers on the edge of the cliff to survey the terrain. Spread out before us is the ocean, the vast ocean, reflecting the white of the sky like a limitless pail of milk. The sun breaks through a crevice in the cloud picking out that small tortoise island rising from the water. Mattie and Overalls are studying the map book. Sammie is pointing at the island with his stick – he knew the stick would come in handy for something – having a wecce with the animals on such matters as tewain, twoops and twansportation. Nevaeh is hovering just to our left, apparently busy considering the situation herself and looking approving. Then she drifts out towards the island.

That island...

The white ocean glistens around it like a stage awaiting the arrival of the dancing girls.

And then, before you can say reconnaissance mission, the ocean *does* become a stage and before the astonished eyes of the surveillance crew, one by one, actors enter the scene and assume their places!

And more and more are now arriving until it seems there are hundreds of bejewelled figures, honourable and magnificent, assembling to one side of the island. Then, powerful avaricious beings, furiously uttering war cries, make their entrance, claiming the other side of the island. A huge serpent bursts forth from the ocean. The parties on either side of the island seize hold of the serpent! One takes the tail, the other the fire spewing head.

And now! Behold! The island rises up. It is indeed a massive, lumbering tortoise. With the great serpent wound around the tortoise's shell, both parties strain to haul the serpent rope back and forth, back and forth, churning the shimmering white ocean. The waves surge and swell, crashing against the cliff and showering us with milky droplets.

But then, what is this? A stream of black liquid rapidly begins to expand in all directions, obliterating the white sea. There's a collective gasp both from the churners and their audience. The black liquid glistens leaving a slick trail as it ebbs to and fro on the beach together with lifeless bodies of fish. It is the treacle from the two dollars shop! Gulls pick through the trail to find the fish but become entrapped. And now a dolphin arrives lifeless on the shore! Ah!

Voices and cries sound from the island. "Poison!" "Get out!" "Run!" "Escape!"

But the blackness now extends as far as the eye can see and is fast hurling its toxic secretions further and further up the cliff.

The crying becomes more desperate, "Help!" "Save us!" "Please!" as the resplendent beings find themselves overwhelmed by the surging venom. More creatures lie stranded and gasping on the shore, half in and half out of the water. Fish with fangs, half-animal half-fish. Backing away from the edge of the cliff, we gaze helplessly at the scene of devastation. All except Sammie, who lunges forward to the very brink of the cliff, brandishing his stick. No!

But in less than a truti, before I can even think, a monkey mother has leaped after the boy and grabbed him round the waist. Chattering and squealing, she drags him back to us, not a moment too soon, as the black starts to creep over the edge of the cliff. She gives him a quick biff and he sits chastened. Meanwhile, the cries from the Tortoise island become fainter and more creatures perish below. My arms begin to tingle.

Then all at once, a man appears upon the horizon... the man from... no. But... yes! Can it really be the man from the ugly furniture? The man from the computer monster? He has a river cascading onto his black locks, where sits a crescent moon, and yes, around his neck is curled a hissing snake. More poison? But wait...

The beautiful ones' cries become stronger as they fold their hands in prayer, "Om namah Shivaya! Please save us! Oh Lord!"

The glorious bluish man beholding the sea of poison, kneels upon the shore and in thunderous tones proclaims his duty to give protection and safety to all the living beings struggling for existence. "Bewildered by the illusory energy, the living beings are steeped in hatred and animosity. However, the noble ones, even risking their very lives, accept suffering to deliver others and so satisfy the Great Soul present in everyone's heart."

By this time, the black poison seems to have reached the ends of the earth and beyond. The compassionate one extends his palm across the ocean. "Therefore, let me drink this poison, for all living entities may thus become happy because of me."

Thereafter, although it is spreading far and wide across the universe, the black venom begins to recede until finally it is contained within the outstretched palm of the powerful but loving Lord Shiva. For indeed it is he. He lifts his hand, as the onlookers seem to hold their very breath, and slowly pours the terrible blackness down his throat. There is a gasp as a few drops of the poison spill. In no time the shore is teaming with snakes, scorpions, plants and other creatures, fighting to catch Lord Shiva's remnants.

Then a voice rumbles across the ocean like the rolling waves. "Lord Shiva is powerful and beyond death, but others who imbibe such poison will certainly be killed. No one else could tolerate the severe pain experienced by Lord Shiva..."

At this, my breasts begin to tingle and Mattie and Sammie move in close and take my hands.

The compassionate Lord remains upon the shore, his head bent as around his neck appears a vivid indigo line. While the honourable ones and the avaricious ones with great cries grab the ends of the serpent rope, eager to resume their churning.

Who knows what might issue forth? But then the newly rejuvenated ocean begins to boil and suddenly a shining *kamadhenu* cow, like Lucky, appears, followed by a pure white horse and a magnificent gem. Soon after, the splendid goddess of fortune, Lakṣmī, emerges from the swirling white water. Finally, Dhanvantari, whose palace Sammie and I visited together, appears. He is very beautiful, and carries a jug containing the nectar of immortality. Both the honourable and the avaricious scramble to lay claim to the oceans' spoils…

The map book has fallen from Mattie's hand and Sammie's stick is still. He is not asking to watch something. For several seconds no one speaks or moves as imperceptibly, the stage dissolves back into the ocean. Lord Shiva rides off over the horizon mounted on his great bull carrier and one by one, the honourable ones and the avaricious ones fade into sky. The only sounds are the pounding of the ocean at the foot of the cliff, where there lies not a single dead fish, and the gulls wheeling in the blue sky, their legs unencumbered by black venom.

Having reconnoitred the lay of the ocean, we return to the truck in silence, as if to speak might sully the vision. We hardly notice the bumps and lurches on the way back to base, if indeed there are any. Maybe we just fly on the wings of our dream?

Who knows how long after this we arrive back. Time has ceased to exist. When we finally emerge from the thicket into the clearing at base camp, Katy B is setting up silver plates. She glances shyly at Lucky. The rest of the troop, milling around, awaiting their repast, look up eagerly. The Agents hurry over, eyes shining.

"Well?" demands Three gently.

None of us responds for several moments, then finally Sammie pipes up, "Better not to ask too much."

The base camp crew have not been idle in our absence. Panzer and Kampf recruited most of the animals to consult on the prototype for the ultimate transportation model. They walk us systematically through the design process prior to actual viewing, illustrating each step with what they call a power point presentation shown on the few vines still in place near our Queen. Initially we were going to watch it on the waterfall, but no one seemed enthusiastic about that idea, not even Sammie. Sammie is however, very happy to use his stick as a pointer for the presentation, along with P and K's horns.

There were several designs mooted: bullock cart, rejected due to lack of capacity and the risk of alienating modern city dwellers by its unfamiliar nature. Despite P and K having their united hearts set on this idea, they admirably renounced personal agenda for the greater cause. Ditto regarding the original Panzerkampfwagen model, rejected on several counts, but primarily the militaristic first impression, which might run counter to our aims. One day we'll do both of them when all this is over they bellow cheerfully. Tesla: too small, been there, done that, boring. Double trailer truck: on the upside, ample space for everyone but rejected unanimously as far too reminiscent of cattle and chicken trucks.

The final design, although a complete prototype of its kind and thus still at a somewhat experimental stage, was accepted unanimously, for many reasons not least of which it is large enough for us all and it's vital for this mission that we're all together. It consists of a hybrid between a large recreational camper vehicle and a horse float. It's completely self-contained and has areas for all different types of folk. There's a mobile forest for the monkeys, a portable burrow maze for the rabbits, nesting holes for the rats and a self-replenishing wildlife reserve for the cats with soy based remote control mice. There are bedbathrooms and a kitchen, although Lucky who wasn't here during the consultation process questions the need for a kitchen. Katy B however, feels better to have it there as back up. There's a mini barn for the bovines, with no white ribbons, which doubles as a meeting hall in case of wet weather. A composting toilet for all, except the bovines whose dung will be used for heating, and cooking, if, of course any is done. Barney who also wasn't part of the design process suggests it can also be used for ammo just in case, but gets booed down, surely you've/we've learned our lesson etc.

There are two surprise elements to the vehicle. One will be revealed in a minute, but for the other we'll have to wait for tomorrow.

"Any questions or comments before we convert ourselves?" P and K gaze round at their spellbound audience.

The rat and the baby monkey who were with us on reconnaissance, politely raise their hands but all at once, Two is wildly waving her hand saying, "Ooh ooh pick me!" One laughs out loud and Two quickly lowers her hand, blushing furiously. "I was only going to say, it reminds me a bit of Kardama Muni's aerial mansion," she mumbles.

Which is interesting, because I was thinking exactly the same thing.

P and K are a bit put out at first, having thought their idea was original, but then they acknowledge ruefully that there's nothing new under the sun. Their design however being a uniquely twenty first century planet-earth-model, can still claim prototype status. They call on the rat and the baby rhesus to ask their question, but they've now forgotten what they wanted to say.

Then Mattie raises his hand and I think he speaks for the three young lads, none of whom have been involved in the consultation or design process, when he asks very politely, "Excuse me, Panzer and Kampf, sir, might there be any alien pirate spaceship features incorporated into the final model?" I suspect he doesn't want it construed as coming from a place of personal ambition.

Panzer and Kampf wave their horns gleefully at this question and say provocatively, "Better not ask too much! You'll have to wait and find out tomorrow!" But then they both do a double take.

"What are we talking about... you know all about those features... you were a major part of their design."

Mattie considers this for a while. He seems to be conducting a consultation process within. Then his brow clears and he grins. "Oh, I forgot."

It seems that Mattie has just cut his first Voice. Everyone congratulates him.

Then for the grand finale P and K convert themselves and we see the model in action. Everyone except Mattie groans as we behold the tiny size of the vehicle. We'll never all fit into that! But then we climb aboard and find ourselves in a space the size of a small forest.

"Surprise!" chorus P, K and Mattie.

The second noteworthy development to report from the day is that Tiger's body is lying in state. While we were away, Shakti and Barney constructed a casket of woven vines and flax fronds lined with moss. The brave cat now sits at the feet of our Queen, who has revised her opinion regarding the burial. She now decrees in her wisdom, that we should preserve Tiger's body, adding that from her vantage point she is witness to everything. At which she smiles mysteriously at the returned reconnaissance party.

We will carry Tiger with us tomorrow, so she can be a part of our final operation: Operation Ocean of Milk.

## Chapter Twenty Two

## Operation Ocean of Milk (OM)

Four hundred hours: "Wake up, Goddess." Overalls is shaking me anxiously. "Our special guest isn't allowing me to sleep. She's very intent. She says there's a lot to do and we don't have the luxury of sleep."

Everyone is instantly alert, especially Three who is ashamed to be caught napping. The wonderful facility of the O.M. bus (or Ombus), is that we don't have to spend valuable time arraying ourselves or looking after our stomachs before we leave. We can do it on the way. P and K, new code names for this mission – Ocean and Milk, or O and M for short – beg our indulgence on the road down the hill, while we're still in the wop-wops, to spend a little time as a bullock cart and a Panzerkampfwagen just to get it out of their system. Nevaeh, our Field Marshal acquiesces, as flexibility is a useful skill to have. However, by the time we reach the end of the stony track, they must convert themselves back into the Ombus.

Four ten hours: We say farewell and bow to our Queen, requesting her blessings for the successful completion of our mission. We wish we could take her with us. She reassures us that she will be with us. She says she will be able to witness everything from her vantage point and that we must be sure to make the acquaintance of her great-granddaughter who is stationed at our destination.

With solemn attention, we situate Tiger in a position of honour on the Ombus, then the rest of the brigade file aboard with varying degrees of sobriety and excitement.

Four twenty hours: Depart.

Five hundred hours: Our first stop is Lord Buddha's sanctuary where we have a brief update on the bare essentials with the Dean. 'We' being One, Two, Three and me. Despite being our Field Marshal, Nevaeh prefers to keep herself in the background. Not in the 'not-getting-her-hands-dirty- or-nails-wrecked' sense though. We couldn't tear anyone else away from the Ombus. We might have to use the no personal agenda card later. Husband brings us herbal tea from the garden, while Three blushes and simpers in an un-Three-like manner. Although I tell him we don't really need it as we have a small garden area on Ombus. He says yes but you know how much I like to offer hospitality. Not that he's not keen to check out Ombus and he's inspired to see me arrayed in full battle dress. The Dean suggests a brief meditation session. One says why not on Ombus, then everyone can join in and get the benefit? He thinks that's a super idea and brings Buddha along too. The Dean seems most impressed by how we've managed to organise everything and says he had his doubts last time we met. He hopes the day will continue as positively. We have an uplifting meditation session. Everyone participates in their own way. Afterwards we mention we did have some chaos. But Overalls quickly changes the subject to the moon landing, does the Dean know about that hoax?

Five forty-five hours: Second stop: A white house near the water. O and M park overlooking the estuary. No one can be tempted to get off even for a quick swim or the view. This time it's Mattie, Sammie and I alighting. I catch a slight hint of "it's not fair", but when I tell them where we're going, they cheer up. I'm a bit worried about leaving husband to the mercy of Three, but try to put aside my personal agenda. The escapee animals are a bit anxious too.

By the road, there's a board on a post with a picture of the house, yelling 'For Sale!' There's lots of smaller bossy writing too but we don't have time to read it. We walk up the familiar driveway; Mattie seems to have grown out of handstands. A dark leafed bush amongst the towering trees is now dotted with pink and white flowers, pervading the whole atmosphere with their heady aroma. The grass is dank with wet leaves. My stomach churns. I've never been to this door before. Cobwebs dot the corners, Mattie's bike lies on one side and Sammie's pink bike stands jauntily with its trainer wheels.

Mattie reaches up and rings the bell. In a few moments, Nani opens the door wearing tiny slippers and a flowery nightdress. She stares at us in disbelief, opening and shutting her mouth wordlessly.

Mattie flings his arms round her. "Nani!"

Sammie sidles up shyly and holds her hand. Silent tears stream down her face.

Prof shouts from upstairs, "Who is it at this hour?" The sound of a nose being blown hard reverberates down the stairs.

Still Nani seems powerless to move or talk. At that moment, twenty rats come scampering up the driveway and stream over Nani's bare feet into the hall and up the stairs. Behind them come One and Overalls.

One says, "I told them if you weren't back in five minutes we'd have to send in reinforcements."

Overalls adds, "They had to put aside all personal agendas too. They're an inspiration to us all."

Nani is rushing into the house after the rats, uttering little screeches. But the rats are on a mission, and following them upstairs we find Prof sitting on the floor crying into his handkerchief, surrounded by his old lab rats nibbling his toes affectionately and climbing over his shoulders.

Overalls points to his watch free wrist. "Come on, there's no time for sentimentality."

He catches me looking at him warily and sighs. "I'm just repeating Field Marshal's orders."

Nani will just have to bring her clothes with her and get dressed on the Ombus.

Because we still have eight stops to make before breakfast.

Six thirty hours: Dora, Bruth, Tony Hardcastle, the pilot and Stanley. We tell him it's a special trip to a sort of library. But since Renée and Rachel don't come in this early that adds on two more stops. Can't you go any faster O and M? We're trying our best.

Six forty-five hours: Toothless is already up for some reason and says we came just in the nick of time like, and not to ask too much. Neville is still sound asleep but one of Shakti's three missing kittens that Prof brought, nudges his nose and wakes him up.

Seven hundred hours: Luckily Irene has been doing lots of extra hours to make up for her bungle, Fern likewise. How are we all going to fit in that thing?

Seven twenty hours: Superette is twenty-four seven. The family are there all the time. Can't leave it for one whole day. Priya miss a day of school? Never! We have to lure them on with the promise of fresh milk and how that feeds the brain cells and the assurance that we'd make it up to them, just wait and see.

Seven thirty hours: A diminutive man accompanied by two large loudly chattering tomes, three spiders, a centipede and several ants.

Seven forty-five hours: Just unlocking the black gate for the first arrival.

Eight twenty hours: Just having our morning *hot chocolate*. No, none of us drink coffee any more.

Nine hundred hours: Leakey Lane Clinic, not there. Finally locate target at gym.

Nine thirty hours: Various stops, school etc.

Ten hundred hours: Gather on the shore for second OM surprise: O and M convert to Omboat! Most of us very excited.

As the animals troop aboard the Omboat, Nani claps her

hands and says, "It looks just like Noah's Ark!"

Barney and Mattie take the other children on a guided tour pointing out the various distinguishing features identifying the vehicle as a genuine Pirate Spaceship.

I'm remembering a different sort of ship, the ship created by the fish incarnation Matsya at the time of universal dissolution, when all the planetary systems are inundated by water. As I meditate on this vision, the boat appears golden. Three smiles, offering her little finger. Do I shake it? Meanwhile, Husband joins little fingers with hers and they shake them, both exclaiming, "Jinx!"

Okay, I think I get it.

Prof is standing up a bit taller. "In my youth I was a naval seaman. I used to navigate ships across the ocean. Maybe I could..."

Mattie and Barney, the first mates, take him by the hand and lead him up the gangplank to show him the engine room.

PC Richard Starling, PC Penny Taylor and PC Mike think it looks just like a police boat. Irene wonders if there's smoking on board? Stanley wants to know, is this the library we were telling him about?

Finally, we're all on board Omboat. I brought my sparkly dresses for the children and anyone else to array themselves as space pirates or whatever fresh persona they might imagine. We may not be the same people when we return from our trip.

Ten thirty hours: Set sail. Nevaeh, our Admiral, floats at the bow of our beautiful vessel like a celestial figurehead, leading us to the island.

The Dean stands up and announces that when we

disembark we are to leave everything behind on Omboat, cell phones, timepieces, handbags, money, drink bottles, sweets, cigarettes, books, weapons, sticks. He sees Sammie's downcast expression and says kindly, "There'll be plenty of sticks where we're going should anyone need one. In fact, there'll be plenty of everything anyone could desire. Especially time. We'll have all the time in the world. Because," he beams agreeably round at us, "we will be operating beyond the jurisdiction of this world's laws…"

The PCs exchange worried glances.

Ten forty-five hours: Breakfast and final time check.


Mattie and Barney lead the way, hurtling down the gangplank with cries of, "Ooh arr! It be a Treasure Island!"

We carefully carry Tiger in her vine casket down the gangplank and place her on the sand.

The now quite sizeable throng waits on the golden sand in silence, while the ocean laps at our feet. Although we're not sure what we're waiting for. We keep an eye on the Dean, who has his eye fixed on Admiral Nevaeh hovering just above the water. A half fish, half land creature with fangs lands on the beach, then some glistening seaweed. We wait in silence. The children's laughter rings out. A seagull shrieks. A turquoise bird dives into the water. A shell floats onto the beach sparkling in the sun, but then dries out and becomes dull. We continue our vigil.

Suddenly, Govind Mistry the superette owner, cries out, "Hey, Ram!"

His wife gasps.

"Ooh! Arr! Treasure!" roar the pirates.

A large blue sapphire sits unassumingly, tossed this way and that with each new surge of water in the runnel carved out by Sammie's new stick.

"It's mine!" declares Mattie.

"No! I got it first, I'm the Captain," protests Barney. "You said you didn't want it. Anyway."

The Dean smiles and everyone steps back to let him pass. "Please, oh merciful gentlemen, Pirate Leaders, would you kindly bestow your spoils upon this Pirate Queen?" He turns to the resolute young girl by his side. "Priya, I do believe the treasure is now rightfully yours."

So Priya becomes the Pirate Queen and bearing the effulgent gem she leads the flock up the beach. When we reach the brow of the sand hills, we stop in amazement. Before us is a grassy clearing amidst groves of trees and all around the clearing are several silvery rocks in the formation of an arc. The rock at one end of the arc tapers away to a point. At the other end stands a rock resembling a serpent's head, with two bulges for eyes, two holes for nostrils, two protuberances for fangs, and a rocky projection forming a long tongue. At the head of the arc is a solitary rock overhung by a huge tree. Although she's not quite as tall as our Queen, she still towers above the clearing, soaring like a beacon into the blue vault of the sky. Some of us bow in reverence to our Queen's great-granddaughter before carefully proceeding across the clearing to place Tiger in her casket at her feet.

Our Pirate Queen, after bowing, takes her position on the solitary rock beneath the tree, while every adult takes a seat on a rock around the serpent arc. There is a perfect number of rocks, and everyone sits in a perfect place depending on their heart's desires. Irene sits on the head of the serpent. The tail rock and one other may appear to some to be empty, but are not. The children cluster round Priya.

When everyone is silent, the Pirate Queen holds aloft the sapphire and in a clear voice, proclaims, "Whosoever holds the blue stone must speak the truth. The Great Soul will hear the message of your heart as well as your words."

Mattie and Barney look at their Queen with respect. Akul, Sammie and Frank follow their lead, while Sofie and Lulu present her with a flower crown.

Meanwhile, the animals continue to wait upon the shore.

After a few moments, the pirate brigade depart on important missions. The Agents make ready to follow. I ask them why they're not staying with the adults. But they tell me I'd better not ask too much and skip off.

Finally, the Dean rises and stands before the arc. "This conference has been convened for peace talks, to negotiate a truce, to go beyond what we may think of as possible." He looks into each person's eyes in turn. "Let us begin." He offers the sapphire in his palms. "Who would like to take the speaking stone?"

The sapphire goes to the head of the serpent and Irene stands. "My name is Irene. I have worked for Child, Youth and Family Services for thirty-seven years. I feel I have helped too many children to count. I am very proud of my accomplishments. I always wanted to help children. Ever since... I wanted to get back at the people who didn't help *me* – the people who fucked my life up." She peers at the jewel in her hand, clenching it tight. "And locked me in the bedroom. Bedroom? Huh, prison more like, while my so-called goddamn mother, god don't give her soul any rest, was drinking downstairs with my," her face twists in anguish, "fucking, fucking uncle, who used to come at me in that grotty room, day after fucking day. He… he… was a monster!" she cries, stuffing her hands in her eyes. "I was only six years old!" Then she speaks quietly, barely more than a whisper, "He destroyed me." She writhes in the agony of remembering. No one speaks or moves. In the distance, we hear the children's laughter as they chase each other through the trees and down to the beach. Irene gradually becomes still, held in the silence.

"Who would like the speaking stone?"

The next person in the arc is Prof. He remains stubbornly on his rock. We wait. Time stretches to infinity. Irene passes him the sapphire with uncharacteristic gentleness.

He rises hesitantly like a frightened rabbit, paralysed in the laser of the group's focus. "I do not have anything to say. Life is what you make it. We cannot always have what we are wanting. That is life. Of course, you are having your ups and your downs but you do not need to be telling everyone your private things. We like to be private in my culture and not to hang out our dirty laundries on the line for all to see." He shudders. "We have made a good life for ourselves, Nani and I. It has not always been easy but everything is okay. Thank you very much for listening." He prepares to sit down, avoiding eye contact with anyone. Everyone is focused upon him. He has never known this before, this undivided attention. He feels like a rhesus monkey under observation. He squeezes the jewel nervously and coughs.

"Yeah right," murmurs Husband.

The silence builds.

Prof stands up again. "Okay. Maybe I can say one little thing only." He kneads the sapphire as though he's making his homemade bread. "I remember when I was five years old. Every time I do not know the answer to a question, the teacher will beat me with his cane. That is all. Not a big thing." He looks into the distance and his hand tightens on the sapphire. "I was so afraid. I was not able to learn my tables at home because I also was afraid there. My mother was very afraid of my father and if we will be naughty or make noise, she will beat on us with roti griddle or broom. Right on our head. Then we were hiding in the almirah. When my father returned to home evening time, he will roar for my mother for his meal and if she is not on time, he will be very, very angry. He will seize the ladle from her hand and beat her all across her shoulders. Then we, we means my three brothers and myself, will all be in the almirah crying, listening to the ding ding of the bell as my father performs his pooja." He lowers his eyes. "Once I stole something from the money tin of my mother which she was keeping on the shelf by the door. She discovered my act and pressed the hot iron on my palm. I was not able to do my writing at school for some time so my teacher beat on me. Then my mother died and my father sent us away to school. At far distant place. I got locked in a cupboard for one month because I had not learned my seventeen times tables." The whites of his eyes are rolling against the brown of his skin. "We were given old rice only to eat and I always had dysentery; the stools would pour out of me; I almost died." He laughs. "But it is okay. It is no use to cry over spilled milk, isn't it?" He attempts a shaky smile and sits down abruptly, dropping the sapphire in the next person's lap like a hot roti griddle or scalding iron.

"Who will hold the speaking stone?"

The sapphire continues its process back and forth.

"My father was so angry it was like a tsunami… I was terrified."

"My mother never gave me any attention. I was always a naughty girl. Don't get your dress dirty. I'll never ever take you out again after that behaviour. You look terrible in that… she never looked pleased to see me, on the contrary…"

"I was in hospital for two years when I was three years old and my parents could only visit me once a month."

"My husband is cheating on me… with underage prostitutes…"

"I never wanted to have kids. I'm just an unpaid slave… I never have any life or do what I want to do."

"My mum left my dad and shacked up with a different boyfriend every month and they beat the crap out of me."

"My dad left me and my mum because he didn't love me. He never loved me. He wouldn't care if I died."

"I had an accident and couldn't move. Then I got fat. Everyone laughed at me, I was the fat boy. I swore I'd never be fat again and I'd get my own back."

"I was stupid in school. I had dyslexia. I was always last in the exams. I couldn't spell. My father was ashamed of me and then when I was a teenager, I realised I was gay and he almost killed me. I could never go home again. He wouldn't let my mum talk to me."

So the sapphire rises and falls like waves, passing around first this way and then the other, churning the ocean.

"It's all your fault." Nani is like a she-demon. "You have ruined our lives. Daksh, the kids, Jay and me. Innocent children! You've done something with our daughter. What did you do? Where is she?" She lunges at me as if to rip me apart. The silence and the Dean's gentle understanding and focus hold her. She falters and looks at the sapphire in her hand.

"Yes!" Jay grabs the sapphire from Nani. "My whole life has turned totally to shit. I always thought it was Prof and the government. But no, it was you who really stirred the crap and fucked up my chances at uni. I can't teach any more and now I'll have to go to prison! I'll never get my boys back..."

"You destroyed my career!"

"You fucked with my head..."

"You didn't deserve Jay. I should have had him..."

"Witch..."

"I experience you as a manipulating, scheming she-devil."

"Sorceress! You should be burned at the stake."

The sapphire rises and falls, churning the ocean. Churning out all the darkness. Churning out all the poison.

We wend our way silently to the beach, where the animals continue to hold vigil. The children have made a huge boat out of sand, complete with a sparkly flag with skull and bones. The Omboat is nowhere in sight. We wait by the ocean. Who knows what for. A shape comes bobbing on the water and lands at

Prof's feet. He stoops to pick it up, clenching his lips defiantly.

However, before we can speculate about this, the sea swells and suddenly explodes before our eyes. What? A great head drenched in seaweed surfaces, followed by immense barnacled shoulders... A torso as broad as a mountain and finally colossal legs erupt from the depths sending waves crashing to the shore. A giant! Clutching to its chest a great copper cask. There are screams as the frightful behemoth, its head touching the clouds, crashes towards us.

As it gradually bears down upon us, its features become clearer, and I realise to my horror that the figure is *me*. Oh no! Now they'll hate... they'll *blame* me, even more! She bears the cask aloft as several drops of mercurial liquid spill over and land on the fanged half fish.

Scattering all in her path, the ghastly ogress ploughs her terrible way up the beach, over the sand hills to the serpent, the earth shaking with her every step. We follow fearfully after. However, by the time we reach the clearing, she's disappeared. Only the copper cask remains, flashing in the sun, by the solitary rock at the head of the arc.

"The children! Where are the children?" cries someone. We rush to protect our vulnerable children, but find them still playing contentedly in their boat. The sand all around them is smooth, rippled only by the wind.

The Dean stands at the head of the arc next to the copper cask. "In this cask is a secret elixir for controlling the mind. The side effects cannot be predicted and it is poison. You may make your case for possessing this product of the churning of the ocean."

Renée lays claim to it for helping those with mental challenges. "We could patent it!"

Rachel, Dora and Bruth aren't convinced. The teachers and Irene see possibilities for children with special needs. Toothless and Neville want it for themselves. The pilot and Tony Hardcastle are wary. Prof wants it for Mattie. The PCs recommend it be confiscated immediately; they know what to do with things like that. Husband and Overalls declare it should be destroyed. Nevaeh hovers anxiously. Chicken Monster gazes out of sightless eye sockets. Everyone starts arguing and yelling at each other.

Dean stands up and raises his hands. Everyone quietens down. All eyes are upon him.

"It cannot be thrown away. It must be consumed by somebody. It has been produced by your churning, it must be taken by you. We will leave the cask until later. When you churn the ocean further, you will know what to do."

"Now. Who will hold the speaking stone?"

Everyone has moved to a different place in the arc.

Nani is seated at the head of the serpent. She rises, clutching the sapphire to her breast. "I saw someone horrific coming in over the ocean to destroy us all."

Oh no. I wait for a further rain of recriminations.

We strain to hear her as she whispers, "It was me."

What?

But she's only just started. "Because I didn't speak up, we came to this God forsaken country and because we came to this God forsaken country, I lost my whole family as surely as if they'd been gassed at Treblinka. When my father became old and decrepit, I wasn't there for him and then he was looked after by carers who didn't care and left pans full of burned food in the cupboard and didn't give him soft towels and allowed him to get a bed sore on his heel which was like a black crater and because of that he had to go to hospital and because of that they didn't get him up to walk and because of that his legs seized up and because of that he never walked again and because of that he had to stay in bed for the rest of his life and because of that he died and because of me being on a different planet, I *wasn't there!*" She takes a huge gulp of air, then relaunches. "I didn't speak up at Mattie's birth and because of that, the midwife interfered and broke Am's waters and because of that they ended up in hospital and because of that she ended up on a drip and Mattie had a big pin gauged into his head and because of that he was stuck in the birth canal for four hours with *Pitocin* going through his brain crossing the delicate blood brain barrier and because of that he got Asperger's and because of that he was antisocial and hit all the other kids and because of that Am couldn't join in any social activities and because of that she got depressed and because of that she got the fugue and because of that she turned into another person and because of that I lost my daughter and the kids lost their mother. And because of that I got custody of the kids and because of that Mattie got his vaccinations and Sammie got his anaesthetic and because of that Sammie will probably suffer developmental delays and Mattie will probably get worse and who knows what will happen in the future and it's all *my fault!!!*"

There's silence apart from the rumble of distant thunder

and Nani's wailing. Her neat little form is ragged and twisted. We listen through her storm.

Her wailing subsides. "I believe I was responsible for CYFS. I'm so sorry."

Catherine leaps up and seizes the sapphire. "No! It was *me* coming over the ocean. I saw it distinctly. And I think I was responsible for CYFS. I know I have been very... fearful. I see that now. I don't have the courage to do what I know is best for the children. I put the Ministry's demands and the parents expectations before the children's welfare. I'm sorry, Akul, for forcing you to write when you weren't ready and destroying your confidence and your love of learning. I'm so sorry, Mattie. You didn't want to come to school. I didn't listen... But I was afraid."

Irene grabs the sapphire. "You're so wrong. It was *me* coming over the ocean. Couldn't you see? She had my scruffy old top on and she was fat like me. Yes, I am fat. I'm fat and unlovable. And I've hurt more people than I've helped. I've been kidding myself all this time. You see after that... uncle... I couldn't have children. I couldn't have children and I didn't want any one else to have children, especially not people who wouldn't care for them properly or didn't appreciate them. It wasn't fair. Don't you see? I made your life hell. I'm sorry. I don't know what's going on here. I don't even want a smoke."

Toothless stands and takes the sapphire tightly in one hand and then in the other. His jaw is working. "You must be blind, Irene, like. He definitely had a scruffy black top on, Irene, that's correct, like. However, he was a scrawny bastard, just like me. I was shitting myself, like. That's what I looked like advancing on the scrawny guys in Treblinka. Impending doom. Poised to turn on the gas. Infiltrate their systems with poison fumes instead of oxygen, like. Mmm. Irene." He hikes his trousers up. He's so thin they keep falling down over his hips. "I should drink the poison. I like drugs. I've been on drugs for forty years, like. Injections. Makes me so sleepy. More poison wouldn't make much difference, like. I mean look at me..." He stands before us, gaunt and yellow, a vulnerable wreck of a human being.

Nani is weeping. So are Dora, Bruth and Rachel. Renée looks down, blinking. The silence extends. Finally, Fern stands up.

Toothless drops the sapphire into her hand and smiles. "Your turn, like, Fern," he says, clamping his lips over his empty gums.

Fern pushes her hair out of her eyes and gazes into the sapphire. "I take responsibility for CYFS. I didn't exactly call them, but I did mention the situation to Irene in a sort of casual way. I was always jealous of Am. She has such a lovely husband, not an abuser like Frank's dad, and she never appreciated him. I wanted her to suffer a bit. I didn't really think Irene would do anything about them. I mean such a great dad to his kids. I didn't think..." She sniffs. "I've been such a fake, pretending to be their friend when all the time... You guys are all totally blind. How you could mistake a giant with long blonde hair for... God, I'm such a bitch. I should drink the poison. Maybe I should let Irene have Frank. I also took a kitten. Those boys didn't need five kittens. Mattie was always hitting Frank... I'm so sorry... I..." She tugs at her clothes as though she wants to escape from the prison of herself. The silence holds a mirror to her and the long blonde hair looks no more beautiful in that mirror than Irene's honest bulk or Toothless's gaunt humility.

"Who will hold the speaking stone?"

"We use patients as guinea pigs."

"I gear my academic papers and scientific studies. Just tweak them slightly. Everyone does it."

"I don't mind accepting money from pharmaceutical companies. I sit on the board of a pharmaceutical company and sure you might say there's a conflict of interest but I rationalise it."

"I have mistreated vulnerable patients who had no one to stand up for them."

"When I joined up, I wanted to help people, look after the citizens, protect them. It's turned into something else. The system... But I'm responsible. I don't need to go along with it. Now all I care about is getting my quota of speeding fines and nailing somebody, *anybody,* as long as we get our man... When I saw that fucking giant pig striding across the water, a sadistic grin plastered on its face, I knew how they felt... I knew..."

Shakti materialises on the head rock. Her gaze sweeps the assembly. "Only the ferocious animal cannot hear the Great Soul within," she whispers, "because he or she fails to listen." Her gentle message is clear, transferred through the heart. She looks sorrowfully down at Tiger's inert body.

The sapphire rises and falls like the waves of the ocean, ebbing this way, flowing that way, churning the water.

"Who will hold the speaking stone?"

Prof gets very slowly to his feet as though his whole body

is concrete. He folds his arms almost turning his back on us.

"I am not an emotional man. I am a scientist." He regards the sapphire in his hand as though it's an object of some faint interest, scientifically speaking that is. He seems barely able to squeeze the words out through his lips. "I took three kittens to my laboratory at home and the rats from the compost heap. I believe it is justified. I am almost on the point of making some discoveries. What is the suffering of small, small kittens? What is the suffering one rat? We all have to suffer, isn't it? But when I saw that colossus, that towering figure of a man in a white coat looming over me in the water, I was experiencing like I did in the almirah of my childhood. I understood for one tiny fleeting moment," he presses his thumb and forefinger together close to his face, "what it must feel like to be a small, small mouse, in a cage." He drops his hand and his whole body sags. He looks at us through hollow eyes. "But now I cannot feel it. I am separated from you all, from your humanity. I have no feelings inside at all. I am a wooden father for the rhesus monkey, a heartless grandfather for my family. Nani complains I have no heart. I am afraid," his attempt to smile is like the rictus grin of the Pirate flag, "maybe I have no soul."

The Dean waits. The silence expands. Then he gently leads Prof into the centre of the arc. He beckons to me. I feel my arms tingle. Everyone draws closer.

Neville says very gravely, "Which hand to you want?"

Prof looks up in terror, a little child hiding in an almirah as I produce my weapons, not to destroy but to bless – my lotus flower and conch shell. I touch the conch shell to his head and the lotus to his heart. He closes his eyes in anguish, his face working wildly.

Suddenly he lets out a great howl as he rocks back and forth, back and forth. He rocks and wails for many minutes. I keep my lotus touching his heart and my conch blessing his crown. The Dean motions for the assembled witnesses to gather round, to cradle him and soothe him.

Then a curdling torrent vomits forth from deep, deep within his hiding soul, "Do not abuse your children! Do not abuse your children! Do not abuse your children! Please. Oh, please do not abuse your precious children!"

We stretch loving hands to the sobbing scientist as Husband cradles him in his lap.


The pirates on lookout duty witness the events from tree top crows nests. The sun appears to have stopped his traverse of the heavens. We have all the time in the world.

Finally Prof stands up, "I have one more thing to say..." He goes to his rock and picks up the object washed up on the shore earlier. It is a coconut tied up with a scrap of disintegrating paper.

"In the privacy of my home laboratory, I have performed one Tantric rite. It is to make someone go away. When all that very difficult times were happening with the children being kidnapped and the animals escaping and what all. I do not really believe in this. I do not know what possessed me to do it. Maybe it will not work. I chanted the mantras and then placed it into the sea. The picture on this paper... was... was... of..." he looks at me sadly, "you."

On the brow of the sandy hills overlooking the ocean, we partake of the fruits growing ripe and full on the trees, accompanied by other delicacies delivered by Lucky and Katy B. O and M are lying down peacefully chewing over the cud. The pirates swoop amongst us purloining sweets or fruits at their whim then retreating into trees to gloat over their ill-gotten gains. The animals are hanging out in trees or creating underground labyrinths in the sand. Though the rabbits say that they keep filling up with ocean, and guess what, the water is actually... Before they have a chance to tell us, however, the ocean begins to boil. We all jump up, repast forgotten, fearful of what might appear.

We breathe a collective sigh of relief as a host of frisky lambs come gambolling out of the waves, but the ocean continues to boil. What next? Again we hold our breath. But the lambs are followed by an apparently endless stream of white chickens, plus a whole clutch of fluffy golden ones. It's like the Easter Show. Sammie gleefully runs down to the water's edge and scoops up a fluffy ball. After the chickens comes a cavalcade of pigs, snuffling through the sand. Discovering the rabbits' burrows mixed with white foamy water, they roll onto their backs waggling their legs in ecstasy. The exodus continues with a pageant of myriad shiny beetles, butterflies, bees and crawling vines. I turn to Toothless to convey my realisation that this must be where all the animals from the facility go, but he's not there. Several bewitching lotus-eyed women with flowers in their hair then surface from the deep, bearing richly patterned velvet and satin cloth. The Voices from my shopping expedition! They dance off into the trees. I wonder where all these beings are going to go on this small island? How will they live? Won't it become overcrowded like the library? I look round for Three or the Dean or Neville. Maybe Nani would know? Or of course Husband, he's studying for his masters. At least, he was. And his masters must surely know... But everyone seems to have wandered off. Shakti is still gazing anxiously out to sea, eyes like slits, her tail flicking. I'll ask her. The Great Soul always tells her everything.

"There's plenty of room for everyone. The Great Soul will provide for everyone. Did you think the island was limited?" she says tersely. She doesn't seem her usual self.

"I guess I'll go and find the others then," I reply. She obviously doesn't want my company. I start towards the arc.

"You're going the wrong way," growls Shakti.

I turn back to the ocean. Oh! How...? What...?

Before my astonished eyes, the ocean has again become a stage, whereupon a joyous carnival unfolds. The white horses of the breakers have become pure white ponies. The pirates have claimed them and are galloping along in the shallows, along with Irene on a huge white mare, and Georgina and Sammie on a gleaming black stallion. Husband and Three are delivering rousing orations from the highest rocks, then leaping headlong into the water crying "We will find out how to unfold our wings as we fall..." then falling into each other's arms. Valerie, having rediscovered the box of dental implements from Karachi, is diving into the water and emerging with pearls, which she attempts to place in Toothless's mouth. Neville and Stanley are riding on dolphins with One and Two. And now the PCs, Renée and the facility folk enter the scene, suffering the waves on sharks! Nani and Prof are frolicking like children, garlanding each other with seaweed, playing leap frog with rats and monkeys and throwing starfish back into the ocean one by one. Fern is sporting with the Pilot and Tony Hardcastle is dreamily floating along on his back. Catherine, assisted by several rabbits and ants, is drawing what appears to be massive letters and numbers on the beach, which are periodically scattered by the galloping ponies. From time to time Mattie dismounts and joins her. They seem to be doing very large calculations. Jessica Wilson and Dr Ganesh are in serious discussion, scooping samples of ocean water from first this rock pool then another using shimmering turquoise shells. They take a taste, gazing at the horizon before resuming their earnest exchange. Several kittens are following suit, minus the shells and the intense discussion. Overalls, way out in the ocean, appears to be having a summit meeting with world leaders.

I say to Shakti, "Why don't you join everyone?"

She briefly turns her proud head to the arc and the granddaughter tree. "Cats don't like water."

I wander down to the ocean and scoop up a palmful of water. It's not salty! It tastes of...

But just then, the Dean blows a great blast on my conch shell and the tableau fades as one by one the members of the troupe make their exits to reassemble at the arc. Only Shakti maintains her solitary vigil, gazing out to the vacant sea.

Everyone gathers for the final churning of the ocean. The gentle animals who can hear the Great Soul, minus Shakti, the ferocious animals who have become gentle by hearing the

Great Soul, and the small people who have not yet forgotten how. Each member naturally assumes the perfect sitting place in the order of the arc.

The Dean offers the lotus to hold to our hearts, the heart of operations. "Who will listen?"

Everyone seems to be inspired. Some press the lotus to their bosom and talk of creating a healing facility with beautiful music, others talk of helping people to break free from the cycle of offending. Irene, surrounded by pirates, declares that she's going to work with Catherine and Fern to create schools where children can do handstands all day and never lose their curiosity. She's also going to foster children in her home. Prof, at the heart of a menagerie of rats and monkeys declares he's going to do animal research in a meadow, utilising environmental and behavioural enrichment strategies so he can non-invasively study animal culture and society. He hopes to make some breakthroughs to help improve human behaviour. Would be a good thing, no? To improve human behaviour?

Toothless, radiant after his dip, smiles widely revealing a beautiful set of pearly teeth. He hugs the lotus to his heart and declares, "I'm going to forgive myself for the Third Reich. I think I've done my time, like."

Everyone cheers, claps, and stamps their feet.

Nani's finally going to do what *she* wants for a change and finish her damn book. She even has a title for the next one.

Husband takes Prof's hand. They do a dance never before seen in this world in the centre of the arc and everyone gradually gets to their feet and joins in.

After who knows how long, a night of Brahma at least, we quieten down. A contented silence cloaks us like a warm embrace.

The Dean, with the children gathered at his feet, stands up by the central rock. "It takes a tribe to raise a child. These children are your children. Look after them well. They are the future hope of the world." Then he looks out over the ocean.

All eyes follow his gaze. Across the water glides a ravishing doe-eyed girl, bearing a golden pot. In her belt are tucked a flaming sword and a ruby and diamond encrusted scimitar. It is our Admiral, Nevaeh. She floats up the beach to the head of the arc, followed resolutely by Shakti.

Everyone stands to attention. She motions to Overalls to convey her message. Overalls stands very erect before the assembly. "Our Admiral, Nevaeh would like to reassure her parents that they are not to blame and she is now free. However, she states that only when we stop poisoning the children of our Mother Earth, will her work here be complete."

She holds aloft the golden pot of nectar. Everyone turns to me. Me? The Dean nods imperceptibly. Moving to the head of the arc in a dream, my feet barely touch the ground. Nevaeh transfers the precious pot into my hands with all solemnity and reverence. It is time to rectify wrongs. I remove the lid and gently tip the golden vessel.

Afterwards, Lucky presents me with five jewelled chalices, which I fill to the brim with the molten gold elixir of immortality. The Pirate Queen claims one and delivers it to the educators and Irene, who then delivers it to the rest of the pirate gang. Toothless claims the next and gleefully distributes it to the facility folk. Overalls shares one chalice amongst the law enforcement and any world leaders who've stayed around. Prof makes sure every animal has his or her share, even the centipede. Lucky presents it to Valerie, Jessica and Dr Ganesh. I hope he will consider it adequate recompense for all the remedies I took from him that night... The last brimming chalice I offer to my dear family, accompanied by many tears and embraces.

Draining the last drop from the cup, I exchange glances with my little Sammie. The elixir tastes just like ice cream.

The ocean has been churned. The elixir has been partaken. The sun is descending towards the horizon as I take my place on the head rock.

And behold! I am borne aloft by one never more powerful, never more sinuous. I am borne aloft by none other than the fully rejuvenated, hissing, tail-flicking form of the now immortal Tiger!

My arms tingle. In less than one truti, Neville is before us. "Pick a hand, any hand!" he commands.

And lo, my ten arms manifest. And in my ten hands, my ten weapons. My bow, my spear, my chalice of fire, my shield, my mace, my disc, my lotus, my conch... and my reinstated sword and scimitar inlaid with diamonds and rubies. The tableau is complete.

The Pirate Queen chants a haunting ode to Kali, which sails off on moonbeams into the night, while the assembly lift their voices in harmonious response.

A honey-tinged moon rises behind the island, spreading her ethereal glow. No one is hungry or tired, as the tribe lingers on the shore waiting for O and M to perform their conversion routine. Some baby monkeys are sitting on children's shoulders. One is perched on Prof's shoulder, while several rats poke their heads out of his pockets, making themselves comfortable amongst his handkerchiefs. The mood is jubilant, as though we'd just discovered Treasure Island, replete with several kegs of rum. But now it's time to take down the pirate flag still fluttering on the breeze, for on the horizon appears Nevaeh at the prow of our pirate spaceship, our Omboat, our ark, ready to speed us over the waves, forward into the arms of normality.

In the gentle beams of the moon, the boat glistens like Matsya's golden vessel. I look round for Three to jinx, but she's not here. Where can she be? Maybe she's still at the rock circle? I skip up the beach to find her. Wandering across the now familiar dunes, I feel as though I've been here for a night of Brahma. The aroma of parijata lightly perfumes the night air. Reaching the arc, I make out a dark shape silhouetted against our Queen's granddaughter. Alone and forgotten near the head rock, for all the universe as though the serpent had disgorged it from its fangs, lurks the copper cask of venom.

On the journey back over the water, the assembly is more subdued. People come to me singly or in groups and declare their promises for the future. The PCs have reconnected with their phones and are talking urgently into them, as we head forward to normality. Lucky and Shakti do not leave my side.

Mattie and Sammie hold my hands, while One and Two in turn hold *their* hands. Husband holds my head in his lap and strokes my hair, while Three places her hands on his shoulders from behind. Prof and Nani hover nearby. One, Two and Three hurl comments back and forth to each other.

Two hisses to One, "You finally got your way, didn't you?"

One retorts, "This is so not what I had in mind. If I'd been there…"

Three says, "Have you guys learned nothing in all of this?"

Omboat seems to have lost some of her sheen. As she draws into the harbour, people wonder if the day has all been a dream. But they've made their promises. I've witnessed them.

# Chapter Twenty Three

# Fugue II

Over the next few days, I am to witness many more things.

Four men by my bedside, two each side, engaged in a blazing argument. The two on the left are hideously ugly, with stunted bodies, matted hair and sunken, angry eyes. Their limbs are covered with hair, or possibly fur, half their teeth are missing, and the rest are fangs. Decked in animal skins and necklaces of skulls, they brandish nooses and whips. Could they be pirate twins?

The two on the right by contrast, are the most beautiful men I've ever seen. Swarthy and dazzling of complexion, their effulgence illuminates the entire room. They have raven-black hair and flashing golden clothes, helmets and jewellery. In their four hands, they each carry a lightning sword, a weighty mace, a whirling disc and a lotus flower.

One of the ugly pirates snarls, "Her soul is ours. She has not learned her lesson. Yamaraja our master, the Lord of Death has seen. His intelligence is infinite. Do you imagine he could miss the slightest detail? Let him be the judge! We're following his orders. Let us do our duty. Move aside, sirs."

An adonis intones in a voice of thunder, "She chanted the sacred mantra with her dying breath, and *we* follow the instructions of *our* master Vishnu who declares that whatsoever the soul shall remember with its dying breath to that state shall it return. Do you not know this, sirs? Her soul is ours!"

Pirate number two growls, "She drank an ocean of poison imitating Lord Shiva. Do you think it's possible that this body could still be viable after that? It was decreed that if she exploited her heavenly powers in the earthly realm after having knowledge of them, she would never return to her heavenly abode. We say she must have illegally utilised her heavenly perfections to be lying here intact. Not us... Yamaraja! You can't pull the wool over *his* eyes. She's ours!"

The second adonis proclaims in a voice of liquid honey, "She risked her life for others and the Great Soul is very pleased by one who takes on suffering for others. Therefore, I say unto you, we have authority!"

Pirate number one then cackles, "Aha! So you agree she *did* imitate Lord Shiva. Are you not aware, sirs, that those who are *proud* enough to think they can imitate Lord Shiva may not have learned certain lessons they were suppose to learn? What do you say to that, huh?" Then he and his comrade proceed to dance round the bed in a victory war dance. Thus, the battle rages on.

Meanwhile, Husband comes in. He cries and holds my hand. "I never told you I loved you. I didn't even take the opportunity to apologise in the arc. I'm a fool. It's been a roller coaster for sure, but it was exciting being around you. My bed feels very lonely."

Three puts her arms round him and weeps as well.

Sometimes he brings the boys.

Mattie, half way up the curtain rail, declares, "Dada you don't need to worry. Sammie and I go travelling on the moonbeams at night and our other Mother says everything's going to be fine. This Mama can't come with us yet because of these silly men."

"Attaboy, Mattie!" cheers One halfway up the opposite curtain rail.

"What men?" Husband looks round the room suspiciously.

Sammie brandishes his stick at the hairy pirates. "You leave her alone do you hear me? I don't like you. You're vewy ugly."

Two stands at his shoulder. "Go, Sammie! You tell 'em!"

Prof and Nani come in too.

Nani refrains from mentioning the coconut. She sits writing her book by my bedside. "I don't know if you can hear me. You probably can knowing you. I think if you'd just stayed a bit longer I might have become more accepting..." She wipes her eye. "Anyway, I promised you I'd get on with my book. So here I am. I'm going to sit here and write it. I'm sure that will help you more than me rabbiting on. You can probably read it over my shoulder."

So, the Agents peer over her shoulder and give me a word by word account. All of which, of course, I remember...

From where I'm lying, I have a better view of Prof's eyes, even though he has a hard time looking me in the face.

"You know I did not really intend for the coconut to work. I do not believe in it. It was sort of... an experiment." He produces a massive handkerchief, riddled with holes and proceeds to blow his nose and wipe his eyes.

Over the edge of his pocket appears a twitching nose, two twinkly eyes and bristling whiskers.

"Oh... aha... Look, Beti, here is Charles the rat come to see you." Prof tenderly takes Charles from his pocket. "Charles fared a little better than... er... the others from the compost heap."

Charles the rat takes a tentative step onto my pillow.

"He was in the control group of nil vaccinations, nil empathy, whereas the group that received a good beating every day..." He shakes his head as Charles' whiskers tickle my nose. "This is a good experiment, no? To see if animals can bring back people in comas? We could have set up something in Renée's facility..." He smiles. "But fortunately we can now afford to buy our own facility. We are thinking of some land in the north. You know, for the animal research in a meadow. I will have my shed four times the size of Mark Anderson's! So much golden utensils we found in the forest..."

The Agents don't say much when Prof and Nani come in. However, they seem pleased to see them. Of course, in the days when I spent time with Prof and Nani, they were just a synapse in someone's brain.

Nevaeh hovers sometimes. Although she says she has a lot to do elsewhere now that her task with me is complete.

Then one day, I receive an unexpected guest. Someone I thought would not be able to come to this world again. She barges in like a she-demon.

Meanwhile the four men are at it again. But not for long.

"You men!" screams the guest. "You're all the same, arguing back and forth with your... your logical brains. Problem with you, is you just don't know how to *listen*! Now move over and leave us women to sort things out. Go on! Scam! I want my boys back and I'm not waiting any longer."

And with that, she marches straight in.


As I step onto the swan aeroplane, I wait for the Agents. But they remain as if welded to the ground, arms folded, faces set in silent mutiny.

"Come *on*," I tell them, "you'd better get on board quick or I'm going without you!"

"We're not coming!" they chorus.

"I'm not leaving Mattie!" declares One.

"I'm not leaving Sammie!" insists Two.

"I'm not leaving Husband!" states Three.

"And we're keeping the weapons."

"So hand them over!"

My arms tingle. "Why do you need them?"

"Better you don't ask too much," replies Three darkly. "We're not out of the woods yet."

And indeed, when I think about those I'm leaving behind, it's not so hard to give up my weapons. I wouldn't want to have any personal agenda.

# Epilogue

By the time I arrive, the Honourable Ones have feasted to their full satisfaction and are casting their golden utensils into the ocean. I pull my sparkly shawl around me and shiver. I've certainly served my penance. I have also fulfilled my sacred mission. What's more, I will not even miss the dancing girls' performance. However, I no longer care. No. Why should I? By not missing the dancing girls, I am missing something far, far more precious.

Ah, well. I treasured the other mother's family for a season by earth time. Now what is rightfully hers has been duly restored. Together with my weapons! And the agents! That's fair. Is it not? It must surely constitute adequate recompense.

And so, while the ivory waves swirl and toss their generous gifts at my feet and the birds utter their final symphony, I gaze out over the wondrous assembly. The flashing eyes are welcoming, and yes, forgiving, even eager, in the dying rays of the sun...

Oh Spiritually Powerful Ones, you who have attained the perfect stage of mystic power, you are tri-kāla-jña, you see everything in the past, in the present, in the future.

And I? I bring with me no red journal filled with words, writings on walls and labels of despair. Being sruti dhara, I have no need. Oh Wise Ones, rest assured, I will forget not the slightest detail in the recounting of my tale. Oh Masters and Mistresses seated before me, I beg your full attention, as I humbly narrate, in fulfilment of your great order, The History of the Ocean of Milk...

# About the Author

Belinda Aycrigg has a degree in Social Anthropology from the University of Cambridge and a Masters in Creative Writing from Auckland University of Technology. She has taught, written plays and maintained a fascination for alternative realities and life styles. She has a grown-up daughter and two grandsons and lives in Auckland with her husband. *Ocean of Milk* is her first novel.